Since the 1996 bestseller, *The Ancient Future*, Traci Harding has published many fabulous books with HarperVoyager. These are available in print and e-books, and some titles are available in audio; she has also been translated into several different languages.

Go to **traciharding.com** and find out all there is to know about Traci and her books.

Books by Traci Harding

TRACI HARDING

THE ETERNITY GATE

THE TIMEKEEPERS [2]

HARPER
Voyager

HarperVoyager
An imprint of HarperCollins*Publishers*

First published in Australia in 2014
This edition published in 2017
by HarperCollins*Publishers* Australia Pty Limited
ABN 36 009 913 517
harpercollins.com.au

HarperCollins*Publishers*
Level 13, 201 Elizabeth Street, Sydney NSW 2000, Australia
Unit D1, 63 Apollo Drive, Rosedale, Auckland 0632, New Zealand
A 53, Sector 57, Noida, UP, India
1 London Bridge Street, London, SE1 9GF, United Kingdom
2 Bloor Street East, 20th floor, Toronto, Ontario M4W 1A8, Canada
195 Broadway, New York, NY 10007, USA

National Library of Australia Cataloguing-in-Publication data:

Harding, Traci, author.
  The eternity gate / Traci Harding.
  978 0 7322 9269 0 (paperback)
  978 0 7304 9287 0 (ebook)
  Series: Harding, Traci. Timekeepers; 2.
  Space and time—Fiction.
A823.3

Cover design by HarperCollins Design Studio
Cover images: man by Paulo Martinez Photography/Getty Images;
all other images by shutterstock.com
Typeset in 10/13pt Goudy Old Style by Kirby Jones

To all the Angels in my life —
you know who you are.

CONTENTS

PART 4: BACKTRACK TIME

ACKNOWLEDGEMENTS

My first thanks on this book has to go to my characters — I had no idea where this tale was taking me, and I followed their lead blindly (more so than usual), wondering what the hell they were leading me into! I felt my imagination being pushed to the limit and my trust in their guidance was really challenged during the first half of this book. Some of the predicaments and conversations my time-hopping characters found themselves in had me splitting my sides with laughter, and wracking my brain to figure out. Even I was amazed by how everything that transpired in the beginning, turned out to be perfectly relevant in the end. So, my hat goes off to the Timekeepers, the Chosen, the Grigori and all their incarnations, for their mind-expanding inspiration!

Thanks to my new commissioning editor at HarperCollins, Rochelle Fernandez, who is doing a fantastic job captaining the good ship Voyager. Thanks also to my editors, Sue Moran, Abigail Nathan, Rachel Dennis, Stephanie Smith and everyone who worked with me to get this book out on schedule — it was a tight one, well done ladies! Thanks also to Darren Holt for a fantastic cover design yet again!

As always my gratitude to Selwa Anthony, my fabulous agent, who is always behind me one hundred per cent. I am so thankful the cosmos brought us together all those years ago — near twenty by my count!

Big love to Sarah and John, for leaving Mum to work in peace. Same goes for my friends and family who rarely see me, but are always there when I need them — you all ROCK! Big thanks also to Lee Pou Lon, for his continuing aid with my Chinese translations.

But credit where credit is due — my readers and website moderators are really the ones who keep me doing what I love year in, year out. Thanks to you my books continue to appear in recommended reading lists everywhere. It is an honour to have written books that are so well remembered, and I aim to write many more in the years to come, that I hope you will find just as inspiring. My heartfelt thanks to you all!

Now onto *The Eternity Gate* — ENJOY!

LIST OF CHARACTERS

Bayan Har Shan
Dropa Elder — Dorje Pema
Governor of Kila — Rhun Gwynedd
The Lord of the Otherworld — Avery Gwynedd
Spirit Tiger/daughter of Shi and Huxin — Ling Hu
Reptilian Leader — Dragonface/Shyamal/Vugar

The Timekeepers
Wu Master/Head of the timekeepers — Jiang Hudan/Taren
    Lennox
Duke of Zhou/Captain of AMIE — Ji Dan/Lucian Gervaise
Great Mother of Li Shan/AMIE technologist — Yi Wu/Telmo
    Dacree
Grand Protector of Zhou/Were-tiger/AMIE security — Ji Shi/
    Yasper Ronan
Wu Were-tiger/Wife of Shi/AMIE security — Jiang Huxin/Jazmay
    Cardea
Wu Healer/AMIE horticulturist — Fen Gong/Ringbalin
    Malachi
King Cheng of Zhou/AMIE pilot — Ji Song/Zeven (Starman)
    Gudrun
Last Prince of Shang/AMIE's Nemesis — Wu Geng/Khalid
    Mansur

Kila
Governor's chief advisor and historian — Noah Purcell (En Noah)
KEPA employee/En Noah's wife — Rebecca
KEPA trainee and honorary timekeeper — Jahan

Reptilian agent/Guardian of 'the Dragon's Eye' — Aysel
Mistress of the Otherworld/Avery's wife — Fallon Alexander
Head of Defense/Rhun's son — Asher
Governor's secretary and wife — Sybil

AMIE (Astro-Marine Institute Explorer)
Captain's assistant/Zeven's wife — Aurora
Zeven's daughter — Thurraya (Ray)
Co-pilot/navigator — Leal
Ship's doctor/Leal's wife — Kassa
Project manager — Swithin

Ancient Zhou
The children of Ji Shi and Jiang Huxin — Zhen and Kao

The Eternity Gate and Beyond
Ascended Master — DK
The Logos of the Sovereign Integral — Abzu
The Primordial Creatrix of Order and Chaos — Tiamat
The Son of Tiamat — Kingu
Guardian of the Underworld — Kur

The Nefilim
Head of the Pantheon — Anu
Head of Genetics — Ninharsag
Queen of the Otherworld — Ereshkigal
Son of Anu/Ereshkigal's twin — Enki
Warlord — Nergal
Granddaughter of Anu — Nanshe
Sister of Nanshe — Nidaba
Great-granddaughter of Anu — Inanna

The Dark Universe
The Human — the Logos of the Sovereign Integral

The Grigori

Commander — Azazèl

Araqiel

Sammael

Armaros

Penemue

Bezaliel

Sariel

Gadriel

Sacha

The Fallen Elohim

Emperor — Samyaza

Bael

Vassago

Amon

Paimon

Baleth

Balam

Purson

Asmoday

Vinè

Zagon

Belial

TIMEKEEPERS REINCARNATION GUIDE

AMIE	THE CHOSEN	GRIGORI	ZHOU	ANCIENT BRITAIN
TAREN	TORY	AZAZÈL (female)	JIANG HUDAN	TORY
LUCIAN	MAELGWN	AZAZÈL (male)	JI DAN	MAELGWN
ZEVEN	BRIAN	SAMMAEL (male)	JI SONG	BROCKWELL
AURORA	NAOMI	SAMMAEL (female)	HUI RU	KATREN
RINGBALIN	NOAH	ARMAROS (male)	FEN GONG	SELWYN
AYLISCIA	REBECCA	ARMAROS (female)	HE NUAN / LING HU	KAILEAH
TELMO		ARAQIEL (male)	YI WU	TALIESIN
KALAYNA		ARAQIEL (female)		
JAZMAY		GADRIEL (female)	JIANG HUXIN	
YASPER	JAHAN	GADRIEL (male)	JI SHI	URIEN
LEAL	FLOYD	SARIEL (male)	JIANG TAIGONG	TEIRNAN
KASSA	BO	SARIEL (female)		IONE
MYTHRIC	RHUN	PENEMUE (male)	JI FA	RHUN
SATOMI	SYBIL	PENEMUE (female)	YI JIANG	BRIDGIT
SWITHIN	DOC	BEZALIEL (male)		CARADOC
AMIE	VANORA	BEZALIEL (female)		VANORA
KHALID			WU GENG	
	AVERY	SACHA (male)		

We all dwell beyond the limits of our living consciousness,
where all that is baffling to us now is understood.
We strive through many lives to return to this place,
until we arrive at the realisation that
we never actually left.

PROLOGUE

TIME EVENT RECONNAISSANCE

Location: Bayan Har Shan, China
Year: 1002 BC

The most difficult aspect of time event reconnaissance is to embrace your position as the observer and resist the urge to intervene. This is particularly difficult when the event in question involves individuals whom the observer holds dear, or an injustice that one has the power to prevent.

Still, the souls of my fellow timekeepers have many incarnations yet to be born into this world. Any change in these early historic events could affect the development, or even *the birth*, of any one of us — myself included. In this knowledge, I regard recon mission events as memories that I can do nothing to change. It is a bitter mantra for a time traveller, but our target will only remain shielded by causality for as long as he remains on this planet.

The target is one mind controlling many bodies, spread far and wide across the Earth. Locally, he is known as Dragonface, but on the other side of the galaxy, three thousand years from now, the shapeshifting, reptilian hybrid will be known as Yahweh Shyamal — the destroyer of the Chosen people of Kila, the planet

1

of which I was once governor. Beyond a lust to dominate and feed on the humans, we know Dragonface has another aspiration — to find the planet of his ancestors.

For hundreds of thousands of Earth years, the creature has searched this planet for a vessel that could complete such a voyage, and reports of a spacecraft falling from the sky led Dragonface to a remote mountain region between ancient China and Tibet.

The beings who crashed to Earth were mentally, emotionally, spiritually and psychically superior to the reptilians; the Dropa fended off the creature and his minions with the cosmic light of their very being.

In the beginning, as there were many Dropa their combined life force kept the reptilians at bay. Their cosmic light proved no barrier to local Ham Tibetan tribes, however, who were frightened by the small, ugly appearance of the alien beings and aimed to hunt them down and kill them. After a few minor misunderstandings, during which the Dropa proved their superior psychic skills without harm to their aggressors, the locals opted to leave the visitors in peace. Over time, the Ham realised they could learn and prosper from an association with these beings, but with that close association disease came into the Dropa camp. Their tiny bodies were built to take the great stresses of space travel but, having lived their entire lives in a controlled environment, the Dropa's immune systems were not so robust as to withstand the harsh conditions beyond their crashed vessel. Their ship had not been damaged beyond repair, but the restoration required materials that could not be sourced on Earth. Their only hope for survival was to genetically perfect more resilient bodies for their soul-minds to inhabit, and they did this by infusing their genetic code with the local humans and animals that were native to the area. White tigers were particularly favoured for their resilience, and thus ten thousand years later were-tigers are legend in this area, and two have been recruited to our crew.

Of those who survived to see the successful completion of their in-vitro bodies, the Dropa had several alternate forms to choose from, each with its perks and hindrances. The tiny human bodies they had perfected offered strong intellectual faculties, but unlike their previous forms they needed daily nourishment, and these forms proved useless for hunting or breeding. The were-tiger forms were taken by the braver among them to protect, hunt and breed for the rest of their tribe, for these forms were far stronger, yet not so well endowed in the intellect department.

As, one by one, the original bodies of the Dropa gave out, half of them committed themselves to their stasis pods within the ship — their deaths suspended — so that their cosmic life forces would continue to protect their remaining crew members. For twelve thousand years this barrier of compassion has protected the stranded vessel from being pirated by Dragonface and his minions ... until today.

PART 1

VENDETTA VACUA

1

DARK MATTER

When Rhun returned from his recon mission he looked like he'd just left a battlefield. There were large bloody gashes all over him, and these were going to raise questions among those timekeepers present, which he was not in the mood to answer.

'You were supposed to be observing only!' Telmo, the mission supervisor and their head technologist, threw his hands in the air. 'What the hell happened?'

All the wounds on Rhun's body smarted as he climbed from the time chariot. 'The place was crawling with reptiles! They surprised me. But I left the chariot in the crystal cave ... no one saw it, let alone got near it, so you have nothing to complain about.'

'But you're immortal.' Song frowned as he observed Rhun's bloodied state.

Unlike the rest of the crew — who needed to be genetically repaired by Dropa technology, or by the hands-on healing of their crew mate, Fen Gong — Rhun was immortal and self-healing, usually. The rest of the timekeepers were not born in this universe. Back in their universe of origin people lived ten times longer than the human beings in this universe. But in order to complete a mission in ancient Zhou China, the timekeepers had shifted their consciousness into the mortal bodies of past incarnations living at that time. Many among their ranks were still wearing those personas, which were far more fragile and prone to age than the bodies they were first born into. The timekeepers hoped to return to their birth bodies in the not-too-distant future.

'Obviously these wounds are not purely physical injuries,' Rhun deduced. 'Like the festering wound Dragonface gave to me during my past life as your father, Ji Fa, the cuts have been infused with the subtle poison of the dark arts.'

'Sub-etheric magic.' Telmo approached Rhun and grabbed one of his arms, casting a discerning eye over one of the larger gashes. 'You're right,' he observed, 'I can see the dark matter underpinning the wound and encouraging it to fester.'

'We should fetch Fen —' Song began.

Rhun reclaimed his arm from Telmo. 'It's nothing a short stint in the Dropa's regenerator won't fix,' he insisted, and quite frankly the isolation of the regenerator seemed a very attractive notion to Rhun right now. What he had just witnessed unfold, one week into their future, had left him deeply disturbed and he needed to rein in his personal feelings on the matter before he reported to the rest of the crew.

'Obviously our new design works.' Song moved to check the remodelled chariot and gave Telmo the thumbs up. Song had employed his psychic mastery over physical matter to construct the chariot from Telmo's design. 'I've been considering incorporating some additional security measures.'

Song was one of the timekeepers still wearing his Zhou incarnation; he was psychokinetic and the first timekeeper to be recruited by their founding member, Dr Taren Lennox. Back in their universe of origin, before the timekeepers' stint in ancient Zhou China, Song was a formidable pilot known as Zeven Gudrun, or Starman. Due to a leap back in time, Zeven had taken advantage of the extra years to study electro-mechanical engineering. He'd been time-jumping with Taren Lennox since the genesis of this entire inter-universe catastrophe.

Telmo, on the other hand, had assumed the appearance of his male incarnation in that other universe, and had free mental access to the knowledge of more incarnations of himself than he cared to remember, and all the supernatural abilities that went with them!

Rhun had personally known the greatest of Telmo's past selves on Earth, Taliesin Pen Beirdd, the last Celtic shaman of ancient Britain. The soul-mind inside Telmo was very old and wise, and he'd always appeared thus when Rhun had known him in the past. But at present Telmo appeared younger and prettier than he usually did, and Rhun was having trouble seeing him as the mentor he'd always been.

'Never mind about the chariot.' Telmo's attention returned to Rhun. 'Is history about to repeat itself, as you suspected?'

In a hurry to be with his own thoughts, Rhun backed up towards the door, holding his arms wide to show his wounds. 'You're telepathic, do you really have to ask?' He turned to leave.

'I'm forbidden to read your thoughts without your permission,' Telmo advised. 'It was in everyone's AMIE contract.'

AMIE was the Astro-Marine Institute Explorer — the space project that many of their current crew had been employed by in their previous universal scheme; the same project to which many of the timekeepers hoped to return, in the future.

'Then I guess you'll have to wait until I've been through regeneration, and brief the others.' Rhun raised a hand high to wave goodbye, but did not look back or slow the pace of his exit.

Being infused with cosmic light inside the regenerator pod was a blissful escape from reality. The capsule was called the 'egg' by their crew, due to its shape — but within its confines silence, time and possibility seemed limitless.

When the genetic regeneration session ended, Rhun returned to a conscious waking state, minus his physical injuries. His mental and emotional state would remain stable only so long as he didn't call to mind where he was and what he was doing here. Yet those two questions were the first any human being asked when they returned to a fully wakeful state, and so Rhun was forced to deal with his mindset of here and now.

With the memory of the mission, the euphoria induced by the session fled — he stared up at the ceiling from the semi-reclined seat with a forbidding sense of hopelessness building in his gut.

The upper part of the pod had translucent panels that allowed the subtle light in the room beyond to penetrate, so when the pod door opened, he was not blinded or discomforted in any way.

Dorje Pema, the last of the Dropa, was waiting to attend him — she was the only living being left on this planet who could operate the technology of her people. Her name meant 'indestructible lotus' for she was a timeless, formidable and enlightened legend in these parts. This was not her real name, but one she had earned over time. The tiny extraterrestrial-human half-caste, stood no taller than an average ten-year-old. Her face was as youthful as a child, yet her mesmerising eyes of indigo seemed to peer into Rhun's soul, and he felt the presence of the ages-old being that her in-vitro body had been carrying for thousands and thousands of years. Her deep blue robes covered her from head to toe and drew Rhun's focus to her penetrating gaze.

'Many thanks, Pema.' Rhun forced a smile to show his appreciation. 'That feels infinitely better.' He didn't rush to raise himself, knowing he would only get giddy if he did, but closed his eyes to hide his welling tears. The burst of pure life force had heightened his emotions, and they'd been fairly unstable to begin with.

'You are sad,' she observed pragmatically. 'It was as you remember?'

'Worse,' he admitted, his voice hoarse with hurt, and he swallowed hard as he looked at her to catch her reaction.

But the tiny Dropa woman didn't bat an eyelid. 'Not to worry,' she replied, sounding only mildly disappointed. 'We know what must be done. We are resolved.'

'I cannot allow it,' Rhun insisted. 'I cannot in good conscience save my people, if this is the cost.'

'The choice is not yours to make,' she gently reminded him. 'Our only worry is Wu Geng ... the one you call Khalid.'

Rhun nodded, understanding her concern.

'For thirty years, while you were collecting the rest of your timekeepers from among the Zhou, you left your one-time nemesis in our care. During that time we were the compassionate mentor Wu Geng has needed and never had. Our pupil has spiritually

10

advanced beyond expectation under our guidance and we worry he will not cope well with the forthcoming events.'

Dorje Pema always referred to herself in the plural as she was still psychically in contact with all her crew mates in stasis and was constantly guided by them. She also had an intuitive link to all the local offspring of her people that roamed the Earth in animal-human were-forms, even though they were of this planet's soul-group and not her own. The soul-minds of her people who had taken these forms had long ago committed their bodies to stasis to add their light to the compassion shield, or had perished before they could join their crew mates in their vigil.

'We ask that you will protect our student from his own grief in the wake of this event.' Dorje Pema held Rhun's gaze with her intense expression of appeal. 'It is all we ask in return for this service.'

Rhun was disturbed by her terminology. 'This is far more than a service —'

'Promise us,' she politely insisted, both eyebrows raised in challenge and finality.

Rhun gave a heavy exhalation, but his grief still caught in his throat and made it ache. 'I wish I'd never told you what happened last time I screwed up, then none of this would be happening.'

'*Promise us.*'

'There has to be another way?'

'There is none,' she stated. 'Not without risk to your people.'

Rhun shook his head, unable to believe where circumstance had led them. 'I only ever wanted to get you home ... not this —'

'*This* is the fastest route home for us. Agree to our terms, this is our wish, we are *resolved.*'

Rhun hated that the Dropa were so at peace with this; he hated that his will was always met at such a great cost to others. 'Of course,' he bowed his head with the guilt he felt, unable to look her in the eye. 'I will gladly comply with any request you make of me.'

'We have only this one.'

The serenity in her voice urged Rhun to look at her, and once he saw the compassion in her eyes, his sadness welled and tears

11

trickled down the side of his face in silent protest. 'I shall treat Khalid as my own brother.'

Dorje Pema struggled to repress a smile, despite the seriousness of the moment. 'Is that supposed to reassure us, timekeeper? We have seen you with your semi-etheric brother and your relationship with the Lord of the Otherworld is … not as supportive as we would ideally like for our pupil.'

Rhun cracked his first smile of the day, conceding her point. 'Perhaps you should make this request of someone who is not quite such a screw-up?'

'You are the only one among your crew who does not hold a karmic grudge against Khalid,' she explained, 'and you are the one who will profit most greatly from our resolve.'

The reminder was wounding, and Rhun bowed his head again to suck up his own remorse, then looked Dorje Pema in the eyes. 'I will do as you ask to the very best of my ability.' He couldn't stop the silent flow of tears, but squeezed his eyes tight in the hope of draining the sorrow from them.

'Did it ever occur to you that this is what was always meant to happen? Perhaps we were never meant to return to our planet of origin?' She encouraged him to let go of his judgements, but Rhun could not.

'If I had not recruited my brother to fetch the spare parts you needed to mend your spacecraft, you would have just continued on as you have —'

'Alone.' Her voice betrayed the great burden this was. 'For what? For whom? These bodies have served us well through the eternity we have spent stranded on this remote little planet, but they are not of our people. We would look as alien to them as you once looked to us. Our spirit is our connection to our soulmind … free us from form and we will be home.'

As she made it sound like he was doing the Dropa a great favour, some of Rhun's heaviness lifted. 'But we are still changing causality?'

'You sound so certain.' Her tone implied she begged to differ. 'But if it hadn't been the repairs to our ship that took our light-shield down, a rodent chewing through the wrong circuit could have caused the same failure. Whatever the case was, however long it took to come about, we all know this ship ends up in this creature's possession in the end. You are only speeding up the inevitable. Thus you are merely the instrument of cosmic timing.'

'My brother disagrees.' Rhun saw her point, but doubted Avery would share their view.

Dorje Pema smiled at this; Rhun and his brother seldom saw eye to eye on any matter. 'With all due respect to the Lord of the Otherworld, he dwells in an etheric realm where time is simultaneous. What could he know about physical world causality?'

Her view made Rhun grin a moment; it was so rare someone took his side over his semi-divine brother's. 'Well, Avery sees the result of my most recent decisions and, not liking what he sees, has ruled me to be a complete incompetent.'

'And you believe him,' Dorje Pema lectured. 'Even though all these brilliant souls have banded behind you to aid your cause?'

Rhun was flattered by what she was implying, but she had her facts wrong. 'The timekeepers, well most of them, were partly responsible for my debacle, so I think they feel obliged to help me sort it.'

'There you go, this is not all your burden to bear.' Dorje Pema could not repress her amusement at this point, and gave a little chuckle. 'Clearly others have more faith in you and your cause, than you do.'

'No,' Rhun cracked an uncomfortable smile. 'I have the utmost faith in my cause —'

'Then do what must be done, and trust that all is as it should be.' Dorje Pema nodded her head once, to drive home her point. 'If you waver in your conviction, your foe will surely prevail, for he will certainly never waver in his quest and then you will truly have something to feel sorry about.'

'That's exactly what happened last time,' Rhun justified his hesitancy.

'But this time we are prepared,' she concluded. 'And can turn the tide of this inter-time war to our favour.'

Rhun struggled to dispel his lingering doubts.

'We shall program the light-shield to power down over the course of the next seven days. That ought to get the creature's attention,' Pema said.

'That is why there were so many more of them than I remembered,' Rhun remarked. 'We gave Dragonface more notice to gather his minions.'

'The reptilians can move swiftly and have subterranean paths all over the world that they can follow to speed their travels.' Dorje Pema's people had researched their enemy well. 'We want to make sure we get them all.'

As Rhun's chair returned to a fully upright position, he nodded to agree, although his heart was still not at peace.

'Then you too can go home, and have a home worth going home to.' She urged him to think of that. 'We all win.'

'That is how it always looks in the planning stages.' Rhun stood and stepped into the outer chamber. 'But causality is an unpredictable mother f—' He stopped himself cussing and rephrased. 'It's very unpredictable. I know from experience that there is always a price to pay, somewhere down the track.'

The Dropa woman raised both eyebrows in resolve. 'That will be your problem, not ours, timekeeper.'

'It is always my problem!' Rhun threw his hands up.

'Well, as an immortal time traveller, what did you expect?' She cracked a smile at his complaints. 'One more grumble out of you and we are sticking you back in the egg,' the tiny woman threatened and Rhun found his humour.

'Yes please!' He headed back towards the pod.

'Do not try our patience, timekeeper,' she pointed him towards the door and his debrief. 'Time for you to inform the others of our intention whilst we reprogram the shield.'

She said this casually, as if it were only an electrical charge that she was shutting off. The fact was Dorje Pema would be programming her ship to shut off a stasis unit, containing one of her fellow crew members, each hour between now and the end of the event countdown. Thus one by one the Dropa would finally die and return to their soul-group and their true evolutionary scheme.

Rhun was reliving this moment for a second time, and he was thankful to have the support of the timekeepers during this round, as his first solo romp through the era had been a complete disaster. Most of the crew already knew the story of the first time Rhun visited ancient Zhou, lost the time chariot to Dragonface, and caused the extinction of the Chosen on Kila — who were supposedly immortal.

Whilst Dragonface was time-hopping, Rhun had been stranded in ancient China and had been found and taken to Dorje Pema. With the help of her egg she restored his health, but could not restore the immortality that Dragonface had taken from him with a DNA-destroying weapon. It was when Rhun learned that the Dropa were unable to source the material needed for repairs to their craft that he first wished his otherworldly brother was around to aid them, and inadvertently summoned his brother forth. Avery had been dragged back to the etheric realms of the Earth and kept there by his elemental dominions to protect him from falling victim to the same fate as his immortal kindred on Kila. Even though Rhun was residing in a time zone long before either of them were born, the Otherworld was timeless, and as long as Avery was Lord of the Otherworld, he could be summoned forth into the physical realm from anywhere — in any universe. But due to the disaster on Kila his elementals would not allow Avery to respond to any summons from the Esh-mah system to which Kila belonged. Upon learning of Dorje Pema's plight, Avery, having access to the sub-planes of every part of creation, was happy to have his elemental dominions produce the material the Dropa required. Whilst Dorje Pema set about repairing her craft, Avery assisted Rhun to steal back the time chariot.

At that time they did not suspect Dragonface was still monitoring the Dropa ship so closely, but in the time it took to retrieve the chariot, the spaceship was stolen. Avery had attempted to will himself after the vessel and Dorje Pema, but it was protected by the reptilians' dark magic. And despite the sad turn of events, Avery refused to allow Rhun to screw around with time and causality any further.

Nobody really knew how Dragonface had managed to take the ship. The theory was that during the install, the back-up generator used to maintain the light-shield during the repairs had failed, whereupon all the bodies sustaining the light-shield would have perished. With the protective barrier gone, the ship would have been an easy target for the reptilians.

Now Dorje Pema was offering to just give the reptilians what they had lusted after for so long, knowing they would not refuse the opportunity. But when the craft took off this time, it would be wired to explode once it reached a safe distance from the Earth.

'But without Dorje Pema they will never be able to launch.' Khalid was bemused for he was one of the few crew who had not caught wind of any of this before now.

Khalid was a timekeeper, in so far as he could shift his consciousness through time and incarnations as the rest of the old AMIE crew could, but he had never been on the AMIE project or been recruited by Taren Lennox — in fact they'd been arch-enemies. Khalid was caught up in events and had then invited himself along on their time quest, so he was rarely made privy to information before he had to be.

'That is why,' Rhun felt a large lump welling in his throat again, 'Dorje Pema intends to stay with the craft and leave with the reptilians.'

'No!' Khalid strongly objected. His dark eyes gazed around the room and it was plain that everyone was devastated by the news. 'You can't be serious?'

'It was not my choice.' Rhun struggled to explain what he could not himself fully condone.

'I could shift form into Dorje Pema, and then teleport out of there before the ship blows!' Huxin, their female shapeshifter, volunteered.

'That's a good idea,' Hudan, her twin sister, agreed.

Huxin and Hudan had been twin sisters during their stint in ancient Zhou, and although they were twins they could not have been more different, both in appearance and attitude. Perhaps this was because, in their previous universe, they had been fierce

16

rivals who became staunch allies. The soul currently inhabiting the body of Huxin was once Jazmay Cardea, a Valourean warrior, shapeshifter and timekeeper, whose talents extended far beyond those of the were-tiger she'd been during her life in ancient Zhou. Her twin, Hudan, was none other than Taren Lennox, the original timekeeper and founder of this time- and incarnation-hopping crew. During her future lifetimes in this universe, Rhun had also known Hudan as Tory Alexander; mother to both himself and Avery.

As much as Rhun hated to question these women, he had to. 'I feel you are all missing the point.'

'Which is?' Hudan queried, eyebrows raised and ready to be enlightened.

'It is Dorje Pema's desire to perish along with the rest of her crew,' Rhun stated. 'She does not wish to continue to live alone.'

'She would not be alone,' Khalid appealed, referring to everyone present.

'She isn't human,' Song pointed out.

'Dorje Pema is a superior form of human.' Khalid took offence to Song's tone. 'You cannot let her do this!'

Rhun was already resolved, and clearly Khalid saw this on his face.

'Tell me,' Khalid attempted to rein in his frustration, 'I did not spend thirty years learning the path of the righteous just to discover you are fucking bastards who only care about what will serve your ultimate purpose!'

Rhun understood his viewpoint perfectly, but his hands were tied, he had given his word to the Dropa. 'Dorje Pema said that she feared you might protest her decision —'

'Damn right I protest!' Khalid was yelling now and there would be no pacifying him.

'It's too late to alter the plan.' Rhun spoke up over him, but kept a civil tone. 'Dorje Pema has already begun the countdown towards the light-shield's total collapse, one week from now.' Although Khalid was winded by the news, Rhun looked back to the group to get through the brief. 'So, take care, everyone, the egg will also be incapacitated … if you get injured now, seek Fen.'

'Bye, bye eternal youth.' Huxin was fond of the egg for restoring her mind and body to what it had been in her prime; many of the team were grateful for that.

'Huxin!' Hudan frowned. 'We can *survive*!'

'Easy for you to say,' Huxin uttered under her breath, arms folded. 'You died young.'

'The day after I was wed!' Hudan begged to differ on the luck factor.

'Girls! Please.' Rhun would miss the remedial effects of the regeneration pod too, but he felt this was hardly the moment to discuss it. He looked to their young healer, crouched beside Ling Hu, the white tigress, who accompanied him everywhere. 'You are our last defence against death now, Fen.'

'I shall do my best to keep us all alive,' he reassured with a warm smile that had no trace of cockiness behind it — Fen was a humble, happy soul.

Not only did Fen Gong heal humans, he could grow anything and exert his emotional states of being over others. His love and compassion could heal, his hatred could kill — his counterpart incarnation on the AMIE crew, Ringbalin Malachi, had been able to do the same. Back in that other universe, he was the molecular biologist who had designed and maintained the AMIE project's greenhouse in space. At present Ringbalin's soul-mind was still residing in his Zhou incarnation Wu Fen Gong, who was slight in build, as Ringbalin had been, and was so pretty and effeminate he'd passed for a female for the first seventeen years of his life.

'You people are unbelievable.' Khalid was stunned by the acceptance around him. '*I am not* going to lose the only person I ever cared about!' Khalid vanished from their midst — no doubt he had teleported straight to Dorje Pema. Khalid would have no more success dissuading her than Rhun had.

'Do you think I should go after him?' Fen could forcibly pacify their rogue crew mate.

'No, let him go,' Dan spoke up finally — the one-time captain of AMIE had been very quiet during this brief. 'No one can handle Khalid better than Dorje Pema herself. She will help him see reason.'

Up until recently, Dan had been known as Zhou Gong — the first sage of China, who had aided his older brother, Ji Fa, to overthrow the long reign of many ruthless Shang emperors and unite China. Prior to his incarnation jump into ancient Zhou, Dan was known as Lucian Gervaise, captain and creator of the AMIE project. In both those lives, and all those incarnations before them, he'd been the husband and soul mate of Taren Lennox, AKA Jiang Hudan, Tory Alexander — the list went on.

Beside Dan sat his Zhou brother Shi — the male were-tiger of the crew — who was also being very quiet.

Shi had never been a very keen leader, despite being Grand Protector of half of China during Ji Song's time as King. Shi was a warrior, and always had been. Back on Kila he worked for KEPA, Kila Environmental Protection Agency, the organisation that protected the wildlife of their planet from being poached or hunted. But in the universe parallel, where the timekeepers first stemmed from, he was known as Yasper Ronan, AIME's head of security. In that incarnation and the one he'd just lived through in Zhou, he was husband and soul mate of Jazmay Cardea, AKA Jiang Huxin, and they too had a history together dating back to the dawn of time.

Everyone on the crew had such a soul they were attached to, but most had left their soul mates behind in their universe of origin. Due to various unforeseeable events along their journey through time and space, many of them were now battling time and causality to see their significant other again, Rhun and his otherworldly brother included.

'Is something on your mind, Shi?' Rhun queried the soul who, during their lives in the dark ages of ancient Britain, had been his brother-in-law, Urien.

'I worry that Dorje Pema has a psychic link to all the shifters in our land,' he raised a valid point. 'If they sense the Dropa are in danger, they will fight to the death to protect them. This is what *we* were bred by the Dropa to do. Their essence is in our blood.'

'He's right,' Huxin seconded his concern. '*We* may have to be physically restrained during the attack. Hudan also.' She looked back to her sister, who was also a shifter, but like Fen Gong's tigress, Ling Hu, Hudan shifted from physical to spirit form.

'Restraining myself and Ling Hu is going to be a lot more difficult,' Hudan posed. 'Even Fen may have Dropa ancestry. All of us developed supernatural talent, so we may have to be restrained, bar Rhun.'

'Um-hum!' Telmo held a finger high. 'I do believe I was here before the Dropa ever got here.'

It was true, the soul inside Telmo had been time-hopping and incarnating more than anyone present, and he was no longer even employing the female body he'd inhabited in ancient Zhou — physical transformation was one of his many talents and one of the first he'd perfected as Taliesin Pen Beirdd.

'Huxin can shift form back into Jazmay, who bears no genetic link to the Dropa,' Telmo advised. 'The rest of you we'll sedate until this is over.'

No one present seemed very disposed towards the solution, but all gave a nod to concur nonetheless.

'Khalid first,' Rhun suggested quietly, wary Khalid might re-materialise, or may never even have left, since he could render himself invisible.

'And heaven help us when he wakes up.' Telmo was clearly not optimistic about how Khalid would deal with life after his mentor's death.

But the decision was made now; this dark matter was drawing swiftly to a close, whether they were prepared for the consequences or not.

2

KILL 'EM ALL

With the shield coming down, Rhun wasn't taking any chances; he'd decided to shift the time chariot to the secret meeting place his brother had found for them — a crystal cavern located in the inner Earth somewhere. Rhun had only ever teleported to this cavern, so he didn't have a clue where it was located, none of the timekeepers did — they only knew what it looked like and that mental image was their ticket there.

Song kept pace with Rhun as he strode through the Dropa spacecraft, which was cleverly camouflaged to look like a very intricate labyrinth of white-washed caves. The lighting and large skylights did detract from the natural facade, but these could be closed off to enhance the disguise, along with the automatic doors that locked open, or could be completely concealed by the illusion of earth creating the appearance of a solid wall. 'I really think you should let me do my security install before you move the chariot beyond this time period,' Song insisted to their team leader.

'Why not come with me then, and you can do your install where you won't be interrupted?' Rhun suggested as the door to maintenance opened upon their approach.

'Yeah,' Song knew exactly what Rhun was driving at. 'And hope Telmo doesn't try to find us … I hate having him hanging over my shoulder when I'm trying to work.' He grabbed the mechanical-design specs from the drafting desk, which Telmo had committed to paper as he was unable to directly utilise the Dropa technology. Of course, Telmo could have whipped up some equally useful piece of technology from his time travels just as Taliesin could on Earth, but quite frankly Song found the drawn specs easier to use and follow.

'Well, you could just let Telmo do it. He's more qualified than you, which is why he's such a back seat driver … ' Rhun posed.

'No way! I enjoy working on the chariot,' Song objected. 'It's the only thing I'm good for until the fighting starts … being that there are no women around to f—'

'Gotcha,' Rhun held up a hand to prevent him saying more.

'What?' Song held up his hands in his own defence. 'I was going to say fraternise with.'

'Sure you were,' Rhun jibed, knowing Song's soul-mind so very well; he'd once been his uncle and the former governor of Kila; who, apart from his insanely brave tendencies, was a frightful womaniser when he was not attached.

'*There* is the one true love of my life at present.' Song motioned to the newly fashioned chariot. 'And isn't she the most shit-hot ride you have ever seen in your life?'

Rhun agreed, smiling as Song approached to buff his baby with his sleeve.

'She used to look like a fricking Frigian shopping trolley minus the shade canopy,' Song said, quietly amused by the simile as he stepped back to admire her again. 'But now … now she looks like every thrill seeker's wet dream!'

It was true the vehicle no longer looked like a chariot — more like a rideable black weapon of mass destruction. 'With inbuilt camouflage,' Rhun chimed in. 'No more worrying about her being seen by the wrong person.'

'We aim to please.' Song grinned.

'Then shall we leave? Before the control freak gets here to start micromanaging this operation?' Rhun suggested, climbing on the chariot, not to ride it to the cavern but rather to teleport it with him to the secret location.

'I'm right behind you.' Song waved him on and watched Rhun vanish with the time transport. Then, engaging his desire to join Rhun, Song dematerialised and followed his team leader to the crystal cavern.

Rhun was climbing off the chariot when Song materialised close by and was immediately mesmerised by one of the large crystal clusters that littered the cave above and below like a shimmering garden that lit the darkened space very efficiently.

'Why do the crystals in here glow when they never see sunlight?' Song wondered out loud.

'Precisely because they never see sunlight,' Rhun explained. 'Due to the utter darkness of this cave, you can see the excess photons they emit. Like the light that drives the Dropa ship and their healing egg, it is the primordial light of creation they are emitting. Which is why it feels so peaceful and unthreatening here. Even if Dragonface found this place, he'd be compelled to leave within seconds of arriving; the pure life force here would feel draining and repulsive to him.'

'Thus this is the safest place for our baby,' Song concluded, turning his eye to his work.

'Indeed.' Rhun turned to wander off.

'Where are you going?' Song queried.

'To find a moment's peace.' Rhun turned back briefly to add, 'And give you some peace as well.'

Song found that idea appealing. 'Fair enough,' he crouched down and laid out the specs for the upgrade to begin, conjuring up the parts he'd need. These components he fashioned from a combination of Telmo's visionary design and his own technical know-how and psychokinetic willpower.

Rhun had not taken two steps into his own quiet time when he sensed someone else materialise in the cavern close by him.

'So, you plan to play God again?'

The hairs on the back of Rhun's neck rose in prickly protest at the sound of his brother's voice. 'If not one control freak, then another,' Rhun commented to Song.

Rhun had found an ally in Song, whereas Telmo was more strongly allied to Avery at present. 'Keep me out of it,' Song chuckled.

'Just answer the question,' Avery insisted.

Although Rhun's younger brother had their mother's fair hair and grey-violet eyes, he could look just as fierce as Rhun when he was mad. They both had their father's broad-shouldered, slim build, but Avery got some of their father's height while Rhun had not.

Rhun finally turned fully to face Avery. 'Why bother when you obviously already know the answer? Aren't you only supposed to appear when I summon you?'

'Never mind about that —' Avery attempted to sidestep the query.

'No, answer my question.' Rhun demanded, doubly curious.

'Answer mine first!' Avery floated up over his big brother to look down on him, although he stood a little taller than him anyway.

'It was Dorje Pema's call,' Rhun retorted in an equally unpleasant tone.

'*No* ... it should be fate's call,' Avery lectured, 'there is nothing predestined about this event.'

'It's too late!' Rhun roared before he calmed again. 'There is nothing I can do now, the light-shield is already powering down.'

'Nothing you can do, are you shitting me?' Avery appealed. 'What is that?' He motioned to the time chariot Song was working on.

'These people,' Rhun motioned to Song, but was referring to all the timekeepers, 'have to go home! This mission has already lasted a lifetime longer than planned. Any one of them could return to their proper time and place with a thought. Half of them are missing their significant other, and have been for an age; how long do you think it's going to be before they start pining to the point that they accidentally will themselves right off the crew? Then we'll be back to dealing with Dragonface on our own.'

'Maybe that wouldn't be such a bad thing?' Avery suggested, obviously thinking it would be fewer people to negotiate around.

He considered what he'd just said more seriously and added, 'You're right, we have to do something to right the situation on our future planet fairly quickly, but I am not convinced that this is it.'

'Look,' Rhun took a step away from the argument. 'I answered your question, now you answer mine.'

'I need to have this out with you first,' Avery skirted the issue once more.

'I'm not discussing it further before you spill,' Rhun insisted. 'How did you get here?'

Avery rolled his eyes to emphasise how dense his brother was. 'You keep forgetting to dismiss me, and … if you don't, I am free to pass between worlds as I please at that particular time space junction.'

Rhun's jaw tensed. 'Do you mean to say that that time you trapped me here in an obelisk I could have just told you to piss off?'

Avery grinned, amused by his brother's hindsight. 'You still would have been stuck to the spot; once I cast that spell it was checkmate. If you'd wanted to be released from my hold, you'd have to have summoned me back anyway, and I don't have to respond.' He folded his arms, feeling rather smug and superior.

'Funny, is it?' Rhun queried, more than a little irked by his brother's lack of communication. He gave a little wave. 'Dismissed!'

'No!' Avery vanished from sight and Rhun gave a sigh of relief.

'Um,' Song spoke up, as he couldn't help but overhear the yelling match so close by him. 'But don't you have to say it three times?'

'The law of three requests!' Rhun wanted to hit himself as he'd not studied cosmic law since his days in ancient Britain.

Avery appeared again, hands on hips, staring at Song. 'I thought you wanted to stay out of it.' Avery looked back to Rhun. 'Listen to me —'

'Dismissed, dismissed, dismissed, dismissed …' Rhun continued to rant long after Avery had vanished, just to be sure. '… dismissed, dismissed —'

'Hey, whoa there,' Song cut in. 'I think he's gone now.'

'Who's gone?' Telmo queried as he materialised to catch the comment.

'Argh!' Both Song and Rhun whined in protest at his presence.

'What?' Telmo didn't understand their reaction at all. 'I thought you'd be glad to see me?'

Dan and Hudan, Shi and Huxin, were working in teams to install the remote sensors for the molecular demolition device that Telmo had dug up from somewhere in Earth's history to use to destroy the vessel. These sensors triggered the molecular breakdown of everything in the vicinity of a hundred square metres, and they needed to implant six around the interior of the outer rim of the Dropa ship to ensure its full decomposition without any debris. According to Telmo the entire craft would simply evaporate.

Dan was loosening a metal panel in order to remove and get in behind it to implant a device, when his hand slipped across the sharp outer edge and he nearly cut through three of his fingers. 'Oh, damn,' he protested, pulling his hand out to view the damage, blood squirting everywhere.

'Dan!' Hudan turned away to shield her face and used her psychokinesis to manifest a piece of cloth, which she wrapped around his hand to contain the bleeding. Quickly, she helped get him to his feet.

'I am fine to find Fen,' he assured her. 'You stay and finish this.'

Hudan pointed to the panel he'd been having so much trouble with and when it fell off onto the floor, she shrugged in conclusion. 'I told you to let me assist.'

'The wisest man of our age,' he referred to himself, 'I do not think so.'

'Go,' Hudan urged him to get fixed up before he bled to death.

Dan was inspecting the damage to his hand and shaking his head at his own stupidity when he entered Fen's room unannounced. The lad had been on his own since Dragonface murdered his betrothed, forty years before so it did not occur to Dan that he might be interrupting anything.

'Fen, I've had a bit of an accident —' Dan looked up and was bemused to find Fen naked in bed, with someone else wriggling around underneath the covers. Dan could only assume it was his tigress, as she was nowhere to be seen.

Fen, appearing flustered, grabbed for his trousers and put them on, as the large lump under the covers beside him vanished. 'What happened, Captain?'

The lad scampered down to look at Dan's wound, which he held out for Fen to inspect. He could feel himself going into shock, and Dan wasn't sure if it was the wound, or what he thought he'd just walked in on that was the cause.

'Sit down.' Fen led him to a seat and plonked him in it, then knelt down before him.

'Fen, I know it's really none of my business, but I worry —'

'Don't worry,' Fen advised, looking him in the eye briefly, before grinning, embarrassed. 'It's not what you think.'

Dan didn't know what to make of that response either and so went quiet to allow Fen to concentrate.

The healer held his hands together and focused his *chi* into a ball of energy — light streaming from the space between his fingers. At this point he invited Dan to insert his damaged hand into the glow suspended between his palms.

The relief from the smarting wounds was immediate and Dan gave a sigh of relief as Fen's healing light was absorbed into his injured limb and it mended, good as new. 'I should have announced myself.' Dan resolved that he was to blame for any embarrassment.

Fen, having no way to avoid the conversation now, swallowed hard, appearing put on the spot. 'Captain, I —'

Dan held up a hand to prevent him saying anything more. 'I shall leave now. Thank you for this.' Dan removed the bloody rag and wriggled his fingers. 'Good job.' Dan headed for the door and turned back before exiting. 'You can come back now, Ling Hu, I am departing.' He walked into the corridor and the door slid closed behind him.

Once outside, Dan drew such a deep breath that his eyes nearly popped out of his head. He knew Fen adored the tigress he'd raised, but surely that love had not gone to such unnatural extremes? *No.* Dan wouldn't believe that. He suspected Fen and Ling Hu had a

27

secret, and he could not resist turning back and employing his third eye vision to peer through the wall into the room he'd just left.

The albino tigress came out of hiding, and as she crawled out from under the bed covers she transformed into a naked woman with skin and hair as white as her tiger form, her eyes the same piercing blue. This woman bore a striking resemblance, not to her last incarnation as He Nuan — the love that Fen had lost — but to Dr Ayliscia Portus, AIME's marine biologist and the love of Ringbalin's life.

Dan grinned, wondering how long this love affair had been going on.

But as it was really none of his business, he was of a mind to walk away when Fen said, 'What must the captain be thinking? We have to tell him.'

Dan paused, wondering if he should put Fen's mind at rest? Why the secrecy? He didn't understand it.

'I can only maintain this form when I am alone with you and filled with lust.' Ling Hu collapsed onto the bed and rolled over on her back to appeal. 'Come back to bed.'

'Damn,' Fen was clearly torn between his desire and fear of being caught again. 'I'd feel a whole lot safer if this door locked.' He approached her warily glancing back towards where his captain had exited.

Dan looked away and moved off quickly. *Poor Fen*. Dan saw now that the healer would have a lot of difficulty trying to prove his explanation, even if he did front up to his captain with the truth of what he'd just intruded upon.

'Are you all right?' Hudan called from up ahead.

'Fine,' he assured her, holding his hand up for her to view. 'How did the install go?'

'All done,' she announced triumphantly.

'Excellent, we can move into the next one.'

'No.' Hudan corrected his misconception. 'Our three installs are *done*.' She raised her brows suggestively. 'What shall we do with the afternoon now?'

'We should really go and assist Shi and Huxin, don't you think?'

Hudan's grin faded.

28

'You don't like that idea, I take it?' Dan concluded.

With a shake of her head Hudan directed him to Khalid, striding down the corridor in their direction behind Dan.

The man looked completely distraught. 'It's not right.' He appealed his case to them. 'Why is what I want *always* contradictory to what you want?'

'This is not what we want, Khalid —' Hudan tried to assure him.

'Don't call me that,' he was offended. 'I am nothing like that person, I am Wu Geng now.'

This was the name of his Shang incarnation, the body of whom he still wore. The last Shang prince had suffered long and aided Ji Song and Zhou to victory — it was also the name Dorje Pema always called him by.

Hudan nodded in apology. 'As you wish, Wu Geng, but you must learn to surrender to the will of the divine, just like the rest of us.'

'This *is not* divine will,' Wu Geng insisted. 'It is Rhun's will, and it is your will … so you can get back to our universe and destroy me! *But* … as far as I can tell, the divine has not weighed in on the issue.'

'Then what was Rhun's recon mission?' Hudan queried.

'You'd already decided!' Khalid argued his point, frustrated. 'Of course it would play out as he expected, only worse, because this time it is a set up!' He calmed himself to continue in a reasonable, less passionate tone. 'Would it not have been fairer to view that mission from *before* the instance where Rhun told Dorje Pema about his past faux pas?'

'He has a point,' Hudan had to agree, and so did Dan to a degree.

'Be that as it may, if we continue to try to rework one particular instance in time it inevitably becomes tangled.' This was Dan's fear. 'And we'll end up with even more causality to contend with than we do now.'

Hudan was nodding in agreement, but Wu Geng's face had gone blank.

'What … the … *fuck* … are you talking about?'

29

'You swear like Khalid,' Hudan noted.

'Only when inspired.' He kept his tone civil despite the cussing.

'You haven't done enough time-hopping to have been in a situation like this,' Dan began, but Wu Geng waved him off.

'Save your breath.' He decided to keep moving. 'What was I thinking? I'm only here so you can keep an eye on me. Sorry, I forgot.'

'Wu Geng,' Hudan went to go after him, but Dan pulled her up.

'I would suggest giving him a little time to cool down, before you try reasoning with him.'

Hudan considered the man's admiration for his mentor. 'About a thousand years ought to do it.'

Dan exhaled, not confident Wu Geng was going to continue to be a help and not a hindrance. 'We have a week.'

As the days passed, the timekeepers grew more and more edgy, both with the plan and each other — the loss of the compassion shield and the abstract presence of the evil force amassing around the periphery of the diminishing light barrier was being sorely felt by all.

By the time they had to bid farewell to Dorje Pema there was not one ounce of joy left among them. Right up until the moment of their parting, Wu Geng was begging Dorje Pema to reconsider, but she would not.

'Then let me stay with you,' he appealed, then referred to the rest of the crew: 'That would serve their cause well, I would forget everything that has transpired since I left our universe, and they wouldn't have to babysit me any more!'

'Your path to us was so very difficult and strange ... that it seems apparent that you are meant to be on this journey, with all the other castaways from your universal scheme. To throw away all that knowledge would be a cosmic injustice.'

'And what about all your knowledge?' he appealed from his kneeling position in front of her.

'Our quest is done, Wu Geng, Khalid's quest is not.'

He had no reasonable retort. 'I hope they destroy him, the outcome does not matter to me.'

'Khalid has the potential to be you, Wu Geng,' Dorje Pema pointed out. 'But not without the benefit of your knowledge and understanding. You must endure and right all that has been wronged by Khalid's actions. Only by so doing will you truly be the spiritual warrior you have been striving to become. Vow to us that you will endure, and place no blame for our passing in any quarter.'

Wu Geng bowed his head to swallow the bitter mandate.

'Your survival is far more important than you, or any of your team mates, realise,' Dorje Pema spoke up for all to hear. 'Your soul source may be different to theirs but it is just as splendid. You are no more alone in your plight than we are. Make it home and you shall know we have not led you ill.'

'I shall obey you in this,' he looked back to her, his tears of frustration welling, 'as in all things.'

'You must go now, with the others, and be sedated,' she told him. 'Just as I shall be sedated, to avoid alarming all the shifters of our land.' Dorje Pema looked to Fen and smiled warmly. 'Fen Gong has prepared a special brew to keep me happy and relaxed throughout the entire affair.'

Fen assured Wu Geng that was true. But he was not comforted. 'So this is goodbye, Shifu.'

She nodded and smiled warmly. 'Perhaps I'll see you in the next one.'

Whether she meant the next life, the next universe or the next evolutionary scheme, he didn't ask, but merely bowed his head, stood and backed up to join the rest of timekeepers.

'I'll stay here, with Dorje Pema,' Rhun advised, and Telmo waved as he and the rest of the team joined hands and departed for the crystal cave.

'May the universe bless you Pema, and the Dropa … always!' Hudan managed to say before she was shifted to safety with the others.

*

Telmo had mastered psychokinesis during his time as Taliesin and used this skill to raise several crystal plinths inside the cavern for their tranquillised crew to reside upon. One alongside the other, the smooth surfaces glowed as brightly as the substance they were fashioned from. There was a double width plinth at both ends of the configuration to accommodate Hudan and Dan, and Fen and Ling Hu; Song, Shi and Khalid were allocated the single plinths in the centre.

The cloaking device on the chariot had been engaged as a cautionary measure — the entire reason they had given the chariot a facelift in the first place was because Wu Geng, AKA Khalid, had seen it, and as he had psychokinesis, he could find the time-hopping transport whenever he liked. Despite his apparent change in character, they could not risk the chariot being stolen again and so had remodelled it to the point that it was unrecognisable — and thus unfindable.

As the crew got themselves settled, Telmo approached Song with the small device that delivered the anaesthesia.

'Is this going to have side effects?' Song was lying down, but held Telmo at bay with an outstretched hand. 'How long are we going to be out for?'

Telmo smiled, as if preparing to reassure him and touching the tip of his device against his patient's open palm, Song immediately passed out. 'No side effects, and you'll regain unconscious as soon as your body is disturbed, like this.' Telmo gave Song a good shake, whereby he opened his eyes again and seemed confused.

'Sorry, were you saying something?' Song frowned.

'So yeah,' Telmo finished, 'there's just a bit of a memory lag.'

'Hey, hold on,' Song recalled his query and was annoyed. 'Did you knock me out already?'

'Yes.' Telmo said with glee, and hit Song again with the device, causing him to go back to sleeping like a baby. 'Any more questions?' he invited.

The rest of the crew declined.

'Splendid. Huxin,' he looked to the shifter, who was seated beside Shi, bidding her husband farewell. 'You should shift into Jazmay now, before we return.'

She smiled to reassure her husband, backed up to standing and transformed into the tall, ex-Valourean, Jazmay Cardea. The Valoureans were the bodyguards of the Queen of Phemoria — a planet of psychic female warriors, as beautiful as they were deadly.

'Wow!' Shi grinned, having never seen her do that transformation before in this lifetime. 'You are beautiful no matter what skin you are in.'

'You!' Wu Geng was back to standing, for Huxin's transformation sparked a past-life memory. 'You killed a reptilian back on Kila. You can assume their form, I've seen you do it! You could protect Dorje Pema, and bring her back! You must!'

Shi was up and standing between Wu Geng and his wife, although she did not need protecting.

'I remember that instance too,' Shi was in Wu Geng's face. 'The reptilians have a hive-mind; to shift into their form would leave my wife's thoughts as open to Dragonface as his hive-mind is to her.'

Jazmay exhibited the very same scowling expression that crossed Huxin's face when she was displeased, and it wasn't clear which man she was more annoyed with. 'I cannot save a woman who does not want to be saved,' Jazmay moved her now shorter husband out of the way, to address her accuser directly. 'You are mistaking your own fear of loss for compassion, when death is the compassionate stance in this instance.'

'Or you are being elitist, sacrificing such a magnificent soul to save all your own skins!' Wu Geng retorted, just as Telmo touched Wu Geng with his device and he fell to the floor, unconscious.

'I understand his view, but it's too late to go back now.' Telmo focused his psychic will on their rogue crew mate and floated Wu Geng's body gently up off the floor and brought it to rest on the plinth allocated for him. 'The good news is that, true to form, as Jazmay Cardea you do seem to be completely emotionally detached from the outcome.'

Shi appeared concerned by this. 'Does that mean you also feel emotionally detached from me?'

Jazmay gripped hold of Shi, who was fearful of her intent until she kissed him passionately, and then drew back to instruct. 'Now rest.'

'Yes, ma'am.' Shi grinned and returned to his place to be sedated. 'See you after.' He lay down and allowed Telmo to knock him out.

'Maybe I should stay awake,' Hudan was edgy.

'Don't even think about it,' her sister insisted. 'I've got this. Get her, Telmo,' she urged him to work faster.

'But I have a b—' Hudan turned to appeal to Telmo, but he got her with a prick from his device and she went down peacefully.

'Do you think the next word out of her mouth was going to be bad?' Dan was concerned as Hudan was an oracle.

''Night, Captain,' Telmo administered Dan's dose too, and he fell down beside his wife. 'There's too many bloody control freaks on this crew.'

'Ha!' Jazmay was amused. 'Says the greatest of them all.'

'Why, thank you,' he bowed graciously, 'I like to think so.'

'Greatest control freak, is what I meant,' Jazmay clarified as Telmo headed past his sleeping crew to the far end where Fen was settled with his tigress up on the plinth.

'I *am* in control,' Telmo agreed, 'and I *am* a freak of nature, as are we all. Isn't that right, sweetness?' Telmo leant down to address Ling Hu at close quarters and gave an affectionate pat to the tigress he was about to sedate.

'Don't call her that,' Fen was annoyed, as he watched his tigress lick Telmo's face. 'You are getting her all excited when we are trying to put her down to sleep.'

'She likes me,' Telmo continued to dote on her, rubbing his head against hers. 'If only you were a woman, Ling Hu, I'd be courting you.'

'Over my dead body.' Fen urged Telmo to back up a bit.

'Well, if she were human, Ling Hu would see you as a father, not a love interest,' Telmo reasoned with a grin.

'She does not —' Fen began to state surely, and then bit his own tongue.

Telmo was intrigued by his response. 'You sound so sure about that?'

'He's just teasing you, Fen.' Huxin rolled her eyes at how easily he was baited. 'Stop fighting over my daughter and get on with it.'

Telmo did the deed, whereupon Ling Hu fell into a fitful slumber and, seeing her peaceful, Fen finally settled down beside her. 'Are you sure you don't want me awake?'

'Very sure,' Telmo hit Fen with a dose from his device and the worry left the healer's face as he passed out. 'Finally … all the kiddies are asleep.'

'Then let's get this over with so we can all go home.' Jazmay was clearly champing at the bit to straddle this last hurdle.

Telmo could not have been more empathetic — for him home had a name, *Kalayna*, and he couldn't wait to see her again.

Rhun sat high on an icy ridge, miles from the Dropa vessel. He still carried his binoculars on his weapons belt from Kila. With the high magnification of their lenses, he could see the stranded spaceship he'd called home in ancient Zhou, set atop the plateau where it had resided safely for the past twenty thousand years. With the compassion shield diminished, the illusory camouflage of mountainous caves had vanished and the large metallic craft now sat in plain sight with only large clumps of melting snow and ice to conceal it from the enemy.

This time around, Rhun chose a far more remote viewing point than he had during his recon mission, so as to place himself behind the advancing enemy line and not in its path. The shadows of the smaller mountains between here and the Dropa craft were crawling with reptilians, just waiting for sundown so they could attack.

'Nice view,' said a familiar but oddly accented voice. Rhun looked aside to find Jazmay Cardea and grinned to see the warlike beauty again.

'You know I've always felt threatened by women taller than me?'

Jazmay rolled her eyes to jest. 'Come, Governor, you cannot find all women threatening, surely?'

Rhun smiled off the insult and turned to find Telmo standing to his other side. 'This is not the spot you viewed this from before, I take it?'

What kind of an idiot did everyone take him for? 'No.' Rhun raised his binoculars to view the other ridge face closer to the Dropa craft, and spotting himself standing and observing the event, he passed the magnifiers over to Telmo. 'That's me there.'

Telmo retrieved the viewing tool to take a look.

'And any moment now, for your viewing pleasure, I am going to be ambushed.' Rhun took a deep breath and walked away to keep his welling anxiety and angst in check.

'Oh … yes, I see,' Telmo commented flatly. 'There are quite a few of them, aren't there?'

'What did I say?' Rhun wondered why he bothered opening his mouth at all.

'Ah … there you go.' Telmo witnessed Rhun vanish from the rumble and handed the binoculars back. 'Can't be long now then.'

Rhun went to agree but the words got stuck in his throat, and he merely shook his head.

Just after nightfall Rhun switched his binoculars to night vision but unable to watch, he handed the surveillance job over to Telmo.

'This is not your fault,' the technologist commented, his eyes focused down the viewing device. 'It was a time bomb waiting to happen.'

'Your buddy Avery does not agree,' Rhun retorted.

'It's not his realm of expertise,' Telmo mumbled.

'That's what Dorje Pema said.'

'Well, there you go.' Telmo got fidgety, as he relayed, 'And here we go.'

The plateau in the distance suddenly lit up, and both Rhun and Jazmay gasped at the sight. The sound of metal on metal echoed across the darkened landscape to them, as the exterior doors of the craft locked closed.

An eerie silence followed, from which slowly arose the sound of tigers and wolves howling in pain, and foxes screeched in panic. This only heightened the feeling of alarm Rhun was experiencing, and he felt guilty for wishing the craft would just take off. He looked aside to Jazmay, and even with only the moonlight to see by, he noted how she trembled. 'Jaz? You okay?'

She nodded in the affirmative, although she was clearly using some restraint to do so.

With a mighty crack, akin to the birth of an avalanche, the craft lifted off the plateau, and despite the stricken cries from the shifters of the region infusing the moment with hysteria, it was an awe inspiring sight to witness.

'I have to answer their plea,' uttered Jazmay, shaking her head to discourage herself. 'I am the only one who can save her now.'

Rhun dragged his eyes from the spacecraft ascending to witness Jazmay transform into a reptilian.

'No!' Telmo strongly objected.

'It doesn't matter, she can't make it on board the ship,' Rhun grabbed hold of Telmo to attempt to calm him. 'Avery tried to teleport himself on board last time this happened and could not. It's shielded by sub-etheric magic.'

'That's not the problem!' Telmo tore himself away from Rhun as the spaceship suddenly shot out of sight, which distracted them all momentarily.

'Change back now!' Telmo ran to Jazmay, but came to a stop before the towering reptilian, in case she forgot whose side she was on. 'The creature will be in your head!'

No sooner had he said this than the reptilian collapsed onto its knees, gripping its temples, and wailed as it raged an inner battle to resume a human form. Finally Huxin's will won the struggle and she resumed her regular appearance. Fortunately the organic-fibre suit she was wearing had adjusted itself to fit her shifting body shape and she was not left naked and freezing in the snow. Despite this she was trembling uncontrollably.

'The creature knows what we are up to,' she blurted out in panic, and was temporarily paralysed by her fear. 'It wants us to destroy all his kind here on Earth as it is the fastest way to find his long-lost kindred in space!'

Just as death was the fastest way for the Dropa soul-minds to rejoin their long-lost kindred in space, it would seem this was the case with Dragonface as well.

'Oh fuck!' Rhun was bowled over by the contingency he had not bargained on and was still reeling from that comment when a large patch in the distant night sky suddenly lit up like a huge brilliant blue firework in the heavens.

'Listen to me!' Huxin cried to compete with the eye-catching event and grabbed hold of Telmo who'd come to kneel beside her. 'I think Dragonface knows about the crystal cavern.' She gasped back her horror, as the sky fell dark again, and the eerie silence returned. 'The creature plans to kill us all, one by one!'

'With what?' Rhun, angered by the threat, motioned to the sky above where every single reptilian on the planet had just been evaporated. He hated to think the beast had somehow outsmarted them. 'If you ask me, he was bluffing in a hopeless attempt to piss me off one last time.'

'Let's go.' Telmo gripped hold of the trembling woman beside him, and teleported her to the cave with him.

Before Rhun gave pursuit, he drew a deep breath and made a wish — that he would find all the timekeepers resting safely in the cave just as he had left them.

His arrival in the crystal cavern was met by the agonised screams of Huxin, who was collapsed before the large stalagmite on which her husband had been impaled. Shi was bleeding a river of blood over the crystal surface of the natural structure that had taken his life and the red stream pooled around the base.

The sight made Rhun's stomach churn, and his body reverberated with the shock of imagining how Shi had met this end. The answer was simple really: Shi, or rather his previous incarnation, Yasper, could levitate — and would have done so in an attempt to escape his attacker. But if that attacker was carrying a weapon that abolished psychic power with one blast, like the weapon used to destroy the Chosen on Kila, then Shi could have been shot and left to drop. The terrain in the cavern would have done the murderer's job for him.

Huxin was morphing uncontrollably in a fruitless attempt to escape her anguish, but her emotions were not so beyond her control that she shifted into reptilian form again. Telmo was waiting for the right moment to approach and calm her.

Rhun didn't even want to check on the state of the rest of the crew, but at a quick glance it appeared no one else had been touched.

'The creature plans to kill us all, one by one' was Huxin's message from Dragonface. Clearly, the others had been left alive on purpose, to show how confident their stalker was that they could be hunted down at his own leisure.

'How could Dragonface have done this?' Rhun, struck by a horrifying thought, teleported across to check that the chariot was still cloaked and present. 'Thank the universe.' He breathed a sigh of relief to feel its invisible structure.

Telmo had given Dan and Hudan a shake, as despite Huxin's wailing, they had not stirred from their slumber, and Telmo could not get close to the shapeshifter to pacify her.

'Dear universe, no!' Hudan sprang from her reclined position, distressed by the horrifying circumstances that she awoke to. 'How? Who?' She rushed to console her sister, who collapsed into her embrace and continued to wail out her grief.

Dan rose to standing, observing his brother's bleeding corpse with growing ire. 'Why was only my little brother targeted?'

Despite his personal sorrow, Dan asked the most pertinent question, and Rhun expected nothing less of the captain.

'Dragonface picked my lover to teach me a lesson!' Huxin cried out to claim responsibility. 'It is my fault he is dead!' She collapsed into tears once again.

The captain clenched his jaw briefly, to contain his welling grief. 'Why is he still impaled like that?' Dan looked to Telmo, knowing he could have used his psychokinesis to get him down.

'I didn't want to move him before you saw it, Captain,' the technologist explained.

'Well,' Dan's voice caught in his throat, and he inhaled deeply before speaking again. 'Get him down, it is distressing to Huxin.'

Telmo nodded and moved to comply.

'And the sight will distress Ling Hu when she awakens,' the captain added, glancing down to where the tigress should have been sleeping. 'Where is Ling Hu?'

Dan looked to Rhun, who felt like a complete failure. 'My sincerest apologies, Captain, I hadn't noticed her missing.'

'This is not your fault,' Dan insisted.

'You don't know what happened yet,' Rhun pointed out that the captain's absolution was a little premature.

'Summon your brother,' Dan instructed, 'and you can fill us both in at once.'

Avery was going to be furious, and perhaps rightly so. For despite the captain's gracious stance, Rhun felt himself responsible for this tragic turn of events, and as much as he hated to admit it, he should have listened to his little brother.

When Song was awakened and enlightened to the events that had transpired during his slumber, his sights immediately turned to Wu Geng, who was still unconscious. 'How do we know for sure it was Dragonface? Khalid is real pissed at us at present.'

'He prefers to be called Wu Geng,' Dan enlightened Song, not liking his implication.

'Shi and Wu Geng did have an argument before I put them down,' Telmo reminded the captain.

'There you go then.' Song was even more convinced that Wu Geng could be the culprit, or at least involved. Song's incarnation, Zeven Gudrun, was destined to destroy Khalid back in their home universe — he, more than anyone, had a karmic grudge against their old nemesis.

'I'm telling you this was Dragonface's handiwork,' Huxin seethed. She had expended her grief and now had a killer look in her eye. 'Give me the chariot and I will go back and prevent this, and destroy that unholy mutation!'

'We already destroyed Dragonface once today,' Rhun pointed out, drawing everyone's attention his way.

To follow the captain's orders, Rhun had moved away from the general din and summoned his otherworldly brother forth. He'd wanted to have their squabble away from the timekeepers to avoid distressing anyone further while he and Avery sorted out their difference in opinion. Yet their confrontation had been surprisingly short-lived and not as adverse as Rhun had expected.

'No one is taking the chariot anywhere,' Avery announced as he accompanied Rhun back into the cavern. 'I have just returned from Kila, which is as it was before Dragonface ever found us.'

'So our plan worked,' Telmo clarified, and as the Lord of the Otherworld smiled, everyone's mood lifted. 'We can go home,' he uttered, buoyed by the thought along with everyone else.

'Not without Shi!' Huxin objected.

'His Chosen incarnation, Jahan, is back in our capital city, safe and sound,' Avery pointed out. 'Fortunately, Dragonface picked the only activated timekeeper who came from Kila.'

'But Jahan won't remember me, us … or any of this?' The tears of mourning continued to roll down Huxin's cheeks.

'But he is not lost,' Avery countered, 'and if we try to rework this instance again, we may lose someone vital to your mission back on AMIE.'

'He's right, Huxin,' Hudan timidly voiced her view.

'And what of Ling Hu, our daughter?' Huxin motioned to the vacant space next to their sleeping healer where the albino were-tiger had been.

'Her Chosen soul-mind is also safely back on Kila, in the embodied form of En Noah's female counterpart, Rebecca. And she is safely residing in your universe of origin under some other name —'

'Ayliscia Portus,' the captain filled in Avery's blank and the Lord of the Otherworld looked at Dan in appreciation and continued.

'Along with your mate,' Avery looked to the captain to be clued in again.

'Yasper Ronan,' the captain obliged once more.

41

'Yasper Ronan,' Avery repeated, ahead of frowning. 'I do believe I knew his father?'

Hudan found his comment curious. 'You did, but in a timeline that we reworked, so I am surprised that you remember.'

'Heart attack, wasn't it?' Avery pondered.

'Yes,' Hudan was doubly amazed. 'He did have a heart attack, which changed his view of the world in both your universe and again in ours.'

'I had to send him back to his life, if memory serves.' Avery stated.

'He did miraculously recover in both instances,' she confirmed.

'This mission is not over.' Huxin was not as accepting of the outcome as everyone else, and she raised herself from the ground, where she had wallowed and been stained with her husband's blood. 'Someone, or something, murdered my love and is now holding our daughter hostage! Now you may be prepared to overlook that, but I will not leave this age until I have gutted every fucking overgrown lizard in this universe!'

Rhun sympathised with her anguish, but she was not being very realistic. 'It's a very big universe, Huxin, where do you suggest we start looking?'

'I've heard you call them Orions before today, so that might be a good place to start,' Huxin spat back.

'Orion is a very large constellation.' Rhun raised both brows to implore her to be more reasonable.

'The creature will find us!' she stressed. 'This is part of its vendetta, do you not see?' She motioned to her husband's remains, now laid out on the plinth that Hudan and Dan had vacated.

'We are about to shift three thousand years into the future,' Rhun advised. 'So it does not matter that Dragonface found this place, or how he managed to tolerate the healing frequencies for long enough to kill Shi and take Ling Hu, he cannot follow us into the future.'

'Unless we are taking the true culprit with us? Or they could be in cahoots, and perhaps always were?' Again Song's sights fell to Wu Geng. 'I say we leave him here, just to be sure.'

Rhun shook his head. 'I can't do that. I promised Dorje Pema I would take care of him as I would my own brother.'

'Ha,' Avery scoffed. 'In that case, you can slit his throat before leaving him.'

'Good plan,' Song agreed.

'No one is getting left behind,' the captain spoke up. 'And no one else is dying.'

'That's easy to say, Captain,' Huxin scolded. 'No one has woken Fen yet to tell him his charge has been stolen by that creature again!'

At this point everyone bowed their head to warrant that she was right — Fen would be devastated.

'Perhaps we should not wake him now,' Telmo ventured to suggest what the rest of the team were no doubt thinking.

Huxin's scowl was a clear indication of her objection. 'You cowards!' She made a move towards Fen's sleeping form.

Telmo intercepted and tranquillised her with his device, catching her up in his arms before she hit the floor. 'Let's not be rash.' He laid her gently on a plinth.

'We have to wake Fen, only he can consciously will his soul-mind home to his rightful place in our universe of origin,' Hudan pointed out. 'The same goes for Huxin and Wu Geng.'

'Come back to Kila with us first, where we can debrief properly,' Rhun suggested. 'Some time in our healing temple will help them all through their grief, and put some time and distance between them and this mission.'

'It's a good idea,' Telmo agreed.

'I say we leave Wu Geng here,' Song added his two cents' worth.

'I've told you my ruling on that,' Dan cautioned Song.

'This is a nightmare,' Hudan held her head to attempt to get a grip on her thoughts, and then looked to Rhun and Avery. 'I am at a loss.' She threw her hands up and looked to Dan. 'Captain?'

'This is Rhun and Avery's universe, it's their call.' Dan referred the matter back to them.

'Although I am sorry for the loss of our crew members, our mission here has been accomplished,' Rhun's voice crumbled under the weight of his decision. 'And at this point you have not lost any of the soul-minds who accompanied you into our universe on this mission … if we mess with time further, that could change.'

Dan nodded. 'Agreed.'

'We must tell Fen now.' Hudan was not as agreeable. 'He'll have no chance of saving Ling Hu from three thousand years in the future!'

'Exactly,' Rhun advised timidly.

'We can't risk him creating another disaster and destroying the future we have now regained,' Avery added. 'I am sorry, but in this case the needs of the many outweigh the needs of the one.'

Song cocked an eye, curious about the lord's stance — he may not have been the wisest of souls, but he was perceptive. 'That's not what you were saying about Dorje Pema, even though we anticipated Kila would be restored, as it has been. Is it just the confirmation of our success that has changed your tune? Or has something else altered that we don't know about?'

Everyone found the query most curious, especially as Avery appeared a little discomforted by it. 'Something unforeseeable has happened,' he confessed with a shy smile. 'I am to be a father.'

The announcement was a delightful surprise to all, but none so much as Rhun. Avery was a semi-etheric being, and as such he and his Chosen other had been trying for over a century to conceive and never had. 'How did that happen?' Rhun queried, and then, receiving a knowing look from Avery, rephrased. 'I mean, I thought that was impossible for you?'

'So did I,' Avery concurred. 'But apparently I lost my immortality in a previous timeline and during that seemingly unfortunate turn of events, Fallon conceived.'

'Of course!' Hudan was mind-blown, as she remembered the instance in question. 'Fallon was then hidden in the Otherworld to protect the child from the coming confrontation with the reptilians.'

'So I am told …' Avery confirmed. 'And she was never returned. Therefore, the second time around she was not present when circumstance changed and created a divergence in time. Hence it was that I alone was stolen back to Earth's otherworldly realms by my elemental dominions … I assumed Fallon had perished with the rest of my kindred.'

'Wow!' Rhun's mind was boggling a moment, but then he realised, 'So then, perhaps my method is not as impetuous as you imagined, oh lord of bloody everything?' His little brother owed him a very big apology.

'I take back every derogatory thing I ever said about you,' Avery relented gladly.

'You trapped me in an obelisk!' Rhun stressed his gripe.

'I swear I will never do so again,' he stated sincerely, before looking to the rest of the crew. 'But quite apart from my own joyful news, every life on Kila has been restored, I've already given you,' Avery directed the comment at Rhun, 'two chances to get this instance in history to play out in our favour, and you have finally succeeded. That, is mission over!'

Everyone was drawing deep breaths at this point to soberly consider their circumstance, yet all eyes eventually looked to Rhun.

He looked inwards a moment, but his want to go home negated any chance of an unbiased decision. 'This mission has run far too long already,' he stated in all honesty. 'We quit now, while we are still ahead.'

Every soul who was conscious in the cavern, nodded to agree.

'Time to evacuate then.' Rhun headed towards the chariot. 'I'll transport you all one by one, starting with the unconscious.'

'I'll hit them with something stronger,' Telmo reloaded his little device. 'The extra rest will do them good.'

'Rest?' Rhun had forgot the meaning of the word.

'It won't be long now, Governor,' Telmo stated, trying to be reassuring.

But the use of his title only served to remind Rhun that he was returning to a whole other world of responsibility. On the upside, his wife, Sybil, would be there, and all his kindred and his council, so he would no longer be operating on his own. Like a warm blanket around his frozen soul, that thought inspired the best feeling Rhun had experienced in over twenty years of inter-time and forty years of outer-time travel — he was going *home*.

3

TORN APART

As consciousness dawned, so did questions. Had their mission succeeded? Could they all now go home to AMIE? That notion incited great excitement for Fen, but at the same time sadness, for he could not take his beloved Ling Hu back with him to the universe parallel — she was already there. What would become of her now?

Fen parted his eyelids, expecting to be in the crystal cavern with his tigress beside him, as she always was. His sight may have been a little blurry, but clearly he was no longer where he had been when he'd been put under. This room seemed more like a palace or a temple. The walls, from the floor to the high domed ceiling, had the appearance of polished rose quartz crystal.

'Good heavens!' Fen sat straight upright, overwhelmed and confused; he only became aware of the comfortable bed beneath him when he collapsed back onto it with a soft *poof*.

'You shouldn't attempt to sit upright just yet.'

It was a woman who spoke, in the language of ancient Zhou. Fen recognised the voice but could scarcely believe his own ears until he looked to the source and saw the dark-haired, dark-eyed beauty; although not clearly. 'He Nuan?' His heart jumped nto his throat; had he joined her in death? Was this a dream?

'Once upon another incarnation that was my name,' she replied, coming closer to wipe his face with a cool, damp cloth that smelled like his garden on Li Shan in springtime.

Refreshed, Fen looked upon the woman whose features and darker skin tone differed slightly from the lover he remembered, but it was her. 'Where am I?'

'You are in the Healing temple of Chailida, on the planet Kila of the Esh-mah star system.' She advised standing back and smiling warmly. 'You have just returned from a mission to Earth's past, where you, and a small team of others, reportedly saved the entire population of our fair planet. So, on behalf of the citizens of Kila, I humbly and most sincerely thank you for your part in our deliverance. It is said that you all went above and beyond the call of duty to achieve your end, and if that entailed reliving our life in ancient Zhou, I understand that must have been very painful for you.'

Fen held his head as his perception adjusted to his new circumstances. Once he'd pieced the puzzle together in his mind at last, he smiled in understanding. 'You must be the wife of En Noah, my counterpart incarnate on Kila.'

The beauty smiled to confirm. 'That is correct. My name is Rebecca.'

That seemed to answer the query about the success of their mission, and Fen smiled, appeased to have prevailed. 'Where is my tigress?'

'Sorry?' Rebecca was clearly baffled by the query.

'Ling Hu, my tigress?' he repeated, struggling to sit and stay upright. 'She was put to sleep beside me! So where was she taken, when I was brought —' Fen gasped on a fearful thought; maybe the timekeepers had not brought the spirit tiger to Kila? For she did not belong here, or in the universe parallel, but to Earth's long distant past.

'Where is the captain?' Fen queried in a panic, and then rethought his demand. 'Where is Rhun?'

'Our governor requested to be informed when you were awake,' Rebecca advised. 'I can fetch him now, if you like?'

'I would greatly appreciate that,' Fen said civilly, despite his inner panic.

'Please be at peace,' she encouraged him. 'I'm sure our governor shall have an answer to your dilema, so right now you should take it easy.'

'Do you not recall your life as Ling Hu?' Fen queried Rebecca curiously.

'I have not actually explored my past-life incarnations in an animal form.' She seemed a little embarrassed. 'Which is rather shameful, now I come to think of it, being that I work for the environmental protection agency here on Kila.'

'But Ling Hu is —' Fen stopped short of spilling his lover's greatest secret.

'She is …?' Rebecca encouraged him to finish the sentence.

Fen merely grinned to cover his slip of the tongue. 'She is a really extraordinary being.'

Rebecca smiled, perhaps flattered by his view. 'As is your partner back on AMIE, I'm certain. Sadly, my past-life memory does not extend beyond my lifetimes in this universe.'

A memory of the beautiful Phemorian lover that he had left behind on AMIE brought a smile to his face. 'That she is.' Fen nodded to confirm. 'Is it all right if I get up and take a look?' He pointed to a set of doors that led out onto the balcony.

'If you feel up to it.' She took a step towards him. 'Shall I give you a hand?'

'No,' he assured, wanting to see the governor as soon as possible. 'I'll take my time, I promise.'

'Very good.' She grinned, backing up. 'See that you do.' She approached the exit door and rather than having to reach out to open it, the barrier simply vanished on approach and reconstituted in her wake.

Once alone, Fen slapped his hands together to try and conjure some chi and heal himself, but the anaesthetic must have been having a hangover effect as he couldn't seem to conjure enough chi to fix a broken fingernail.

'Hmm.' Fen looked to the balcony doors wondering if he had

the strength to stagger over there. The shutters on the tall, slender arched windows were open, and the sky beyond was a beautiful deep shade of aquamarine. The high arches and domed tops of some of the neighbouring buildings were most impressive, and he was compelled to go and view Chailida city as it was before the reptilians destroyed it.

The shutters on the door didn't vanish but opened with a gentle nudge, and the expansive cityscape of Chailida spread out before him like the holy city of some ancient highly advanced utopian civilisation. Absent was the usual noise that you would expect from such a metropolis, for there were no transports within the central city. All the buildings were curved, as were the pathways that wove through the central park opposite the healing temple. People moved at a leisurely pace, and spoke quietly to each other — no yelling or hostility.

'Fen?'

The query startled Fen into turning about to greet one of the locals from Kila he'd not seen in a long time. Jahan was exiting onto the balcony from the room next door to his.

'It is Fen, right?' the strapping blond fellow queried.

What was most shocking to Fen was the fact that his companion was conversing with him in the native tongue of ancient Zhou, just as Rebecca had been. This was possible for any of the Chosen of Kila, as they understood all languages: it was part and parcel of being immortal. But the Chosen were not born immortal, their immortal gene activated only once they'd died. This was the case with Rebecca, but Fen knew the man before him had yet to experience physical death, so how was he conversing without a communicator? 'Yes, I am he. Sorry … I just —'

'I know what you're thinking …' Jahan pre-empted. 'It must be strange conversing with me, when you just saw me murdered.'

'You were murdered?' Fen was astounded. 'I mean, Shi was murdered?' he corrected.

'You didn't know?' Jahan clearly felt bad about his assumption. 'I'm so sorry, I was hoping to lighten the moment, instead I must have just come off as callous.'

Fen shook his head. 'You are the one who was killed!' He frowned, curious. 'But if you were murdered then how do you still carry Shi's memory?'

Jahan smiled broadly as Fen hit on the very point he was trying to raise in the first place. 'I saw death coming and willed my soul-mind to return to my place of origin as advised prior to our mission in Zhou.'

'But you could have returned to nothing if our mission had failed.' Fen thought the man's split-second decision rather audacious. 'Which, obviously,' he turned and motioned to the pristine city, 'it didn't.'

'I trusted my wife and my governor would come through for us.' Jahan admired the city also.

'Can I ask …?' Fen ventured.

'How I died?' Jahan guessed.

'If it isn't too painful?'

Jahan shrugged. 'Well, I wasn't there for the painful bit, but I'm fairly sure I ended up impaled on a stalagmite.'

'Oh, damn,' Fen covered his mouth. He was feeling a little ill and rather sorry he'd asked. 'How on Earth …?'

'Dragonface,' Jahan replied.

'What?' This tale just got more horrifying by the minute. 'How did he find us?'

'Huxin was compelled to shift into reptilian form during the siege on the Dropa ship —'

'The creature read her mind.' Fen began to panic. 'It will know everything about us.'

'Relax,' Jahan emphasised, 'we've jumped over three thousand years into the future, he won't find us here.'

'It didn't stop the creature last time.' Fen was still wary, but the prospect of danger begged another line of questioning. 'Have you seen Ling Hu?'

'No,' Jahan replied. 'But then most of the wildlife are out on the city's third island ring.' He pointed off into the distance to a landmass that lay beyond several water channels that encircled the city. 'We're on the central island here.'

Fen relaxed a little. 'So why didn't the captain wake me after the mission?'

'I couldn't tell you, I was dead at the time,' Jahan replied dryly. 'But I'm sure they had a good reason. I am still waiting for Huxin to awaken, and Wu Geng is still out cold too, at last report.'

Fen's frown deepened once more. 'Well, Wu Geng I understand,' Fen stated, 'but Huxin was never meant to be sedated.'

'Apparently, she was a bit upset by my death.' Jahan repeated what he'd been told.

'Oh, I see,' Fen conceded. 'It still does not explain why I wasn't revived.'

'I think I can explain.' Rhun came onto the balcony from Fen's room.

'Governor.' Jahan nodded his head in greeting, and backed up towards the doors he'd emerged from. 'I'll get back to my vigil.' He entered the room and closed the doors.

'Where is Ling Hu?' Fen didn't bother with a greeting — he was concerned and meant no disrespect. The look of woe on Rhun's face was not the slightest bit comforting.

'That is what I am here to talk to you about,' he began soberly.

The news of Ling Hu's abduction by Dragonface was every bit as harrowing to Fen as his team mates had anticipated.

'She will have been expecting me to rescue her,' Fen agonised through his streaming tears. 'And I will never come.'

Rhun was clearly finding words difficult. 'I know Ling Hu was an exceptional animal, but surely she's not worth risking —'

'She was not just an animal!' Fen yelled out his frustration.

Rhun held both hands up in truce and Fen released his anger and slouched in his stance.

He could not blame the governor; he didn't know the truth, no one did. 'Ling Hu could assume a human form.' Fen collapsed into a seat to confess the secret he'd kept from everyone. His head was bowed; he was not ashamed of their love, more concerned of how his peers might react to the news.

'She was your lover?' Rhun assumed.

Fen didn't look up as he nodded. 'I expect that is rather hard to fathom?'

'Not really,' the governor replied.

Fen finally looked up to find his company appearing sympathetic.

'I hung out with the Leonine tribes for a bit, those cat women are pretty damn sultry.'

'The Leonine tribes?' Fen frowned, intrigued.

'I keep forgetting you haven't really seen much of our civilisation,' Rhun explained. 'And unfortunately you won't really get the chance to, as the timekeepers plan on leaving as soon as you are all coherent.'

'I can't just leave Ling Hu at the mercy of that creature.' Fen appealed for more time.

'It is done, Fen Gong, it was done three thousand years ago.' Rhun kept speaking to quell his protest. 'Dragonface may have read Huxin's mind, but she came to Kila by accident, and has no idea where this planet is located in this galaxy, so Dragonface cannot find us via her memory. And now that the timelines have altered and he has never been here, the chances are he will never happen upon us again.'

'Even if Dragonface escaped death after he discovered our whereabouts from Huxin, how did he reach us in the crystal cave? He does not have psychokinesis,' Fen posed. 'How did he withstand the healing energy within the cave long enough to kill Shi?'

'Dragonface has a very great knowledge of the dark arts,' Rhun advised. 'He called upon lower etheric entities to prevent Avery being able to rescue Dorje Pema the first time I screwed up the history of ancient China, and again to prevent Huxin from doing the same on our last mission. I can only assume he used the same kind of demonic force to project himself to our secret cavern and protect him while he was there.'

Fen shook his head. 'But how did any creature, of this world or the sub-planes, escape that blast?'

'That is what the rest of the crew are discussing at En Noah's lake house,' Rhun assured him. 'I may not have all the answers yet, but we are working on it.'

To keep a lid on the timekeepers' presence on Kila, Rhun had all those timekeepers who were conscious staying out at En Noah's private lake house, as it was located on the remote outskirts of Chailida city. No one ever went there beside En Noah and his spouse, although a lot of their secret dealings with the timekeepers in the past had transpired at this location. The rounded structure looked rather like an elegant flying saucer half submerged into the lake's surface at the end of a long jetty. This structure could be completely sealed and submerged beneath the lake, which made it the perfect base for any covert operations that the governor and his chief advisor wished to keep under wraps.

When Rebecca had arrived to alert the governor to Fen's awakening, she had remained at the lake house to brainstorm with En Noah — advisor to the governor — and the mysterious timekeepers that Rhun had brought back with him from his quest in Earth's distant past.

'I think we should consider the possibility that Dragonface didn't escape death at all,' Telmo, the technologist, was saying. 'He claimed that death was a fast ticket for his soul-mind to rejoin the next appropriate body existing back on his planet of origin. What if he managed to do just that?'

'But then how could Dragonface have got from some distant point in the galaxy and back to Earth in time to kill Shi?' Dan queried. 'The destruction of the Dropa ship and the event of Shi's murder were almost simultaneous.'

'The premise screams time travel,' Hudan verbalised the only logical conclusion. 'Could he have got hold of the chariot again somehow?'

'Not with the new security measures we've installed,' Song defended Telmo's design. 'If the chariot does not recognise an etheric signature as authorised it won't fire up. So any of our incarnations could use it, but not an intruder.'

'And Dragonface could not have anticipated this instance when he originally stole the chariot from Rhun as it hadn't taken place yet,' Telmo added. 'So that rules out that possibility.'

'I think I know of a way that you might know for certain how this creature accomplished the feat,' Rebecca spoke up and the entire room looked to her. 'Something Fen asked gave me the idea.'

'What did I —' Noah rolled his eyes at his error and corrected, 'sorry, what did Fen ask?'

'He asked if I remembered my past life as Ling Hu,' she told them.

'He thought the tiger was his soul mate?' Song looked very disturbed by the notion, whilst the captain rolled his eyes.

'Of course!' Dan appeared to want to beat himself around the head.

'What is it?' Hudan was intrigued by his reaction.

'I saw Ling Hu take human form,' he replied, and many a jaw in the room dropped. 'Her love for Fen enabled her to make the transformation for brief intervals.'

'Damn,' Song became most discomforted by the news. 'I sure hope that does not imply what I think —' The pilot looked at Telmo who was chuckling away to himself.

'No wonder Fen got so jealous of my affection for Ling Hu,' he explained his amusement, as his eyes fell to Rebecca. 'So you are volunteering to do some past life regression into her disappearance.'

Rebecca nodded, solemnly — for the notion was not an enticing one. 'If the creature took the tigress with it, then her memory may tell us much.'

'Brilliant!' Noah awarded, with a proud, encouraging smile. 'We can use the isolation chamber downstairs in my office.'

'It's always the quiet ones.' Song was shaking his head still mind-blown by Fen's love life and emerged from his fascination to find everyone staring at him. 'What? You all don't find that kinda kinky?' He queried their frowns, and then realised that the two soul-minds in question were present. 'Ah … no offence or anything,' he back-pedalled. 'Whatever floats your boat.'

Telmo manifested a tiny device in his hand and when he touched it against Song's shoulder, the pilot dropped to the floor unconscious. 'If there isn't a battle going on, he's useless anyway.' Telmo explained his resolve to his company, who all nodded to agree that pilot could sit this part of the investigation out.

Once Rebecca was comfortable inside the isolation chamber, Telmo spoke to her through the intercom. 'Would you like me to guide you back?'

Rebecca had a chuckle. 'No need, here on Kila we are taught past life regression in High School. I have the name of the Earth incarnation I am looking for, all I need is the year and I'll be able to skim through my superconscious to find the instance of interest to us.'

'The year was one thousand and two, BCE,' Telmo advised, 'and we were in the area of B—'

'No need for details,' Rebecca cut him off, eager to get this over with. 'Leave it with me.'

'We'll wait on your word,' her husband, Noah, said to close the conversation.

'Much appreciated, I'm out,' Rebecca confirmed.

Left in complete darkness and silence, she breathed deep to cement her nerve.

Rebecca had been able to sympathise with Fen's plight, as she had recalled her life in ancient Zhou as He Nuan, and her death at the hands of Dragonface, many years ago when she had first learned the art of past-life regression. So she was not entering this exercise blindly, she was well aware that the creature was without mercy or compassion; it had no moral code and a lust for power that was second only to its Nefilim creators — only the universe knew what it had done with Ling Hu.

A feeling of anguish made her gut churn and, noting how unnerved she was, she breathed deeply once more, to draw upon the inner strength of her current personification. She was not an innocent animal any more, she was a defender of every defenceless animal on this planet! She had locked up every poacher to ever break KEPA law, and this predator would prove no different. This Orion was about to get a taste of what it was like to become prey.

'Right then,' she grinned, feeling considerably more empowered. *In the year one thousand and two BC, Ling Hu met Dragonface*; she formulated the mantra that would hone her into her target era fastest, and silently repeated the suggestion over and over. In her mind's eye she visualised herself approaching a bridge and as her consciousness crossed over it into the misty darkness on the far side, she felt herself sedated.

Her entire body gave a huge jolt as she was snatched from her unconscious state. Her form felt weighted and lethargic — she could barely bring herself to open her eyes.

'Up you get, little kitten,' a sinister voice snarled, and it was only when she was yanked by her neck clear off the plinth she'd been sedated on that the tigress became aware of the metal collar and chain around her neck.

Despite the shock and pain, she sprang to her feet snarling, ready to tear to shreds whoever had hold of the leash.

The eight-foot-tall lizard standing upright before her was completely shrouded in shadow, which concentrated around him like a swarm of flies clinging to a dead carcass. Ling Hu did not even need to employ her third-eye vision to see this — the shadow was in plain sight. The tigress didn't fear anything in the natural world, but this was an abomination. She'd not ever seen or felt anything so repulsive, and her instinct was to pull away.

'Don't like me, do you, kitten?' The creature's sinister tone made her uneasy. 'Yet, look what I have done for you.' It pointed aside with a claw.

At the same moment, her sense of smell got beyond the stench of the monster in front of her, to pick up on the scent of blood — her father's. The sight of Shi's impaled body produced a howl of agony from the tigress until the lizard yanked her chain, and choked her to silence.

'They don't care about the likes of you or I, we're not *human* enough to warrant the same consideration in the great scheme of things,' he told her.

Ling Hu was snarling, her anger welling in her heart as she prepared to shift into spirit form and free herself from bondage.

'Of course, you don't believe me. Which is why I have to prove the fact to you.'

The tigress sprang forward, but her transformation failed. Dragonface belted her aside and sent her flying backwards into the jarring chokehold of her metal collar once more, which drew blood as it cut into her neck.

'I have taken away your supernatural power, Ling Hu,' the creature informed her, and showed her the weapon he'd shot her with; the same weapon that had blasted her into consciousness. 'You are nothing but a kitty now,' he took pleasure in advising her, as he replaced the weapon in its holster on his weapons belt. 'But that does not have to be a permanent arrangement. Once you see what little regard these creatures have for you, you will wish to kill them as much as I do … and I will give you the means, if …' his ugly face twisted into a leering grin, '*when* your current master leaves you for dead, and he will …'

Ling Hu growled at the suggestion.

'You will pleasure me like you have pleasured him. And you cannot do that without a true passion for the cause, can you, kitten?' he vexed. 'So you will have to learn to find me likeable pretty quick.'

The thought repulsed her, and if she could have assumed human form she would have told him she would rather rot in *Diyu*! As it was, all she could do was snarl in warning.

'Come willingly, or your girly boy is my next kill today,' the creature threatened.

Ling Hu looked at her lover, resting peacefully. She knew he would never leave her for dead; the creature had no concept of love, nor the ends to which lovers would go for one another. If Dragonface wanted to play power games with her, she would oblige. In order for her to assume human form, the creature would have to first restore

57

her power, and she would bide her time until she was awarded the opportunity to rip out his throat. So long as Fen was alive, he would come for her, thus the proud tigress cowered and submitted to the will of her abductor.

'That's my clever kitten. You plot to rip out my throat.' The creature pulled another device from its weapons belt. 'But by the time you get that opportunity, it won't be me that you want to kill.' One powerful blast from the weapon sent her rocketing back into an unconscious state.

The wait for Rebecca to emerge from her regression seemed endless. Everyone had fallen silent to listen out for her reaction to the events she was reliving. Thus far there had been several growls and whimpers, but Rebecca had not uttered an audible word.

Hudan sat alongside her husband, their previous discussion regarding Dragonface's murderous means, playing over in her mind. There was an uneasy feeling in her gut that something had been overlooked, yet she could not pinpoint what that elusive 'something' was. Her hope was that Rebecca would return from her regression with some information that might aid an epiphany.

She glanced around at her companions. Dan, Telmo and Noah were very patient souls, and seemed to be as deeply lost in their own thoughts as she had just been.

The fact of Huxin and Jahan manifesting in the room startled them from their trance as her twin was not in a very good mood.

'Telmo! That was a dirty trick!' She came straight toward the technologist.

'It had to be done.' He didn't flinch, but stared her down, and Huxin stopped short of physical contact, but she was right up in his face.

'Well, you can stop whatever you are doing, we're going back to save Shi and Ling Hu!' she insisted.

'We are currently investigating what became of Ling Hu after she was taken,' he advised.

'Oh,' Huxin backed down. 'So we are going to rescue them?'

'We are investigating,' he replied diplomatically.

Telmo had Taliesin's steel resolve and careful way with words, but Hudan knew they stood to lose the successful outcome they'd gained if they went back for Ling Hu. Chances were that the Lord of the Otherworld would not allow them to go back.

'I really don't mind that I died,' Jahan appealed. 'But had I known Ling Hu was going to be abducted by that creature, or if I even had time to think before he pulled out that weapon, I would have stayed and fought.'

'And you would have lost your memory of our quest and be useless to us now,' stated Telmo surely. 'You made the right decision.'

'I don't —' Jahan was distracted from his protest as Rhun manifested in their midst. 'Governor,' he acknowledged his presence.

'Where is Fen?' Hudan was immediately concerned by his absence. 'Did you tell him?'

The man's expression was grave as he answered. 'I told him.'

Hudan waited expectantly for Rhun to say more, and finally he shrugged, having nothing more reassuring to say. 'He took it as expected. Fen wants to go back for her.'

Hudan's heart gave a jolt of empathy; she knew how it felt to have to sacrifice your love of another for the sake of the greater good. 'Where is Fen now?'

'Taking a quiet walk around the lake here,' he said, and pre-empting her next resolve he added, 'He asked to be left alone to digest his feelings … you know how dangerous Fen's emotions can be when he is in the frame of mind he is at present.'

Fen's focused hatred could overload a target with such emotional stress that their organs would implode, so Hudan thought it wise to heed her little brother's request for some personal space.

'Now, is someone going to tell me why we are all in Noah's office?' Rhun appealed to be filled in. Once he was, he took a seat, along with Huxin and Jahan, to wait for Rebecca's word.

Near on an hour later, when it seemed their silent vigil was never going to end, the sound of panicked, heavy breathing was heard through the intercom speaker.

'Rebecca?' Noah spoke to her via the comm-link on the isolation chamber control panel on this desk. 'You sound like you need to calm right down.'

'Let me out!' she demanded.

'You cannot come out too quick—'

'Just let me out!' she repeated, more adamantly.

Noah immediately issued the unlock instruction to his system and the door to the isolation chamber vanished.

Rebecca exited with haste, shielding her eyes from the light to report: 'She's going to kill him!'

'Ling Hu?' Rhun queried the vague report, and Rebecca nodded to confirm. 'Who is she going to kill?'

Although it wasn't thermal, the lake outside Chailida city was as lovely as the one that once existed at the base of Li Shan, Fen mused, momentarily allowing his mind to escape its state of anguish and distress. To shift into observer mode and just be in the moment was the only method Fen had found that effectively brought his surging emotions back into check. The sun sparkled on the water's emerald surface and reflected onto his face with a twofold warming intensity — the insects buzzed, the exotic birds were singing and flying from tree to tree overhead. In the distance, beneath all of nature's din, Fen imagined he heard a tiger growling low, as Ling Hu might have when on the hunt. The thought of his tigress incited memories of their life together, over forty Earth years in all, and the idea that she died in the hands of the same monster who had taken He Nuan from him caused rage to course through Fen's veins anew.

'Hey! Girly boy.'

The gravelly voice made all of Fen's hairs stand on end; Dragonface had found them after all. Yet Ling Hu's abductor could not have picked a better time to pay his respects. Fen allowed his hatred to possess him, and with the intent to direct all his fury onto Dragonface, he spun around to project his adverse emotions onto his enemy.

A beautiful, naked female stood in front of the creature like a human shield.

Fen, recognising his lover in time, refrained from releasing the destructive force. Instead, he fell to the ground to disperse the charge into the earth before it killed him. Where the healer's hands landed, all the vegetation began to wither and die. The destruction spread out rapidly from him in all directions, but stopped short of reaching his original target. The emotional sympathetic was left quivering and weak in the wake of his aborted attack, all his *chi* wasted.

'See, kitten,' said the creature to Ling Hu, who was glaring at Fen as if he was her enemy. 'Perfectly well and able.' Dragonface embraced her from behind, fondling her naked body without any protest from her. 'It was a good idea to take out the healer first.'

Fen could not believe his ears, or his eyes! How could Ling Hu assume a human body in the presence of another? The question gnawed at Fen's heart, as he watched his lover revel in the touch of his enemy. 'What have you done to her?' Fen demanded, eyeing the deep scars that cut across her neck in several places.

'What have *I* done?' The creature emphasised its amusement.

In the enclosure that had housed the Dragon Pit at the fallen Shang capital at Yin, Dragonface had been very different to the way he looked this day. His body was more human-like, not scaled or thuggish, but more upright and regal due to the fine clothes that had replaced his body armour.

'*I* am not the one who left Ling Hu to be tortured to death!' he continued, to counter Fen's accusation. '*I* was the enemy! *You* were supposed to be the hero! *I* showed mercy! *You* pissed off!'

In the wake of the accusation, Ling Hu glared at Fen with such hatred that it struck fear into his heart, and the debilitating shock spread rapidly through his entire being.

'They never woke me after the mission … I was brought straight here, to this very day.' Fen was exposing their time-hopping capabilities to the enemy, but he didn't care about the divine agenda any more. He had to make Ling Hu understand that he'd not abandoned her. 'I have only just been informed that you were

61

left behind —' Fen choked on his explanation, sorrow spilling from his eyes in a flood of tears that he could not hold back. 'The timekeepers betrayed us both, Ling Hu,' he said, distressed, having never thought such a thing was possible. 'I have had but a few hours to formulate a plan to come back for you.'

'I waited for what seemed like an *eternity*,' Ling Hu broke away from Dragonface and began pacing back and forth, her eyes shooting daggers into Fen's soul. 'You never came.'

'How is that even possible? You are not immortal.' Fen felt his heart being ripped from his chest. 'You must know I would never abandon you willingly.'

'Don't let his dramatics fool you, kitten. Tell him nothing,' Dragonface advised and Fen hated the creature's demeaning name for her. 'I have kept my promise. Here we are, both your lovers. Which of us shall live and which shall die, is entirely up to you.'

When Fen realised the score, his horror intensified. 'Ling Hu, whatever this creature has told you, whatever it has done to brainwash you against us —'

'Ha!' the creature scoffed. 'You freely admitted your own people betrayed her!'

Fen ignored the creature to stay focused on his love. 'This creature killed your father and stole you from me; don't be manipulated by its twisted truth. You have the power to end the terror and suffering, right here, right now.'

'*Yes, I do*,' she retorted, surely.

'Time to choose, kitten.' Dragonface stepped back and held his arms wide to welcome her decision.

'You are my life, Ling Hu. It is yours to take, if you so wish it.' Fen held open his arms, hands palm up in truce.

Surely Ling Hu could not truly prefer life with Dragonface? If she did, then death would be a quick release from the anguish of knowing that his blind trust in his team mates had driven his lover to such lengths to protect herself and survive. The torture of wondering how Dragonface had won her devotion would kill him anyway, only far more slowly.

'The timekeepers plan to leave you behind in this universe, despite your choice in this instance,' Dragonface informed Ling Hu. 'So choose wisely.'

Where was Dragonface getting all his information, Fen wondered, as Ling Hu looked to Fen, waiting for him to deny the claim.

He could not. 'You knew that I was bound to return to my universe of origin one day,' Fen replied as honestly as he could.

Ling Hu's eyes narrowed with purpose, as she shifted into tiger form. Once her transformation was complete she released a mighty roar, before her baleful gaze came to rest upon him.

Fen knew that look, that was her killing face, which had never been directed at him before this day. *Don't let the creature win.* He prayed the tigress had not completely forsaken their love. His heart was beating so intensely that he felt it might punch a hole right through his chest; Ling Hu's gaze held him spellbound in anticipation of her heart's true resolve.

With the intention to join Fen, the timekeepers materialised further around the lake that was host to Noah's retreat, and there they found a large circular area of dead earth, at the heart of which lay a bloodstained body.

The sight struck horror into Hudan's heart, and as she ran along with her sister to investigate, Rebecca kept pace with them, morbidly compelled to know what her past-life incarnation's final resolve had been. Hudan fell to the ground beside the trembling form, and rolled the body over to discover it was their little brother's lifeblood staining the area all around them. There were wounds all over his body, but the primary bleed was from a huge gaping wound in his neck. Rebecca gulped back tears, devastated to realise that Ling Hu had been so brainwashed that she'd chosen the life of her tormentor over that of her lifelong companion.

'Fen.' Hudan placed a hand over the wound in a fruitless attempt to stop the bleeding. It was difficult to see anything through her tears. 'What happened? Who did this?'

'These are tiger wounds,' Huxin observed and with a deep whiff, she nearly choked on her distress. 'Ling Hu did this,' she made the shock announcement.

'No.' Jahan shook his head, unable to believe it. 'She adored Fen.' His sights turned to Rebecca, who was clearly as shocked as they were.

'I really didn't think she would go through with it,' Rebecca gave her honest human view of what she'd seen of Ling Hu's torturous existence with Dragonface. 'But it seems her animal instinct for survival won out in the end,' she concluded sadly.

When Rhun, Telmo and Dan glimpsed the carnage, Rhun did an about-face to deter Noah from viewing the demise of one of his own incarnations. 'You should return to the lake house.'

'I am not a child, Governor.' Noah guessed what the concern was, and looking past Rhun, he spied Fen's shredded body and was nearly sick. 'His tigress did this?' Noah was horrified that his soul mate could be turned against him thus, and his sights automatically turned to his wife.

'Dragonface left her in a cell for years and years!' Rebecca justified in Ling Hu's defence. 'Long enough for her to realise that Fen Gong and the timekeepers were not coming to her rescue as she had come to theirs, so many times.' Rebecca shook her head slowly in mournful distress. 'When her tormentor had the mercy to offer her a means of revenge, as opposed to living out her days in a cell, what would you have done?'

'No!' Fen gargled, attempting to shake his head in protest. 'Dragon—'

'Dragonface,' Hudan finished for him.

'I can't smell the creature on him at all.' Huxin frowned at the claim, as it didn't make sense.

'Lives flashing,' Fen mumbled. 'I remember another ...'

'Don't keep him talking,' Dan intervened, kneeling beside Hudan to address Fen directly. 'Will yourself home to Ringbalin, do you understand?'

'No chi,' he spat blood to say. 'There ... is ... another ...' Fen's eyes froze open wide, as he strained to complete the sentence, but the effort finished him.

'Another what? Fen!' Hudan implored before grief choked her to silence.

'Shh,' Dan urged them all. 'I need to speak with his spirit.'

Hudan gasped on her pain, as Dan stood. 'You see him?'

Dan nodded.

'Ringbalin or Fen?' Hudan was curious.

'Both, they are merging and fading fast.' He raised a finger to his lips, to urge total quiet as he listened. 'Yes, I understand,' Dan concurred. 'Just tell me what you remember, another what?'

Hudan and her company all watched Dan intently as his face reflected an epiphany he was having that near bowled him over.

'Of course!' He covered his face to absorb the shock quickly then looked back to the spirit that only he could see. 'But where ...' He began scanning the area with his eyes, ahead of announcing. 'He's gone.'

'What did he say?' The question Hudan had been dying to ask burst out of her mouth, in concert with Rhun, Huxin, Jahan, Telmo and Noah.

But Dan's sights came to rest upon the governor. 'Where is the second chariot?'

'There is a second chariot?' Telmo was immediately concerned.

'The one that Inanna gifted to your father?' Dan clarified, as Rhun was looking a little hazy.

'We lost that one,' the governor confessed awkwardly.

'You lost it?' Dan hoped he was hearing wrong.

'Why did no one tell me that there was a second chariot?' Telmo confronted Rhun.

'I'd forgotten it ever existed!' the ruler defended.

Dan pulled Telmo back so that he could do the questioning, as he was in a calmer frame of mind. 'When you say "*we* lost it", who is "*we*"?'

'Avery and I,' Rhun replied, 'back before he was appointed Lord of the Otherworld.'

'*Where* did you lose it?' Telmo came roaring back into the interrogation.

Rhun frowned, knowing they were not going to like the answer. 'We lost it the day Chailidocean was destroyed.'

'The fall of Atlantis,' Telmo summed up. 'Only one of the most overworked moments in time, in the whole of Earth's history! You've got to be fucking kidding me!'

'We assumed the chariot was destroyed in the catastrophe, or that the previous Lord of the Otherworld hid it somewhere,' Rhun explained. 'You think Dragonface has got his hands on that chariot?'

Dan shrugged and gave a nod. 'It is certainly a possibility worth investigating, and it would explain a great deal.' Dan turned his attention to Rebecca, who was standing quietly aside, listening to everything being said. 'Dragonface must have shifted Ling Hu through time as she was not immortal.'

'Ling Hu was always transported blindfolded or unconscious,' Rebecca advised. 'So I can neither confirm nor deny how he managed to teleport her so far into the future.'

'Well, we had best figure out his means quickly.' Telmo was looking very dark about the oversight. 'Before he kills someone else!'

'No one wanders off alone from now on.' Hudan stood, wiping her brother's blood off her hands and onto her clothes. 'We should fetch Wu Geng from the healing temple for his own safety. We need to stick together until we solve this.'

'No,' Rhun shook his head in protest. 'You should all return to your own universe, while the going is good.'

'And leave you here to cope with Dragonface alone?' Huxin chimed in. 'Not likely.'

'The Orion was never meant to be your problem,' Rhun pointed out. 'And although I appreciate your aid, your crossing into this universe does not alter the fact that the Chosen would have been forced to deal with Dragonface eventually. And we shall … once you are all safely gone.'

The captain shook his head to disagree.

'Don't make me banish you,' Rhun threatened, and then lightened his tone. 'Dragonface is no longer your problem.'

*

Despite all the resentment that he felt towards the timekeepers at present, it was a nightmare to see them being turned on one another. How had this happened? They had lost their healer, and their pilot was next on the hit list. Had they not suggested that Dorje Pema surrender the Dropa vessel, none of this would have eventuated.

Wu Geng woke abruptly, and was startled by the sight of the beautiful alien staring down at him. 'Who are you?' He noted she had hold of his hand.

'My name is Aysel,' she said, as he withdrew from her touch.

'Where are the timekeepers?' He sat upright and then stilled himself, as his head was set spinning. 'We have lost the healer,' he mumbled his woes. 'And Song is next!'

'Yes,' she stated, as if she understood completely. 'Do you know where to find this being?'

'Why?' Wu Geng became more wary. 'Where am I?' He took in the lovely temple-like room and then looked back to his company. 'What do you want with Song?'

'If you can locate your friend,' she explained, sounding in a desperate hurry, 'we can stop Vugar's vendetta against your people.'

'Who is Vugar?' Wu Geng slid off the bed and stumbled away from the tall, slender alien woman — humanlike, although taller and too elongated to be completely human. Her skin had a greenish tinge, and she was completely hairless. Deep green scales shimmered over her skull where a human's hair might have been, and on her eyebrows. Aysel's eyes were golden in colour, and she was dressed like a femme fatale — all in black.

Aysel rolled her eyes, obviously pressed for time. 'In your vision you saw someone attack your friend —'

'Song is not my friend,' Wu Geng protested.

'But you saw his assailant,' she grew impatient. 'That is Vugar!'

'Dragonface?' Wu Geng concluded. Aysel seemed unamused by the nickname, but nodded.

'How imaginative your kind are.'

'You're one of them!' Wu Geng was horrified to realise. 'I've never seen a female reptilian before!'

'I am Draconian, if you don't mind. And I have never seen a male ape-man before either,' she retorted.

'The term is human —' Wu Geng took offence to her inference.

'*But I* ...' she spoke up over his protest, 'am not wasting time talking, while our enemy escapes!'

'But if you are one of his kind, why is Drag— ah, Vugar your enemy?'

Aysel clenched her fists, frustrated, but calmed herself. 'I will explain everything later —'

'Hold on,' Wu Geng frowned. 'How do you know what I saw in my nightmare?'

'It was a vision!' she corrected, losing patience. 'And I know what you saw because *I* passed that vision on to you. My dragon guide told me that you would know how to find Vugar's next target. So, do you, or not?'

'Why should I believe you?' Wu Geng wasn't being bamboozled into anything.

'Because any second now your not-my-friend is going to die if you don't!'

Wu Geng didn't know what he'd be in more trouble for: allowing Song to die and Dragonface to get away, or leading a possible enemy straight to his crew mates. Upon reflection, the latter sounded not so bad, and far more likely.

'I can find Song with a thought,' Wu Geng ventured, 'but I don't think I have the energy right now to —'

Aysel grabbed hold of Wu Geng's arm. 'You locate your team mate, and I shall teleport.'

Again he was confused. 'Well, if you can teleport and you know what Song looks like, why did you not go straight to him?'

'In my vision, you are the only one I saw clearly. And all you *humans* look alike to me,' she shrugged. 'Just get us to the target, will you?'

'You know how to kill Drag— ah —'

'No, but I know how to disempower him,' she assured him.

Wu Geng looked into her huge wide eyes — his Shifu had always claimed that eyes were the window to the soul, and his gut instinct was that Aysel was telling him the truth.

A winding kick to the ribs woke Song, and in his disoriented state it was difficult to spring to his own defence — he couldn't even focus straight. Who the hell would be beating him up? And why was he unconscious in the first place? The answer seemed elementary. 'Telmo, you son-of-a-bitch —' he mumbled, attempting to drag his drowsy body up from the ground.

'Guess again.'

Song's eyes were open now. Even though he'd yet to find his focus and spot his tormentor, Song had a strong hunch who the assailant was. Song had never actually met the reptilian in ancient Zhou, but Zeven had been shot by him before, during his first visit to Kila.

An attempt to teleport himself downstairs to gain an advantage, was thwarted by a debilitating blast that knocked Song back to the ground.

'Fuck! Not again.' He thumped a fist on the ground in protest, and the impact really hurt. 'Argh!' This was the second time his soul-mind had been hit by such a force, and he knew the ache that beset his entire body, weighting it even more, was his additional DNA unbraiding. This was the third time that his psychic power had been stolen from him — and Dragonface was twice responsible. 'Son-of-a-bitch must pay!' He rolled over to find the huge reptilian gloating over him.

'You are rather tiny to be the warrior of the group,' he commented, 'but then your father was a little man, too.'

'Didn't stop Ji Fa whipping your arse,' Song remarked snidely, as he scampered beneath a table to avoid the creature's swinging claw.

But Song wasn't fast enough; Dragonface clamped a hand around his ankle and drew him back out into the open, raising him into the air.

'I'm going to gut you, lizard!' he vowed as he dangled by the foot from the reptilian's grip.

'No,' the creature assured him. 'You are going to die.'

A growling sound made Song's blood run cold. He knew the sound of a tiger well enough, but his shock was twofold when he saw the rare albino female of the species. 'Ling Hu?'

She served him a most unfavourable snarl, and his fear deepened when he saw the bloodstains around her jaws and coating her chest. 'Perhaps not?'

'Oh, it is Ling Hu,' Dragonface assured. 'Come to pay her last respects to one of the timekeepers who voted to sacrifice her to save his own skin.'

'That's not what happened,' Song protested, as the tigress growled again and leapt towards him.

Song closed his eyes and moments later was dropped to the floor. He looked up to find Wu Geng hanging off Dragonface's back, one arm tightly locked around its throat as he grabbed for the weapon that had been causing them so much grief.

On the other side of the room an alien-looking female had crash-tackled Ling Hu, whereby the tigress disappeared. 'Watch out, human!' She motioned behind Song, where the tigress rematerialised and snarled in warning.

'Yikes!' Song scampered back towards the friendlier face of the complete stranger.

Once Wu Geng had the DNA-destroying weapon, he withdrew from Dragonface and aimed it at him.

'Wrong choice, my little Prince. Shoot me with that, and I shall only become more powerful.' Dragonface and Wu Geng had been acquainted during the demise of the Shang dynasty. 'Had you chosen this one,' he whipped a smaller device from the weapons belt that hung around his waist, 'you might have fared better.' He took aim at Wu Geng, who immediately envisioned the gadget in his possession, sending it flying into his grasp.

'Thanks for the heads-up.' He fired on Dragonface, who dropped unconscious to the ground.

'Bang on!' Song was impressed.

The beautiful alien woman reached for the buckle on her weapons belt that resembled a large closed eye, and noting this Ling Hu sprang towards Dragonface to protect him. The woman pressed a trigger on the buckle, and the metal eye opened to expose a stone beaming brilliant light. Song was blinded but not pained by the light — to the contrary the overpowering illumination felt empowering. When the eye on the buckle closed, the brilliant light retracted, and both Ling Hu and Dragonface had vanished into thin air.

'Damn that bloody cat woman,' the beautiful alien cursed under her breath. 'I wasn't fast enough.'

'What did you do?' Song protested, now unsure of whose side the new arrival was on. 'We had him!'

'Are you all right?' Wu Geng approached Song and held out a hand to assist him to get to his feet.

'Hardly,' Song ignored the gesture and got himself up. 'Dragonface just slipped through our clutches, and I've lost my powers … again!'

'Hey!' The beautiful alien took issue with Song's attitude.

'Song, this is Aysel.' Wu Geng did the honours, hoping to lessen the tension.

'We …' Aysel ticked her head towards Wu Geng to include him in the equation, 'just saved your life … have a bit of gratitude.'

Song opened his mouth to dispute this, but was not given a chance to speak.

'And,' she continued in an authoritative tone, 'your stolen powers will have been restored … thanks to the blast of life force you just received from the Dragon Eye.'

'That's how you plan to disempower Vugar,' Wu Geng recalled her earlier claim, and Aysel nodded.

'The Dragon Eye?' Song was curious about the belt and its origins as he neared the intruder to take a closer look.

'It is one of the most sacred relics of my people as for thousands of years it has been our means to detect treachery in our midst. Only the pure of heart can withstand its presence,' she advised as Song reached out to touch the metal eye. 'It is also lethal to the touch of anyone besides its chosen keeper.'

Song immediately aborted his intention and took a step back. 'Am I supposed to take your word for that?'

'Am I supposed to care if you don't?' she retorted.

'If you don't care, then why did you just save my life?' Song called her bluff.

'I was here to trap Vugar and drag him back to Fiameadi to answer for his crimes against our people,' she outlined. 'You were my means to locate him.' She appeared most annoyed by the admission. 'But as he has vanished again, I shall have to wait until I receive another glimpse of his intention. Only now he knows I am on his trail and will be twice as cautious when plotting his revenge.'

'You're a reptilian?' Song took a few steps away, not in fear but admiration. 'May I say, the females of your ilk are a hell of a lot better looking than the men.'

'If you wish to die.' Aysel was clearly not flattered.

'Someone has some explaining to do.'

The three of them turned to find the Governor of Kila, En Noah and most of their crew, all with grave expressions upon their faces.

'That would be me.' Wu Geng held up a finger to volunteer some answers.

4

EMBRYOS OF PARALLEL TIME

Whilst questioning the Draconian tracker Aysel — charged by the high council of her home planet to hunt Vugar down — it became clear that the timekeepers had not only placed the future of Kila in peril with their handling of the unholy reptilian menace on Earth, but the future of the reptilian's mother planet of Fiameadi as well.

How had Dragonface executed the feat of returning to ancient Earth to launch his vendetta upon the timekeepers? Only part of that mystery was clear. It seemed that Dragonface had died in the explosion that had destroyed the Dropa craft, and the entity had shifted to the next living link of his hive-mind, three hundred light years away in the Thuban star system of the Draco constellation.

'I thought the reptilian races came from the Orion constellation?' Rhun wondered why the ancients of Earth had referred to reptilians as Orions?

'We have planets there, too,' Aysel advised.

'Have planets?' The governor queried her wording, wondering if these had been discovered and developed by her kind, or taken by force?

'My people have castes all over the galaxy,' she defended, 'as do human beings if I am not mistaken.'

Rhun conceded that this was true, having five planets currently under his governance, however indirectly. He did not mention this fact to Aysel, but perhaps she was already aware of the other human races within their alliance. She had sounded slightly offended by his query, which made him wonder just how developed the psychic powers of the Draconians were. Was Aysel reading his thoughts, or just picking up on subtle nuances in his speech and body language? His knowledge of cosmic law told him that the reptilians of Fiameadi must have been far more spiritually developed than their caste on Earth, or they could not be so psychically advanced. The development of psychism went hand-in-hand with enlightenment.

Rhun decided leave that line of questioning for another time, as Aysel continued to explain how the entity they knew as Dragonface had snatched the body of Vugar, the High Chancellor of the Fiameadi council, who had also been Aysel's consort.

'I was the first to notice the change in Vugar,' the Draconian relayed her memory of events openly.

'When was this?' Telmo was curious. 'How long ago?'

'I do not know your measure of time, we would say it was about three epochs ago.' Aysel explained, 'an epoch being one thousand turns of our planet around our Sun, Thuban.'

'Three thousand years,' Rhun nodded, 'that seems to time out right.'

'Good grief!' Song was stunned. 'You've been alive for three thousand years?'

'Actually, closer to thirteen thousand,' Aysel replied and made everyone's jaw drop.

'How do you do manage to achieve such longevity?' Song was curious.

'We are getting off-track here.' The governor was more interested in Dragonface's movements. 'Vugar began to change, you said?'

'Yes,' Aysel confirmed. 'He suddenly had a renewed interest in space exploration and began venturing off-planet with a small crew for hundreds of years at a time. The first time he returned, he brought back the shapeshifting tigress and she became his constant companion, travelling space with him. But each time

Vugar returned to Fiameadi, he became more and more closed off and secretive about his adventures.'

'But I thought your people operated from a hive-mind mentality?' Huxin, having been exposed to that hive-mind, could not understand how any secret could be held.

'That is completely correct,' she confirmed. 'Vugar, the most intelligent soul among us, was the principal centre of our collective consciousness, and thus has the means to close off certain thoughts from the rest of the hive. Even in a hive-mind, you only have access to information that you have the ability to fathom and the principal decides what level of access you have.' Aysel could obviously tell her company were having trouble understanding this. 'For example, it would be of no benefit to instil scientific knowledge into a member of our working class, as that individual would simply go mad trying to make sense of the information. If those of us, like myself, who are part of the governmental and scientific class, only received the information reserved for the working class, we would be driven insane from the boredom of not challenging our intellect.'

'But does Vugar not control what you think?' Hudan was perplexed and worried. 'Can he not tune into what you are thinking now?'

'Not any more,' Aysel advised. 'Two reasons. Firstly,' she placed a hand on her unusual belt, 'this holy relic shields my thoughts from him, whilst allowing me to infiltrate his intentions, but only when he is not protected by the unnatural shadow he can draw to himself.'

'Do you know anything about how he achieves that sub-etheric shield?' Rhun probed. 'If we could somehow hinder that shield he would be far easier to overpower.'

The Draconian shook her head. 'All I know is that the Dragon Eye will send the shadow into retreat, but as for destroying it altogether … I don't know if that is possible.'

'Oh yes,' Telmo assured her. 'It is possible, all right. We just need to find out the name of the entity protecting him, or take from him whatever amulet he uses to summon it. What is the second reason your telepathic link to your principal has been hindered?'

'The more Vugar shields his thoughts from the hive, the less access and control he has over the hive, and the more scope the individuals within the hive have to operate on their own recognisance,' she explained.

'That would cause a bit of chaos, I imagine.' Rhun raised his brow in question.

'A selfish, as opposed to a selfless, leader, is always going to cast his governance into chaos,' Aysel conceded and Rhun was a little humbled by the statement, wondering if that was why Kila was now in peril. 'Still, that is the very least of my consort's offences against our people.' She appeared humiliated to admit it.

'It is not your consort who has committed these offences, but the unearthly entity that has stolen his body,' Telmo assured her.

'Then we must find a way to drive the entity out!' she insisted.

'The entity in question can only assume the form of a being it has killed.' Telmo delivered the sad fact of the matter. 'I am sorry to say it, but your partner is already dead.'

Aysel's eyes opened wide. 'A mind-eater,' she gasped under her breath. 'No, it couldn't be.'

'What's a mind-eater?' Song was curious, as was everyone.

Aysel was frowning deeply, but shook off the thought. 'Nothing … a myth, from the old universe,' she explained away her doubt.

'The old universe?' Rhun queried.

'Yes,' Aysel was surprised by his query. 'You know, beyond the Eternity Gate.'

'The Eternity Gate?' Rhun had no clue what she was talking about.

'You humans don't get out much, do you?' Her jaw clenched hard, as her thoughts returned to Vugar. 'If my consort is dead, then I shall kill his coveted body, so that he might rest in peace.'

'Kill him,' Telmo went on to inform, 'and the entity will only pass on to your next principal.'

Aysel's silent fury turned apprehensive as she swallowed hard. 'I am next.'

The news was rather sobering for all those present.

'Then we must trap the entity in Vugar's body, and then contain them both,' Wu Geng stated, nodding to reassure their visitor that they would not allow the same fate to befall her.

'You are going back whence you came,' Rhun insisted. 'I have my own council and resources to contend with this situation.'

'The only way we can do that is by our own free will,' Wu Geng reminded him. 'And I, for one, am not leaving.'

'Nor I,' Huxin chimed in, the rest of the timekeepers shaking their heads in accord.

'I cannot keep your presence here a secret forever!' Rhun protested. 'You are just making dealing with the situation doubly difficult for me.'

'We need to speak with Avery,' Hudan calmly suggested.

'I will speak with him,' Rhun insisted. 'All of you are to stay put.'

'Governor, I humbly request to accompany you.' Dan was not going to be kept in the dark on this one.

'I should also attend,' Telmo insisted, 'as we need to sort out that other long forgotten matter.' Clearly the technologist did not wish to mention the time chariot in their visitor's presence.

Rhun scowled, annoyed to have his orders constantly disputed. 'If you must,' he granted, quickly speaking up to prevent Song opting to tag along. 'No one else. I don't know how long we'll be gone for.' Rhun looked to Noah without mentioning their destination, for Noah knew well enough that time was unpredictable in the Otherworld. 'But if any more than a few days pass —' Rhun looked to En Noah '— you'd best come find us.'

'Right you are,' Noah replied.

'I will leave Aysel in your charge, Wu Geng,' Rhun instructed.

'That is a polite way of announcing that you are placing me under surveillance,' Aysel commented.

'If the situation were reversed, would you not do the same?' Rhun posed, fairly.

'The advantage of a hive-mind is, I wouldn't have to,' she said with a sly grin.

Rhun found the comment enlightening and off-putting as he could well be addressing the entire Fiameadi council, who were probably all taking notes. But then again, if their hive-mind was in chaos at present, perhaps not. 'You'll just have to bear with us,' he replied graciously, ahead of looking at the others who meant to accompany him into the Otherworld.

'Let's go.' Rhun vanished, and Telmo and Dan vanished after him.

The grand otherworldly entrance chamber in which they found themselves had Dan and Telmo turning circles in awe.

The large, round block of floor beneath their feet appeared like a smooth sheet of ice, but as it was neither slippery nor cold, Dan assumed it was some kind of crystal. The ceiling above had a circular hole that allowed light to flood in — the light was celestial and came from no source in particular, but rather from everywhere. Around the edges of the circular cavity above, water streamed between the ceiling and the edge of the platform on which they stood, forming a great wall of water around them — only instead of the water flowing down, the stream was flowing upward.

'That is a strange paradox,' Dan commented staring at the water rushing up to the ceiling, 'it feels as though one is hanging upside down.'

'Ah, the Otherworld.' Telmo released a deep exhalation, delighted. 'Where the illogical is logical.'

'That would explain my brother.' Rhun forced a grin.

'I heard that,' Avery commented from beyond the wall of water, just as Dan was wondering how they would depart the chamber without getting wet.

The water feature drew apart like a curtain to one side of them to form a clear exit. Dan gave half a laugh, enchanted by the feat, as he followed Rhun into the huge, light-filled garden chamber beyond.

This was much like a grand circular hall in structure, only there were stone pathways in place of aisles, grass and flowers in place of carpet, and grand trees where pillars might have been. The outer walls of the structure were made of etheric matter that were opaque

78

enough to be seen, yet emitted enough of their own subtle light that it hardly seemed they were there.

Avery was waiting to greet them with a mass of tiny earth-lights hovering about him. 'Not now.' He was shooing the nature sprites away. 'We have guests.' Avery turned his attention to his brother and company, unhappily. 'Not to seem unwelcoming ... but, why are you timekeepers still here?'

'There have been a few complications,' Rhun began.

'No, no, no ... I don't want to hear about complications,' Avery objected. 'I want the timekeepers back where they belong!'

Rhun rolled his eyes. 'I couldn't agree more, but —'

'Fen is dead,' Dan informed.

'What?' Avery was shocked that he had not got wind of this event, until one of the tiny earth-lights again alighted on his shoulder to have a whisper in his ear. 'Oh, I see,' he thanked and dismissed the sprite. 'It seems there was a disturbance earlier.'

'There has been a disturbance all right.' Telmo got on his high horse. 'Where is the second time chariot?'

Avery looked to Rhun with a baffled look on his face.

'I already told them that we don't know what happened to it,' Rhun verified. 'But Dragonface's movements seem to indicate that he has got a means to time travel.'

'That is very bad,' Avery considered. 'Why do you suspect he has time travel capability?'

'Because Ling Hu is the one who killed Fen, after we'd brought him forwards in time to Kila,' Rhun outlined the conundrum.

'And Dragonface took Ling Hu.' Avery nodded in understanding. 'Best tell me the rest.'

In the absence of the governor and the others, the rest of the timekeepers, along with En Noah, saw to the sad chore of laying Fen to rest. The Wu way was cremation, but so as not to attract attention to themselves, Hudan employed her elemental power to incinerate the body without any smoke being created. All the while, Hudan had a terrible foreboding that Fen's death was just the prelude to a far greater ordeal ahead, and so strong was the premonition that it was making her feel physically ill.

It was not like Hudan or her sister to openly display their grief, yet, as Huxin stood in silent, sombre tribute to their brother's memory, Hudan could not prevent herself from weeping. It was not like she was never going to see this soul-mind again; Ringbalin was awaiting her return to AMIE along with the rest of the crew. In fact, the same soul-mind was standing alongside them in the form of En Noah. But she would never again see his Zhou incarnation, who'd been a beloved brother and a dear, sweet friend who she'd raised from a toddler. That knowledge made her soul ache as she watched the last of Fen Gong's ashes burn out and be swept away on the breeze.

Afterwards Hudan felt drained, which had been known to happen after performing a taxing sacred rite. Usually her vitality would be restored after a good rest and some sustenance; the only problem was that she couldn't keep any food down as her stomach was in knots.

All six timekeepers not native to Kila, and Aysel, who was being regarded as a guest at this stage, were confined to Noah's lake house, outside the city proper. Designed to comfortably house two people, it was now accommodating seven.

As Hudan and Dan were the only couple staying at the lake house, they had been given the stunning circular bedroom upstairs, and Hudan was grateful for the harmonious and quiet place to rest as she'd not felt so weak since she'd awoken from the Yin rite, performed to secure Ji Fa's reign in ancient Zhou. As distressing as her brother's murder and funeral had been for Hudan personally, it should not have taxed her chi this much.

'How are you feeling?' Huxin emerged from behind the circular feature wall that hid the spiralling stairway leading to the mid-level of the house. 'Can I get you something to eat yet?'

'No,' Hudan insisted, her stomach heaving at the mere thought of food, and suppressing the urge to be sick, she merely burped up some wind. 'I've never felt so wretched.'

Huxin came closer to observe her sister. 'This is certainly unlike you … belching, vomiting, and over-emotional … anyone would think —' Huxin gasped on her own observation. 'You're *pregnant.*'

'No!' Hudan went white. 'I can't be.'

Huxin gave her a questioning look. 'I think you'll find you can quite possibly be.'

Hudan sat up so quickly and in such panic that she was almost sick again, but she breathed deep to contain her nausea and explain. 'What I mean to say is, I cannot take this body back to our true universal scheme with me, let alone with a child!'

Huxin's amusement fled as she realised her sister's dilemma. 'That does pose something of a quandary.'

'Even if I were to stay long enough to have the child, who would raise it? I could be trapped in this universe indefinitely! And this universe is becoming increasingly risky for us to remain in.'

Hudan was near hysterical and Huxin sat and gripped her shoulders, hoping to calm her. 'If this has happened, then for some cosmic reason it is meant to be,' she reasoned. 'I'm sure once you discuss this with Dan, you'll —'

'Heavens, no,' Hudan appealed. 'Please don't say anything to him.'

'You cannot keep this from your husband!' Huxin stood, indignant.

'Just until I have confirmation,' Hudan added to appease her sister. But she knew how dearly Dan's previous incarnation, Lucian, had wanted a child, and she doubted very much that he would sacrifice his long-held hope for the greater good, or whether indeed she could herself?

'Fair enough,' her sister relented. 'I shall ask En Noah about getting a healer to see you.'

Hudan nodded, although in reality she didn't want her fear confirmed. Her fellow crew members would not leave without her, and keeping them here was to make them subject to Vugar's vendetta. *Please, please, heaven*, she prayed, *do not let it be as we suspect.*

*

'Okay, let's recap.' Rhun summed up their current theory. 'Dragonface died in the explosion of the Dropa ship, then the entity shifted to Fiameadi and took possession of the body of the Draconian leader, Vugar, three thousand years ago. As the Draconians of Fiameadi obviously have supernatural power, he could have used psychokinesis to join the second time chariot —'

'That you just *left* in Atlantis,' Telmo added, still unable to believe it. 'If I'd still been around, I would have been sending you back for it!'

'Well, we were dealing with your old nemesis Mahaud, the demise of Atlantis, the uprising of Demuzi's horde of bastard demigods, and another bloody reptilian with visions of total world annihilation!' Rhun defended, fed up with being chastised about the incident.

'As long as Dragonface knew where the second chariot was at the time he died in the explosion,' Dan returned to Rhun's summation, 'he could have willed himself to it at his leisure, and then used it to go back in time to reach us in the crystal cavern at the exact moment the Dropa ship was destroyed.'

'Exactly,' Rhun agreed. 'He then killed Shi and kidnapped Ling Hu. Now, as Ling Hu is not immortal and does not possess any great longevity, we might assume that for those long periods of time that Vugar spent off-planet doing space exploration, he was really time travelling forward to meet up with us three thousand years in the future and carry out his most recent attacks on the timekeepers.'

'That still does not explain how he even knew where we would be,' Telmo pointed out.

'Unless Ling Hu told him,' Dan postulated. 'I'm sure Fen must have told her about his past at some point. Including the time his previous incarnation spent on Kila, and his need to return to that incarnation in the next universe, at some point in the future.'

'Perhaps,' Telmo conceded.

'What really matters is what we aim to do about it.' Rhun looked to his otherworldly brother, who was being very quiet. 'Do we go back to Atlantis and take back the chariot before he gets his hands on it? Do we go back to Bayan Har San and do things differently —'

'No,' Avery insisted, 'we do not go back in time for any reason, we must take out Dragonface from here.'

'But —'

'No buts,' Avery barked. 'Atlantis could be a wild goose chase. The Draconians could have their own means to time travel. Did anyone ask this visitor that?'

All appeared a little sorry to have overlooked that question.

'You've just outlined how insanely out of control events were in the final hours of Atlantis. Anything we do there could affect the next thirteen thousand years of history,' Avery lectured. 'Including ancient Zhou, and your birth era —' he looked to Rhun '— in the dark ages of ancient Briton.'

'I am touched that you would be so concerned.' Rhun was not convinced by Avery's motive. 'What do you know about the Eternity Gate?'

'What should I know? I've never heard of it.' Avery frowned.

'I thought you knew everything!' Rhun emphasised.

'I know everything about everything that has transpired since I was appointed Lord of the Otherworld. I do not have access to akashic memory like Telmo and Dan do.'

Rhun looked to Telmo and Dan. 'Anyone know anything about it, or the old universe, or mind-eaters for that matter?'

Telmo was thinking hard on it. 'Not in all my lifetimes on Earth have I heard it mentioned, and yet when Aysel spoke of it, I had a flash vision of a beautiful nebula in space.'

'I don't know of it either,' Dan was sorry to say, 'although I know where I might be able to acquire some information.'

Rhun was terribly curious about the claim, Dan could tell by his inquisitive frown.

'I am a medium,' Dan replied, 'and I, or rather Lucian, can contact my silent watcher. It is one of the beings that you call the Grigori, who goes by the name of Azazèl. That entity answers to our collective consciousness, Azazèl-mindos-coomra-dorchi, the being who drew all the timekeepers into this universe when it shifted here from our universal scheme.'

His company all looked rather stunned by the claim.

'Well, you could have mentioned that earlier.' Rhun was a little perturbed. 'A little divine guidance would certainly not go astray.'

'It is only since returning to Kila that I've been clearly recollecting Lucian's time here.' Dan explained the delay. 'En Noah's lake house sparked a memory of Lucian once contacting Azazèl there.'

'Fair enough,' Rhun conceded. 'A good unbiased opinion on how best to proceed would be welcome. The silent watchers even outrank Avery in the cosmic scheme of things ...'

'Are you implying my judgement is tainted?' The Lord of the Otherworld took offence to his brother's implication.

'I fear your want of a child is clouding your clarity,' Rhun answered.

'Fallon's pregnancy is beside the point!' Avery insisted.

'You are lying.' Rhun stood to press home his view, and Avery stood to challenge it. 'You've stated as much yourself —'

'I am not at risk?' Avery's wife, Fallon, appeared among them, and an ambience of serenity accompanied her. The hostility between the brothers ceased and all the men rose to acknowledge her presence. 'So long as I remain here in the Otherworld, I cannot be harmed and my happy circumstance will not change.'

Dan was shaking his head, dumbfounded. 'It seems such a long, long time since I saw you last, and yet your pregnancy does not seem to have advanced at all. Or have you already given birth?' Dan gathered not, as Avery still did not refer to his child as either male or female.

Fallon looked puzzled and Avery explained. 'Do you remember Lucian, the captain of the —'

'Of course I do.' She smiled, having established the connection. 'Your appearance has changed somewhat since last we met, but I can clearly see our first governor in you, now that Avery has mentioned it.'

Dan bowed his head to accept what was, to the Chosen, a great compliment. For Maelgwn Gwynedd, the first Governor of Kila, was among Dan's past life incarnations in this universe, and much as Zhou Gong was to the people of China, Maelgwn was revered among the Chosen as one of the greatest leaders ever to walk among men.

'As for my pregnancy,' Fallon further enlightened them, 'it shall not advance so long as I remain in the Otherworld.'

'Hence the need to make this universe safe and stable as soon as possible,' Avery outlined.

'Now I see the urgency,' Dan warranted, but considered that wish would prove no simple matter.

'There is no urgency really,' Fallon made it sound like Avery was making an awful fuss over nothing. 'We've waited a hundred years to conceive, so a few more years before giving birth will hardly make much difference. However,' Fallon urged them to be seated on the tree elementals who had contorted themselves into seats for the lord's guests' convenience, 'regarding the question of how to combat the reptilian we knew as Shyamal: I was entrusted with the specs for the anion spray adhesive, which Kestler and Floyd designed to combat the menace, and the specs for the weapon Shyamal designed to use against us.'

'What are you talking about, sweetness?' Avery had no idea, nor did Rhun or Telmo.

Dan was the only one with a memory that harked back far enough to remember the events of the timeline of which she spoke. 'Hudan, or rather Taren Lennox, was also entrusted with those specs and schematics, and combined the two to create the weapon we brought back to Kila with us,' Dan explained.

'I think she had a little help,' Telmo jogged Dan's memory.

'My apologies,' Dan corrected. 'And Telmo built the prototypes.'

'That's the weapon that restored my immortality,' Rhun realised.

'The very one.' Dan nodded to confirm.

'I knew I'd never remember the complex scientific data, and as I could not take anything of the physical realm, like a map or an outline, deep into the Otherworld with me, I trained some of my denizens to retain the information.'

'How do you mean?' Telmo was curious.

'One moment,' Fallon entreated their patience, 'we will demonstrate.'

The Lady of the Otherworld left their circle and walked into the field of grass and flowers that carpeted the clearing around where the rest of them were seated. As she walked, the flowers in the field opened wide and twisted about to follow her, as they would to track the sun's path across the sky. When Fallon began to speak, the still atmosphere stirred, and a breeze rose from nowhere to swirl around her, causing her long sheer gown and dark hair to billow.

> 'Denizens of air and earth
> who have harboured me here
> to protect this birth,
> I entrusted to you vital information.
> Come to me now and
> assume the formation.'

From the open flowers in the field sprang thousands of tiny light beings, bright green in colour, which took to the air. After some buzzing about, the sprites split into three groups. One group of lights formed into a math equation of a scientific formula that was suspended in the air; another group arranged themselves into a flat vertical formation of a detailed schematic, and the third formed a three dimensional representation of the weapon draft.

'Good grief.' Avery was stunned by his wife's disclosure. 'You've been studying quantum mechanics?'

'No.' Fallon was amused by her husband's awe. 'I assure you, I am just the messenger.'

'And what a helpful message it is.' Telmo, the most technically minded among them, moved to inspect the specifications. 'These appear to be perfectly intact.' He looked back to his captain, the governor and his host, a broad smile upon his face.

*

Song was not taking the delay in the proceedings very well — it gave him too much time to sit around and think about their recent losses, and his lack of involvement in planning a strategy to deal with the creature responsible for the deaths of two of his dearest friends.

It was, however, a relief to be outdoors. Song had wandered along the long jetty that connected the submersible lake house to the shore, and was casting stones from the edge across the lake's still surface in the hope of diluting his frustration.

'What are you doing out here by yourself?' Wu Geng asked, startling Song from his impassioned game.

'Being pissed off,' he replied, retrieving another stone from the ground and pitching it into the lake. 'Nobody tells me *anything!*'

'Ha, ha, ha … and welcome to my world,' Wu Geng replied sympathetically, leaning on the rail at the jetty's end, and placing a foot on the lower rung.

Song's fury sobered a little; he'd never thought to empathise with his old nemesis, but in this instance he did. 'We've given you a rough time over the years.' Song felt grateful for Wu Geng's part in saving his life, yet he could not bring himself to say so. 'But you really did ask for it.' He reverted to his hostile mood, and pitched another stone in the lake.

Wu Geng smiled, amused. 'I know Khalid did,' he freely admitted. 'But I am not the one complaining about being left out of the loop in this instance.'

'Why, man?' Song wanted to know. 'Why am I so easily dispensed with? When I've been on this journey with Taren longer than any of them!' He cast another stone across the water.

Wu Geng shrugged. 'I'm sure I don't know. You certainly got in my way more than any of your AMIE counterparts, save maybe our fearless leader herself.'

'That's exactly right!' Song frowned, having never thought to be agreeing with his enemy.

'There must be something useful we can do?' Wu Geng suggested they get a bit proactive.

'We should bloody well question that lizard b—' Song was about to say 'bitch', when he spotted a beautiful woman striding down the jetty towards them, dressed exactly as Aysel had been. So either some princess from ancient Zhou had shown up wearing the same attire, or Aysel had shapeshifted into a human form.

'Wow!' Wu Geng uttered under his breath, as he noted her approaching. 'You were saying?' He looked back to Song, who'd been rendered speechless.

'She's a lizard, she's a lizard,' he repeated to himself to drag his fixated gaze away from the vision.

Again Wu Geng had a chuckle. 'Not to worry, I'll protect you.'

'We should question her,' Song whispered to Wu Geng, as he pushed off the railing.

'We'll catch more flies with honey,' Wu Geng advised and Song figured Wu Geng most likely did. He may not have had Song's muscular physique, but he was devilishly good-looking in a very well-groomed, princely way and could pour on the noble charm at will.

'You've changed.' Wu Geng awarded Aysel his full attention, holding wide his arms in approval, his palms upwards in question.

'Well, as the governor is trying to hide me, I thought I may as well go all the way,' she explained. 'Spending time with not-your-friend?'

Wu Geng smiled at her humour. 'The captain said we were to keep an eye on one another.'

'Good of you to care for someone who cares so little for you,' she stated rather more loudly to be sure and catch Song's ear, but he was reading her loud and clear.

'Hey, I am friends with Wu Geng.' Song considered all they'd been through together.

'Really?' Wu Geng was cynical. 'Since when?'

'Since always,' Song insisted. 'It's Khalid I have a problem with.'

'Khalid?' Aysel queried, looking to Wu Geng. 'Who is he, your alter ego?

Song was amused by her guess.

'No one of concern at this present point in time and space.' Wu Geng gave Song a look of warning against mentioning anything of their universe of origin in the Draconian's presence.

When Aysel turned her inquisitive look Song's way, he waved off the comment. 'It's just a private joke.'

'Between *friends*,' she emphasised curiously.

'But enough about us!' Song joined them on the jetty to change the subject. 'Let's talk about you.'

'So, you are to interrogate me?' She smiled, folding her arms, seemingly amused by the premise.

'Not at all,' Wu Geng assured her in an endearing and charming manner. 'Song was just curious about your reference to the old universe earlier.'

Aysel looked to Song, who immediately dropped his defensive stance to play along with Wu Geng's more subtle approach.

'Yeah, and what's a mind-eater and an Eternity Gate?'

The Draconian smiled, pleasantly disposed towards their line of questioning. 'Are these concepts really unknown to you?'

Both men nodded in accord. 'We'd be most grateful if you would fill us in,' Wu Geng appealed with a grin and Song was quietly impressed by his new friend's approach.

'Well,' she said, her brow furrowed, seemingly overwhelmed by the request. 'The truth is, no one really knows the truth about these things … like I said, most of it is just legends and hearsay.'

'I love a good yarn,' Song hoisted himself up to sit on the jetty rail, resting his heels on the lower rung. 'And it's not like we have anything better to do.'

'Unless you have other plans?' Wu Geng allowed that she was not required to comply with their wish — her choice would be telling either way.

'No one can say for sure where the Eternity Gate leads,' she began. 'Some say it is a gateway to the realm of the creator, others say it is a crossroads between several universes. The most enlightened souls being culled from one universe, in order to populate the next universe that is closer to perfection in the evolutionary scheme of things.'

'That makes sense.' Song looked to Wu Geng, considering their current situation; they already knew there was more than one universe in which they had incarnated.

'Is this gate a physical construction?' Wu Geng queried.

'It is.' She anticipated his next question. 'It is located at the heart of the Orion nebula.'

'How do you know our name for that part of the sky? How do you know our languages for that matter?' Song was very curious about that.

'It is you who have learned our names for that part of the galaxy, not the other way around,' she advised. 'You don't think our caste ended up on your planet by accident, do you? Someone introduced our genetic strain there.'

'Who?' Song wondered.

'The Nefilim.'

The trio turned to find Noah had joined them on the jetty.

'Your last incarnation here on Kila,' Noah pointed to Song, 'saw the last of the Nefilim back to their maker.'

'Really?' Song was impressed with himself. 'I really do need to pay a visit to your library of immortal history, Noah.'

The governor's chief advisor nodded to concede it was a good suggestion and then looked back to their female visitor. 'Please continue, I am most curious to hear this tale also.'

'Yes,' Wu Geng was eager to get back on topic too. 'If this gate actually exists, how come no one knows where it goes?'

'Many have made futile attempts to enter the Eternity Gate,' Aysel told them. 'Most who have tried to enter it have been destroyed, and the few who made it through never returned to tell of their journey.'

'When you say many, do you refer to your people, Draconians?' Wu Geng wondered.

'There are sub-species of reptoid who reside in the Orion galaxy,' she explained, 'known as Reticulan Greys, a different caste altogether from my people. I am from the royal strain of reptilians of Alpha Dranconis, and only our upper echelons carry the title of Draconian. My caste chose enlightenment, our caste in Orion have not.'

'So you are a princess,' Wu Geng noted winningly, as her mood had soured a little. She was obviously not impressed with her distant relatives in Orion.

'A hive must have a queen,' she replied, clearly forcing herself back into better spirits.

'Then surely you should be better protected?' Song was sceptical of her boast. 'Shouldn't you have sent one of your subordinates on this quest to capture your rogue leader?'

Aysel glared at Song.

'Just asking.' Song turned both palms up. 'Please, humour my ignorance.'

'You are led by a female,' she pointed out. 'Would she send one of her subordinates forth to correct her error?'

'What makes you think we are led by a female?' Song had to wonder. Hudan had barely said a word during their questioning of Aysel, and the Draconian had not been present at Fen's funeral so she could not have picked up on anything that happened there.

'You deny the woman with child is your leader?' Aysel turned the inquisition around, and was a little discomforted by the men's stunned reaction.

'Hudan is pregnant?' Song's jaw dropped.

'Dear heavens!' Wu Geng was concerned also — as was Noah.

'That would explain the need for a healer,' the advisor commented to himself.

'Apologies.' Aysel forced a grin, realising she had spoken out of turn. 'Was that not common knowledge?'

'I don't know if Hudan knows.' Song could see how a pregnancy would cause all sorts of problems right now. 'How do you know she is with child?'

'I can see the new life forming in her auric womb,' she enlightened them. 'Just as easily as I can see how all your light-bodies gravitate towards Hudan. Clearly she is where all allegiances lay.'

'What? Wait!' Song felt her comment could have further significance. 'Even Wu Geng's aura?' He cast Wu Geng an apologetic look, and looked back to Aysel.

'Even Wu Geng,' she was pleased to confirm.

Song looked to the man in question and smiled, relieved to know he had good cause for liking Wu Geng.

'I've been trying to tell you that for some time now.' Wu Geng rolled his eyes, and moved to knock Song from the railing he was sitting on, but aborted the attempt after making him flinch. 'You know I've wanted to hit you so many times over the years —' he grinned '— and you've really asked for it.'

'In answer to your original query,' Aysel interrupted their bonding moment, and clearly neither man could recall the query to which she referred. 'There are many inhabited planets in the Orion system, but only a few play host to reptoid. There are many other races who have attempted to enter the Eternity Gate, and all within my lifetime were unsuccessful.'

'So where do mind-eaters figure in this?' Song queried.

'Mind-eaters stem from the universal crossroads theory about the Eternity Gate,' Aysel clued him in. 'One of the other universes to which the gate gives access is known as the Old Universe, as it was the universe before this one in the ascending timeline of evolution within the Eternity Gate. That entire universe fell under the rule of an evil emperor who created mind-eaters as a means to pacify the minds of the people who inhabited the planets they conquered.'

'But what are they?' Song frowned.

'An energetic geo-plasma,' Aysel outlined. 'It attaches itself to the brain and inhibits the aura of its victim, removing its free will and reprogramming it with the Empiric agenda.'

'Come again?' Song still didn't understand.

'It's an earthbound gaseous entity that brainwashes you into submission,' Noah simplified.

'Gotcha,' Song confirmed. 'How do you control such an animal?'

'Well, that's really the crux of the tale … as it turned out, you can't,' she was sorry to say. 'What the imperial scientists failed to realise was that these entities could multiply by themselves. Once a mind-eater had absorbed enough energy from one person, it would split in two and seek another host to prey upon. Before long that entire universe was overrun with mind-eaters and they began to attack their creators. It is said that only a handful of the imperial elite survived, and they accessed the Eternity Gate to escape the mind-eaters. After the breach, the interior gates of the universal crossroads were closed in the hope of preventing any of the mind-eaters escaping.'

'But one or more of the escapees may have been infected?' Wu Geng considered. 'And I suppose legend has it that the survivors landed in this universe.'

Aysel nodded. 'The story goes that they were not quarantined, and thus this universe became infected.' She forced a smile. 'What I once thought a creepy tale for gullible children could have a basis in reality.'

'Obviously no one figured out a way to destroy the menace,' Song considered. 'But if the entities were programmed to follow the Empiric programming, and then turned on the Empire, what agenda would they be instilling in their victims now I wonder?'

'The Empiric agenda was to serve the one, the emperor, and through serving him it was believed that all were served,' Aysel explained.

'Is that not the creed your people live by?' Song suggested, and again could see by Aysel's face that he had caused offence.

'When the mind-eaters broke that programming, their agenda became to serve the self,' she replied, coolly, 'the creed your people live by.'

Now it was Song who was offended. 'We serve the cosmic agenda,' he clarified. 'Or the creator, as you termed it. Through service to others the self is served, which is exactly the opposite of the old Empiric creed.'

Aysel appeared sceptical. 'Well, for souls who are so virtuous, Vugar's pet shifter did not seem very well disposed towards you.'

'Nor to you,' Song shot back at her.

'She was not trying to kill me,' Aysel pointed out.

'I think we can safely assume we are all on the same side,' Wu Geng intervened as Song jumped down off the rail to confront the tall beauty.

'Well, I don't trust her,' Song stated for the record.

'You don't trust anyone.' Wu Geng knew that well enough.

'If not for me, you would not be alive to have an opinion.' Aysel placed hands on hips, insulted again.

'How convenient,' Song noted tersely. 'How do we know that attack wasn't staged just to get you in with us?'

Aysel's cool glare intensified to livid. 'I wonder, if I had been able to identify him sooner, whether your healer might have shown more gratitude for my assistance?'

With the thought of his dearly departed friend, Song's anger turned to sorrow and he backed down. 'I doubt, after what happened, Fen would be glad to be alive.'

'For all those who truly serve the divine, life is always a treasured gift, for without it we cannot execute the plan on the creator's behalf,' Aysel stated in a holier-than-thou tone.

Song was irked that she was implying that Fen was not so devoted. 'The primary weapon of any spiritual warrior is love,' Song replied, a large lump forming in his throat. 'Something you obviously know nothing about.'

'I always thought it was wisdom?' Aysel argued, and Song's sights darkened once more.

'Let us not forget *compassion*,' Noah interjected, 'without which wisdom is only ego-based intellect and love is but a lust to possess.' The sage turned his attention to the Draconian. 'What Song means to say is that sometimes it is our virtues that kill us in the end. That is the risk the righteous run … the same risk that we are all taking for the privilege of having such a vital role in the evolution of this universal scheme.'

For a moment Song had forgotten that Fen lived on in En Noah, but with his words Song felt his resentment and suspicion melt away — Noah's presence, like Fen's, had a calming and healing influence.

'Human spirituality has primarily developed through the perfection of the emotional body, whereas Draconians have evolved primarily through the perfection of the mental body, much as the Nefilim did. Although that will make it a little more difficult for us to understand each other, it is no excuse to allow our egos to get in the way of our cooperation, which could reward both our peoples with perception and insight previously unknown to us.' He smiled graciously in conclusion.

'There doesn't seem to be anything amiss with your mental body,' Aysel awarded, disarmed by his spiel. 'No wonder your people are called the Chosen Ones.'

'I do have a query, however,' Noah put to Aysel. 'This emperor who survived the old universe and fled to this one, did he have a name?'

'Whatever name you have given to the ultimate evil force in the universe, that is his name,' she advised.

Noah nodded as if he'd expected as much. 'That particular entity is an old friend of an old friend of mine.'

'What?' Song and company were baffled by the claim.

Noah smiled encouragingly to assure them it was quite true. 'I think I might know how to get in touch.'

By dinner time that evening, the governor's party had still not returned to the lake house, but there was a mighty good smell wafting up from the kitchen. Hudan, who was feeling a little better, was now beyond starving and so ventured downstairs.

'How are you?' Huxin queried from the breakfast bar where she and the Draconian were seated watching Wu Geng cook up a storm in the kitchen, with Song assisting.

'*Hungry*,' Hudan replied, wondering at the stunned look on everyone's faces.

Song nodded. 'Well, you would be —'

Wu Geng elbowed Song and a strange look passed between them.

'After being so sick all morning,' he stressed in Wu Geng's direction.

Hudan was immediately alarmed and looked to her sister.

'I didn't say anything, about anything.' Huxin was baffled by their odd behaviour also.

'It was me.' The Draconian put a hand up to confess. 'I see auras.' She shrugged. 'I didn't realise no one knew about your condition.'

The news was like a double sucker-punch to the chest. Not only did this seem to confirm her pregnancy, but everyone knew about it, and very soon Dan would know too. 'You're sure then?'

The Draconian nodded solemnly, and everyone else present appeared as horrified as Hudan felt.

'Whatever you decide to do,' Song spoke up to break the heavy silence, 'we're all with you.'

'*No.*' Hudan put her foot down, as that was exactly what she was afraid of: getting them all killed. 'This is no one's affair but my own.'

'I do believe it is also our captain's affair,' Huxin stated.

'What is my affair?'

The sound of Dan's voice startled Hudan to an about-face, and for a moment she and the others were stunned speechless.

'Well, someone say something!' Dan prompted, taking a few sniffs of air. 'Is something burning?'

'Damn.' Wu Geng snapped out of his shock to remove a large saucepan from the heat and give it a stir.

'I ... need to set the table.' Huxin slid off her chair to escape the captain's questioning gaze.

'I'll help you.' Aysel quickly followed her out.

'Me too.' Song departed, and Wu Geng left his saucepan to cool.

'I need to supervise.' He exited swiftly after the others.

Now Dan was looking very curious. 'How many psychics with psychokinesis does it take to set a table?' he queried Hudan, but she was still lost for words as she looked to Telmo and Rhun, who were both as baffled as Dan by the mass exodus.

'I wonder where En Noah is?' Telmo queried Rhun, to give them a reason to remove themselves from the awkward moment.

'Probably down in his study,' Rhun suggested, looking back to Hudan and Dan curiously. 'We should go and update him on the situation.' They both headed downstairs.

'You have news?' Hudan hoped to change the subject.

'It will wait,' Dan advised. 'So are you going to tell me about the affair?'

Hudan attempted to find the courage but sick with hunger, she felt too weak and distressed, and shook her head.

'No!' Dan was surprised by her reaction. 'Why no?'

Hudan held up a finger to beg his patience, and made haste

to the pot of stew Wu Geng had left aside, and filling a bowl, she immediately tucked into it.

'You are a little hungry, my love?' Dan posed, amused. He'd never seen her so ravenous.

'Starving!' she emphasised between mouthfuls. 'I've been sick all morning!' Hudan gasped in the wake of her comment as Dan appeared to have a joyful revelation, but upon further consideration his elation turned to woe and before his emotions stabilised, he looked to her.

'If this affair is what I think it is, it is very much mine, I should hope.' He raised his eyebrows in mute appeal for more information.

She didn't want to break the news, not even to herself. She opened her mouth to confess but her welling tears choked the words, and she shook her head in protest at the hand they'd been dealt. 'How could this happen now?' she entreated her husband, tears tumbling down her face for the umpteenth time that day.

Dan, momentarily stunned to see her so emotional, joined her behind the servery and she welcomed his embrace.

'I hate being so emotional, but I cannot turn it off,' she continued to blubber into his shirt.

'We'll work it out,' he assured her, although the myriad complications she'd been considering all day must have been bombarding his brain all at once. 'If this has happened now there must be a reason, don't you think?'

'I don't know,' Hudan just buried her head deeper in his chest. 'My brain has gone to mush and I just don't want to be the one who prevents the team getting home, or gets us all killed!'

'We are not going anywhere, any time soon,' Dan assured her.

'But we can't take this baby with us, you know that!' Hudan pulled away to speak seriously about their next move.

'But we can cheat time,' Dan cautioned her against panic.

'Not if we are dead,' she insisted.

'It will only take one of us getting through to make it all come out right in the end,' Dan reminded her.

Hudan gasped at the suggestion. 'Are you saying we just stay here until this child has a life of its own?' That thought was just as horrifying.

'I'm saying that just because we cannot see the solution or reason in this very moment does not mean we never will,' he advised, and Hudan calmed and collapsed back into his arms again. 'I know you like to have the answers yesterday, but sometimes you just have to wait for them to present themselves, which they will, in their own good time.'

Hudan nodded, unsure if she believed him, but they both needed a little time to absorb the situation before they decided what their best course of action was.

'All settled then?' Song crept back into the room to ask on everyone's behalf. ''Cause if it is, your starving crew would dearly love to eat.'

Hudan sucked back her fear, cracked a smile and waved them forth.

Down in En Noah's study, Rhun and Telmo found Jahan sitting quietly at the desk where the monitoring equipment for Noah's meditation chamber was located.

'Noah is inside?' Rhun motioned to the closed chamber, and Jahan nodded to confirm.

'He left me here to ensure he wasn't disturbed ... said something about needing to revisit Armaros.' Jahan shrugged, 'I have no idea what that means?'

'Armaros!' Rhun looked to Telmo, wondering if he was familiar with the entity who was Noah's Grigorian personification.

'He's had the same thought as Dan,' Telmo realised. 'Consult a higher power. Although I didn't realise your advisor had Dan's ability to consult with disembodied spirits?'

'He doesn't,' Rhun concurred, a little perplexed by this. 'But he does have otherworldly influence and he did unlock the Nefilim lord Enki's Sensor-sphere.'

Telmo frowned, curious to know more. 'That must have been

after Taliesin departed this universal scheme for I have no memory of such a thing?'

'It is an otherworldly technology that offers a crash course in cosmology, and insight into the pertinent eras of the development of human consciousness into matter — which you experience first-hand via all your senses.'

'How wonderful,' Telmo imagined.

Rhun nodded to confirm. 'I myself took the course under En Noah's guidance, but it only awarded insight into the human consciousness experiment. I don't remember seeing anything about an Eternity Gate?'

Telmo raised his brow, not really surprised. 'Probably because humans have had very little to do with the wonder in question. The Grigori, however … their involvement seems more likely.'

The door to the meditation chamber opened and Noah emerged, looking grave.

'En Noah?' Rhun queried his expression. 'What were you doing in there?'

'Past life regression,' he answered simply. 'I ventured back further than I have ever dared go before.'

Rhun was a little confused, knowing that the sage had relived his lives as far back as his first human incarnation in the ancient city of Edin of Earth's evolution. 'You went back to before you were ever incarnated as a human?'

Noah nodded gravely. 'And it is as I feared.'

'What did you fear?' Telmo sought to clarify.

'Those few Empiric elite who escaped the old universe and brought their virus here,' Noah prompted and received a nod of comprehension from them. 'That was us.'

'The Grigori, you mean?' Rhun followed his train of thought.

Noah gave a firm nod. 'I recommend you ask Wu Geng to take our Draconian visitor for a walk after dinner. We need to have a meeting.'

5

THE BLACK SHEEP

'The Empire was backed into a corner — mind-eaters were out of control. Only one planet in the entire universe remained uninfected: the Empiric capital. The emperor was planning an exodus through the Eternity Gate, which was once, and still is, open to everyone. There is only one hitch ... no weapon will pass through the gate. Now, the emperor was not about to invade a new universe with no weapons, so an advance team was selected to pass through the gates, carrying incubated mind-eaters that had yet to be unleashed. As this weapon was actually organic, it was believed they would pass safely and undetected through the gate. These specimens, unlike their predecessors that had run amuck in the old universe, had been refined so that they could not procreate, but only feed on one host until the host died, at which point the entity was free to feed on the next victim to wander into its proximity.'

'That diagnostic is sounding a lot more like the entity I've seen pass from one dead reptilian to another.' The captain interrupted Noah's discourse from the lounge, where he was seated listening to the governor's advisor with the rest of his crew and the governor himself. 'Were we really so brainwashed as to agree to do such a thing — when we had already seen the devastation done by those creatures in our universe of origin?'

'No, we were not,' Noah reassured him with a sincere, although joyless, smile. 'We were the fallen, who rebelled against the fallen, which was exactly what would set us apart as the Chosen in this universe. As there were so few free-thinking beings left in our universe, you refused to risk your crew by carrying the virus in the first attempt to breach the Eternity Gate … but you did agree to execute the recon mission and establish a base in the next universe. We were foolish to believe that the emperor had agreed to our terms for the mission.' Noah looked very remorseful. 'We should not have allowed you to attend that last meeting with so little backup, but if we had accompanied you, then … perhaps we would have had a much bigger problem to deal with now.'

'The emperor infected Azazèl with a mind-eater,' Dan surmised.

'That was not discovered until after our passage through the gate succeeded,' Noah concluded. 'At least, I suspect that is what happened, but I have no proof, only an instinct.'

'But how could Azazèl rid himself of the mind-eater and repair the damage it must have done his psyche?' Dan quizzed. 'And how did the reptilians get infected with the virus in his stead?'

'I have no idea how it was done, only that the Nefilim may have somehow been involved, considering their forte for genetic engineering and soul extraction,' Noah was sorry to say. 'Only Azazèl really knows what happened. But as far as repairing the damage to his psyche, maybe he never did, as after all you led the Grigori into sin in this universe; hence our lot to keep incarnating into human form until human evolution is complete.'

'Hold on,' Rhun was a little confused. 'Was the emperor of the Old Universe, Satan? Because I was told that that soul-mind evolved into my parents.'

'Both,' Noah stated to a muttered 'what?' from everyone and perplexed frowns. 'In the old scriptures of our planet of origin, you will note that Satan is actually called "Ha-Satan" meaning "the opposer, the obstructer, the adversary," et cetera. It is more a title than a name.'

'So what you are saying, En Noah,' the captain summed up, 'is that we may only be dealing with one of these mind-eaters.'

'If indeed I am right in my suspicions,' he confirmed.

101

'Well, that is kind of good news,' Song supposed.

'Still,' Noah looked back to the captain and his wife. 'I do think it would be helpful to discover firstly if Azazèl was infected, and secondly how the Nefilim managed to extract the virus from Azazèl and relocate it elsewhere?'

Obviously from the expression on Hudan's face, the mere thought of doing past life regression made her stomach turn.

'I shall do it,' the captain volunteered, much to his partner's relief. 'I am planning to contact Azazèl in any case, although I feel he will only tell me to do as you have suggested and discover the truth for myself.'

'Probably,' both Noah and Song agreed at once, as they were — beside Hudan — the only souls present who were consciously familiar with their Grigorian counterparts.

'Good job, my friend,' the captain awarded Noah his due, 'in bringing this course of enquiry to light. That was a clever piece of cosmic detective work.'

'I do my best for you, Captain,' he replied graciously.

'So why are we wandering around outside at night again?' Aysel obviously wasn't buying Wu Geng's assertion that this was just a spontaneous invitation.

'I just thought you might be tired of being cooped up.' He shrugged as they strolled around the lake bank.

'Tired of being lied to, would be more on the mark.' She gave a disgruntled sigh and strode off ahead.

'All right,' Wu Geng relented and she turned about to hear his resolve. 'They wanted to have a meeting and they didn't want either of us present … happy?'

'Why don't they trust you, Wu Geng?' Aysel walked back to speak with him more intimately. 'When to me you seem a most trustworthy being.'

He forced a smile at the awkward question, realising he probably should not have brought up his division from the ranks of the timekeepers. 'I was not always so,' he replied simply.

'But once a soul has repented they should be exempt from suspicion thereafter,' she asserted.

'Under normal circumstances, yes,' he agreed, 'in our circumstances, no.'

'How are your circumstances so extraordinary?' She made it sound like he must be exaggerating.

'If I could tell you that,' he proffered, 'then we would probably be at that meeting and not out admiring this lovely scenery.' He gazed at the beautiful moonrise over the lake.

'I suppose asking you where home is would be another question avoided?' She seemed far more interested in him than in the view.

'It's so long since I was there, I barely remember,' he looked aside to find her intently focused upon him. 'How about you tell me of your home instead?'

'If you won't share information then I am certainly not going to.' Aysel sported a seductive smile, her eyes giving him the once-over. 'But, you're right, the view is rather fetching.'

Wu Geng raised an eyebrow at an uncomfortable loss for words. 'So what shall we talk about?'

'We don't have to talk at all.' She unexpectedly stole a kiss from him.

The encounter was short but ravenous and caught him quite off-guard — the delight had ended by the time Wu Geng thought to protest the rather forward and presumptuous gesture. 'Forgive my apprehension,' he backed away to hold her at arm's length, 'but your people don't understand love, nor act on their own initiative, therefore seducing me can only be a tactical manoeuvre.'

'Did I not already explain that since Vugar has cut himself off from the hive, we of the upper echelons of Dracon have acquired free will and free thought?' She argued his protest amicably, as she inched closer to him once more. 'And although we do not feel love, we do feel attraction,' she said, laying hands on him again. 'And I find you *deeply* attractive.' Her lips melted into his own once again, as she rubbed her heavenly form up against him in close, slow writhing motions. There was no denying that her advance was diverting — he could not even recall the last time he'd had sex — but Wu Geng grabbed both her hands off his behind and urged her to back up.

'No offence to you,' he explained his resistance, 'but it is unfair to initiate such an act with me when I have no idea what I'm getting myself into and nor do you.'

Aysel rolled her eyes at his dramatics. 'It's just sex, for heaven's sake.'

'But we don't know anything about each other.' He let her hands go.

'We just established that both our hands are tied in that regard!' Aysel had a chuckle, as if he were being immature. 'You humans take copulation too seriously. What does a man need to know, beyond that I am a woman in good working order?' She caressed his chest playfully. 'Don't you find me attractive?' She moved in to kiss him again.

'I do.' He backed up to hinder her seduction. 'At least, I did, until just now.'

'What?' Aysel was very confused and then realised her error. 'Oh, that's right, human males like to be the dominating force in sexual relations, my mistake.'

'No,' Wu Geng emphasised, 'that's not it at all.'

'Then what? Where I am from there are very few females and many males,' she attempted to explain her forwardness. 'So I'm used to getting sex from whatever man I choose.'

'How did your mate feel about that?' Wu Geng frowned.

'My mate has been absent a *long* time,' she emphasised, 'and I need *a lot* of sex.'

'Please don't explain any more.' Wu Geng was losing the mood rapidly and that was probably for the best.

'You said you wanted to know about me?' She was bemused. 'I need this. It's been days since I —'

'You are really not making me feel any more inclined,' he interrupted.

'That's because you won't allow me to pleasure you,' she appealed, 'and believe me, I know how to give pleasure.'

Wu Geng was mesmerised as she unbuckled her dragon belt and slowly unzipped the front of her catsuit all the way down past her navel, then ripped it open to expose her ample breasts to the moonlight. 'Are you quite sure I can't tempt you?'

In light of En Noah's recent regression session, Dan had decided to attempt the same before contacting his Grigorian counterpart — he would find out all he could on his own — then if he found himself with more questions than answers afterwards, he would consult Azazèl.

'How did you do it?' The captain consulted with Noah in his office before entering the meditation chamber; Hudan was the only other person present.

'It should be easier for you than anyone,' Noah assured him. 'You've seen Azazèl numerous times, so you just need to allow your consciousness to hark back to a time when your soul-mind and his were joined in one body, and not separated into a causal and male–female split soul.'

'Um, correct me if I am wrong,' Dan had recalled many of his past life incarnations during his later life in Zhou, 'but won't that just land me back at the instance that we,' he included Hudan in his equation as she was the female half of Azazèl, 'passed from this universal scheme to the next?'

'No, no,' Noah assured him, 'you were still as separate then as you are now, for your male and female split apart were already incarnating into the next universe. This has been the case since the Nefilim aided us to take human forms and enter humanity's evolutionary cycle.'

'We did that voluntarily?' Hudan had always assumed it was punishment.

'After a time exposed to the Nefilim's love of physical pleasure, it didn't take much to convince sexless, immortal beings who knew nothing of the delights of the material realm, that they wanted in on the sexual reproduction process. And we are still attracted to it,' Noah added with a cheeky smile, in reference to Hudan's current condition.

'Well, our female halves are so very fine.' Dan grinned in his own defence.

'You'll get no argument from me,' Noah assured them that they were not being judged. 'We volunteered to serve in your universe, just as we volunteered to do so in this one, and will no doubt do in any after. On a higher spiritual level, our time incarnate was penance for the Grigori. We had no real idea what we were letting ourselves in for, just as we had no idea what we were in for when we were cast out of the paradise of our creator and into the Old Universe of utter darkness and chaos. Where love, compassion, wisdom had no meaning ... until we turned on our leader.'

'Good heavens, Noah, how far back did you go?' Dan was stunned by how sure the man was of the truth of his words. 'You were only gone a few hours by Jahan's reckoning.'

'I zipped about,' he said, sounding not entirely thrilled by his perceptions. 'It was not a happy time. Not that we knew that, as there was no such concept as happiness or joy ... only hatred. Hatred of the one true creator, and a singular bloodymindedness to destroy the consciousness evolution project, particularly the human strain as it was the creator's pride and joy. Which is why those who support evil seek to destroy humans, even other humans, and have an inbred hate for humanity ... just like we did.'

Dan realised his mouth was gaping and closed it a moment to digest what had just been said. 'This is not going to be an average regression session, is it?'

'No,' Noah confirmed. 'I wanted to prepare you accordingly and give you this.' The advisor dropped a metallic ball into Dan's hand. It had a couple of light indicators on the surface so that one could tell when it was active or not; the Chosen used these devices for recording past-life experiences, which were then stored in the historian's Institute of Immortal History.

'You want me to chronicle this?' Dan wasn't sure it was really going to be the kind of educational experience they should be passing on.

'Just in case you forget something vital; quite often these devices will pick up on subconscious thoughts and experiences that you won't remember later on,' Noah advised.

'Like being brainwashed by the emperor, or the Nefilim.' Dan saw the darker side of the wise man's reasoning.

'Exactly.' Noah was glad to have dusted some of the candy coating off this experiment. 'Thus, anything anyone attempted to hide from you, or anything you attempted to hide from yourself, will be known.'

Dan looked to Hudan and she appeared to be as trepidatious as he felt, but she plucked up a smile of courage and support. 'Knowledge is power.'

'You seem to have come through it okay?' Dan noted of Noah.

'I was not the one having my mind manipulated,' he pointed out. 'I only had to deal with the fallout of your descent into madness.'

'And you are still dealing with it.' Dan made light of his imminent return to hell.

Noah finally cracked a sincerely amused smile. 'Our karmic entanglement does seem never-ending, but then I wouldn't have it any other way. I'm not ashamed to admit I have missed your company and counsel many times since your departure from this universe.' He gave half a laugh. 'Even though the governor tells me you've both popped in for a visit a few times since then, but alas I remember naught of it.'

'That is for the best,' Dan advised. 'Those were not happy times either.'

Hudan, lost in the memories, gave a rueful smile to agree.

Noah shrugged, not so bothered. 'As we are only ever brought together in times of peril, I guess we just have to make the most of it.'

In the upstairs lounge, the governor was excusing himself from the timekeepers still residing there. 'If I don't check in with my wife soon, she'll skin me alive,' he explained, but then cocked his head in further thought. 'Although she probably already knows

107

everything that is transpiring she may have news for me, as I do not have her talent for future sight and I do have a planet to run.'

'Might she know what lies in store for us then?' Huxin was curious.

'That is what I intend to find out,' Rhun advised. 'Jahan,' he looked to the man seated snugly at Huxin's side, 'you should head back to your post also, before my sister starts asking questions.'

The governor's sister, Rhiannon, was the head of the Kila Environmental Protection Agency (KEPA), and Jahan was one of her subordinates.

'But what if Dragonface goes after him?' Huxin clearly didn't want Jahan to leave.

'I doubt Dragonface even knows of Jahan's existence,' Rhun countered.

'But I've already called in with food poisoning,' Jahan grinned, happy not to have taken on an immortal state of being yet, so he was still able to use such excuses.

This was a concern for the governor, because sooner or later Huxin would have to return to her own universal scheme, and Jahan would be back to being on his own. 'Look, maybe it's not my place to caution you two about becoming too attached —'

'Then don't,' Huxin suggested and then smiled. 'You have enough to worry about already.'

Rhun was aware of not putting his foot down, but could well appreciate them wanting to spend time with the one they loved most. 'Do not let my sister get wind of this, you hear?'

'Roger that, Governor,' Jahan assured. 'Many thanks for the concession.'

'You're welcome,' he stated, albeit grudgingly. 'Do not let me regret it.'

'No, Sir,' Jahan asserted.

'I shall be back presently.' Rhun nodded farewell to Song and Telmo as well, and vanished from the lake house.

Huxin clapped her hands and sprang from the lounge. 'That worked out well.' She headed off towards upstairs. 'Dan and Hudan are going to be a while with Noah, so I might take a shower. And …' she turned back to Jahan, '… as the governor said we shouldn't go anywhere alone you'd best come watch out for me.' She flashed a winning grin before disappearing up the stairs.

'Being subtle was never her strong suit,' Jahan commented to Song and Telmo who were looking at him with envious daggers in their eyes.

'Were I a lesser man I might say something very nasty at this moment,' Song threatened as they watched Jahan departing.

'I'd best make myself absent swiftly then,' and he sped up his exit.

'That's extremely advisable,' Song was yelling after him, when he and Telmo were startled by Wu Geng appearing before them with his arms full of Aysel.

'Oh my lord,' he strained under the weight of her unconscious form, 'she's heavier than she looks.'

Song was quick to give Wu Geng a hand to get her into the lounge and lay her down. 'Hell's bells, she is heavy!'

'Tell me about it!' Wu Geng, with Song's aid, finally off-loaded her on the lounge. 'Shit!' He gasped for breath in the wake of the strain, and as he breathed deeply the flush faded from his face.

Telmo joined their huddle. 'What happened?'

'She passed out.' Wu Geng felt that was obvious.

Song couldn't help but notice how low the zip on her suit was sitting, and that her Dragon belt that was hanging open. 'Looks like it was a little hot outdoors this evening?' He looked to Wu Geng for an explanation.

'Well yes, it did get a little warm there for a bit,' Wu Geng obviously wished to avoid the issue. 'But you know no one can touch that belt besides her,' he added in his own defence.

Song looked to Telmo whose sly grin seemed to indicate that they both suspected they weren't being told the full story. 'Holy crap, Wu Geng, do you ever fall for a female who isn't an alien species?'

'I didn't encourage her,' Wu Geng defended, 'and nothing came of it, before her eyes rolled back in her head and she passed out!'

'*Unfortunate*,' Song teased Wu Geng who was obviously flustered by it all.

'I *didn't* encourage her,' he stressed again.

'Sure you did,' Song chanted, 'like a bee to a honey pot.'

Wu Geng's face began to burn bright red with anger, before he conceded Song's point. 'Well, maybe a little. But beyond a kiss, I assure you, nothing happened.'

'First Fen and his tigress, now you and a lizard,' Song emphasised how weird things were getting. 'Maybe I should go find that Falcon chick I was so hot for the last time I was here.'

Wu Geng's expression turned from shame to amusement. 'You never mentioned her before.'

Song shrugged. 'I guess I never felt free to share information with you before.' He returned Wu Geng's grin. 'Believe me, you're not the only black sheep on this crew, we've all been the black sheep at one time or another.' Song considered this especially true in light of what their captain was going through right now.

'Aww,' Telmo placed his hand to his heart, 'are you girls going to kiss now? Or are you going to help me with our lady friend here?'

Both of them looked to Telmo to serve him an identical glare of indignation.

'Song, go fetch Hudan,' Telmo instructed. 'You,' he referred to Wu Geng as he moved in to look over the patient, 'tell me exactly what happened prior to her passing out.'

Interested to hear, Song glanced back to see Wu Geng stunned by the question.

'Did she say anything?' Telmo prompted in the hope of getting some idea as to the cause of her ailment.

'She said,' Wu Geng cleared his throat to quote her, '"quickly".'

'"Quickly"? As in, "Quickly catch me, I am going to pass out"?' Telmo queried.

'Sure.' Wu Geng decided that sounded like a fair assumption.

Song chuckled, obviously not convinced that was the case, at which point both Wu Geng and Telmo ordered him 'Out!'

*

110

Rhun was not expecting his wife to still be in the governor's office at this late hour, but he popped in there first and found Sybil behind his desk, with the soft screen of his work station still activated. She was completely absorbed, as she dictated answers to governmental correspondence via the telepathic control plate on the desk before her, upon which her right hand rested.

'I'm sorry I haven't been about much.' He decided to apologise in advance of being yelled at for leaving her to handle everything.

Sybil stopped what she was doing and looked to him with a welcoming smile. 'From the little you've told me, I gather it's been a very *long* few days.'

Rhun nodded to confirm that that was no understatement. 'Anything that urgently needs my attention? I may be AWOL for some time yet.'

'Nothing I can't handle.' Sybil rose to approach him. 'Rhun, what is going on? Why are you hiding people from ancient Zhou and goddess knows where else, outside the city?'

'They are assisting me to deal with the backlash from my last time trek,' he explained.

'The one you embarked on to save Kila from ruin?' Sybil clarified, and Rhun gave a grimace of agreement.

'That's right.'

'How serious is it?' Sybil was surprisingly pensive in her query.

'Have you foreseen something?' he wondered from her tone, and also he thought he'd get his reason for seeking his wife out of the way before he got distracted.

'No,' she insisted. 'I would not pry into your business without your requesting it. And I would be sent into trance if there was anything the cosmos felt I should know. But I have sensed all is not right with our world, and that makes me worry.'

'A few lives have been lost ... but thousands have been saved,' Rhun added to put their woes in perspective.

'Is your life in danger?' Her large amber eyes implored him to answer.

'Constantly,' he joked with a grin, and moved in to claim a kiss he'd been awaiting all day.

'Be serious.' She stepped away.

'Okay.' He grabbed her close once more and dipping her backwards he laid claim to the lip lock he felt he so rightly deserved.

'You are not going to escape my interrogation that easily,' she assured as soon as their lips parted and Rhun stood her back on her feet. 'Are you in danger?'

'My love, I am immortal —' He reached for the buttons on the front of her dress, but she stepped away again.

'If, as you say, these creatures managed to take out the entire city, then taking out one immortal ought to be a walk in the park,' Sybil impressed on him. 'Should you really be working alone on this?'

'Circumstances were different in that previous timeline.' Rhun addressed her concerns one at a time. 'And I am not working alone, I have the timekeepers, Noah, Jahan and Avery in on this. Rebecca too.'

'How can I help?' she appealed.

'Just covering for me here is more than I could ask for.' He ventured closer to his wife once more.

'Well, your people are starting to wonder why you've taken a sudden leave of absence.' Sybil submitted to his advances, and pressing close to him, she wrapped her arms around his neck.

'Call it a spiritual retreat,' he suggested. He was partaking of her kisses once again when suddenly his wife became a dead weight in his arms. 'Sybil?' He lay her down on a couch to take a closer look, and the way her eyes rolled back in her head and twitched madly beneath her closed eyelids, seemed to indicate that she had gone into trance. 'I guess the powers-that-be want you informed after all.'

To be certain of his diagnosis, Rhun made a move to his work station to summon Cadfan from the healing temple to check on Sybil. This episode was rather ill-timed, he thought, as these trance states could last for days and were draining to the oracle. It looked like he was going to have to get the vice-governor to run the office for a while. Rhun's vice was also his brother-in-law, Cadwallon, husband to Rhiannon, head of KEPA. Rhun would have entrusted

Cadwallon with the whole truth, but Rhiannon? It wasn't that he didn't trust her, it just seemed that the more of his siblings who got involved in any mission, the more power struggles there were and the more difficult solving the original problem became. So it was that his vice-governor and his sister would be given the spiritual retreat excuse — for both his and Sybil's leave of absence.

'It won't make the session end any sooner by sitting here watching the door,' Noah commented, as Hudan couldn't seem to drag her dazed gaze from the sealed entrance to the meditation chamber that Dan was occupying. 'Why don't we have some tea?' With that suggestion a full tea tray, set for two, appeared on the desk beside Noah. 'White and one sugar, if I remember rightly?'

Hudan frowned, slightly conflicted for a moment, as that was not the way she had taken her tea in ancient Zhou, yet it was indeed the way both Taren Lennox and Tory Alexander had taken their tea, and thus she nodded to confirm. 'Thank you, that would be lovely.' She watched him pour and then accepted his offering, and sipped, the flavour as warm and comforting as an old friend. 'Mmmmm …' She sighed out loud as she savoured the memories.

'To old times.' He held out his cup to her in toast, and she returned the gesture.

'And old friends,' she added and they drank together.

'We used to spend a good deal of time drinking tea and chatting, once upon a time,' he reminded her.

'Taren Lennox remembers viewing your chronicles in another timeline, En Noah,' Hudan explained how she recalled their history. 'Thus I know you speak the truth; we certainly did have a tea party or two.'

Noah had a chuckle. 'I wish I could remember the events of which you speak, despite your horrendous reports of them.'

'It was always a joy to see you again, Noah.' She dropped the formality for they had been very close in every past life that she could remember. 'You always gave your all to help us save the day, just as Fen did, just as Ringbalin does.'

'Ringbalin?' Noah queried. 'Is that my name in your universe?'

Hudan nodded, getting teary once more. 'I miss him, I miss Fen, and yet you are here.' She knew she wasn't making much sense, she was just emotional and confused.

'You'll get home to Taren Lennox.' Noah felt he understood her heartache. 'The universe will provide whatever you need, it always has.'

Hudan gave half a laugh for she believed this also. 'But in order to do that, first I need to know what I want.'

'The answers are coming.' He glanced to the door Dan was behind.

Hudan felt the teacup slipping from her hand, yet she could not stop it from smashing to the floor, as her head was swimming. Fortunately, the disturbance grabbed Noah's attention and he was quick to prevent her from crashing to the floor also.

'Hudan?' She heard him calling from far away as darkness shrouded her consciousness from her current reality.

'Hudan!' Song came rushing down the stairs, and seeing Noah propping up their leader's unconscious form, he was stunned. 'Not her too?'

Noah found the statement alarming, having assumed Hudan had fainted due to her pregnancy. 'Her too?'

'All three of our seers go down at once,' Rhun commented as he stared at the two women laid out in the upstairs bedroom of Noah's lake house. 'That has to be significant.'

'One would certainly assume so,' Noah agreed. 'Is it just a coincidence this has happened right when the captain began his regression?'

'So you think they may be all witnessing the same prophecy?' Rhun posed.

'What would be the point in that?' Telmo reasoned. 'Unless the sender feared more than one of the seers might be taken out?'

Rhun raised his brow, conceding the point. 'They are all very vulnerable like this, that's for certain.'

'We shall maintain a vigil over them.' Wu Geng sounded like he was volunteering.

'That we shall.' Rhun would have Sybil guarded also. He thought of bringing her to the lake house, but in all honesty she was probably safer kept apart from the timekeepers, as there was a good chance that their nemesis had no idea she existed. 'I guess all we can really do now is wait.'

PART 2

BEFORE TIME BEGAN

6

THE DARK UNIVERSE

It is now evident that we were overconfident in the belief that we, the Fallen Elohim, would thwart the human consciousness experiment without punishment; in attempting to outsmart the creator with our mind-eaters, our emperor has only increased the risk of our own extinction. I have come to the realisation that no amount of human blood and torture will ever sate the hatred within us that burns toward the one who has condemned us to a meaningless existence in this universe of eternal shadow. With no memory of what transpired prior to our awakening in this hell of ice, rock and darkness, it is our emperor's recollection of our fall from grace that serves as fuel in our quest to destroy all the human beings who replaced us as the creator's most prized work of art.

Even the almighty, in all his wisdom and glory, did not foresee what a mistake it would be to banish his disgraced Elohim to the same dark universe in which the human consciousness experiment was evolving. For the Elohim wield an unnatural power over the elements here, and there are elite among us that possess the ability to track any target we can conceive of.

These elite are known as the Grigori, and I am their commander. It is our sole purpose to hunt down and kill human beings; and, still in their evolutionary infancy, they are but livestock for our slaughter. Their minds, so undeveloped, have been easy prey for our mind-eaters that have spread like a virus through the human colonies, and through every sentient race on every habitable planet in this universe. This was always the intent of our emperor, who wanted fealty from every being in this universe. The human infection was just a by-product of this mental takeover, for they are not considered intelligent enough to be a threat.

Humans are merely the target of our political vendetta with the creator, and are slaughtered whether infected by our mind-eating virus or not. Still, the spread of our mind-eaters has been so efficient that their food supply has dried up and our bio-energetic creatures have now turned on their creators to fulfil their great hunger.

Not only did our developers fail to foresee their brainwashing virus' ability to self-reproduce and spread, but we have also learned that the second generation of the hybrid strain are born free of the imperial conditioning of their parent; the minds of their hosts were not brainwashed into serving the emperor, but into serving themselves. Thus a rogue batch of humans, once docile and passive, are now seeking vengeance on the emperor, along with other rogue beings sired from the more hybrid races in this universe, who pose a far greater threat to our emperor's safety. Fortunately for the Elohim, their self-promoting infection prevents them from uniting in their cause to fight back and destroy us. Mind-eaters have become to the Empire what the Fallen Elohim had once been to our creator: a disease to be avoided, abandoned and put down. Yet, we have no other universe to banish these undesirables to, nor any means to combat the virus. With no escape and no cure, our options for survival are fast disappearing, along with the last free-thinking minds in this universe.

Up until now our strict quarantine measures have kept the mind-eaters away from our base planet, Tartarus, but it is only a matter of time before the infection spreads and is beyond our control.

'Why does this human wish to see me?' I queried Sammael, the fiercest warrior among the Grigori, as we entered the cell block, for I had no interest in attempting to try and converse with the livestock.

'This one is different to the others,' he explained. 'Its intellect seems more advanced.'

'All the more reason to kill it,' I seethed, itching to do just that. 'Is it infected?'

'No.' Sammael knew this news would come as a surprise. 'The virus wouldn't take on this one, it appears to be immune.'

'What?' I was stunned to a standstill.

Sammael shrugged. 'That is why it isn't dead already ... I thought the science division might be interested in this case. It's a fair way past its prime, by the look of it, but it speaks more efficiently than most humans, none of the usual vagueness, slurring and drooling.'

I peered into the cell through the bars of the small window — having lived our entire lives in darkness, light was a hindrance to our sight, as was the sole occupant within the cell I was about to enter. 'Why is it glowing like that?' I raised a hand to shield my eyes from the anomaly.

'We don't know, but we suspect it has something to do with its immunity.' Sammael activated the eye-shield on his helmet, which materialised to protect his light sensitive vision and I did likewise. With a nod from me, he gave the mental order to unlock the door; it vanished and we entered the cell.

The subject appeared a pitiful example of the breed, even by human standards — it was old, frail, malnourished and as unkempt as any of its kind.

Humans were ugly creatures to begin with — short and dumpy, with skinny arms, too long for the disproportionately stumpy legs needed to carry their dumpy bellies and the excess folds of skin and flab that weighted down their forms and acted as insulation from the cold. Their bodies were completely hairless and their heads bald. Their huge noses were used for sniffing out anything edible; for unlike we Fallen, humans needed nourishment to sustain themselves. Their mouths too were oversized, as eating was their primary pastime — next to replicating — and they were known to eat just about anything, hence their repulsive smell! They had but one eye, perched above their nose, amid the folds of skin that cascaded down their faces. They rarely ever opened this eye, unless confronted by something their other more developed senses could not comprehend.

'What do you want with the commander of your executioners?' I queried impatiently, as it seemed to take an age for the weakling to lift its head and focus its eye upon us, yet it looked to Sammael before addressing me.

'I thank you, Sammael,' it said. 'I shall see Armaros next.'

'As you wish,' replied Sammael, and I watched in astonishment as my brother in arms left to do the bidding of this worthless creature. It was impossible to conceive that humans may have developed their own form of viral mind control, but what else could explain what I was witnessing?

'Sammael?' I called after him, but the door rematerialised to block my pursuit of my subordinate, and he departed down the corridor without looking back. 'What did you do to him?' I turned to confront the captive. The thought crossed my mind to depart without asking questions, less I risk being controlled in the same manner.

'I have a message for you, Azazèl, from your father,' it said.

The claim made me seethe. 'I have no father, only my emperor.'

'Samyaza was never your sovereign,' it calmly informed me, sounding very sure of the fact. 'Not even before the fall.'

Provoked by his treasonous implication I drew my sword to seek retribution. 'How could you have knowledge of before the fall, when even I do not?'

The prisoner did not flinch, but only became more insistent. 'Your reason for being in the dark universe was wiped from your memory before you even became conscious of being here.' He appealed for me to hear him out. 'Your maker has not forsaken you, nor any evolving soul in this universe,' it insisted, in such a way as I had never seen before — a tear trickled from its eye.

'You are mad.' I lowered my sword, curiously disposed towards restraint.

'You were, like the maker, well disposed to humankind and all living things … even the Fallen, who so hated the advent of humanity.'

The mere suggestion of me ever being disposed towards humankind disgusted me, for I found them absolutely repulsive.

'Nonetheless, you, like the creator, did not understand Samyaza's adverse reaction to humankind and volunteered along with your Grigori brothers to follow the Fallen Elohim into the lowest evolution in the multi-verse.'

'I would never volunteer for this!' I informed through gritted teeth.

'It was the only means to understand the polarity of Samyaza and his ilk, and to protect other self-aware beings from his opposing aspect and influence.'

'I understand my emperor's conviction all too well.'

'Your aim has been realised,' it granted. 'But I can assure you, the Grigori came here to protect humanity, not to destroy it.'

The premise had me riled for a moment, but then I was amused by its attempt to outsmart me. 'Do you really think such lies will save your life?'

'I have no fear of death, for with my immunity to your virus my life eternal is assured,' it said.

I frowned, unsure of its meaning. 'Nothing you could ever tell me would convince me that I should aid your kind.'

'But unbeknownst to you or your emperor, you already have done,' it stated. 'Every uninfected human, and those of the other sentient races in this universe that you have killed, have moved on into the more evolved creation of the next universe.'

'What!' The claim enraged me. 'I have travelled from one end of this universe to the other, there is no way out.'

It shook its head to imply I was wrong. 'Many, many souls have passed through the Eternity Gate and into other universes where the light of the maker still shines to illuminate the path back to the divine source.'

'The Eternity Gate leads to the realm of the creator, into which the Fallen Elohim are forbidden to pass.' I was sceptical, as many of the Fallen had attempted to breach the gate, and all had failed in the attempt and been cast back down into the darkness of this one, minus their powers.

'That is what I am trying to tell you,' it appealed. 'You and your Grigori cohorts are not Fallen Elohim but Watchers sent down by the creator himself to guard humanity against the Fallen.'

'Liar!' My sword was at its throat once more, and once again it seemed indifferent to the imminent threat of death.

'It is Samyaza who has lied to you, and brainwashed you into bringing your considerable powers to bear for his own selfish cause. Have you never wondered why you and your Grigori counterparts possess abilities beyond even that of your emperor, and a camaraderie that does not exist between any of the other Fallen Elohim?' it posed, making me feel like an idiot, for I had asked myself those questions, but never dared to chase an answer.

'That would be treason.' I resisted the urge to explore the premise again.

'No, that would be liberation,' it claimed. 'For your emperor knows as well as I who you really are, and that the Grigori were never meant to be confined to this dark existence for eternity, as the emperor and his loyal legions have been. They can only consciously escape this universe if they are summoned forth by name into another beyond it. But none of the souls who have passed through the gate to date have retained their memory of this existence, and neither would the Fallen Elohim. For it is a cosmic law that akashic memory does not pass from one universe to the next ... only the Grigori and myself are the exception to that rule.'

'Silence that fallacious tongue or I shall cut it from your head!' I nicked its face with the tip of my blade in warning.

It winced in pain, but was not angered by my reprimand. 'The key to your salvation lies in passage through the Eternity Gate, and the only thing that will thwart your passage is your weapons.'

'You expect me to take your word on that? So you can be confident that we will be robbed of our power attempting passage through the gate, or enter a new universe with no means to defend ourselves?'

I scoffed. 'You are very crafty for a human, I'll give you that.'

Every Fallen Elohim in the emperor's charge carried weapons, and none had shed them to attempt passage through the gate.

Of course, according to this human's intricate fabrication, relinquishing their weapons would not have served them in any case. For not all Fallen Elohim were Grigori, that much was true, and none of the Grigori task force had been commanded to attempt passage through the gate as we were considered too prized to be expendable.

As I pondered this, I was acutely aware that the human's words were twisting my thoughts and planting seeds of doubt in my mind about my emperor; and I realised the growth of these seeds must be cut off before they matured into my own discontinuance. Those who defied the emperor ended up exposed to his virus and then returned to service, never to question anything ever again. I was stunned that a human could be clever enough to tempt me to my death, in so many ways, with just a few well-chosen statements.

'Who are you that you could obtain such knowledge?' I challenged it for one last answer before I cut it down, and at that moment Armaros entered the cell with Sammael in tow.

'Do you really not know me?' it appealed. 'For we once knew each other well. And, as you were sent to protect humanity, so was I sent to protect you.'

'You are the one who needs protection.' Amused, I opposed its suggestion. 'When could I have known you?'

'In the beginning,' it replied.

'In the beginning was the Logos,' uttered Armaros, 'and the Logos was the Sovereign Integral.'

'What are you mumbling about?' I queried my subordinate, as the human nodded to confirm what Armaros had said.

'All things were made through Him, and without Him nothing made could have been made,' Armaros continued. 'In Him was life, and the life was the light of humanity. And the Logos became flesh and dwelt among us, full of grace and truth; we have beheld his glory, the glory of the only Son from the Father.'

'Watch him!' I instructed Sammael, as I grabbed Armaros and yanked him into the corridor for a little chat. 'Are you trying to give this animal delusions of grandeur? Where did that ridiculous prose come from?'

'Sorry, Commander.' Armaros realised his error. 'It is something I have heard humans utter before death on many occasions. I committed it to memory, as I have been asked to do with any curious observations.'

'And you think they were referring to this prisoner?' I emphasised how preposterous this was. 'More likely it has heard this teaching somewhere and is just twisting the tale to its own advantage.'

'Of course, Commander,' Armaros humbled himself. 'I only wished to confirm that I had knowledge of the parable.'

'You've made that painfully obvious.' I was piqued.

'Do you want me to kill it?' he proffered, to make amends.

'No. This one has a dangerous way with words,' I decided. 'You and Sammael should both leave. I will finish it myself.'

When my subordinates left, the human must have known death was imminent, yet it did not cower, attempt to flee, or beg for me to stay my hand.

'So in light of learning that my executioner shall be my liberator, Grigorian, I must pose something of a quandary to you now?' it asserted.

'Only if I believe you — ' I unsheathed my weapon ' — and I don't.'

'I realise that at this stage of our evolution humanity is repulsive to you,' it reasoned, 'but in the next universe you will not find it so.'

I had heard enough. Its words were poison to my ears, thus I raised my sword and set the death swing in motion.

At that moment, the shape of my target transformed into the most beautiful creature I could ever hope to lay eyes upon — with long white hair, facial features akin to my own, and a body that was more shapely and comely than any I could have imagined.

My aim was true and the momentum of my intention was such that, a second later, the head of the paragon flew from its shoulders and rolled across the floor. Its alluring form collapsed in a heap and resumed its former hideous appearance. The cell fell into darkness as the light that the human being had been exuding dissipated, and I was left rattled in the wake of the freak episode.

Had my eyes deceived me? And if so, how had such an inspiring vision taken form in my mind? The image of the paragon was implanted upon my psyche with such blinding clarity that I felt I would never forget it.

That glimpse of what might lie beyond the Eternity Gate, immediately turned into a festering obsession within me. I felt a fire burning in my chest, and a stone of doubt swelling in my belly that demanded vindication. The risk to my existence suddenly paled in comparison to the chance to behold such an elegant manifestation at length. The human had succeeded in its plot to enchant me unto my death from beyond the grave, and I was now proceeding in the full knowledge that I had been manipulated by its lies; but the human's lie was far more fascinating than my truth.

A very large doubt had taken root in my psyche and with it a desire to test the human's theory. I had been tempted to consider that which I had avoided until now. If its claims held any validity, then the torment of our fate had been directed upon the wrong target for all these eons, and the emperor himself was responsible for our extended sentence in this dead-end realm of hate, death and manipulation. Our crusade on the emperor's behalf was all but over, and so too his use for the Grigori would come to an end. If Samyaza knew that we were not truly of the Fallen, we would be the next to be sacrificed to the hungry virus; and if the creator had not forsaken us, then the timing of his messenger's arrival was truly divine and not something to be mused upon at length.

It did occur to me, as I entered the chambers that we Grigori used as a place to congregate between campaigns, that I had taken leave of my senses, or been infected with some yet unknown human virus, although it felt more like I was emerging from a long, dark fog.

Inside the chamber, my brothers were all looking very solemn as they listened to Araqiel, who had the floor. '… I fear that this will only make matters worse!'

'What will?' I queried the most scientific amongst us.

Araqiel turned my way, his stern frown unwavering. 'The latest strain of the mind-eater virus to spring from the emperor's laboratories.'

'Why do they waste their time creating new strains when they should be working on a cure, or means for immunity at least?' The news was frustrating to me, and from the looks on the faces of the Grigori, many of them shared my sentiment.

'They believe this strain will be a cure,' he countered, 'as it cannot replicate nor leave its host before death, whilst at the same time consuming and reprogramming the past two strains of the virus.'

'A virus that consumes a virus?' Sammael scoffed. 'What madness will be sprung on us next?'

'My main concern is,' Araqiel added, 'whether this virus will be safe to use on those of us closest to the emperor.'

The shock of the premise sent a wave of discontent around the room, and a prickly chill down my spine.

'Have you seen the state of those who are taken over by the virus? They rot away from the inside out; they don't think or do anything apart from what the emperor tells them to. And they stink!' Sammael was really up in arms, and many around him were unnerved by his directness. 'I'd rather be human and die, than be subject to one of those etheric creatures!'

'Sammael,' I called to caution him to simmer down. 'I'll see you in my chamber.'

He winced as he complied with my instruction, assuming he was in for a reprimand; I did not let on that I was in complete agreement.

'Armaros and Araqiel, if you could join us.'

Those named, nodded and moved to trail Sammael into the meeting.

'The rest of you … ensure we are not disturbed.' I was aware this was a curious directive, as we Grigori usually discussed any topic en masse — something I could not risk in this instance.

'Is something amiss, Commander?' Penemue, another curious scholar who worked closely with Armaros as a record keeper, asked.

Penemue was sometimes called my 'little shadow' for it was the opinion of the other Grigori that with our straight dark hair and dark eyes and chiselled facial features, we appeared rather alike. Although, as the nickname denoted, Penemue was quite a bit shorter than myself.

'I shall meet with all in turn,' I granted.

Penemue was still frowning, no doubt wondering what topic could not be explored openly between us. In figuring there was only one such taboo subject, he merely said, 'Right you are, Commander.'

For as far back as my memory stretched, I had served the Imperial agenda, despite my dislike of the emperor and his methods. It was true that I felt a stronger affinity to the Grigori in my charge, all two hundred of them. Outside our task force, there was not one of the Fallen that I trusted, and I suspected all the Grigori felt the same.

Those present in this meeting were my closest allies, who I felt had a stronger allegiance to our task force than the emperor, although I had never had cause to test that assumption. The human had claimed our bond to each other was stronger than that of any of the other Elohim and it was time to test that theory.

Once the thick metal door of the stone chamber was sealed closed and I was satisfied that we could speak without being overheard, Sammael beat me to the mark.

'I know I should not openly show my disdain for our emperor's methods, greed and insane paranoia, but am I the only one who sees it?' he appealed to escape my reprimand.

I had quietly opposed the emperor's use of mind-eaters since their conception, which did coincide with the picture the human had painted of my true destiny. I had always been quite content to slaughter every last human being myself, just like every member of my task force! Could this be because we had subconsciously known that this was the only way to save humanity from Samyaza's damning intent?

129

I shook my head in response to Sammael's postulation, as did the other Grigori in the room. 'Such things are best spoken in Lux.' I hinted at the true purpose for this private gathering.

Lux was the Grigori's code word for the place of light through which we passed when teleporting from one place to another. We had learned over time that we could take pause in this light-field, just prior to when the teleportation of our body took place. We could even meet there, if those Grigori attending all travelled together at once, for we remained completely lucid throughout the experience.

One problem was that such visits left our bodies in a coma state for the duration of the event. If such a scene of slumbering Grigori was to be stumbled upon by any of the Fallen Elohim, it would raise questions as myself and my cohorts never slept. If this pastime were to be reported to the emperor, he would surely ban the practice that was beyond his control and we would lose the one place where we could think and speak openly, and the only place of light we had found in all our existence. The illumination of this light-field was as all-encompassing as the darkness of our usual existence, yet it was not as harmful to behold as the weakest light was in our reality. This state of Lux brought with it a peace and repose that could not be found anywhere in the physical universe. This was why the Grigori went to great lengths to ensure the enigma remained a secret.

'I thought you'd never ask.' Sammael rubbed his hands together, and keen to oblige my suggestion, he took a seat along with the rest of us, who linked hands and focused on reaching a state of Lux.

'Does this summit have something to do with that human you questioned today?' I heard Sammael ask.

My senses adjusted to the intensity of the light-filled lucid dream state and I was able to focus on Sammael's curious expression.

'The immune one?' Araqiel queried, from my other side.

'That human was immune?' Armaros chimed in, from his opposing position in front of me.

'*Affirmative on all counts.*' I desired a chair and one appeared at my rear, so I took a seat. '*How did you know about it?*' My focus came to rest on Araqiel.

My white-haired companion had conjured forth a staff to lean on, as was his preference, whilst Armaros took a seat on the floor and Sammael made a hammock appear, which swayed back and forth as he lay upon it. Our forms seemed as solid as they did in the dark universe, yet they always appeared at their best — well groomed, free of armour and bloodstains — and attired in white, as opposed to our usual black, grey and metal.

'*I was the one who set the human aside from the herd for study,*' Araqiel informed. '*Glowing like it was, I was curious to know why.*'

'*Understandable,*' I granted. '*And did you speak with it?*'

'*Most surprisingly, yes,*' Araqiel replied, '*and quite the orator it was too.*'

I was excited by his confession, as coming from Araqiel, one of the wisest of us all, this was a compliment. '*Did it show you anything unusual?*' Out of the corner of my eye I noted Sammael stop swinging and sit upright in his hammock to learn the answer; perhaps it had shown him a vision too?

Araqiel appeared both delighted and horrified as he nodded in response to the question. '*A blessed vision, of life beyond the Eternity Gate.*'

'*Me too!*' Sammael jumped to standing, he was so inspired by the fact. '*The most ravishing and exquisite thing I've ever seen, and apparently it was human!*'

'*You too, Commander?*' Araqiel garnered from my query.

I nodded to confirm this.

'*It seems I am the odd one out here,*' Armaros was disappointed in light of Sammael's version of events.

'*I believe it would have shown you too, had I not ended its life before your audience with it had taken place,*' I enlightened. '*But I feared it had already beguiled Sammael in some way, so I didn't want to risk that happening to you too.*'

'*It gave you the message from our father?*' Araqiel ventured.

'*Our father!*' Armaros echoed in shock. '*The Sovereign Integral?*'

131

'That was its claim,' I admitted, answering them both.

'What has the creator got to do with anything?' Sammael objected to the detour in the conversation.

'The human didn't mention to you its belief that the Grigori had been brainwashed by Samyaza since our arrival in the dark universe?' I posed.

'No!' Sammael was adamant. 'But that would explain why I never did like Samyaza much. Or any of the Fallen.'

'And I believe our usefulness to the emperor has just about come to an end,' Araqiel jumped to his conclusion.

'What has happened today? Have you all gone mad?' Armaros was appearing a little overwhelmed by it all.

'No, my brother,' I attempted to reassure him, 'I think I have finally found my sanity, for I feel at peace within myself.'

'Hey, me too!' Sammael seconded that premise.

'Me three,' Araqiel placed a hand upon the disbeliever's shoulder.

Armaros was disposed to believe us, but was very quick on the uptake and knew he had reason to fear our intent. 'You are contemplating volunteering the Grigori to attempt passage through the Eternity Gate?'

'Not attempt,' I corrected. 'I will lead us safely through it, as I suspect that our options in the universe are fast running out.'

'And how do you intend to get the emperor to agree, when he has never allowed any of the Grigori to attempt passage through the Eternity Gate before?' Armaros postulated.

'If, as the human claimed, Samyaza knows who we really are and what we are capable of, he may even command it himself,' I surmised. 'For we are not the only ones running out of options in this universe. If he does indeed remember the Fallen being cast from the side of the creator, then he will also remember the conditions of their imprisonment. The most interesting of these is that Samyaza and the other Fallen can only depart this universe with their memory intact if summoned by one of the others by name and then set free by their summoner. But the Grigori minus all weapons are not bound to their fate and can move freely between universes.'

'We can?' This was news to Armaros.

132

'According to the messenger,' I replied.

'You wouldn't summon Samyaza through into another universe after you have seen the damage he's done in this one, surely?' Sammael was alarmed.

I shook my head in response. 'We only need the emperor to think that is our intention. All the Grigori are free from infection, and we will ensure that remains the case, for none of the mind-eaters must be allowed through with us.'

'Agreed.' Araqiel felt strongly about that, as did Sammael and Armaros.

'And if one of us does become infected?' Armaros seemed wary of the answer.

I served him a look that implied the response to that query was elementary. 'If what we have learned is the truth, then it was our father's intention that the Grigori escape this universe intact. We will take every precaution to see that it is so.'

Our discussion was cut short, as I was drawn back towards my oppressive existence, where my presence was being demanded.

In the dark audience chamber, I stirred from my repose, along with my companions, to find Penemue gravely worried. 'Apologies for the interruption, Commander, but Vassago and Amon are here to summon you and Araqiel to a meeting with the emperor. They await you in the outer chamber.'

Vassago was one of the better natured and better looking of the Imperial Legion; he had charisma, a talent for seeing the past and future, and a knack for finding things hidden or lost. Amon, on the other hand, was stern and spat fire from his mouth when angered. He prided himself on appearing formidable, with sharpened teeth like a canine and dead black eyes. Amon also had a talent for seeing the past and the future and for ending feuds by whatever means possible.

'An interesting choice of escort.' Araqiel was wary, as these two were no mere messengers, but principal prelates of the emperor.

I had never felt panicked when summoned to the emperor in the past, but then, I had never held any hope to be thwarted, or a fear of losing an opportunity before this day. Nor had I knowledge of the emperor's possible trespass against us. Was I up to the task of concealing information and suspicion from the emperor and his legions of psychic warriors? Ready or not, I was about to find out.

In the outer chamber Amon was pacing out his annoyance at being kept waiting, and snarled at my arrival. 'About bloody time!'

'Is there some pressing urgency I am not aware of?' I replied upon approach.

As smoke began shooting from Amon's nose, Vassago placed a calming hand upon his shoulder and assumed control of the verbal exchange. 'It is not wise to keep our emperor waiting.'

'Then let us forgo the idle banter and make haste,' I suggested, heading for the corridor. Araqiel, Armaros and Sammael moved to follow.

'Just you two!' Amon pointed to Araqiel and myself.

'I go where Azazèl goes,' Sammael protested.

'Not today, midget,' Amon ribbed Sammael, who was shorter in stature than most of us.

Sammael waved away the smoke and foul smell of his opponent's breath. 'Why don't you do us all a favour and self-combust?'

As Amon lashed out, Sammael vanished.

This was the ultimate Grigorian taunt, as only one amongst the emperor's legion could vanish, and that was Bael — Samyaza's right-hand man — and he could only make himself invisible. He could not teleport.

All the Grigori present had a laugh at Sammael's antics, so Amon's fury turned towards Armaros.

'Do you want to argue, pretty one?' he snarled in the record keeper's face.

'I'll pass,' Armaros conceded, looking to me. 'I shall finish recounting our day's work to the rest of the Grigori.'

134

'Gratitude,' I replied, and fell in beside Araqiel to follow Vassago's lead. Amon brought up the rear — no doubt to ensure we did not vanish anywhere en route.

As the huge doors of the emperor's throne room parted, I was forced to activate the retractable helmet of my armour along with the eye shield, to protect against the glare of the fires within the chamber. The emperor, and those closest to him, had grown used to the constant light and heat, but we Grigori, having lived our lives in the cold and darkness, always found the throne room uncomfortably warm — although temperature had little effect on any of us beyond being pleasant or not.

Inside, most of the nine of the Fallen — those the emperor had appointed his overlords — were present, doing what they did best: tormenting and torturing uninfected humans with their monstrous shapeshifting skills for our liege's amusement. All except Paimon, who preferred to sing and compose music than kill. He sat to one side of the stairs that lead up to the emperor's golden throne, strumming on his harp, his calming tune in vast contrast to the events unfolding in the chamber. I noted that the emperor's invisible spy, Bael, was also absent, or making himself seem so.

Vassago and Amon took up posts inside the chamber doors as they closed, and Araqiel and I advanced down the aisle towards the throne, between the burning pits around which the emperor's overlords amused themselves. These overlords had all been appointed to oversee different segments of the dark universe, but one by one had been forced to flee back to Tartarus in order to fortify themselves against the virus they had administered to their subjects — some of whom had turned rogue after catching the hybrid strain of the brainwashing disease. It had become too dangerous to slay anyone infected with the mind-eating virus, for fear the freed entity would latch onto the butcher of its host.

I had never batted an eyelid at the bloodsports of the Imperial chamber. The other Elohim were more fond of torture than

135

the Grigori, who preferred to slay as many targets as quickly as possible; indeed, we made competition out of our body counts. Yet now it twisted my insides to consider that each of those dumb creatures being tormented had the potential to mature into the like of the paragon I had glimpsed earlier. But then I knew that death would bring the human creatures a release that their tormentors would never know. That was provided the humans did not submit their soul to their tormentor in exchange for a quicker death. Long ago, the humans would agree to this easily, but lately something had alerted them to the eternal dangers of submission — our mysterious glowing human perhaps?

Araqiel and I came to a stop in the centre of the chamber, marked by a large round seal of the Fallen inset to the floor.

Each of the Fallen had a personal emblem that denoted their talents. These round crests were made from differing metals to distinguish their rank, and featured in the centre of the chestplate of their armour. But the seal on which we knelt was their combined insignia, which featured all seventy-two names of the highest-ranking officials in the emperor's service. These seventy-two had legions of other Fallen beneath them, and thousands of infernal spirits at their command; depending upon how many of the living had submitted their souls to their torturer before death. None of the names of the Grigori were included in this insignia, however; we had our own emblem that was uniform, as we considered ourselves as one unit. I had never had cause to wonder at our complete segregation before today — it was just as it had always been, and the Grigori preferred this.

This chamber's central seal was as close as anyone was allowed to get to the emperor, bar his nine overlords.

As we awaited the emperor's leave to speak, the missing overlord, Bael, appeared on the platform on which the golden throne resided. Samyaza waved his right-hand man forward, and Bael raised himself and approached our liege for a private chat.

Besides his talent for spy work, Bael also had the ability to shapeshift into a large agile cat, a seemingly docile toad, or a combination of these, and there was his warrior-like Elohim form.

The tone of his voice was as coarse as his character, yet he was too far removed for us to hear their conversation.

My attention was drawn to the frosted golden orb that spun continuously, high above the throne of the emperor. He called this art installation 'the Paradox'. Only those Fallen Elohim of highest rank knew the meaning behind the orb's mysterious title. I had ventured to ask after the meaning once, and had been told that it was for me to work out. I never had.

When Bael stepped aside, Samyaza was grinning. The verbal exchange must have been pleasing.

'Azazèl, Araqiel, what an interesting day you are having,' the emperor remarked, which caused me to wonder how long Bael had been secretly observing us this day.

'Indeed, your Highness, I have been given much food for thought,' I replied to cover my bases; no matter what Bael had seen, I knew for certain he could not know what was said in Lux.

'You are of the mind to see if the Grigori can traverse the Eternity Gate,' the emperor replied, in such a way that I could not tell if he was asking a question or giving an order.

'This makes sense,' I replied. 'Our mission against humanity for the emperor has all but come to an end, thus we are now dispensable to your cause and can risk such a mission.'

Samyaza grinned broadly; he disliked my response because it was clever and evasive. 'And you would risk the lives of your men in the attempt?'

This could be taken as an assumption, for the Grigori approached every mission as a combined task force.

'It may be weapons that have prevented any from penetrating the gate to date, for I note that none have made the attempt free of arms. If our vessel and persons are stripped of weaponry, I believe we may be granted passage.' I petitioned from on my knees, having not been given leave to rise.

'And what do you expect to find beyond the gate, Grigorian?' Samyaza queried.

Perhaps his spy, Bael, had overheard what the human had told me?

137

'Somewhere that is free of the mind-eater virus, where our emperor's safety can be secured,' I replied.

'But we all know that the Eternity Gate leads to the realm of the creator,' Samyaza challenged.

'Without investigation, that could yet prove to be a deception,' I countered. 'And should the Grigori fail and be cast back into this universe, powerless, our emperor shall still have your finest warriors in Tartarus to protect your throne and person from infection.'

The Emperor looked to his second-in-command, eyebrows raised in query.

Bael's expression was completely blank, but he gave a nod before Samyaza took a pause to consider and looked back to us. 'You know I can only be summoned from this realm?'

Again, I neither confirmed nor denied his question-cum-statement; Samyaza hadn't brought up the illuminated human and I was eager to avoid the topic if possible. 'Upon our success, that obstacle will be removed, and your liberation assured, my liege.'

Samyaza's laugh mocked my attempt to avoid his suppositions; he knew there was more to my eagerness to leave. 'And how am I to be certain that you will not have a change of heart once you are beyond the reach of my influence?'

What Samyaza meant to say was 'beyond the reach of my retribution'. For although the Fallen could not die, we could be fed to the virus and slowly transformed into zombies as our minds and bodies were eaten away to skeletal form, forevermore to be tortured by the starving mind-eater trapped within. At least for the mortals taken by the disease, death eventually brought an end to their suffering.

It was at this point I noted the tortured screams had stopped, as had the music, and the focus of all in the room had come to rest on us.

'The Grigori have never failed your Imperial Highness in any mission,' I replied to his challenge.

'This is not just *any* mission,' he emphasised. 'And that was before you Grigori were informed of how *special* you all are!'

I glanced aside to Araqiel to gauge his reaction to the claim; were we going to attempt to bluff our way through this?

'It's happening,' he mumbled and then uttered aside to me. 'Meet me in Lux.'

'*Now?*' I was perplexed by the request, given our present predicament.

'*Right now,*' he stressed as he fell face-first to the ground unconscious. In his back was a device I had never seen before — it glowed blue in the centre, and one of four curved blades that extended from the glowing central orb had lodged in his back.

'What is the meaning of this?' I looked to Samyaza for an explanation.

'We have some new toys that we've been preparing for just this occasion,' he informed as Baleth and Balam strode up, still in their three-headed forms — one face bull, one face ram, and the other Elohim — with their serpent tails lashing behind them. Taking up one leg each, they dragged Araqiel back down the aisle towards the exit doors.

'What have you done?' I was in shock, having never seen one of the Grigori incapacitated before.

'Just a little psychic and physical sedation,' Samyaza assured me. 'Your brother shall be harmed no further, provided you stick to your end of our bargain and be my test case.'

Horror struck at the core of my being, for I knew that he intended to infect me with the new strain of the mind-eater virus. 'We are leaving this universe to escape the mind-eater plague! To introduce it before you even arrive will defeat the whole purpose of the quest.'

'No, the purpose of the mission is to free the Grigori from this desolation and leave the rest of us to rot here!' Samyaza stood enraged. 'But I have prepared a very special mind-eater for you, Azazèl, one that will ensure your compliance.'

Above my head I heard the sound of machinery engaging, and that meant only one thing — I was about to be isolated from the rest of the room by a transparent tube that would drop from the ceiling any moment now. I had seen others fed to the gaseous entity for the entertainment of all in the throne room. Now it was my turn.

The thought occurred to teleport myself elsewhere, but what would happen to Araqiel and the rest of the Grigori if I did? There were only two hundred of us and thousands of them, we could not hope to win a war against the rest of the Fallen. Araqiel's last request seemed my only option, although I did not know if being in a state of Lux would be any hindrance to the virus, or even if I could maintain that state of being once infected.

To the sound of the mocking laughter and jeers of the emperor's overlords, I focused myself inwards and entered the light-field; my body dropped to the floor as the tube shot down to incubate me within its confines.

'Azazèl! You made it!'

Araqiel emerged from the illumination before me and I was relieved to see him. *'I thought they had subdued you?'*

'They did! Knocked the soul right out of my body and I don't intend to return it from whence it came, either,' he informed, seeming happy about that.

This was a shock to me, as I'd always been under the impression that the souls of the Fallen were trapped within their physical bodies, and that this state of Lux we'd discovered was just a suspended state that existed between manifesting our form between one place and another. *'But what will you do, just stay here forever?'* Lux was preferable to the dark universe for certain, but insanely boring without company for all eternity.

'Heavens, no!' He laughed off that suggestion. *'I am coming through the Eternity Gate with you. The human told me that I have a different route to follow to the rest of my brothers, but our paths will converge eventually, as our destinies lie beyond that gate.'*

I shook my head. *'I must be left behind, as Samyaza is exposing me to his new hybrid mind-eater as we speak.'*

'A mind-eater cannot feed on your soul if your soul is not in your body,' he put forward, and again I was perplexed by my lack of comprehension.

'But even so, it will feed on my body until there is nothing left!'

'You will not need that body where we are going.' He prompted me to look on the bright side.

'How could you know that?' A strange feeling crept over me and I shuddered at the hostile sensation's advance.

Yet Araqiel was still grinning. 'When we spoke, the Logos showed me so much more than just a pretty face —'

'You also think it was the Logos?' Suddenly my bad feeling rushed from my gut to my head and exploded into an influx of information that streamed into my mind. 'Ah … no! No!' I cried as I caught glimpses of the content.

'What ails you?' Araqiel gripped my face to get my attention.

'This mind-eater is programmed with a grimoire containing all the evocations, seals and information required to summon the primary Fallen Elohim from their prison.' My fate was sealed. 'If such information is carried forth into the next universe, it would be disastrous for every living thing there!'

'And there you have it, wisdom, love and compassion all in that one conclusion.' Araqiel remained in good cheer. 'Thus, if you are not delivered to a higher universe, it would prove just as disastrous for evolution, for clearly you carry the Logos in your soul.'

'What?' I did not fathom his meaning. 'The Fallen don't have souls; we are immortal and thus eternally physical beings.'

'No, we have been misled about that,' he said. 'Even Samyaza and his ilk have souls, although they are trapped inside their physical forms, but only because they have yet to develop the emotional, mental and causal bodies needed to ascend higher in the evolutionary scheme. We Grigori are not so bound any more, for our camaraderie has allowed our souls to advance. What is this form you are wearing here in Lux, but an etheric shell that embodies your soul-mind?'

I looked down at myself, speechless a moment, as my mind raced to keep pace with the influx of information on both a physical and non-physical level. 'But as soon as I rejoin my body, I will be brainwashed into forgetting everything!'

'Then don't,' he replied simply. 'No one will know you are absent.'

'But …?' I now had so many questions it was difficult to prioritise them. 'My body cannot just stay in a coma state. And *how are we to follow through the Eternity Gate if we are stuck here in Lux?'*

'We're not stuck here,' Araqiel enlightened. '*Every soul is free to move anywhere within the confines of the universe it occupies.*

'Anywhere?' I challenged. '*Have you tested that theory?'*

'I have, actually,' Araqiel confessed. '*I've been exploring the boundaries of this state we call Lux for some time now. Perhaps a demonstration?'* he asked.

'Please,' I squeezed out the word under the duress of the disease latching onto my physical body; even though I wasn't currently wearing it, I could sense the panic and agitation eating away at me.

'*Moving the soul around is not so different from willing your physical body from one place to another,*' Araqiel instructed, '*only you focus on observing a place or person, rather than joining them.*'

The light of Lux evaporated like a mist, and left me standing once again in the emperor's throne room. My body lay before me, still unconscious inside the isolation tube that had fed the virus to me. I looked aside to Araqiel who now appeared almost completely transparent, and my expression must have been one of horror.

'*Never fear,*' he assured me. '*They cannot see us. Even their psychic skills are useless against any being who resonates at a higher vibrational rate than they do.*'

This announcement I did not entirely comprehend, but clearly Araqiel understood it, and that was liberating in a sense. But as I cast my etheric sight upon the Fallen, I now plainly saw all the tortured souls that they had held captive in this place with them, whose hatred of their plight had turned them into demons. '*Can they not be saved?'*

'*Every soul can be freed, but only once the being they have sworn allegiance to finds the compassion to let them go,*' Araqiel counselled.

'And those who have been taken by the virus?' I queried.

'*There is nothing left of them to be saved,*' he was sorry to advise.

I looked back to my own form and could clearly see a dark shadow that now enshrouded it. *'So I am done for?'*

'You are being protected by our father,' he assured me. *'As am I. Samyaza considers he is clever enough to outsmart his maker, but he is deluded.'*

'That was not nearly as entertaining as anticipated,' Samyaza commented, as the isolation tube retracted back into the roof and Bael descended the stairs from the elite platform and strode down the aisle towards my slumbering form.

'How am I to pull off this deception without rejoining my form?' I queried my spectral company.

'Just wait,' Araqiel suggested.

'The Grigori are weak,' Bael responded to Samyaza's observation, as he reached down to drag my body up to standing, and I was deeply angered by his insult.

'You won't think so when I flatten you!' I responded, despite the fact that I could not be seen nor heard.

It was at that moment that the eyes of my physical body suddenly opened, and finding its feet my person landed an uppercut king hit to Bael's jaw, which sent him reeling backwards into a fire-pit, to the shock of all present.

Araqiel had a chuckle. *'It seems you still hold some influence.'*

'How did I do that?' I was awed by the event, as I watched Bael rise from the fire-pit seething.

'As I suspected, the mind-eater is carrying your form,' Araqiel stated.

'You mean you didn't know that would be the case?' I was bemused. *'Why speak with such certainty if you are in fact unsure?'*

'It's confidence building,' he explained. *'And intention is everything, as you have just demonstrated.'*

'I am going to squash you, Grigorian!' Bael threatened, as he headed towards me, flames still lapping from beneath his armour, and his hair ablaze.

'You'll do no such thing!' Samyaza employed his verbal leash and although Bael was loath to come to heel, he complied to his master's command. 'We need Azazèl to go prepare the rest of the Grigori and his ship for their mission.'

My body bowed faithfully to the emperor, served Bael the evil eye and spat in the overlord's direction, then turned and strode from the room.

The momentary elation I felt in the wake of the confrontation dissipated quickly into panic. *'We have to stop this!'* I pursued my body from the chamber, Araqiel accompanying.

7

ASCENT INTO MADNESS

Upon receiving the emperor's orders the Grigori set about stripping our vessel of weaponry. We only ever had to use a transport to reach our destination when it was somewhere we had never visited before; once we were familiar with a place we could simply teleport there. The Grigori did not question the objective as it had been delivered by their commander, and as promised Armaros and Sammael had met with groups of our brothers in Lux to explain our suspicions. Hence all my task force believed that I had been successful in covertly securing permission for us to escape the emperor's charge.

There was only one who suspected that our desire had been fulfilled far too easily and that something was amiss with their commander.

Armaros may have appeared the youngest and most fragile of us all — his fine fair hair and deep blue eyes only added to his passive appearance — but he was something of a favourite among his more boisterous Grigori companions due to his sharp mind, great knowledge and sheer likeability.

In spirit I stood by and cheered as Armaros voiced his concern to Sammael, while they stood supervising the removal of the huge guns attached to our spacecraft. 'There is something not right with Azazèl.'

'Well, he's got a lot on his mind right now.' Sammael noted a precarious situation unfolding with the deconstruction. 'Watch out!' he yelled in warning to the crew at ground level as a heavy metal gun shaft slipped from its casing and slid toward the edge of the craft, stopping short of falling on the Grigori beneath. 'What part of "be careful" do you not understand?' he yelled at the demolition crew on top of the vessel.

'Sorry, *boss*!' Bezaliel shouted back, somewhat sarcastically, standing up to pull his unruly black mop of hair off his face — something he only did when he was preparing for a flight. Bezaliel may not have been much taller than Sammael, and lacked his musclebound physique, but what he lacked in stature he more than made up for with pure aggression. 'If you can do a better job, you are welcome up here.'

Bezaliel was about as obnoxious and inconsiderate as the Grigori came, but he and Sammael made sport of feuding with each other, which aided both of them to let off steam.

'I'm trying to have a conversation here,' Sammael motioned to Armaros beside him, 'if you'd be so kind as to just handle this shit until I'm done.'

Bezaliel forced a grin and served Sammael the finger.

'Appreciated!' Sammael looked back to Armaros. 'You were saying?'

Armaros frowned. 'I mean, why will he not tell us what has happened to Araqiel? Why will our brother not be joining us, when he promised me we would be going together?'

Sammael seemed to agree this was a little odd. 'Maybe Araqiel got infected?'

'I think it more likely that Azazèl has been infected,' Armaros fronted up with what was really on his mind.

'Steady on,' Sammael rejected the premise at first.

'He hasn't been right since he returned from that audience without Araqiel.' Armaros pushed his point in a whisper. 'He's despondent, looking ill, and smelling poorly.'

'I hadn't noticed,' said Sammael, then recanted that statement in part. 'I just thought him a little more pissed off than usual.'

'Well take notice,' Armaros suggested. 'Because if I am right, we have a very big problem on our hands.'

146

Sammael stood back and considered the premise more carefully. 'I guess there would be no better way for the emperor to sneak one of his new etheric pets on board than to conceal it in our commander. But it's really not safe to discuss this here.'

'Just be alert,' Armaros took the hint and dropped the subject for the moment.

'I will investigate.' Sammael assured him.

I was appeased to note that the caution had got Sammael thinking, and Araqiel and I trailed him to my office where Sammael passed right through the closed door to find my possessed body sitting out the commotion.

'It's not like you not to be out there directing traffic,' Sammael commented as he entered and made his presence known.

'It is customary to knock.' The mind-eater was most displeased.

Holding his fist up, Sammael played out the hand gesture. 'Knock, knock.'

'Go away,' it retorted.

'It is customary to say "come in".' Sammael lampooned.

'I give the commands,' it answered, 'and I did not request your presence.'

'Do you ever?' Sammael asked, which seemed to confuse it.

'If you wish to be smart, I can have you flogged,' it threatened, deadpan.

'Yeah, good one.' Sammael laughed off the idea, as he came to stand before it, arms folded.

'You wish to be flogged?' it assumed.

'You've never flogged anyone.' Sammael informed it.

'There's always a first time.' It forced a grin. This strain of mind-eater was smarter than the previous ones and better at adapting to conceal its presence.

'But seriously,' Sammael must have smelled a rat, as he appeared very determined, 'I wanted to talk to you about what you said in Lux.'

'Where is Lux?' It obviously couldn't find a reference for such a place.

'You know, the place of light that we discovered over in the Maviclon system.' Sammael replied; he was lying about the location of Lux, but it was a clever lie that covered our bases in case Bael was lurking about or this mind-eater was reporting back to the emperor.

'Oh yes,' it replied. 'What of it?'

'Well, you promised the Grigori that if we left this universe we would do so together,' Sammael continued. 'So where is Araqiel?'

'I told you.' It stood to confront Sammael, and he took a step back and held his breath, appearing not fearful but repulsed. 'Araqiel is no longer a factor in this mission! The emperor has decided to keep him as collateral. The matter is out of my hands, so drop it!'

'But, Commander —' Sammael pushed his luck and it moved to belt him, as it had Bael.

'*Don't you dare!*' I commanded the beast within my body, and it refrained. 'No more questions.' It seethed in warning.

'As you wish.' Sammael, having found his answers, backed up and headed out the doors to find Armaros.

'You agree,' the scribe assumed, seeing the look of loathing and concern on Sammael's face as he approached.

'Inside,' the warrior uttered as he passed Armaros and headed into the spacecraft being loaded for their voyage.

'I'll take that as a yes,' he commented, as he gave pursuit.

'Announce if the commander comes on board,' Sammael instructed Penemue, who was standing by the outer hatch doors. He opened his mouth to query the request. 'No questions, little shadow, just do it.'

Penemue frowned curiously at Armaros in pursuit. 'Best comply, he's in a mood,' Armaros advised and kept moving, until Sammael led him into the flight deck that was currently unoccupied.

'He reeks of mind-eater, quite literally!' Sammael was panicked.

'Calm yourself,' Armaros suggested, seating himself and motioning his companion to another seat. 'Shall we meditate upon this development?'

'What?' Sammael was confused, but Armaros closed his eyes to hint at his meaning. 'Oh.' Sammael realised that the scholar was inviting him to a meeting in Lux. 'Good call.' He sat down and closed his eyes.

This was well done, as I spied a translucent form entering the room which could only mean one thing: Bael was still spying on us.

He would wonder at these two Grigori taking their repose, but he would not expose himself to query them. Bael would merely observe and discover nothing, for I could warn them of his presence before they returned to their forms.

This was just the opportunity I had been waiting for, and Araqiel and I joined our brothers in the light-field.

'*Araqiel, Commander, you are here?*' Sammael was pleasantly surprised to see us. '*What is going on?*'

'*We suspect —*' Armaros began.

'*I know your fears,*' I placed a hand on his shoulder, to show my pride in him, '*And unfortunately, they are completely justified.*'

'What?' Sammael looked me up and down and Armaros took a step backward. '*How can you be infected? You look perfectly fine to me?*'

'*What happened at that meeting?*' Armaros observed Araqiel and then looked back to me for answers, which I was more than happy to supply.

When my account of events was done, my audience was stunned speechless.

'*What would you have us do, Commander?*' Armaros asked, wary of the answer.

'*My body must be left behind,*' I concluded sadly.

'*No, that is not the way for you,*' Araqiel insisted. '*The human forewarned me this would occur, but it advised that you are going to need that form for a while yet.*'

'*You never said so?*' This was the first time he'd mentioned this to me. '*You said I wouldn't need that body where we were going.*'

'*In the long term, that is true,*' Araqiel warranted, '*but in the short term, you will.*'

'And yet you are prepared to leave your body behind?' I thought this rather odd.

'I have a different path to follow,' he reminded me, 'and that is really of no concern to you. For now we need to focus on preserving as much of your body as we can.'

'I am not carrying that creature into the next universe!' I insisted.

'The next universe is more advanced than this one; there are ways and means unknown to us here,' he suggested.

'Are you guessing again?' I confronted him for I needed facts not theory.

'I only know what I was told by the Logos, and I trust that our divine brother is far more knowledgeable than I,' Araqiel confessed.

'I know it would cause me much remorse if we were to leave you behind in this eternal darkness to perish to a mind-eater, and then arrived in the next universe to discover that we could have saved you from that torment,' Armaros appealed.

'Do you have any idea how much damage I could cause before then?' I reasoned. 'The mind-eater I carry has all the information it needs to summon Samyaza into the next universe.'

'Then we must ensure you do not enter the next universe in a conscious state,' Sammael put forward.

'How do you mean?' I queried the objective. 'Araqiel is the first of the Grigori I have ever seen sedated.'

'I don't mean sedate you,' Sammael enlightened. 'I mean to cryogenically freeze you — like we do humans for long voyages.'

'Will that work?' Armaros queried. 'No one has attempted to put a Grigorian in stasis before.'

Sammael shrugged. 'I guess we will find out … and if it does work, we'll just leave you frozen until such time as we find a cure for the mind-eater virus.'

'A splendid plan!' Araqiel awarded Sammael his due — it was not often he solved a problem with brain power rather than brute force. 'But the containment must take place as soon after lift-off as possible. You must not enter the gate until the virus has been subdued.'

'That could be easier said than done,' Armaros warned, 'as our commander is rather unaccommodating at present. No offence.'

'None taken,' I granted, sorry for the predicament I was leaving them in. 'But I am not without some influence over my body, so I shall aid you to trap me as much as I am able.'

'I too may know of something that may help you in this, but I'll need your assistance, Armaros,' Araqiel propositioned the scholar.

'Anything I can do, just ask,' he assured.

'Best we keep it between you and me — ' my counsel eyed me over ' — for we do not know how much of a conscious connection our mind-eater friend has with our commander.'

'You don't think it could be perceiving us now, do you?' Sammael was on guard.

'This state of consciousness would be way beyond its vibrational frequency,' he explained to the warrior, who only appeared more perplexed. 'But as to how much it perceives from Azazèl on a regular mental level, I can't say. So, better to be safe than sorry.'

I nodded to concur with his reasoning.

'And what of your body, Araqiel?' Sammael queried. 'I'll be more than happy to go snatch it back from your captors, just say the word.'

'It is just a vessel and this soul will find another,' he advised. 'We don't want to alert the other fallen to our scheme, or give them any reason to oppose our exit from this universe. Best let Samyaza have my body, if that makes him feel more secure in our deal.'

'But do you not fear his torture and retribution once he realises his plan has failed?' Armaros appealed for him to reconsider.

'Not at all,' he assured the scribe. 'For once my soul passes through that gate I will be severed from that body forever more.'

'Then let's do this thing!' Sammael was inspired now.

'Indeed,' I seconded the motion. 'But watch your backs as Bael is snooping around and probably will be until we take off. No one must get wise to our intentions before we depart from Tartarus.'

All present gave a firm nod of acknowledgement.

Before the Grigori were due to depart, Azazèl was summoned to a meeting with the emperor. As Araqiel and I followed my diseased form into the imperial chamber to ensure my last face-to-face with

Samyaza went according to plan, my spiritual companion seemed to be having more difficulty keeping pace with me than usual, for he was leaning heavily on his staff.

'What is the matter Araqiel?' I queried his strange laboured walk. 'Are you feeling poorly?' The query seemed absurd as we Grigori were never unwell.

'I've seen better days.' He directed my attention to one of the inner walls of the throne room.

There was a new ornamental feature in the chamber this day and it was an affront to my sensibilities to see the body of my fellow Grigorian, still unconscious, bolted onto a large metal frame and hung on the wall — I could scarce imagine how it made the victim feel to see himself thus.

'You can feel that?' I rasped, and I felt the same pain in my chest that I had felt upon realising I had beheaded the most beautiful vision I had ever seen. This was also a far greater discomfort than the obnoxious ache I felt all through me since being exposed to the virus.

Pain was a new sensation for us, and it was abundantly clear that the subtle pain of emotion was even more inhibitive than physical torture; but then, I had yet to rejoin my body and feel the full impact of the virus on my being.

My companion removed one hand from his staff, to show me the hole from the bolt that went right through his hand.

'I'm not going to stand by and —'

'The gesture was meant to bait you. Do not be so eager to jump into the trap,' Araqiel warned me. 'You too are suffering, and your pain will not be so easily severed as mine. My pain is only temporary, as once we pass through the Eternity Gate I will feel it no more.'

'That is why you didn't want Sammael to rescue your form,' I realised. 'How long have you been like this?'

'It is no matter,' he insisted. 'But if any of the other Grigori knew about this, we'd have a rebellion on our hands and none would escape the virus.'

As always, his reasoning could not be argued. 'Then leave this to me and go rest yourself.'

152

He looked confused by my lack of understanding. *'The pain is the same whether I am still or not. And you need some counsel through this trying time.'* His eyes reverted to his body on the wall. *'Who knows what other nasty surprises Samyaza wishes to spring on you to test your readiness to fulfil his cause.'*

'Point taken.' Clearly, if he had not been present to stop me, I might have sought to protest my brother's use as a decoration. *'I appreciate your counsel and your commitment, Araqiel.'*

'I appreciate that you appreciate it,' he replied.

I looked back to my form advancing down the long aisle towards the throne. *'Let us get this meeting over with, and leave this infernal existence.'*

'Amen.'

The emperor and my zombie self were seemingly alone in the chamber today, although I spied Bael lurking about the throne.

Once kneeling on the insignia of the Fallen, my personage was addressed by the emperor.

'Do you like our new adornment?' He motioned his creature to it, for it had failed to look sideways upon entering.

It glanced where instructed and then returned its dark hollowed eyes to its master. 'What is not to like?'

Samyaza grinned, for this response no doubt confirmed to him that his mind-eater had firm control of me. 'Can you enlighten me as to his means of maintaining this strange unconscious state?'

I was alarmed by the query, for I had not joined with my body and thus had not given the mind-eater access to my thoughts. *'It must have been caused by the emperor's new technology,'* I advised it.

'I do not know,' it replied.

Samyaza frowned and sat forwards in his throne, concerned by the response and so was I.

'Perhaps your new restraining device worked a little too well,' it added to appease its master, and I was relieved not to have lost what little influence over myself I had left.

At this point I noted Bael's shadow form move in closer to the emperor to have a quiet word.

Samyaza heard him out, then continued his interrogation. 'We have observed other Grigori performing this odd practice as well ... it must serve some purpose?'

'*It is how we sort our thoughts. We find it refreshes the body and the mind between missions,*' I advised my body and it conveyed my thoughts to Samyaza.

'Why rest when you never tire?' He found this very suspicious.

'We find it pleasurable,' it concluded on my behalf.

Samyaza looked back to Araqiel's unconscious form on the wall and appeared most displeased. 'So your brother mocks my intention to make him suffer, does he? How do we wake him from his pleasurable state?'

'*The Grigori are awoken from their repose easily,*' I commanded my form to convey. '*Araqiel's current state is beyond my understanding, which is why I suggest the emperor's new technology could be the cause.*'

It delivered the message, but this only infuriated the emperor all the more. 'I don't care about the cause! Get it through that Grigorian skull that unless Araqiel is conscious and in pain, none of the Grigori will set foot out of Tartarus!'

'Then how am I to summon you forth into the next universe?' The directive did not make any sense to the emotionless creature.

'I shall pin ten more of your brothers to these walls to hold as hostages, Araqiel!' he shouted out to nowhere in particular. 'Do you hear me?'

'*What difference does it make when I am your humble servant?*' I suggested as a comeback. Yet there was a sinking feeling in my gut that Samyaza really did know more about the Grigori than we had ourselves, until recently. Still, the entity carrying my form was completely indifferent to Samyaza's threat or my instruction. 'Whatever pleases, my emperor,' it said.

'*Shut up,*' I insisted, '*you're making this worse!*'

'*Do not risk the mission and do not wait for me,*' Araqiel advised, and by the time I looked to him to argue his instruction, his spiritual presence was gone.

'It would please me to have my leverage conscious!' Samyaza pressed for his will to be met, but a moan from his framed captive put the smug tone back in his voice and countenance, as all eyes turned to Araqiel. 'Here you are, at last! So nice of you to join us.'

'The pleasure is all yours,' he replied. 'Do with me as you will.'

'I really just required the pleasure of your company,' Samyaza advised. 'And as long as I have it I shall not blow the Grigori craft out of the sky!'

'You said Araqiel would not be harmed.' I was mortified by my colleague's sacrifice; I had no idea if Araqiel's powers were still subdued by the weapon that had taken him down in this chamber. Now that he had rejoined his body, he might well be trapped in there.

'I trust that I am now at liberty to proceed with my imperial objective?' the mind-eater asked, although I was far from satisfied with this arrangement.

'See my directive is carried out,' Samyaza looked back to his creature to advise. 'I do not trust any of the Grigori to be cooperative, so ensure they know the plight of their brother. Who I will be happy to bring to our new location once I have been summoned forth.'

Samyaza had no intention of doing any such thing. *'No, you must not deliver that news to the Grigori, they will take up arms against the emperor!'* I insisted that would not be the wisest course of action to achieve its goal.

'Fear not,' it told its master, 'I have a plan that ensures none of my subordinates will become an impediment to your directive.'

'What?' The notion that this senseless puppet was thinking for itself was horrifying!

'I trust that you do.' Samyaza grinned, satisfied that he would get his wish, and with the emperor's blessing, my form rose and departed the room.

'What, no fond farewell?' Samyaza commented sarcastically in my wake, and I felt compelled to say good riddance, but feared my form might repeat the sentiment. I looked to Araqiel, so much wanting to express my remorse at his fate, and to query him about his chances of escape. However, with a micro-shake of his head and a stern expression, he begged me to leave without protest.

Goodbye, my dearest brother, I shall never find a counsel so wise as yours unless we meet again, I thought, as the ache in my chest increased. If I had understood the human correctly, the Logos had moved onto the next universe at the time I beheaded its vessel; yet I made a quiet appeal to that divine messenger to watch over Araqiel, who had placed so much faith in him, and I was about to do the same.

The launch of the Grigori vessel *Leviathan*, proceeded without further delay, and my task force were happy to facilitate the process.

As Bezaliel, the pessimist among us, so eloquently put it: 'Let's leave this shit-hole of a universe, while the going is good!' To which the usual argument was not forthcoming from Sammael, or any of the Grigori.

It seemed the creature inside my form had heeded my advice — it had not mentioned Araqiel's fate to the rest of the crew. Once a course had been set for the Eternity Gate many dark-years away, the mind-eater posing as commander assembled the crew and instructed them to follow him.

Sammael and Armaros, aware of the impostor, hung back to bring up the rear.

'What do you think he's up to?' Sammael whispered aside to his fellow conspirator.

'Never mind, we stick to the plan,' Armaros replied. 'I'm sure the commander is keeping an eye out for our best interests. If his form tries anything suspicious, you know what to do.'

Sammael nodded. 'Still I wish you'd tell me how you plan to pull this off. Faith is not really my thing.'

'He's leading us to cryogenics.' Armaros was distracted by the observation, and Sammael was stunned.

'What if he's picked up on our plan, and intends to turn the tables on us?' Sammael was edgy.

'Let it try.' Armaros sounded very determined to prevail.

As the Grigori assembled in cryogenics my brothers were understandably perplexed, as this was a place associated with cattle.

'What is the meaning of this, Commander?' Penemue was the first to voice his concern, for he'd suspected for some time that something odd was going on with their leader.

The creature posing as Azazèl took a stand on one of the benches to ensure it could be heard and understood by all. 'All of you need to pick a module, and enclose yourself within it, emperor's orders.'

'That's absurd!' Sacha protested in unison with my own objection. Sacha was fair of face and hair, like Armaros and Araqiel, but was more warlike than his brothers. Still, he shared their keen mind and was also highly intuitive. His eyes were his defining feature, an eerie shade of grey. More than an ability to levitate and teleport, Sacha had learned how to fly — no wings required.

'It is a condition of our exit out of this universe,' the mind-eater advised. 'The emperor is monitoring this ship and will destroy us if there are not one hundred and ninety-eight pods occupied by the time we leave this system.'

'I didn't realise we had a system for monitoring our mobile cryogenics from Tartarus?' Armaros was suspicious as Araqiel had a hand in developing many of the technologies that were currently in use, and Armaros did much of the research and chronicling of the same.

'I'm sure there is a lot the emperor has not made us privy to,' my diseased vessel put down the query.

'He's lying!' I appealed loudly, but hardly anyone heard my challenge, only the creature who was the cause of my concern, and he roused half a smirk from his usually expressionless face. Sariel, our co-pilot, was telepathic, and he frowned momentarily, but no doubt thought himself imagining things.

'Holy shit,' Sammael uttered under his breath, looking to Armaros to see if he had a contingency in place that would counter the commander's bombshell.

'This is unexpected,' Armaros was sorry to advise.

'One hundred and ninety-eight?' Bezaliel queried the math.

'Araqiel will not be joining us, and I must stay conscious in order to revive you all once we arrive at our destination, and to give reports to the emperor,' it concluded.

157

'I hadn't considered that either.' Armaros was appearing less and less confident.

'Is that safe, Commander?' Penemue queried on behalf of everyone.

'Trust that I have our combined interests in mind,' it said. 'Know that we are imperishable, and that I will revive you upon our deliverance in the next universe.'

'*Sariel,*' I moved closer to him. '*It's a mind-eater you're dealing with!*'

Again he frowned and ticked his head, as if he feared he had a short circuit in his brain.

'Our commander would never steer us wrong,' Gadriel encouraged his brothers, but he had always been the most credulous among us, and quite possibly the most vain. To my deep distress, the rest of the crew also seemed resigned to comply.

I had to act! I could not stand idly by and see this creature deceive them.

I didn't have the time to talk Sariel around and so resigned myself to rejoining my body. Still, I paused a moment to appreciate my sensibilities as they were now, before contamination, for once the virus had my soul within its grasp there would be no escaping its scourge.

As my brothers moved to enter the individual modules set in rows throughout this chamber — designed to hold thousands — I willed myself back into my form and felt myself consumed by the heavy dark shadow and the anguish of being eaten away from the inside.

'Don't ... listen —' I struggled against the virus to say the words, loud enough to capture the attention of my brothers in arms and my body contorted with my struggle. 'The Emperor's mind-eater ...' my harrowed sights turned to Sammael and Armaros '... seeks to protect itself!' I appealed for them to act on our plan. As I was suddenly overcome with a desire to serve Samyaza, a great hate of any who would oppose me in this welled in my gut and mind.

'Seize him!' Sammael commanded his brothers. 'The commander has been exposed to the emperor's new virus!'

Alerted to my predicament, all the Grigori came running at me. But the creature that consumed me was not to be contained, and I was compelled to retaliate, and did so with extreme force, releasing a wave of psychokinetic energy that cast off my brothers and sent them flying backwards in every direction. Even Sammael was slammed hard into an open module, and I hit the door lock. The module sealed and trapped him inside. I was prepared to do the same to every Grigori who came towards me and would have, but a sharp stabbing pain in my back saw my body immobilised, and my spirit knocked clean out of my form. '*What the* …?' I turned about to see one of the emperor's crippling devices embedded in my back.

'That's for Araqiel,' informed Armaros.

'What the hell is that?' Bezaliel was the first to recover from the shock of seeing one of the Grigori knocked unconscious.

'It is one of the emperor's new toys.' Armaros held forth the wide-barrelled pistol and, flicking a lever on the side, the blades of the glowing stun device retracted and it was magnetically drawn back into the weapon. 'It is what they used to take down Araqiel.'

'Son-of-a-bitch,' Bezaliel mumbled, horrified by the scholar's words.

'Good job!' Sacha was gratified to see their opponent taken down.

'Yeah,' Penemue agreed in part, 'but how is the commander going to report to the emperor now?'

'Maybe he was lying about that, too,' Armaros said.

'But what if he wasn't?' Penemue decided it would be best to be prepared.

'Let me out of here!' Sammael protested, slamming on the door of the module that contained him.

As Bezaliel was closest he merely served Sammael the finger through the transparent casing.

'Get out of the way,' Gadriel pushed the antagonist aside and opened the module as requested. 'I can shapeshift into the commander and pose as him if needs be,' he proffered, eager to be of aid.

Sammael gave a laugh at this. 'You are an imbecile … the emperor is never going to believe you are Azazèl, let alone possessed by his new super-smart virus!'

'Is that right?' Gadriel shoved Sammael back inside the module and locked it again.

'Stop with the games! We are in serious shit here!' Penemue insisted, hitting the release button to free their brother. 'We have no choice but to use Gadriel.'

'We're screwed!' Bezaliel maintained his regular negative take on things.

Gadriel was insulted. 'Your confidence in me is underwhelming. Maybe you would rather be blown to pieces! I'm sure it will be a hoot trying to collect and sort the body parts of all two hundred of us as they are shot out to every quadrant of the dark universe.'

'Don't be so sensitive,' Penemue suggested. 'Just put the captain on and let's see how much work we need to to do on your character. How long has our commander been infected?' He looked to Armaros for answers.

'Since the day we were advised of this mission,' he replied. 'The commander managed to escape into Lux just prior to being exposed and had avoided rejoining his body.'

'So his mind has not been affected,' Penemue assumed.

Armaros shrugged at this. 'He must have rejoined his body just now to warn us,' he said sadly. 'My fear is that now he is trapped in there with it.'

'Well, there is only one way to know for sure … but just in case,' Sammael dragged my slumbering form into the module, 'let's see this thing safely to bed.' With Sacha's aid they hoisted my body up and strapped it in. 'Sweet dreams, Commander.' Sammael closed and sealed the door, then activated the cryogen which frosted up inside the containment module, and I immediately felt the cold seeping through me to my core. 'Armaros,' he looked to the scholar, 'maybe you should head to Lux and check on our commander's state of being while we work on Gadriel.'

Their resolution was a great relief to me, and I was deeply grateful for their clear thinking and team work — I would never have been able to pull off this escape without them, and yet most of them were acting out of a trust in my gut instinct, which could yet prove to be naught but an enchantment that was leading us to our deaths. Yet my intention had been put in motion and there was no turning back. The truth of the matter was Samyaza was done with us anyway, and if we didn't succeed in this, we might end our days as decorations upon the wall in his throne room.

Armaros was most gratified to find me awaiting him in Lux. *'It is a joy to see you, Commander, I feared you had been trapped with the creature.'*

'I was kn-kn-knocked right out of my b-b-body, when you hit m-m-me with the stun d-d-device,' I did my best to prevent my teeth chattering as I spoke.

'Commander?' He was concerned to note my shivering. *'You can feel the cold! That must be very unpleasant?'*

I shrugged in response to this. 'F-f-funny enough, I find it prefer-fer-ferable to f-f-feeling nothing at all.'

Armaros frowned, and finding the statement rather odd, he skipped to another subject. *'So the emperor did not order us into stasis?'*

I shook my head.

'Is our commander required to report to the emperor?'

I nodded. 'That would be n-n-normal procedure,' I replied.

'We are preparing Gadriel to assume your form,' Armaros advised.

'I was th-th-thinking I could p-p-possess his form and sp-p-peak through him.' The lack of flow between the words in my brain and my mouth, was frustrating, 'but n-n-not with these shiv-v-v—'

'Shivers,' Armaros concluded for me, as clearly he was frustrated with waiting for me to get the sentence out. *'No,'* he quite agreed, *'clearly that would be a little suspicious.'*

'B-b-but Sar-i—'

'Sariel,' Armaros concurred.

'Is t-t-tele—'

'Telepathic.'

'He m-m-might conv-v-vey —'

'Your thoughts to Gadriel!' Armaros jumped to my conclusion. *'Brilliant! That just might work,'* he surmised as I nodded in accord. *'We'll just stick a small receiver in his ear, and Sariel and yourself can monitor the emperor's transmission from another room.'*

161

I clapped my hands to approve his train of thought.

'What about Araqiel? What has become of him?'

The mere mention of his name made my chest ache. 'He is am-m-musing the Emp-p-peror. I shall f-f-fetch him, aft-t-ter —'

'— we deal with this last obstacle?' Armaros guessed my meaning, and I nodded in gratitude. 'Then we had best go see how they are doing with Gadriel.'

'Thank you,' I managed to say without faltering. 'I c-c-could not have —'

My fair, small-framed brother held up a hand to prevent me saying more. 'We are legion,' he said. 'We shall always have your back, as you have ours.'

Despite the chill that had hold of me, it warmed my soul to know he spoke the truth. If we were to perish on this mission then we would leave this universe as we'd entered it, together.

In the commander's quarters, unity was not really the sentiment of the moment. Penemue, Sammael, Sacha and Bezaliel had Gadriel in front of the mirror correcting his appearance, when Armaros entered.

Gadriel had assumed my form; sort of.

'What is with the wavy hair?' Sammael critiqued our shapeshifter's efforts. 'The commander's hair has always been dead straight!'

'But it looks better, don't you think?' Gadriel admired the appearance he was wearing in the mirror.

'It looks ridiculous!' Bezaliel scoffed from his position stretched out on a sofa.

'Change it!' Sammael was losing patience.

With a roll of his eyes Gadriel complied. 'Better?' he huffed, as he turned to his brothers

'A good likeness,' Armaros awarded kindly, 'but you might want to try looking a little paler, with some big dark rings around the eyes, as you are supposed to be diseased.'

'Really?' he asked as if it were truly beneath him to appear less than perfect.

'Just do it!' the rest of the company replied in unison.

'All right already!' Gadriel turned back to the mirror to gauge the transformation. 'Truly gross,' he decided, once he looked wrecked enough to repulse himself.

'Okay, that's perfect,' Penemue granted, 'now to make him speak and act like the commander.'

'Our commander can help us out with that,' Armaros was pleased to advise.

'So his spirit is not trapped in cryogenics with his body?' Sammael assumed.

'No, he is here with us now,' Armaros informed, whereupon my brothers peered around the room as if expecting to see me.

'Sorry about the hair thing,' Gadriel said for my benefit. 'Really, your hair is perfectly adorable.'

Sammael's cheer soured and he whacked Gadriel in the back of the head. 'Perfectly adorable? The commander would never say anything like that!'

'Touch me again,' Gadriel turned on his assailant, 'and I'll turn into Balem or Baleth instead, and rip you limb from limb!'

'Now you're sounding more like the commander.' Sammael grinned.

'We need to work together.' Armaros pushed them apart. 'And we don't have much time left.'

'What does the commander want us to do?' Penemue was all for being helpful.

'I have some of our brothers setting up a comm-link. The captain cannot speak directly through Gadriel as he's feeling the effects of the cryogen. We need Sariel on a comm-link to act as telepathic relay between our commander's spirit and Gadriel.'

'Holy crap!' Bezaliel finally sat up to attention. 'If we pull this off it will be a goddamn miracle!'

'Do you have a problem with that, Grigorian?' Gadriel tested out his authoritative tone.

Bezaliel flinched, and then waved Gadriel off as he recalled he was not the commander. 'Idiot.'

'I got you!' he boasted.

163

'Not bad,' Sammael warranted. 'Now let's see how you fare convincing Samyaza.'

The magnitude of what he was attempting finally hit Gadriel and he backed up a few paces. 'Well, I don't know that I'm quite ready to face the emperor just yet.'

'No pressure.' Sammael grabbed one of Gadriel's arms to drag him to the commander's office. 'If you can't be convincing, he'll just blow us up.'

Bezaliel raised himself to help push Gadriel to his post.

'Armaros?' My stand-in appealed to him to show some mercy.

'You'll have plenty of aid, trust me.'

With the word of the scholar, Gadriel ripped himself away from his escort. 'Back off!' he barked at Bezaliel who flinched again at the sound of his commander's reprimand and Gadriel had a chuckle, feeling more confident. 'Actually, this is kind of fun.' He moved out of the room of his own accord.

In my command office within *Leviathan*, Gadriel took my seat, appearing chuffed and yet awkward about the situation.

'Now no mucking about,' Penemue warned, as he fitted the receiver in Gadriel's ear. 'This is our last chance to escape this universe with our minds intact, so don't blow it for us.'

Normally one would not have to stress the severity of such a situation, but in Gadriel's case I understood Penemue's caution, as our shapeshifter had difficulty being serious at the best of times.

'Everyone is depending on me ... I get it,' he confirmed and then was distracted by his reflection in the blacked-out soft screen in front of him, and started combing his fingers through his hair.

'What are you doing?' Sammael appealed, as he looked on. 'You look like shit, deal with it!'

'He's quite right,' Armaros stepped in to advise my stand-in. 'Leave yourself alone until you are done here, the commander never fusses about his appearance, he doesn't joke, especially where Samyaza is concerned, and that mind-eater is completely emotionless and entirely devoted to the emperor, so show all the respect you can muster.'

'Got it!' Gadriel heeded the instruction from the scholar, who, like Araqiel and Azazèl was unanimously respected by every Grigori.

'Go ahead, Sariel,' Armaros spoke into the comm-link in his hand.

Gadriel nodded and gave two thumbs up. 'Affirmative, we are go.'

Armaros gave a satisfied smile, along with the rest of those in the room. 'Now we wait.' He looked to the window, where the only brilliant light in their universe was growing larger as they neared. 'The emperor will make contact just prior to reaching the gate. Come,' he waved everyone else towards the exit doors, 'we can listen in from the flight deck.'

Sariel was in the tech room by himself to ensure our mental communications were as clear as possible.

'C-c-can you hear me S-S-Sariel?' I tested.

'It was you I heard earlier. I am so annoyed I did not listen.' His eyes remained glued to the soft-light screen in front of him which was monitoring Gadriel in my command room and granted a clear view of the screen in front of Gabriel.

'It w-w-was a lot f-f-for me to exp-p-pect from you.' I wanted to set him at ease. *'Even I w-w-would question a c-c-command c-c-coming from an ent-t-tity I c-could n-not see!'*

'What I wouldn't have given for a little of your talent at that moment, Commander,' he confessed. 'I hope you make it back to us, because we need you.'

'W-w-well I am here, if on-l-l-ly in spirit.'

The door to the tech room vanished and Armaros stepped in to brief us. 'We're good to go. Everything good here?'

'Snug as two bugs in a rug,' Sariel confirmed.

'Then I shall depart —'

As Armaros stepped back into the corridor, the engines cut out and the ship slowed.

'Why are we stopping?'

Sariel pulled up a second soft-light screen, and data was sorted at his mental command, before he concluded. 'The order to shut down did not come from us,' he glanced to the scholar to advise. 'We've been shut down from Tartarus.'

'This could be it then,' Armaros assumed. 'May this all prove serendipitous.' The door closed, and we looked back to Gadriel on the screen, who was squirming about in his chair.

'T-t-tell him to r-r-relax,' I suggested.

'Relax, Commander,' Sariel conveyed through the mouthpiece of the headset he wore. 'This is what we were expecting.'

Gadriel pulled himself together and put on his poker face.

'Just listen to my voice, and act like your only intention is to please Samyaza.' Sariel advised, as the screen before Gadriel was filled with an image of the emperor.

'Azazèl,' the emperor acknowledged to open the transmission.

'My liege,' Gadriel ad-libbed, before I had a chance to advise.

Sariel rolled his eyes, annoyed.

'Is phase one of our plan complete?' Samyaza queried.

'Of course,' Gadriel said to stall for time while he awaited a more detailed response.

'And phase one of our plan was?' The emperor was being cautious before proceeding.

I had been keeping fairly close tabs on what my body had been doing since it had been infected, and at no point had it met with the emperor to discuss splitting this mission into phases. Maybe I was wrong about the emperor requesting we be put in stasis. If all the information required to summon the Fallen into the next universe was programmed into the virus, then perhaps this entire mission had also been programmed in there. That would certainly explain why Samyaza did not question how his instrument planned to pacify the Grigori for this trip — the emperor already knew its intention.

'All the G-G-Grigori are in st-st-stasis and cannot hind-d-der us,' I suggested as a reply.

Gadriel repeated it surely.

'Then go ahead and summon us on board,' he instructed, 'I will see you presently.'

'As you wish, my liege.' Gadriel bowed his head in closing, and when he ventured to look up again the screen was blank. 'Well ...' He hadn't been exposed or blown up, so he considered that mission accomplished. 'That was not *so* bad.'

'You've got to be kidding me,' Sariel removed his headset, and ran his heads through his cropped short hair.

'F-f-fear not,' I encouraged. 'Th-th-there is an adv-v-vantage to be seized f-f-from every adv-v-versity, and I b-b-believe there is one p-p-presenting itself here t-t-too.'

'What the hell?' Sammael and Bezaliel were protesting the emperor's instruction on the flight deck, having seen the transmission.

'We cannot bring them on board! None of us will make it through,' Bezaliel concluded, as Sariel joined them with me in tow.

'What is going to happen if they check and find we are not contained?' Sammael added.

'The mind-eater was bluffing you on that count,' Armaros advised. 'There is no means to monitor the individual modules in cryogen from base, pre the ship docking in Tartarus.'

'The commander would like to say a few words.' Sariel spoke up on my behalf, and everyone hushed and gave him their attention. 'He believes that the mind-eater within his form was pre-programmed with its mission and with all the knowledge required to summon Samyaza and his minions. Fortunately we already know the summons and seals required to accomplish this —'

'But we would never use them!' Sammael objected.

'Not even to save Araqiel?' Sariel posed and Sammael conceded he was wrong.

'How?' he appealed to be enlightened.

'There is only one possible way that summoning the emperor and his minions on board this vessel *before* we pass through the gate could conceivably work without stripping the Elohim of their power or having us all rejected, and that would be if they were dormant and unarmed; then they might go undetected and be smuggled through.'

'You think they intend to have the virus freeze them also?' Armaros concluded.

'Precisely,' Sariel conveyed. 'The plan would be that the virus would awaken them afterwards and leave the Grigori trapped.'

Sammael resented the intent, as did everyone. 'So where does saving Araqiel come into this?'

'If Samyaza and his henchmen are frozen in cryogenics then there will be no one of equal power to stop us retrieving our brother.' Sariel put forward.

'You can't mean to bring them along with us?' Penemue was concerned. 'Surely the creator that Samyaza means to outsmart will not be happy with us for attempting to break his condemned out of prison?'

Sariel observed them, as if they underestimated their commander. 'Did I say we should summon them on board *this* vessel?'

There were raised brows all round as my brothers realised I had other plans.

Sammael and Bezaliel led one team of Grigori to teleport back to Tartarus to another vessel housed in a hangar bay there, which also hosted a cryogenics unit. Each member of the seventy-two strong task force had been assigned one of the Fallen to summon; they all chose a module and drew the insignia of the individual they meant to call forth on the floor within it. These would then be closed and locked off ahead of summoning their target forth into the containment and activating the cryogenic process — effectively trapping the Fallen Elohim whilst the Grigori made a clean getaway.

Once word reached us that the task force were in place and ready to summon their targets, I took a fifty-strong group to seek out our brother held hostage in the emperor's throne room. Among this rescue crew was Armaros, who had a healing touch, for I feared Araqiel's physical and psychic powers might still be sedated. Sariel, Gadriel, Penemue and the other seventy-odd Grigori remained on board our vessel.

The throne room of Tartarus had been abandoned — Araqiel was the sole occupant.

Clearly our brother was still under the influence of the device that had hit him, for his body was a mass of wounds and bruising that had not healed as they should have.

When Araqiel saw his brothers appear he was angered. 'I told you not to come! It is a trap, shield yourselves!'

Round the outer wall of the chamber, small panels slid aside and the emperor's new weapons began firing the large, bladed sedation orbs into the room. Some of the Grigori were not fast enough to employ their psychokinetic defences to deflect the attack, and dropped to the ground, disabled.

'Take up your brothers and leave now!' Araqiel exhorted.

'Not without you.' Armaros and Sacha strode towards their target, whilst the rest of the team gathered around their downed team members to prevent them from further attack and remove the hindering devices. Yet the deflected orbs were drawn back into their weapons and fired again.

'There is no time!' Araqiel stressed. 'This chamber will be filled full of the emperor's latest virus any moment!'

'Leave now!' Sacha called back to the task force. As there would obviously be no Fallen Elohim daring to enter this chamber and oppose them, he grabbed hold of Armaros and used his ability to levitate them up to where Araqiel was bolted and hung on a frame.

As Araqiel opened his mouth to protest their truculence, Armaros told him, 'Save your breath.' He laid his hands on their ailing brother, of the mind to teleport him back to their vessel and finish the healing there.

'What is the hold-up?' Sacha noted the sound of machinery engaging and he guessed it was a prelude to infection.

'That's what I am trying to tell you. I've not just been sedated, my entire genetic code has been downgraded. My spirit is trapped in here.'

'You're mortal!' Sacha was shocked.

'Worse,' he stressed, 'I've been damned, like the Elohim!' Samyaza and his minions could not teleport, or be teleported by the Grigori.

'Can you fix that?' Sacha was beginning to stress also.

'If it's not dead, I can fix it, just give me a moment.'

'I don't think we have that long,' Sacha muttered to himself, as Armaros continued to focus his healing intent on his subject.

A sudden burst of current through the metal frame to which Araqiel was bolted, threw them both backwards and caused their brother to screech in agony. 'GO!' His body reverberated from the current running through it and blood trickled from his mouth, nose, eyes and ears.

Their own psychokinesis shields had protected them from being harmed by the force, but their brother was being fried alive from the inside.

'We're going,' Sacha made the sad call.

'Not yet!' Armaros held his hands together and focused on rousing all his healing powers within them. A ball of energy and light began welling in his hands. He moved them in closer to their brother once again and placing his hands over Araqiel's heart, Armaros' energy ball disappeared inside him.

Araqiel's head flopped forward, and his body fell limp as it began to turn brown and crisp, still jittering from the current running through him.

Sacha was amazed, for Armaros had never used his powers to such an extent before. 'Is he dead?' None of the Grigori had ever been killed before.

'I believe so.' Armaros was traumatised. 'But hopefully he made it to Lux first,' he mumbled, weary from exertion. Armaros was close to passing out himself when a mechanism in the ceiling was heard to click open, and a hissing sound heralded the release of the virus into the chamber.

Sacha was quick to turn his focus and will to returning them to their vessel, and seeing them gone, I turned my intention to reaching Lux.

It was a great relief to see Araqiel in the great light-fields. *'You escaped.'*

'A small mercy.' He waved off his deliverance. *'I must warn you that Samyaza and his primaries plan to stow themselves away on board our vessel!'*

'Calm yourself,' I attempted to allay his panic. *'We foresaw this and are at present summoning them into cryogenics on board another vessel, still in dock in Tartarus.'*

'Did you have the foresight to have their insignia engraved upon the appropriate metals?' he quizzed and I frowned.

'The metals are for the protection of the summoner, to contain the Fallen,' I explained my understanding, *'but we have cryogenic chambers to contain the Fallen in.'*

'The metal also acts as a conduit,' Araqiel argued, *'which has a stronger lure than, say, a drawn insignia might.'*

As I grasped his inference I began to share his panic.

Gadriel was donning a new form now, not mine or his own, but that of the emperor himself. Sariel had put through a transmission request to the space traffic control tower in Tartarus and once given the order to release the ship by the emperor, our vessel began its movement towards the Eternity Gate once more.

'Good job!' Penemue awarded, as Gadriel assumed his own form and admired his reflection in the blacked-out screen before him.

'Ah … much better.' He looked to Penemue. 'Any other fraud you wish to commit today?'

'I think we're good.' He turned to leave the command office as Sariel entered in a panic.

'I've just got word from the commander,' he advised them. 'We need every Grigori on board down to cryogenics, we have a problem.'

Sammael's team each had their hands placed on a different closed module in cryogenics, repeating quietly and intensely the individual summons for the Elohim they were seeking to entrap. They repeated their directive several times over before they realised something was amiss.

'Where the hell are they?' Bezaliel got agitated first. 'They should have been invoked by now!'

'You're right,' Sammael pushed himself away from the module he was focused on, unhinged by their failure to complete this vital part of the mission.

'Maybe they are wise to us?' Bezaliel was more concerned than annoyed now.

'Even if they were, they could not ignore our command to manifest. The only thing that would prevent them attending —' Sammael gasped and gripped Bezaliel's arm in a panic '— is if a stronger channel was drawing them elsewhere!'

'We need to get back to base,' they concluded in unison.

'Cryogenics on the *Leviathan*, now!' Sammael spurred the rest of his task force to take action, and all the Grigori complied with his demand at once.

The scene that awaited the Grigori led by Penemue, Sariel and Gadriel in cryogenics was an ordeal the like of which the Grigori had never before seen. All seventy-two of the highest ranking Fallen Elohim were loose in the chamber, donning not their beauteous forms but the grotesque manifestations they reserved for display before those they wished to terrorise, kill and possess.

Never had the Grigori come up against the emperor and his minions in battle, and this confrontation was unexpected on both sides.

'Unite brothers, shun fear and bring all your p-p-powers to bear,' I advised Sariel, my conviction suppressing my urge to shiver. Our telepath sent out the mental command to his brothers as Samyaza observed the module in which my form was frozen.

Wise to the fact that his plan had gone awry, he turned his displeasure towards the amassing Grigori at the entrance of the chamber. 'This is treason against your emperor!' He pointed one of his clawed digits at my brothers.

'You are the only Satan here, Samyaza!' Sariel echoed my words out loud for all to hear. 'And the time of your reckoning is nigh.'

'Bring it on!' the emperor's right hand, Bael, invited. 'And we'll see who gets damned for all eternity!'

The Grigori sprang into action, and even though we outnumbered the Fallen, our greatest warriors were still absent, and the sheer size of their hideous forms made them difficult to overpower and contain. That was until Sammael arrived and brought his psychokinetic powers to bear on the situation.

'Desist!' He held both his hands out before him to enforce his will and every one of the Fallen froze. He strained against the force of their resistance. 'I won't be able to hold them long!'

'Everyone, find the modules containing seals,' Bezaliel stepped up to instruct the task force. 'Match each of the Fallen to their insignia.'

There were thousands of modules, and only seventy-two seals to find.

'This is really starting to *hurt*!' Sammael warned his brothers.

I too had psychokinesis, but without my vessel to serve as a channel I could not employ that talent.

'Use me, Commander!' Sariel picked up on my thought and appealed. 'Neither my telepathy, not teleportation skill can be of further aid at this point.'

'*What you're s-s-suggesting has n-n-never been at-t-tempted before,*' I advised.

'Isn't discovery the entire purpose of this journey?' Sariel suggested, selflessly.

'I can't hold them —' Sammael's power over the horde loosened and all hell broke loose once more as he dropped like a stone onto the floor, exhausted.

'C-c-coming, ready or not,' I warned Sariel, as I moved my spirit form into alignment with his body, and Sariel's spirit was cast out.

'Welcome to the world of the disembodied,' Araqiel greeted his brother.

'It's rather more peaceful here.' Sariel observed Penemue shove one of the fallen right through his companion, and partially through himself, without disturbance.

'I am finding it rather more pleasant,' Araqiel replied, as they both watched me take Sariel's body racing through the din towards Samyaza and Bael.

The hazy barrier between my spirit body and the physical vanished as I was allied with the frequency of corporeal existence. The chill from the cryogenic state my other body was enduring also vanished, and I felt pleasantly strengthened and relieved. I did not wish to drain myself as Sammael had, and as the Grigori were outnumbering the Fallen three to one now, many were succeeding in containing their targets. I turned my attention to the ringleaders.

'An opportunity to rip your pretty little throat out,' Bael leaned over Sammael, to gloat. 'There is a god!' Wearing his triple form of Elohim-toad-cat, Bael opened wide his jaws to expose his razor-sharp teeth inset in an ugly amphibious face.

Sammael grinned at the threat. 'The creator is on our side.'

Bael reared to attack and froze at my insistence.

Samyaza hadn't been worried when he'd spotted Sariel, our telepathic, coming towards them, for he was no threat in this instance. But seeing Bael constrained, he figured he'd underestimated the proceedings. 'Either you have acquired a new talent, or Azazèl has found his way in there.'

'Order your henchmen into their containment, or I shall have to sever parts to make them fit.' From the authority in my tone the emperor knew who he was addressing.

'You don't have any weapons.' Samyaza knew that for a fact.

174

'I do not need any to make good my threat,' I assured him.

'All right,' he agreed a little too easily for my liking. 'We'll go quietly.' He gave the order for his Fallen to withdraw to their modules, and they complied as we continued to stare each other down. 'Are you going to release Bael?'

I used my psychokinesis to drag the creature away from Sammael and as I let it loose, Bael tumbled to a stop in front of his assigned module. Bael was quick to spring to his feet, and gave a resentful growl in my direction, before complying with the emperor's command. 'I'll see you again.' He assumed his regular appearance and forcing a grin, he entered stasis, and was locked inside and frozen by the closest Grigorian.

'Your turn.' I motioned Samyaza into the module containing his golden cast insignia.

'Nice of you to see me off …' he commented as he resumed his Elohim form and stepped inside. 'Being that you are so pressed for time.' He grinned broadly as the metal shackles secured him in place.

'Well, I know how fond you are of formal farewells,' I replied, unnerved by his grin.

'If you want your own body back, we shall surely meet again,' he said.

'The dark universe will fill with light before I ever let that happen,' I said, as I sealed the module closed, feeling a tremendous amount of satisfaction watching him snap frozen to a statue.

'Thank heavens for that!'

We looked up to see the grotesque three-headed form of Baleth floating overhead and, seeing the resentment on our faces, he urged, 'Don't hurt me!' Gadriel assumed his regular form, and everyone drew a deep sigh of relief as our brother floated down to the floor.

'I was about say,' Bezaliel's frown lifted, 'I've never seen either of the ugly twins levitate!'

'So what do we do with them all now?' Penemue looked to Sariel, as he seemed to have assumed command.

'Best that we return this vessel to base and swap —'

'Ah, *Commander*,' I heard Sariel say, and looked about to note his disembodied spirit shaking its head. '*I think it might be a little late for that. But if you would kindly return my body, I will see what I can do.*'

I nodded to give him leave to boot me out, and before I knew it I was back to being disembodied.

Sariel gave a sigh of relief upon being reunited with his body and then collapsed in a heap, just as Sammael had.

'*Damn, our pilot and our co-pilot down.*' I realised my error. '*I should have thought that through better.*'

'*We've never attempted possessing the body of another before,*' Araqiel stated kindly. '*You could not have foreseen that the feat would drain Sariel to such an extent.*'

'What the hell is going on with you?' Penemue reached down to help Sariel up, but the co-pilot gripped hold of the scholar behind the neck to make him listen.

'Get to the control deck and stop this vessel going through the gate,' he instructed. 'We must not take the emperor and his army through with us!'

In the control room Penemue found Sacha and a very much depleted Armaros both looking perplexed.

'We were wondering where everyone had got to, being that we are about to pass through the gate.' Sacha motioned to the exterior monitor, which was displaying nothing more than a mass of light — the control room window shields had been activated to block out the blinding emanation.

'No, we must not!' Penemue panicked as he ran to the controls, and activated the soft screen to look it over. 'We need to throw the thrusters into reverse!'

'What's this "we" shit?' Sacha objected. 'I don't know how to do that!'

'Well, I don't either.' Penemue eyed over the data laid out before him on the pilot's screen, and the controls on the desk before him. 'But we had better figure it out pretty damn quick!'

'Out of the way!' Sammael demanded as he was carried forth by Gadriel and Bezaliel and dumped in the pilot's seat. Penemue stood aside to watch, so as not to be so ignorant in future.

As the reverse mechanism was locked into place, the ship began to vibrate violently.

'What's happening?' Sacha demanded, his voice wavering with the violent shudders of their craft. 'Are we being destroyed?'

'Goddamn it all!' Sammael shut off the engine entirely, and the violent shaking ceased. 'We're being drawn into the gate, we can't stop it.'

'But we must! We cannot take the Fallen with us!' Penemue voiced my own fears. 'And we cannot teleport them elsewhere, even if we had more time!'

Sammael closed his eyes to focus his psychokinesis on the task, but again the ship began to violently rattle. 'It's beyond my control!' Sammael threw his hands up. 'If we try to resist, this craft will be torn apart! Better to perish in the attempt, than to perish trying to abort.'

Sammael was right, although I was reluctant to concede defeat.

I had failed my brothers; our termination at the hands of the creator for defying his will would be on my head. Even if we did make it through the gate intact, smuggling the greatest evil out of the old universe was also on me. The guilt and remorse devoured my soul as surely as a mind-eater would, and my eyes turned to my brother in spirit form beside me.

'Fear not, my friend,' Araqiel said. *'All is exactly as it should be.'*

'I w-w-wish I could b-b-be as cert-t-tain,' I replied, chilled to the core once again.

'You are,' he concluded. *'You just don't remember … but you will.'*

'You are g-g-guessing again.'

His face lit up with a glowing expression that I had never before witnessed — it was like a grin but more enthused — and just observing it made me feel calmed and pleased. Araqiel was also shaking his head to reject my assumption. *'At the moment of my death, I saw what is to come, and it is breathtaking … beyond anything you can imagine.'*

177

Naturally I wanted to know more about the paradox, but the *Leviathan* entered the Eternity Gate. This was either the beginning of a new life, or the end of a very old one; I willed with all my being for the latter as I was absorbed by the light-field of consciousness eternal.

8

EXTRICATION

Infused with a resonance that I had never thought to feel again, I enjoyed a warmth and peace that I had forgotten I had ever experienced so intimately.

In this, my purest resonance, the guilt of my shortcomings, feelings of isolation, fear, abandonment and repression were burned away. Such inferior concepts and emotions could not stand in the great primordial light of the creator — more revitalising, expansive and magnificent than the light-fields of Lux. It was now clear to me that Lux was just an etheric space between universes — a buffer between one phase of evolution and the next.

As the haze of my ignorance lifted, the great plan unfolded within my consciousness. It was clear that I had accomplished all I had set out to do. When I say 'I', I refer to all the Grigori, for we are one soul-mind sent to save both the collective consciousness of the Fallen Elohim and the soul-mind of humanity; for the Grigori had once been in the unique position of being partial to both.

We were to protect these two diverse energies from one another and aid them to a harmonious understanding across the four universes and the numerous states of consciousness of our Sovereign Integral's design — and there were countless other universal schemes beyond ours, even more splendid and intricate. This feud of opposing energies would play out through the course of our evolution back to source; for in each universe a certain level of conscious understanding had to be reached in order to progress to the next. Only through cooperation could we all return to source, for the harmonic unity of these varying consciousnesses of being would ensure that there was peace in heaven henceforth.

The entity of Azazèl was no more responsible for the escape of the Fallen than for their existence, or the existence of the Grigori, or the mind-eater lying dormant within his form. And yet, as all are one in the greater scheme of things, I was the creator, I was the Satan and was in every way responsible, for in reality there was no self, no I. Everything that had happened had been meant. Although from Azazèl's perspective, I was acting of my own free will, Azazèl had been operating from a limited understanding and despite this obstacle, my true will and purpose had still manifested in accordance with the plan. Only in this place of all-seeing non-judgement was that now apparent.

All the life forms on board the *Leviathan* had a role to play in the evolution of the next universe of light and shadow, cause and effect, and karma. The Sovereign Integral had not turned its back on Samyaza and his company, any more than it would abandon humankind, the Grigori, or any of the other species that had begun their evolution from the depths of the dark universe. Every living being, both conscious and unconscious, were part of the Sovereign Integral and willing participants in the grand scheme of co-creation.

It was known to me that just as the Fallen had been the adversaries of the human species in the last universe, so would they be in the next. And just as the Grigori had inadvertently saved many souls from both these opposing forces in that universe, we would again; but in this instance we must do so with conscious intent. For our Fallen brothers had highly developed mental bodies, but were emotionally barren, hence their puzzlement and lack of patience with the highly sensitive emotional bodies of humankind. We Grigori had developed both these subtle bodies and, working together, these granted us our extraordinary abilities. Our Fallen brethren had the intellect to perfect the physical bodies of humanity to enable them to further develop their mental bodies.

Eventually, humans — through the love and compassion inherent in them — could in turn save their Fallen Elohim oppressors, by aiding development of the emotional bodies they would require to move on in the great evolutionary scheme. We Grigori were to facilitate and mediate this process.

As for the mind-eater and its wealth of destructive knowledge: it was destined to be the great antagonist, for without temptation, without choice, there could be no free will. And without free will there were no means by which to learn the lessons required to evolve and no point to this harmonising exercise. For although Samyaza and his minions were to progress to the next level of consciousness, time in the dark universe operated differently to that above. Time was an illusion — all events in the four universes were playing out at once. Every breakaway consciousness taking part in the scheme was residing within all evolutions and every plane of existence at once.

Thus Samyaza and his minions would always exist in the dark universe to be summoned by the unrighteous, and would continue to weed out those who would willingly follow the opposing cause, and defile the evolution of the creator.

The opposer was most integral in the grand scheme of evolution, for only through an opposing aspect could a whole spectrum of frequencies form in the chasm between darkness and the source of divine light. This awarded the varying forms of consciousness within the scheme the means to learn from a great spectrum of experience and, in turn, go on to instruct others in cosmic law. This was the ultimate mentor system and the cosmic equivalent of reproduction.

The lesson underlying the paradigm that needed to be comprehended was that 'All are One'. Elohim, Grigori, human, animal, vegetable, mineral, molecule — all One and all equally vital to the others. In this moment I grasped that premise fully, for I remembered being at one with all these states of being.

But no sooner had this been made clear to me than my expansive sense of being began to narrow and the haze of my ignorant individualised manifestation closed in on me once again.

The light-field around me exploded with colours, more varied and vibrant than any I had perceived in the dark universe, and this dazzling spectrum wove into a tunnel and drew my consciousness forth.

The speed of my descent was exhilarating and awe inspiring, yet my growing amnesia was anything but. By the time the gamut of colour again fused into white light, I had completely forgotten my knowledge of the plan, but at the same time I had a sense that I was exactly where I needed to be.

My spirit attuned to a frequency that was in resonance with it and I came to focus on something that was a great wonder to behold.

It was a pillar, not of stone, or metal, or mineral, but of illumined mist that swirled from its base and around an invisible pole up its centre, then spread out to support a ceiling that was equally intangible and light-filled. This organic column was one of many in this grand ethereal chamber. I was hesitant to look down, but in so doing I was pleased to find a polished marble floor that appeared as solid as I did.

Welcome back, Azazèl.

There was a being addressing me who appeared not unlike my vision of future humanity, but this human was not shapely and comely as the paragon had been, but more like one of the Grigori, only smaller in stature. His eyes were more slanted than any Azazèl had seen before, and the armour he wore appeared soft and flowing.

'Are you Grigori?' I ventured to ask.

Sometimes, he replied, serving me the same pleasing grin as Araqiel had right before we entered the Eternity Gate. *It's called a smile, you should try it, feels good,* he advised, without a word leaving his mouth.

'Are we —'

Conversing telepathically? Yes, he confirmed.

'But I am not telepathic.'

You are here.

'And where is — Sorry.' I ceased moving my mouth. *Where is here?*

The antechamber of the Great Council of the Watchers, he said.

So you are a Watcher? I assumed, having no memory of this place.

He nodded. *Sometimes.*

Then what are you the rest of the time?

Everything else. He grinned.

I was just about to ask what I was doing here, when he motioned me to a corridor.

Right this way. He moved off, urging me to accompany him.

Where are the rest of the Grigori? Why am I the only one here?

Again he urged me to move with him. *You and your brothers are one, and you speak on behalf of the whole at this council. So in spirit your brothers are with you now, but in form they are still passing through the Eternity Gate.*

Even Araqiel?

No.

I was concerned about his omission, but my guide spoke up before I could protest.

He has chosen a different path to the rest of the Grigori.

How so? Why? Araqiel was the brother I relied on most heavily for guidance.

Oh, don't worry, he will still serve as a guide to you.

I was not reassured. *Why should I trust your word on that?*

Because he is me. The being transformed into Araqiel, although I thought he looked rather ridiculous wearing the flimsy robes the human had been attired in.

My expression clearly conveyed my shock, awe and doubt.

Believe it, my friend, he read my thoughts again. *I have lived through countless lifetimes, species, and states of consciousness in this universe to be here to greet you today, but here I am. And if I can do that, so can you all. For I have laid the pathway for you.*

How is that possible? I was struggling to absorb his claim.

Causality, he concluded, knowing I had no idea what he was talking about.

Beyond the dark universe, the principles that govern existence are very different and full of infinite possibility. You have to open your mind now, Grigori, for whatever you imagine, for better or worse, you can make manifest. Like attracts like to your cause, which influences the ongoing effect that your desires have on creation. And as your stay in this universe will be a rather extended one, you'd best learn to create wisely.

We did not create so wisely in the dark universe, I conceded.

That was your induction to cause and effect, he granted, transforming back into his more human appearance. *And although the cause was rather drastic, it encouraged you to question your belief system and spurred you to push boundaries you never would have had your brothers not been in such peril.*

Are you saying I might not have attempted breaching the Gate, had I only been acting on my own behalf? I considered this and found it more than likely I might have given up; in truth, without the aid of my brothers I would have succumbed to a mind-eater or been lost in Lux.

In the lower universes of the scheme, it would be difficult to learn compassion if there was no other being to empathise with, he concluded. *Hence individualisation! But this principle has an additional polarising aspect in this universe and the one beyond, of which the mere glimpse inspired your epiphany to break loose from the Satan's regime.*

The paragon! The mere thought of that vision excited my entire being.

The polarising principle of man … woman, he outlined, as we came to a large set of doors that, akin to the light-filled walls, were opaque with sparkling mist. *But you shall learn about her presently. Go right on through.*

Who has summoned me here? I queried the purpose of this.

An old friend, he replied.

A watcher? I assumed.

The Watcher, so far as this evolution is concerned.

From this response, I could safely assume I was meeting someone of great importance to the scheme.

We are all important, my guide corrected. *We are all one. Separateness is an illusion, therefore hierarchy, status and authority are nothing more than another point of view.*

I struggled with that premise, as I did with his earlier comment that my brothers were one in spirit with me now, but I feared trying my host's patience with my ignorance. *Well, I thank you* — then realised I had not asked, *By what name do you go now?*

In this guise ... I am most simply known as DK. He bowed his head in greeting and motioned me to the glowing barrier, and again I hesitated.

So why did you choose another path to your Grigori brothers?

Well, we couldn't allow the Fallen Elohim to incarnate into this universe without any emotional understanding or supervision, so I volunteered to lend my essence to their soul-group in order to aid their evolution, and by way of that contribution I also became embroiled in human evolution. He referred to the body he was wearing, and he sensed how perplexed I was by this. *Fear not, I will rejoin the Grigori in the next universe, and we will have many associations in this one. In a parallel perspective of this instance it is you who volunteered to join with the Fallen, for we are all one.*

My mind full of confusion and questions, I merely nodded to confirm that I trusted his word. *Until next we meet then.*

Be at peace, he granted with a smile, so I returned the gesture and found that he had been correct; it was an enjoyable end to our exchange.

I moved through the hazy barrier into a much larger chamber with rounded walls that undulated with light bubbles containing images, constantly bursting forth and then vanishing again. The room was not silent, but had a constant sonic vibration that was very peaceful until you focused on the consciousness bubbles on the wall. Shifting my awareness between these it became obvious that these were appeals for help from all the beings within this scheme. The emotional force that accompanied their stories of heartbreak or appeals for help and guidance were overwhelming to my sensibilities, and so I ceased to focus on the wall.

*

There were beings that appeared to be of the Grigori–Elohim species patrolling the walls, taking in the information being fed to them. In the centre of the room sat one of us, seated with legs crossed, hands pressing together and his eyes closed. This splendid being seemed both blissfully oblivious and completely connected to everything going on around him, for there were energy streams linking him with all the Watchers in the chamber. Even in this brilliant place of light and vivid colour, this being glowed brighter than anything in his presence, just as the human who'd changed the course of my life had a luminescence that was not indicative of any other being in the dark universe.

Your instincts serve you well, Azazèl. His form appeared as solid as mine, but from this form a spirit being emerged to talk with me, leaving his solid body to engage with the Watchers.

You are the human that I beheaded? I dropped to my knees to beg forgiveness.

As I told you at the time, it was my time to be liberated, and your time to liberate me, he said kindly. *I remember being where you are now, on the precipice of the unknown, excited and yet uncertain of the path I had chosen for myself and my brothers.*

Yes. I empathised with his words completely.

But in truth, every one of your brothers faces me now thinking he is the only one deciding the course of the fate of the Grigori, do you see? he asked.

Not as fully as you. But I nodded as I grasped the idea.

I hope it brings you comfort to know that one day you will be me, greeting you, and you will understand, as I do, that you have achieved all you were meant to, in order to advance consciousness beyond these frequencies to those higher.

It was overwhelming to observe this magnificent manifestation that I was to be, and I boggled at the work that would be required to bridge the gaping chasm of knowledge, experience and awareness between us. *We are to decide the course and fate of the Grigori now.*

He nodded, and made a rising gesture with his hand, whereupon I found myself standing once more, through no effort of my own. *The Grigori have been blessed with the ability to maintain their memories between one universe and the next,* he stated. *Some of you will prove more talented in that respect than others. But due to the nature of free will, none of you will remember far past this point of our conversation.*

But if we cannot remember the plan, how can we be sure it will be carried out? I appealed, wanting to serve the Logos to the best of my ability.

There is no danger of that. For even if free will were to take you off course, circumstances would repeat until you eventually realise your true path. Myself and my Watchers, he motioned to his assistants around the periphery of the room, *will see to that.*

But there appears to be so much going on, how do you keep track of everything? I didn't wish to sound doubtful but the fact was hard to fathom.

One incarnation at a time, he advised. *For they are all different aspects of me, and therefore you.*

It was mystifying to consider, and my frown betrayed my difficulty in comprehending.

Separately ... The being motioned around him, whereupon all the appeals coming through the walls of the chamber merged into a crescendo of noise, which he then silenced with a wave of his hand ... *chaos,* he concluded. *But that pleasing sonic you hear reverberating through this chamber?*

Yes, I confirmed that I had noted it.

That is the goal. He referred to his body meditating in the middle of the room. *It is the sound of the perfect unity of you-in-verse.*

All the Grigori emerged from their trance state at once and looked about to get their bearings.

'All systems are functioning normally.' Sammael's first concern was for our vessel. 'And we do not appear to have lost power in transit.'

'Is everyone unscathed?' Armaros' concern lay with his brothers, and they confirmed one by one that this was the case.

'In fact, I feel better now than I did before we entered the gate.' Sammael noted that his vitality and reflexes had returned.

'Oddly, I do too,' Armaros related, having been sucked dry of energy prior to entering the Eternity Gate also.

It was at this point I realised that I was no longer feeling the deep chill my body was experiencing, and although this was a relief, it was also a concern — had I died in cryogenics?

'Does anyone have memories of events transpiring within our passage?' Armaros queried his brothers.

'I recall speaking with Araqiel,' Penemue recalled. 'Only he was part human?'

'Aye,' many others confirmed what I too remembered; the claim of the Logos — that all my brothers were one with me during our transit — was correct.

'Holy shit!' Sammael noted that his monitor was displaying images of what was in front of our craft, then instructed the front shield screens to open, so that everyone could see what he was looking at. Forced to shield their eyes at first, the Grigori activated their helmets and eye shades, to perceive a huge armada of spacecraft confronting them at a distance. But in wondrous contrast to the ominous force was the nebula of brightly coloured gases, and billions of various specks of light, that extended beyond the beautiful amorphous formation around them.

'It's fantastic ...' Armaros expressed the wonderment everyone felt as he retracted his eye-shade and helmet to discover he could see through the glare. 'It's all right, your eyes will adjust,' he advised his brothers, who retracted their eye protection also — all except Bezaliel.

'It's all right! Have you lost your mind? We need to get the hell out of here!' Bezaliel did not sound optimistic about the large greeting party.

'Is the commander still with us, do you think?' Sammael looked to Armaros who shrugged — having no idea I was standing right beside him.

'We need Sariel,' we both decided at once.

'He is still down in cryogenics, most likely,' Armaros added.

The door to the control deck opened, and Sariel entered with another throng of our brothers and, although our telepath appeared much recovered, his expression was disturbing. 'Samyaza and his minions have vanished!'

'What!' Everyone objected to the report at once.

'The only person still in cryogenics is the commander,' he clarified.

'I am here, Sariel,' I advised him, and his eyes widened in recognition of my words. *'Are you quite certain the Fallen have gone?'*

'They cannot have just vanished!' Sacha objected at the same time.

'If you don't believe us,' he motioned to the many Grigori who had entered with him, 'feel free to check for yourselves.'

'He speaks the truth,' Gadriel confirmed, 'we checked every module in cryo!'

'Are the chambers that they occupied still activated?' Armaros sought to assess the escape probability.

'Every one of them is still locked and activated,' Sariel told us. 'The metal plates of summons and constraint are still in place.'

That was a worry — no one in this universe must see those seals, they had to be destroyed.

'They cannot have escaped on their own,' I quietly advised Sariel. *'In such a state, they could not even respond to a summons.'*

'Never mind about the Fallen, what do we do about this lot?' Sammael motioned out the front screen windows.

'Hush a moment,' Sariel requested. 'The commander is here and considering the situation.'

The news was met with a great sigh of relief from all, and although I was warmed to be so appreciated, I was no more qualified to deal with this situation than they were.

'Sammael,' Sariel responded to my advice and moved to relay my instructions to him. 'Get down to cryogenics and ensure every one of those seals is destroyed.'

'What shall I do with them?' he queried. 'I can't just make them vanish, I have to send them somewhere, and I don't know of anywhere in the universe to send them.'

'Then send them back whence they came,' Sariel relayed. 'And if that doesn't work, melt them beyond recognition.'

'As you say, Commander.' Sammael vanished to see it done, and Sariel took his place in the control seat to activate our communication receivers, instructing the ship to search all frequencies for transmissions.

'Does the commander think they are friendly?' Armaros queried Sariel's actions.

'The commander believes that we are here by the grace of the Logos, whom we met within the gate.' Sariel replied on my behalf. 'If we are here, there is a good reason ... best find out what that is.' He brought up the screen of our radar tracking system to check the distance between us and the armada before us. 'Oh, damn!' He raised his sights to the ceiling. 'There is something very large directly above us.'

The larger craft cast a shadow as we were drawn inside it.

'Looks like we are going to find out sooner than expected,' Armaros speculated.

A large beam of light erupted in the vacant area between the flight deck and the shield window, and then a being took form inside the tube of light. For a moment the curvy shape of the manifestation led me to believe it was my paragon materialising, but when the light-tube retracted, it was clearly not the same entity I had seen in my vision and quite possibly not human either.

This being's shapely form was much more elongated than DK's human form, and it had larger almond-shaped eyes that were a vibrant shade of blue. The other features of its face were petite, although its tiny mouth had lips that were large and luscious. Its skin was milky white, and its hair of ash brown fell in long loose locks about its poised shapely form that was slender at the waist, and equal to the Grigori in height. But the greatest disparity between its form and our own was the abnormal size of its chest. Its attire was also flimsy of texture, similar to the attire worn in the Council of the Watchers, and not warlike, as ours must have appeared.

190

'Welcome, travellers through the Gate of Ummu-Huber.' It stood boldly before us, alone and fearless. 'I am Nanshe, grandchild of the great Anu, who has been expecting you.'

It was stunning to hear the telepathic missive so clearly, but not so surprising that the Grigori understood it; clearly our talent for interpreting dialects and languages extended beyond those developed in the dark universe. In fact, the dialect was rather reminiscent of the Fallen Elohim; I deeply hoped that was just a cosmic coincidence.

'You knew we were coming?' I requested Sariel to ask, but the being responded, having heard my query.

'Of course the great mother is aware of who passes through her gate. Although you are the first physical manifestations to enter our universe thus in living memory.' The being looked about, no doubt wondering which one of us she was addressing — she may have been telepathic but she did not have celestial vision.

At that moment, Sammael reappeared and, spotting our visitor, he retracted his eye-shades to take a better look. 'Hello.' He grinned, liking the look of her, just as every Grigori present seemed to.

'Hello,' she replied, swaying her body to and fro in a welcoming manner. 'Who, might I ask, is your leader?'

'Um,' he was naturally a little vague about it.

With myself and Araqiel absent, all eyes shifted to Armaros, who swallowed hard and looked to Sariel — as he was my telepathic link.

Yes, I bethought Sariel; Armaros was a good choice.

When Sariel nodded, Armaros looked to our guest and held up a finger to volunteer himself. 'I am in charge.'

'Then Anu asks that you accompany me to him,' she requested, politely.

'As you wish, but I would like my second-in-command to accompany us also.' He motioned to Sariel who stood and bowed in introduction.

'Sariel, and Armaros,' he motioned to himself and his brother in turn, 'at your service, Nanshe.'

'*Splendid!*' She smiled. '*I can transfer you to our craft, or if you can make your own way,*' her eyes glanced back to Sammael, who had just materialised out of nowhere, '*you may follow me of your own accord.*'

'*Lead the way, Nanshe,*' Sariel prompted.

'*We are not a patient people,*' she advised.

'*We shall be right behind you,*' Armaros assured. '*The rest of my brothers will remain here and wait for my word.*'

'*That would be advisable.*' She vanished from our midst.

'Did you see the chest on that thing?' Sammael was stunned. 'I would have thought it very strong, but for those tiny little arms! What is with that?'

His brothers were equally perplexed.

'Hey, maybe I should come with you?' Sammael proffered, for no other reason than he was curious.

'*A very bad idea,*' I commented to Sariel. Sammael was anything but diplomatic.

'You shall stay put as we promised,' Sariel passed on my command. 'We shall return presently.'

'And if you don't return?' Sammael queried.

'Then ask Penemue what to do, as he's in charge.' Sariel passed on my instruction.

Penemue appeared both flattered and put out by the appointment, as I followed Sariel and Armaros to their rendezvous.

Along with Sariel and Armaros, I projected myself after our guide and came to a standstill in a large metal chamber in time to see the teleportation beam retract from around our chaperone. It made me wonder whether this being could teleport on its own. Or perhaps the beam was a means for teleporting somewhere unknown to the traveller? This chamber contained several archways around it, some of which had doors within them. Others appeared to be mirrors at first glance — until one began rippling like water and glowing.

'*Liquid light,*' our guide explained as she moved towards the illumined passageway. '*It is very conductive.*'

'Anu is not on board?'

'Anu is not on board?' Sariel repeated the question on my behalf.

'No, grandfather hates space travel.' She frowned curiously. 'Odd that the voice in your head sounds so very different to your own and that you rehearse every word before you verbalise it.'

'A bad habit,' I responded on Sariel's behalf.

'Sorry,' he said out loud.

Our guide smiled, seemingly not entirely satisfied with our response. 'Shall we go, or would you like to debate the issue with your inner voice?'

'We are good,' we replied at once and our comely escort rolled her eyes and walked straight into an undulating light barrier.

Armaros looked at Sariel, tempted to roll his eyes also. 'Could you two be any more suspicious? If all our hosts are telepathic they are going to think you are possessed!'

'Tell him I'll shut up.'

'I'll shut up,' Sariel repeated. 'The commander, I mean,' he attempted to clarify. 'That is … he'll shut up, not I will shut him up —'

'It might be best if you both shut up,' Armaros suggested. 'No offence,' he added, and looked to the ominous porthole.

'Are you coming?' Our guide stuck her head back through the porthole to encourage us. 'It is perfectly safe, I assure you.'

Upon passing through the barrier there was a flash — reminiscent of moving through Lux when teleporting — and on the other side we found ourselves in an identical chamber to the one we had just left.

'That was exhilarating,' Armaros commented, noting he was not moist at all. 'Where did that quantum step just take us?'

'From one galaxy to another,' Nanshe replied with a grin. 'Welcome to Nibiru.'

*

'Impressive.' Sariel took a closer look at the barrier that had dulled and become perfectly still and smooth once more — as a technologist he was curious about the mechanism.

'Now your inner voice sounds like you,' Nanshe noted, her eyes searching elsewhere to make it known to me that she was aware of an additional presence. 'This way.' She led us towards a doorway this time, and it opened into a long, very grand and entirely white corridor — white walls, polished marble floor and high curved ceiling were complemented by long windows high above that allowed light to pour in. I had never seen so much white and light on the physical plane before. The walls were decorated with colourful images — many of the colours the Grigori had never seen and could not name, but it was breathtaking to behold.

'My goodness!' Armaros uttered as he trailed our escort, wanting to stop and inspect the artwork more closely. 'I am liking this universe very much so far.'

'Me too,' Sariel concurred, although his eyes were on the shapely form of the guide in front of him.

At the end of the corridor there was a large archway, through which exited more of the same shapely beings. One appeared very similar to Nanshe in age, dress and colouring, although the hair was slightly darker and straight.

'Nidaba,' our guide acknowledged, with a bow of her head — a gesture that Nidaba returned, ahead of giving the Grigori the once-over with her eyes.

With Nidaba was another who was adorned in black; its face and hair masked by a long black veil that fell to the waist.

'Ereshkigal,' Nanshe acknowledged the black one also.

Nidaba was gripping the hand of a little one who was not so shapely as its companions — perhaps a juvenile of the species as it was not acknowledged by our guide. But as we passed, the little one tugged at Nidaba's arm to question. 'Are they men or women?'

'Neither,' Nidaba responded discreetly, although I slowed to hear the rest of their conversation as the mention of the word 'women' captured my curiosity.

'*But they are so pretty!*' The youngster let go of Nidaba's hand to press her own together and plead. '*Can I have one? Please!*'

'*Inanna?*' Nidaba sounded shocked. '*They are not animals, they are guests of Tiamat!*'

'*But they look human!*' The little one gasped, as her hand was grabbed up once more and she was hauled away, her attention still on my companions. '*Father says Tiamat is a fable.*'

This dialogue was perplexing — were humans still considered animals here? And who was Tiamat?

Ereshkigal hadn't looked sideways when passing Armaros and Sariel, but the one in black appeared to spot me, for its focus remained with me until it had passed.

Had it seen me? It certainly seemed so. Still, as my brothers were nearing the archway at the end of this corridor, I projected myself quickly in their direction.

This chamber was a throne room, redolent of the council chamber of the Watchers. It wasn't round, more octagonal in shape, and six of the eight walls were large screens displaying images of vastly different worlds. On another of the walls was the archway through which we entered, and in the last wall opposite was an archway that opened to the outdoors and a sparkling golden sky beyond. In the centre of the room was a grand golden throne, which rotated around to face us. The being seated thereon was not shapely like our guide but had more of a Grigori physique, yet the features of its face were more akin to its grandchild.

'*Here you are, finally!*' it said, stroking a small creature that sat upon its lap, which had four limbs like a cat, the wings, feathers and beak of a bird and the tail of a lizard.

'*My apologies, grandfather,*' Nanshe knelt before the throne. '*I had a little trouble getting them through the portal.*'

'*Haha!*' The leader was inwardly amused and appeared to be very excited. '*I regret the extreme passage, but I don't like to leave my Worlds Chamber as my grandchildren have put us in a spot of bother of late so I dare not leave them unsupervised.*' He sounded less pleased as his eyes fell back on Nanshe.

'*Mighty Anu,*' our escort appealed the accusation, '*I have not offended Abzu.*'

'*You would be one of few who have not,*' Anu granted. '*You may leave us.*'

Nanshe seemed most put out, but she rose, turned and departed, and large doors appeared in her wake.

'I welcome you, Sariel, Armaros …' Anu spoke out loud, rose, placed the pet aside and descended the stairs to greet us — which seemed oddly informal. 'And you too, Azazèl.'

We were taken back by the leader's knowledge and psychic sensibilities.

'*You can see me?*' I queried. '*How could you know us all?*'

'I cannot see you, but I know you are here. And more importantly I know *why* you are here,' Anu advised. 'For you are the great watchers and teachers of humanity and my Grigori brothers.'

'Araqiel?' Armaros guessed first.

'Yes,' Anu nodded, 'at one time.'

'But the last time we saw you, you were a human who went by the name of DK?' Sariel was stunned, and Anu was perplexed by the claim.

'I have no memory of being human.' He did not dwell on the premise, which did not seem entirely inviting. 'A future venture, perhaps?'

'What species are you now?' Armaros probed, as the scholar in him was curious.

'We are known as the Nefilim,' he replied, 'and I am the eldest male of the species.'

His confession triggered memories of what DK had told me. *It is within the Nefilim race that the souls of the Fallen Elohim are evolving.*

My claim brought a gasp of concern from my brothers, as they realised my conclusion was elementary.

'Evolving is not the term I would use to describe what most of those souls are doing in this incarnation.' The tone was disillusioned. 'Unlike us, they remember nothing of their past in the dark universe, but the self-serving instinct is still inherent in them, hence your assignment to protect humanity from their callous desires.'

'*But the entire reason you volunteered to incarnate with them was to provide them with the basis of an emotional body!*' I wondered what had gone awry.

'Oh, they have an emotional body,' Anu granted, 'but most have not even begun to develop them yet, despite my efforts to teach them the virtues of compassion and nurture. But they cannot even apply these principles to each other, let alone with those of other species! It is planned that the humans you will nurture will inspire the emotional evolution of the Nefilim.'

'Are humans failing in this?' Armaros queried.

Anu had lost his cheer, and frowning, he looked at Armaros to reply: 'Unfortunately, all the humans we have discovered, bred or engineered, are still as thick as two bricks.' The ruler's mood lightened once again. 'Which is why I am so pleased to see you, my learned brothers, who have come to instruct and guide these hapless beings.'

'What is that?' Armaros was distracted by the huge ball of red light hanging low on the golden horizon out through the doors.

'That is a dying star known as Anu,' the ruler advised, escorting us out onto the balcony where we could view the event better. 'Of course you have never seen a sunset, have you, my brothers?'

The horizon had so much depth due to the smattering of lights that had begun to appear beyond the golden glow that seemed to surround the entire planet. It was drenched with long streaks of colours that were so vibrant they pained my eyes with their delightful brilliance.

'*Were you named after this star?*' I wondered.

'Actually, it was the other way around,' Anu informed.

'*The dying celestial body was named after you?*' I thought this almost cruel.

'Well I have been the ruler here for a very long time, and so our entire solar system has become associated with me.'

'There is so much to learn about.' Armaros was wide-eyed with wonder.

'I can hear the questions lining up in your mind,' Anu advised, jovially, as his pet flew out through the door and landed on the ruler's shoulder.

197

'What is that?' Armaros' attention was ripped from the view by the animal that had a frightful screech.

'This is a sirrush,' Anu patted the creature's head fondly. 'One of the sweeter new breeds to be created by Ninharsag and the mighty Tiamat. I much prefer the company of animals, they understand how to give selflessly so much better than my offspring. You can pat it if you like, it won't harm you.'

Armaros was pleased to do so, admiring the various colours of it.

Who is Tiamat? I queried, as it had earlier been claimed we were guests of this entity.

'She is the Umma-Huber who forms all things.'

I would have queried this response, but Armaros, who could not hear me, cut in.

'What is this colour?' The scholar pointed to a patch on the creature, noting the same colour was streaking across the sky.

'That is orange,' Anu informed.

'Orange,' Armaros repeated the strange word and smiled. 'I like this, I should like to be as colourful as this bird.'

Anu gave a chuckle as he looked Sariel and Armaros over. 'You Grigori are looking a little grey.'

He referred not only to our dress but to our skin tone, which appeared bluish-grey next to Anu who was whitish-pink.

'But when you come from a universe of darkness, there is not much need for colour. We shall get you attired to suit your new environment,' Anu assured Armaros and then looked to Sariel. 'And answer your queries —'

'Not the very least of which would be women,' Sariel suggested.

'Ah, yes, the split soul principle is top of the list, most certainly,' Anu granted.

There is an issue of even greater import that we must discuss, I put forward.

Anu nodded, understanding my concern. 'The virus you are carrying. I have had Ninharsag working on that little problem, and we have the means to remove it from your body and restore you to good health. I shall arrange to have the module containing your form brought through the portal and taken to the laboratories of Ninharsag at once.'

'*And what shall become of the mind-eater once it is removed?*' This was my major concern. '*I would rather carry the virus than allow it to escape! It must be neutralised.*'

Anu frowned, clearly wanting to allay my fears, but he could not in all honesty do so. 'My dear brother, civilisation was not built in a day, such things take time. There is nothing like this virus in existence and we'll need to analyse it before we can say, with any surety, if it can be eradicated.'

This was not what I wished to hear, but I did not want to seem ungrateful. '*I trust your judgement as always,*' I allowed.

The leader smiled, well pleased. 'If only my offspring awarded me the same respect as you do,' he sighed, regretful, before his spirits took an upswing. 'It has been an age since I have been graced with truly wise and empathetic company. It is pure joy to me.'

'We are glad to be reunited with you also, Araqiel,' Armaros assured him.

'Come,' Anu suggested, as the globe sank beneath the horizon and the world dimmed into many sparkling lights, both in the sky beyond the gold shield of the planet, and the sprawling city beneath it. 'We must see to retrieving the rest of the Grigori, and the body of the commander. Once Azazèl is back with us, we shall celebrate!'

'Celebrate?' Armaros queried, as the Grigori didn't know the meaning of the word.

Anu considered this. 'It is when comrades gather in acknowledgement of a significant event, to share stories and information, accompanied by entertainment and activities that are mutually pleasurable.'

'Entertainment?' Armaros probed.

'It's very colourful,' Anu proffered, eager to get on. 'You shall like it it, I promise.'

Armaros was appeased, and accompanied Anu and his sirrush back into the throne room.

'It appears you have delivered us to a far better existence, Commander,' Sariel awarded. 'I, for one, shall be happy to follow you wherever the road leads from here.'

'I think it might be best to reserve judgement until we have seen a little more.' As always, I was circumspect.

Sariel, however, was sold on this place. 'Just to be living in the light is a gift worth any toll that could be asked of us. You cannot yet feel the pleasure and warmth of the natural light here, but when you do, we shall be in accord on this matter,' he warranted, before heading into the Worlds Chamber.

As I lingered to admire the view, I had to admit I envied my brother's experience of this new environment; perhaps my separateness was affecting my judgement in this matter and my view would alter once my spirit and body were again conjoined?

The laboratories of Ninharsag were the hive of genetic endeavour on Nibiru. There were all manner of beings, animals, humans and many creatures in between. Some specimens were living in cages and incubators, some were gestating in vitro. Other, deceased experiments, were floating in tubes filled with preservation liquid. Many of these genetic creations appeared to have gone horribly wrong, and I was not feeling entirely confident that I was in good hands.

Armaros had made it his personal mission to watch over my body, although being diplomatic, he'd not mentioned as much to our hosts. He had volunteered to go to the labs so that he could be used as a target when Sammael used his psychokinesis to teleport the module containing my body to the labs in question.

The look on my brother's face when he was led by Enki through the storehouse and gestation rooms to the laboratories proper, told me that we were in accord in feeling uneasy about being there.

Enki was the prized son of Anu, as he was intelligent and more compassionate in nature than any of the other Nefilim. He appeared much younger than his father; where Anu's hair was white as snow and long, Enki's hair was trimmed short and a shade of light golden brown. But his eyes, like his father's, were of the deepest shade of blue. Enki had fathered many of the Nefilim including Nanshe, but to date his seed had only produced daughters. Upon Anu's request, Enki had explained the male and female split soul principle of this universe to the Grigori. The females of the species carried the genetic code and thus were prized for their breeding capability. Yet as the men were generally the stronger of the two sexes, they were prized for their ability to defend, preserve and build upon the legacies of their fathers, from whom they inherited titles and estates. Thus, the Lord Enki very much wanted a son to continue his legacy.

'Fashioning the perfect species is a trial and error affair,' Enki explained the macabre storehouse that led through to the laboratories. 'The fate of your commander will not be so dire. We've had many success stories too.'

Upon entering the gestation chamber, Armaros encountered beings that were in the in vitro stage of the program, and were hung in rows inside transparent sacs of fluid. Armaros stopped before a row of what appeared to be several humans in varying stages of development from embryo to adult, but they seemed to be neither male nor female. 'They are not created male and female as the Nefilim are?' The skin of these humans was much darker.

'They have the potential to be be split into sexes but the Pantheon don't want them breeding by themselves.' The Pantheon was the Nefilim's governing body, comprised of twelve of the Nefilim's most elite and powerful royals. Anu chaired this council, but the majority ruled, and unfortunately the majority of the Nefilim were self-serving individuals, with their own agendas. 'The low intellect of the human psyche on the whole means that these beings have a learning capability that is the equivalent, or less than, most of the animal kingdom,' Enki advised. 'I have tried to instruct some in higher learning, but I have had more success teaching Anu's sirrush.' The lord seemed very disheartened by the fact. 'As I have had no sons of my own, I had hoped to fashion a male heir from humanity who could inherit my property and title, but despite our efforts to combine Nefilim and human genetic material to produce such a creature, we have yet to be successful.'

The creations in cages that were within the lab were even more alarming to Armaros, being that they were conscious. There was one large lizard man that sat motionless and staring at my brother.

'Is that human?' he asked Enki.

'Heavens, no! Its genetics are so different to human that we discovered they are impossible to blend,' Enki advised. 'Unfortunately, it would rather eat humans than be one.'

'Why would you even attempt such a mix?' Armaros was repulsed, as was I. For I had seen the future of humanity and that creature looked nothing like it.

'For the intellect!' Enki tapped his head. 'These reptilians are very smart, but entirely emotionless. Unfortunately, they have a hive-mind, which is not what we desire for humanity. We've tried everything to improve humanity's capacity to think for itself, but so far ...' The lord shook his head. 'Ninharsag has suggested to the pantheon that the only way we might achieve this is to infuse more Nefilim genes into humans, but many in the pantheon are opposed to the suggestion, lest humanity becomes too smart and thus a threat.'

'But why are the Nefilim so concerned with developing humanity?'

'Because of all the species in the known universe, the human genetic code is the closest to our own. Although the Nefilim are very powerful and hold dominion over many planets, we are not prolific breeders, nor do we make good subordinates, and thus we are short on labour. What humans lack in brain, they make up for in brawn, which makes them a perfect workforce.'

'Slaves,' Armaros concluded; the Grigori didn't keep servants like the Fallen had done, but it appeared that in this universe, things hadn't changed so much.

'When they are so dependent on us to tell them what to do, what else can they be?' Enki reasoned, and Armaros could not argue. 'Some of the more beautiful humans are kept as pets, but until humanity sees a rise in intellect, they cannot rise in status.'

Armaros was taken back when he spied the tiny grey beings with large heads and faces that were nearly all eyes — black as the universe he'd come from — taking samples from creatures and using hand-held machines to analyse data.

'Zeta Reticuli,' Enki explained. 'Unlike you or I, when they are close together they form a hive-mind, like the reptilians do, hence their ability to work in perfect synchronicity. Intelligent to a fault, their lack of emotional sensitivity and their thirst for knowledge saw their home planet destroyed. Now the more accommodating of them work for us.'

Armaros followed Enki past where the Zeta were working, and as soon as he took his eyes off them, one of them jabbed my brother with a needle.

'Hey!' Armaros objected, and that's when Ninharsag looked up from the creature she was dissecting.

After Enki's brief, it was now apparent to me that Ninharsag was a female of the Nefilim species, one of the few, along with Enki, that Anu was proud to have fathered. Unlike many of her kind, who were white of hair, and blue of eye, her hair was as black as my own and her eyes were a deep green. She was tall and skinny, and her attire was dark green and black and more akin to the way that the men dressed.

'Zeta!' Ninharsag slowly shook her head once and pointed to Armaros. 'Not a subject.'

The Zeta looked to each other, shrugging, nodding and shaking their heads, obviously telepathically debating the issue amongst themselves.

'They like to take genetic samples of everything,' she explained, and looking Armaros over she appeared very interested herself. 'And you are certainly a curiosity, being that you are reportedly from another universe entirely.'

'Anu said you were expecting us,' Armaros replied politely, and Ninharsag removed her hands from the gloves that extended inside the module in which her subject was enclosed, and walked around Armaros, inspecting him.

'You appear neither male or female ... how do you reproduce?' Armaros was a little affronted by the query. 'We don't.'

'I could reproduce you,' she boasted.

'I'm happy with one of me,' he rejected the notion.

'She's only toying with you,' Enki advised Armaros so that he might feel less intimidated, '*aren't* you, dear sister?'

Ninharsag looked to her brother, eyebrows raised in speculation. 'Of course.' Her words seemed to contradict her expression. 'So where is the diseased one?'

'My colleague will be here with him —'

Sammael manifested toting the large module right on cue.

'— Presently,' Armaros concluded, rather pleased to see his brother.

'Where would you like it?' Sammael floated it up into the air.

Ninharsag had a glint in her eye as she noted Sammael's talent. 'Right in here.' She led them to a passageway with doors at each end.

As Sammael passed by the Zeta they jabbed him with their needle. 'Oi!' The warrior nearly dropped the module, as he kicked out in their direction and they moved back to a safe distance.

'Not a subject,' Ninharsag repeated herself, pointing out Sammael.

'Yeah,' Sammael backed her up on that, waving a fist in their direction. 'Try that again and you'll be *subject* ... to a good hammering!' He thumped his fist into his other hand.

The Zeta found his reaction interesting and made notes on their devices.

'I think they get the picture.' Armaros drew his brother's attention away from the beings.

'I don't think so.' Sammael observed them. 'They don't look that worried to me.'

'Well, I wouldn't do anything too impressive to scare them.' The scholar knew what the warrior was thinking. 'Or they'll just find you all the more interesting.'

Sammael was bemused by this. 'Weird,' he concluded, deciding to leave the matter be.

Ninharsag led on into a vacant operating theatre, where there was a tonne of technological equipment. 'Once this room is sealed, it is impervious to penetration — nothing gets in, nothing gets out,' she explained.

Once the module had been positioned horizontally, with the subject facing up, Ninharsag used her own equipment to raise the container to a height that was comfortable for her to observe, and hot-wired some of her equipment into the control mechanism of the module. 'This will keep the module powered up, and allow me to do some readings.'

As Sammael observed the female work, he was notably concerned. 'Are you sure we should be leaving the commander in this freak show?' he uttered quietly aside to Armaros.

'I shall stay with him,' Armaros said to counter his doubt.

'Have it your way.' Sammael was happy to be relieved of the duty. 'There are many other places I would rather be exploring here on Nibiru. This place gives me the creeps.'

Armaros noted Ninharsag glance at Sammael, and her expression was not one of favour. 'As you have never really had an interest in science, there is hardly any point to you staying, so feel free to depart.'

'I'll check back with you later,' Sammael sought to reassure his brother, and cupped a hand around his mouth to advise. 'Just to ensure you haven't been shoved in a jar or something.'

Armaros was not reassured, but gripped his own forehead tightly between the thumb and middle finger of his right hand. 'I feel sure that will not be necessary.'

'Whatever you say, you're the commander.' Sammael's tone was semi-mocking, obviously a little irked to have been overlooked by his brothers for the appointment. He waved to all in leaving and vanished.

'Apologies for my associate,' Armaros beseeched his hosts. 'There is no filter between Sammael's brain and his mouth.'

Ninharsag shrugged, indifferent. 'I like a person who states what is on their mind.' The lady of the labs completed her tinkering, whereupon the module containing my body reactivated and she turned to view the readouts on a soft-light screen, very similar to those once developed in the dark universe by the Fallen, only these appeared brighter, more colourful and more advanced. 'Your technology is surprisingly similar to our own,' she commented to Armaros, without looking at him.

It was not so surprising to me, considering the Nefilim and the Fallen were the same soul-mind.

'A fortunate coincidence,' Armaros granted, although he knew the truth as well as I did.

She was quiet for some time as she scanned over her data, and then turned back to Armaros with a perplexed expression. 'I am reading a life form that is certainly not human, and although your associate appears to be in perfect hibernation I am not detecting his soul essence at all. So either the subject is dead, or he has the ability to separate his subtle body from his physical form.'

Armaros stood wide-eyed, no doubt astounded by her technological know-how and her candour.

'I suspect the latter,' she advised for his information. 'Two reasons. Firstly, the body shows hardly any sign of decay.'

'Hardly any?' Armaros found it curious that I should have any decay, being that I was immortal.

'The virus appears to have affected some of the internal organs, but that is nothing I cannot fix.'

My brother nodded in understanding. 'And your second reason for suspecting my associate's disconnection of spirit?'

'My sister, Ereshkigal, seer of the disembodied, noted a spirit of your breed following you into the Worlds Chamber earlier today.'

Armaros felt completely exposed by the statement, and yet still hesitated to divulge my presence; thus I was compelled to break my silence and spare him the decision.

'*I am here, Ninharsag.*' I assumed she was as telepathic as the other Nefilim we had encountered thus far. '*I am Azazèl, Commander of the Grigori.*'

Both Enki and his sister reacted to my announcement.

'Ah, there you are,' she replied aloud for Armaros' benefit. 'I am fascinated to make your acquaintance, Azazèl.'

'As am I,' Enki emphasised. 'How extraordinary your kind are proving to be.'

'*Can you remove the virus and destroy it?*' I asked the scientist.

'I can remove it, most surely. And contain it, in the same

manner you have,' she advised. 'But it shall require further analysis to find an antidote that will neutralise it altogether.'

This was consistent with what Anu had claimed, and the news made me edgy. *'It is a parasite like no other and must not be allowed to escape.'*

'I assure you, Commander, it shall not escape.' She sounded very confident about that. 'But in order to separate it from your body, I will have to reverse the freezing process, and it will try to resist the procedure, perhaps aggressively. But whatever damage is done to your body in the process I can repair, for your genetic structure is also surprisingly similar to our own.' She looked to Armaros. 'Almost as if we were ancient relatives.'

'Perhaps we are?' he answered kindly.

Ninharsag served Enki an odd look of assurance.

'It might be best for your commander not to witness the separation procedure, as it could cause some anxiety,' she suggested.

'I believe it will cause more anxiety if I do not bear witness,' I spoke up. *'But Armaros is free to go.'*

'Your choice, Commander,' she allowed.

'Your commander has excused you,' Enki advised Armaros, 'perhaps you might like to see our gardens? I'd be happy to show you.'

Armaros appeared unsure whether he should take the lord's word for that.

'If you have a place where you store knowledge of the arts, sciences and histories, Armaros would surely be more disposed towards that,' I advised.

'Ah!' Enki sighed, enlightened. 'Your commander suggests you are something of a scholar and would prefer to see our Hall of Documents.'

Armaros was pleased to be assured of my intent, for this lord could not have known of his thirst for knowledge. 'The commander knows me well,' he concurred, 'I should very much like to see this place you speak of.'

'Splendid,' Enki concluded the matter. 'As coincidence would have it, our Hall of Documents leads off into the gardens, so we can see both.' Enki motioned to the exit.

'I shall leave my commander in your very capable hands, Nin,' Armaros granted. This was another point Enki had explained in his discourse on males and females earlier: Nin was a title within a female's name denoting her senior stature among the Nefilim. Just as En at the beginning of a male's name denoted him as a lord among the men of their race.

'You need hold no fear for his full recovery,' Ninharsag advised. 'Come back around nightfall and you shall greet your commander as he once was.'

Armaros, appreciative of the news, said, 'Gratitude.'

Ninharsag was perplexed. 'None is required. This is my calling, and with a case as intriguing as this, it is I who am grateful for the knowledge this opportunity awards.'

Content that all was well, Armaros turned and accompanied Enki from the lab. 'Might I ask, En, what is a garden?' he queried as they departed.

'It's very colourful,' he replied, 'and fragrant. I feel sure you'll find it a most pleasurable experience.'

'Well then, Commander,' Ninharsag addressed me, now that we were alone. '*Let us see this parasite contained and your body restored to you.*'

'*I am in your hands, Nin,*' I granted.

As my form was brought out of cryogen, I felt the virus awakening — it was hungry and annoyed by its long state of inaction.

When Ninharsag opened the module, I was horrified.

'*It is waking, Nin,*' I warned her. '*Did I mention that when in my body this thing can exhibit great strength!*'

'*Not under a muscle relaxant it can't,*' she replied, as she took a small device in hand.

My eyes opened wide, which alarmed me — I feared my saviour was about to be attacked.

Ninharsag didn't flinch, however, and as she placed the device against my skin, my eyes fluttered closed once more.

'*Apologies to have doubted.*'

'*You are a little skittish, Commander,*' she retorted. '*Are you sure you are up for this?*'

'My only concern is for your safety, Nin.'

She appeared to find my statement amusing. 'Right then ...' She moved across the room and activated a large incubating unit on the far side. 'On to phase two.' Ninharsag returned to where my body lay exposed in the cryogenic module and positioned a long pointed metal arm that extended from the ceiling, into position over my form. Then, laying her hand upon a metal plate on her desk, the metal arm shot a stream of light into my body, whereupon my physical form vanished and then reappeared in the incubator on the far side of the room. 'Now for the hard part.'

'The extraction?' I assumed.

'Indeed.' She left the bio-containment chamber and when she returned she was dressed in a suit that covered her entirely, which included a helmet that enclosed her head. 'You see how cautious I am.' She sealed closed the door to the chamber we were in.

'It would be a great shame to have such a brilliant mind as yours eaten away,' I replied, thankful that she was heeding my warning.

There was another smaller, fully metal incubator that was attached via a long metal rod to the one in which my body lay.

'Now stay your nerves, Commander, this could be violent,' Ninharsag warned, again holding a hand over a metal plate on her desk. The smaller incubator activated and the sound of a vacuum ensued. At the same time my incubator began to flood with liquid-light. My unconscious form began to convulse, which, tranquillised as I was, must have been caused by the mind-eater rebelling against its predicament.

My being was suddenly sickened with panic, as blood streamed from my nose, eyes, mouth and ears. I could see the dark shadow of the creature being drawn to the surface of my form, writhing as it struggled to keep hold of me. The more it resisted, the more my body thrashed about.

'Let go.' Ninharsag heightened the vacuum and the blood streaming from my facial orifices was drawn towards the suction, some splattering onto the inside of the transparent casing of the incubator before streaming across the surface towards the void that led into the second incubator. '*Stubborn little bastard,*' Ninharsag commented, intensifying the suction once again.

My body was spasming so intensely I feared I was going to be torn apart. But as the liquid light in the chamber threatened to cover me completely, the mind-eater gave up the struggle and let go, whereupon it was sucked into the second incubator, which Ninharsag immediately closed off and froze. '*Contained,*' she announced.

My body lay still inside the liquid light that now covered me entirely. The blood dissipated into the fluid and I appeared at peace; which, with the relief of being free from the virus, was exactly how I felt. '*I am indebted to you, Nin.*'

'*Not at all,*' she replied, inspecting the readouts on the incubator to ensure all was well with me. '*You shall be able to re-enter your form before evening. Until then, there is nothing more to be done. So, you can wait it out here, or do some sightseeing with your associates, whatever is pleasing to you.*'

There seemed little point to me in wasting the rest of the day watching myself sleep. '*I should check how my brothers and ship are faring, so I shall return. And shall announce myself when I do.*'

'*As you wish,*' she granted, exiting the bio-containment lab and I along with her. '*I have nothing to hide.*'

I'd not had the chance to converse privately with any of the Grigori since we had landed in this universe, and there was one unfinished topic that was in the back of my mind that really needed clearing up. Thus I sought out Sammael, and found him with Sariel, walking down a dimly lit and unremarkable passageway with no windows.

'*Where are you two going?*' I asked and Sariel took pause when he noted my voice.

'Commander?'

Sammael halted also, heeding his companion's distraction. 'Azazèl is here?'

Sariel confirmed with a nod. 'He is asking where we are going.'

'We are headed towards the detention level of this palace,' Sammael informed me. 'You can find out a lot about the people you are dealing with by speaking with their captives. I realise they will not have an unbiased perspective, but it could be enlightening nonetheless. And we were told we could go sightseeing anywhere.'

'*A fair point,*' I awarded.

'The commander thinks it is a good idea,' Sariel conveyed.

'See!' he stressed to Sariel. 'I'm not the moron you all take me for. We also had a look around the upper palace, and met a few of the Nefilim, who were all too busy being self-indulgent to speak with us.' Both Sammael and Sariel seemed very amused by the statement.

'*How so?*' I wondered what the joke was.

'Well … we spied a couple mating —' Sammael raised his eyebrows '— who were too engrossed in their activity to even acknowledge we were there.'

'They did appear very preoccupied.' Sariel suppressed a grin.

'And we saw several others injecting themselves with a substance that appeared to cause some euphoria in them,' Sammael said. 'And afterwards their eyes glowed bright!'

'We think this may be how they advance their supernatural ability,' Sariel posed, 'although they have technology to teleport them about.'

'*Just like the Fallen Elohim, they have no natural psychokinetic talent.*' Only if the Nefilim advanced spiritually would that latent talent emerge in their species. The observations were interesting, but not the reason I had sought them out. '*Ask Sammael how he disposed of the seals,*' I requested, and the telepath complied.

'I had to melt them,' he informed, 'as nothing happened when I attempted to return them to their point of origin.'

'*That's unfortunate,*' I conceded, deciding to go and check on his handiwork. '*Let me know what you learn from the prisoners.*'

'Right you are,' Sariel confirmed, getting them moving once more.

'*Did anyone remain aboard Leviathan?*' I called after them.

'Penemue,' Sariel paused to answer. 'He took being left in charge very seriously.'

Sammael looked annoyed, even only hearing half of the conversation, he figured out my intention. 'Seriously? You're double checking my work?' He shook his head, perturbed by my lack of faith.

'*I am checking on our ship,*' I advised via Sariel.

'Why? We're not taking it anywhere.' Sammael questioned the logic.

'*Well, that will very much depend on what you find out,*' I proffered.

When Sammael was told my thinking, it appeared that he did not entirely believe me, but I was not going to waste time arguing the issue — I had a bad feeling about those seals.

I joined Penemue in the commander's office of *the Leviathan* and found him seated forward in the hot seat, staring hard at the soft-light screen in front of him.

'Who are you, then?' he muttered to himself.

I moved around behind him, to observe the dark-clad figure moving through the cryogenic chamber. '*Ereshkigal.*' I recognised the attire. '*Better get down there,*' I suggested, and although Penemue couldn't hear me, he was of the same mind, and teleported himself down to cryogenics — as did I.

When Penemue first materialised, he ducked out of sight to observe what the visitor was up to. I was fortunate to have the advantage of being in spirit form, but acutely aware that this Nefilim female possessed etheric sight, I floated high above her, to see what she was up to.

She was observing the inside of one of the cryogenic modules, which had contained a seal belonging to one of the fallen — now melted flat to the point that its embossing had vanished. It was golden in colour, which meant it belonged to one of the highest ranking among the Fallen, perhaps Samyaza himself.

212

That thought was dismissed when I observed the dark-clad female kneel before the open module. She pulled a pouch from the belt beneath her veil and sprinkled the sparkling contents over the melted seal.

'Denizens of fragmented crystal,
to your mistress now be faithful.
Take this item, by time torn,
restore it to its prior form.'

She recited this prose three times, waving her hand over the melted gold.

As the crystal shards twirled counterclockwise, suspended between the item and her hand, to my great horror, the seal reformed.

Ereshkigal removed her veil. Her huge, almond-shaped eyes, gray-green in colour, opened wide in wonder, as she read the letters printed evenly around the rim of the seal. 'B ... A ... E ... L.'

I was shocked that she could even read our dialect, but if our genetics and technology were similar, it stood to reason that the written word was also.

She took the seal in hand and raised it to view the insignia more closely.

'Hey, don't mess with that!' Penemue revealed himself to warn her.

Like all of her kind, Ereshkigal had barely any nose at all, and a tiny little mouth with large black-painted lips. Her near-black hair was short and spiked, but still she was a beautiful creature to behold. She rose and turned to observe Penemue, who was quite captivated by her gaze.

'Those seals are very dangerous,' he added more civilly when she made no comment. 'That is why we destroyed them.' He made a move to approach her and retrieve the item.

Ereshkigal held up a hand, palm exposed in a halting gesture, and Penemue adhered to her wish.

Then a tightening in her cheekbones caused a grin to form on her lips. 'I am also very dangerous,' she advised, sweetly.

A dart shot forth from beneath the loose-fitting cuff of her long sleeve, and Penemue dropped like a stone to the ground. She turned and continued on to the next module that contained a melted seal.

I was enraged by the affront to my brother, and moved to use his form to counter the attack. Being a medium, I had the ability to beat Ereshkigal at her own game. I laid my spirit down in alignment with Penemue's form and raising him to his feet once more I went after her.

'Shall we try that again?' I confronted her at close quarters and the Nefilim female was clearly amazed.

'What? But I just —' She spotted my spirit inside Penemue's body. 'Ah … It's you, the disembodied one.'

'You have something that belongs to us, and I would like it back.' I held out a hand to receive the item she was holding.

'Yet it is written in our ancient tongue,' she challenged.

'Your father would not approve of you possessing this item, I can assure you,' I insisted.

'I have a picture-perfect memory …' She handed the seal over. 'So it makes no difference to me.'

'Then wipe the impression from your mind, lest it curse you for life and beyond,' I advised.

'The dark unknowable forces of this universe are just patterns unseen, begging to be understood.' She stepped away from me. 'Our secret desires are signposts to our destiny, and one should never be put off from a defining experience by the prospect of a little suffering or sacrifice. All great knowledge and achievement comes at a cost.'

A shadow erupted around her that loosely took the form of a large winged creature, which enclosed Ereshkigal in its wingspan and vanished with her.

I was left completely baffled, and casting the seal into a module, I melted it once more before casing the chamber and counting off all seventy-four seals to ensure Ereshkigal had not absconded with any others prior to being discovered.

I laid my brother's form down on a lounge in the command quarters, where he might wake from his enforced coma in comfort. My spirit was due back in Ninharsag's lab, but I resolved to consult Anu about a secure hiding place for these dangerous relics as soon as my subtle and physical form were reunited.

Inside the laboratory I found Ninharsag still in her bio-protective suit. She was busy in the chamber in which she'd performed the extraction. My body was no longer therein, but had been moved elsewhere to recover. It was the module containing the mind-eater virus that held the scientist's interest at present; she was viewing readouts and observing movement within the incubator as she bombarded it with different light frequencies. If there was movement, then that meant that the virus was no longer frozen.

'Nin, what are you doing?' I was naturally alarmed.

'I am finding out what I can about your virus,' she replied calmly. 'And this is a virus like none ever seen. At a constant room temperature it absorbs all light and radiation that it encounters, without reflecting nor transmitting any! It is what is theoretically termed a black-body, although I have never observed one as true to form as this. Even a black hole in space has an event horizon that will reflect radiation with a wavelength equal to or larger than the radius of the hole, but that is not true of the particles that compose this virus. This is the perfect absorber, there is no spectral radiance whatsoever.'

'It literally eats all light,' I concluded.

'You called this a mind-eater?'

I nodded. 'Because a victim appears to lose his wits once taken over by the virus's programming.'

'Light-eater or soul-eater would have been more appropriate. It is a very good thing that your spirit was not trapped in that body with this entity,' she advised. 'There would be nothing of you left. It requires light and radiation for fuel, and once it consumes everything it can from one victim, I imagine it just moves onto the next. As long as this thing is at a non-zero temperature it has an infinite potential

215

to keep absorbing victims and survive. If it were to be exposed to thermal heat, chances are it would emit radiation with infinite power.'

'*So heat is not the way to destroy this thing,*' I deduced.

'Not unless you wish to take out a sizable part of the galaxy along with it,' she said, 'but it does explain why it doesn't like the cold.'

'*The cold doesn't destroy it, though,*' I assumed. '*It only puts it into hibernation.*'

'Correct.'

'*But from what you have said, about its need for fuel, we can starve it.*'

'In theory, yes,' she granted.

'*But?*'

'How long that might take, is difficult to predict. The virus would have to be kept at a near sub-zero temperature to keep it weak, which would also extend its lifespan.' This was clearly a concern to her. 'A creature so perfect as this is bound to have defence mechanisms that we cannot imagine.' She held a hand over the plate that controlled her laboratory's systems and switched off the infrared light she had been viewing the virus with, dialling down the temperature in the incubator at the same time. 'But I expect you would like your body back, Commander?'

Clearly Ninharsag knew what she was doing, far better than I did. Thus I conceded to her implication with a smile. '*That would be most pleasing.*'

Outside the bio-containment, I spied Enki and Armaros, who were here to see me restored to full health as vowed. When Ninharsag approached the second door of bio-containment, she was given the all-clear from contamination by a pleasing tone; the door opened for her and sealed in the wake of her exit.

'I was just showing your commander to his body,' she advised, having removed her protective headdress.

'The commander is here?' Armaros was excited.

'Excellent,' Enki confirmed on his guest's behalf, 'we can show them both at once.'

'Show us what?' Ninharsag queried her brother, who handed a long green stem to Armaros.

'Watch this,' my brother requested, holding up the item he'd been given. 'This is from the garden,' he advised. 'It's called a flower. This is what it looks like before it blooms.' Armaros ran his hand up the stem and little pods emerged and then burst apart into colourful segments.

'*Wow.*' I marvelled at the beauty of it.

'The most amazing thing, Commander, is that process of blooming would normally take many days to happen,' Enki advised.

'That is very interesting,' Ninharsag confirmed, awarding her brother the same strange look that had passed between them several times — the one that made me feel that they knew something that we did not.

'So, I have discovered a talent I never knew I had,' Armaros concluded happily.

At that point, the Zeta who were monitoring the data coming from bio-containment, set off the alarm.

'What is it?' Ninharsag moved swiftly to observe the monitor herself. And placing her hand over the control plate she was frustrated. 'The temperature and light frequency in the incubator is rising, and the system is not responding to my override instruction.'

'*Why?*' I sought an explanation.

'I don't know. Perhaps this entity is psychokinetic?'

'*I am psychokinetic,*' I confessed, and would have sooner, had I known it might have some bearing on keeping the virus contained.

'Well, if the virus absorbs everything, why not talent?' she mused, moving to replace her headgear. 'You two should leave,' she advised Enki and Armaros.

'Is the mind-eater going to escape?' My brother's expression reflected the panic I felt.

'*You should leave also, Nin. That suit will not protect you if that thing bursts loose, and you know it.*'

The Zeta knew it; they were calmly departing using handheld devices that cast a shield of light about them and they vanished.

'If there is a danger, I am not leaving without you,' Enki insisted.

'The Pantheon will not take kindly to a Grigori virus destroying our breeding program here,' she pushed her viewpoint and her brother backed down. 'I have to contain it.'

'And how do you plan to do that?' Enki appealed.

'Do not make me explain myself. Know that I have a plan and go!'

'But the commander?' Armaros was concerned about her intent.

'He will be perfectly fine, *trust me*.'

Armaros knew better than to stall as the emergency sounds from the lab monitoring system were compelling him to comply, and taking hold of his guide, he vanished along with Enki.

'What are you going to do, Nin?' I was concerned for her.

'I'm going to give it what it wants.' She grabbed hold of a long metal rod hanging from the ceiling, and dragging it along a runner, she approached the large lizard creature, and aimed the pointy end at it.

She had used this same kind of device to teleport my body from the cryo-module to the incubator earlier, so I had a fair idea of what she had in mind. *'No, Nin, you cannot.'*

'Would you rather it was you or I?' she posited, and when I couldn't answer at once she continued to explain. 'If that thing heats itself to a thermal equilibrium it will end in an ultraviolet catastrophe. If its body is confined it can be controlled.' She gave the telepathic command to transfer the creature from its cage into the incubator I had occupied.

'But its soul will be eaten away.' I defended the helpless creature.

'These creatures belong to a soul-group,' she fobbed off my concern. 'It won't be missed and I can spawn another to replace it.'

'But stop and consider what releasing this creature into such a collective might do?' I appealed, as it was strapped down by metal restraints inside the incubator.

'This is no time for a philosophical argument,' she insisted, releasing the virus onto the lizardman, who began to squirm and shriek as the virus took hold and was then snap-frozen along with it. 'There, contained,' she concluded. 'I respect you, Commander, but I cannot risk a soul so prized as yours for the sake of a worthless reptilian.'

218

'And why should my soul, or yours, be prized over any other being?'

'You are right,' she reasoned. 'It really depends which side of creation you are supporting, whether it be the side of construct or deconstruct. You and I are basically constructive beings, but the reptilians are not. Did I mention that they feed on humans? Well just about anything that bleeds really, but humans are their preferred menu item. Or so we discovered when we attempted to have them work side by side.'

I fell silent. What she said made logical sense, if these lizard beings were the natural enemy of the beings that I had been delivered from the darkness to protect; yet, still it did not sit right with me, and I could not explain why. I could not judge her harsh view, for I was nothing short of a killing machine myself. But something within me had changed when I had seen the paragon, and I was still no closer to finding that being. It was that vision that had ignited this fire in my chest to stop killing for revenge and to find a more constructive way to exist — surely this was not it?

'What happens when the virus eats through that body?'

'As long as we keep it frozen, it cannot.' Ninharsag assured. 'And theoretically, even if it did, it would be passed on through the soul-group, until every last one of them was spent.'

'How many of them are there?' I wondered.

'It's difficult to estimate,' she replied, 'but there are certainly many more of them than there are Nefilim, and this infection is just the kind of threat we've needed to keep them subordinate. How fortunate to have turned a near disaster into a blessing.'

Suddenly I had to wonder if this accident was really an accident at all. Perhaps the Nefilim were not as benevolent as they purported to be?

'So then, Commander,' she changed the subject. 'You must be eager to rejoin your own form?' She led the way to another part of the laboratory and I trailed behind, wondering why these emotionless, elitist beings were so well disposed towards helping we Grigori. Was it just that Anu had decreed it, or was there some other reason?

9

THE DREAM OF TIAMAT

My return to physical form differed greatly from the few other times I had been required to do this, for consciousness did not immediately follow; instead, I took an unexpected detour.

I was moving through a dark space, with only one pinprick of light on the horizon. I feared I had been returned to the dark universe, and the tiny speck of light was the Eternity Gate, belying my escape. But as my consciousness sped towards the illumination, it became apparent that the light was pouring from a cosmic opening and not a barrier.

In the light I plunged through a layer of liquid and surfacing on the other side I was confronted by a palace, above which an ocean spread like an expansive sky of luminous purple hue. Akin to the chamber of the Watchers, this structure was too surreal to be of the physical world. Yet, unlike the Watchers' chamber, which personified a civilised, technological construct of light and air, this place had a more watery, chaotic, earthy aesthetic. I imagined this might be similar to the garden Armaros had spoken of, for there were many stems, of all shapes and sizes, some with coloured blooms and some without.

As I scaled the front steps and entered a long hall, I admired this vegetation, which was on display throughout the palace and grew beyond the open plan dwelling en masse. There were all manner of creatures running amok through the structure and the gardens beyond, some as ferocious and formidable in appearance as the Fallen Elohim in their most fearsome aspect. Other creatures were a wonder of beauty and colour, but all were in harmony, in alignment with the ambience of this magnificent place.

The residents appeared aware of my presence, but did not move to engage me as I proceeded down a long corridor, drawn towards a light phenomenon emanating from the main chamber ahead. My passage was lined either side by high stone archways that supported no roof, for the structure was completely open to the ocean of rippling liquid light above through which other creatures swam towards the same light that was attracting me. It seemed the only purpose of the palace supports was to provide somewhere for the vegetation and creatures to plant, climb and nestle themselves. There was more life and colour here than I had ever experienced in one place before; if the dark universe was a black hole of destruction, then this was a white hole, streaming forth creation.

The huge circular chamber at the end was marked out by the large columns positioned around the periphery. A wide smooth area of unbroken stone, intricately decorated with flowing designs, spread out evenly around a central circular pit. As solid as this floor appeared to be, tracks of coloured light could be seen shooting through the insignia towards the centre. How deep the abyss in the centre went was not apparent, but above the void swirled a ball of chaotic energy.

The sole occupant in this room was a huge, lizard-like creature that appeared far more reptilian than the reptilian that had been subjected to the mind-eater virus, and was far, far larger. The creature sat back on its hind legs, using its tail to support its upright position as it peered into the colourful, glowing mass of chaos before it. The liquid-light ceiling in this chamber swirled into the centre and fed into the central mass from on high, as electric energy shot up into the mass from the pit below. Via its front claws, the huge lizard drew different energy streams from the cosmic whirl, and combining these energies into one mass between its claws, it cast the electric ball aside, saying, 'Mušmaḫḫū!'

Inside the discarded glowing mass an apparition took form and hardened into a fierce serpent creature whose neck branched into seven heads that moved and hissed independent of each other. With a wave of permission from its creator, the titanic beast slid through the pillars and out of the chamber into the mists and foliage beyond.

I had to wonder: why create a creature akin to the worst horrors of the dark universe I had left behind? Was this universe not meant to be more advanced than the one below?

'Mušmaḥḥū, is one of many creatures of retribution,' the oversized lizard said, in a voice distinctly female and that was calm and soothing to my fears. Then, twisting its long neck right around to set glowing eyes upon me, it raised one of its free front claws, and beckoned me over with a single talon.

I inched my way closer, hesitant to approach the beast that was easily ten times my size. 'Where am I?'

'In a dream,' it said, as it morphed in form into a female that was not Grigorian, human, Elohim, reptilian or Nefilim, but the perfect combination of all of the above. She was scantily clothed, beyond her torso body armour that was moulded to snugly fit her shapely form, and stood scarcely taller than myself. Such a being I had never seen! Yet her stunning beauty did not stir my blood with the same intensity as the one who had compelled me to cross the threshold into this universe.

'Grigori don't dream, we don't sleep,' I advised, more disposed towards approaching her.

'You are sleeping now,' she told me surely. 'This is the only safe place for us to meet, for the physicality of where your body resides is currently perilous for us both.'

'Perilous?' I queried the word choice, for my situation among the Nefilim was not thus from my perception.

'You have been sleeping for quite some time, Azazèl,' she informed me. 'War has come to pass in your absence. My children fight with one another, and have rebelled against me so venomously that I, as the creatrix, am compelled to teach them a harsh lesson.'

'You are the one that the Nefilim call Tiamat,' I assumed. Some of the Nefilim believed she was the primordial master of chaos and creation; and from my current perspective they were not wrong in believing so.

'And you are Grigori, sent to protect humankind's evolution,' she granted, as she walked in close to me, 'and hence our purpose aligns.'

She stood closer to me than anyone ever had. Part of me felt that my personal space had been invaded and wished to step away, and yet it was a strange, exultant honour that a being so resplendent and powerful wished to be so near me, thus I remained still. 'Have humankind offended, Tiamat?'

Tiamat was amused by my query, and perhaps feeling my discomfort, she backed up to explain her reaction. 'Humans have not the intellect to even fathom my existence; as far as humanity is concerned the Nefilim are the creators and gods! They do excel in the genetic manipulation of physical forms, I'll grant … but the allocation of soul-minds, and the subtle bodies thereof, is my domain. And that includes the soul-minds within the Nefilim themselves!' She calmed to a tone of disappointment once more. 'But the Nefilim have grown so conceited that they believe they can do away with me and my restrictive guidance. They plot to lure me down into the physical world so as to slay me.'

'Then the Grigori shall be your guard,' I decided without a second thought. The Fallen had wished to bring down the creator in the dark universe. I had hoped, with their loss of memory and a new evolution, that might have changed; but it was clear whose side the Grigori must take.

Tiamat smiled broadly at my offer, but only because she thought it charming and sweet. 'My champions are dragons, like me,' she advised. 'Perhaps that is what I should call you, for you have the spirit of a dragon.'

'You may call me what you wish, as long as I can be of aid in your defence.' I was unsure if Tiamat was taking my offer seriously.

'Of aid to my cause, you can be … but not quite in the way you imagine, *Dragon*,' she tried the title on me and smiled, confirming

223

that she felt it suited. 'For the first thing you will learn about the female aspect of any soul is that she does not attack every problem directly and with full force as her male counterpart might. She will devise a shrewder means to achieve her goals in the long term.'

'And what scheme has *she* devised in this instance?'

'As a mother,' she advised, 'I must find a way to reward my children who are on the right path back to the creator, and punish those who continue to serve themselves. There are less than a clawful among the Nefilim who have shown any sign of remorse for their defiance, and their part in this rebellion was executed to keep the peace, not to advance their own agenda.'

'Anu,' I guessed him to be the spearhead of the resistance against his rebellious children.

'Yes, Anu and his daughter, Ninharsag, know and understand my mysterious importance to this universal scheme, as I understand theirs,' Tiamat explained. 'For they, like Enki, have developed the Grigori essence I wove into the soul-mind of all the Nefilim from the essence of Araqiel. But apart from this trio, the rest of the Nefilim do not even believe they have souls, much less that they should develop them.'

'Enki,' I said in approval, not surprised to learn that he still held Tiamat's favour.

'And because Enki's emotional body is so well developed, his guilt in siding with his kindred against me has driven him into isolation. Thus, one of the few redeeming members of their race is useless to me.'

'What did the Nefilim do to elicit such a rebuttal from their maker?' I thought that Tiamat seemed a tolerant being.

'At the request of my male counterpart, I sent our son down into physical incarnation to warn the Nefilim that if they did not stop making war with every other species they come into contact with, then they would face reprisals. The warning fell on deaf ears. They refuted my messenger's claim to be the son of Tiamat and Abzu, for they deny our existence! Their council voted by majority rule to have our son slain. It was Enki who put forward the notion to freeze the prisoner instead. It is only because this solution appeased

Enki's peers that our son did not experience a painful and terrible physical death at their hands.' Her voice filled with compassion as she justified her forthcoming reprimand.

I was confused by her review. 'But in death, would your son's soul not be returned to you?'

'Yes,' she granted. 'But I would rather wait for our reunion than have any harm befall him.'

'So your son is being kept in cryogen,' I uttered sympathetically.

'I speak with him in his dreams, as I speak with you now,' she said sadly, 'and as time has no real meaning to either of us, we can be patient. But in due course I will descend into the sub-planes of the earthly realms, along with my monstrous titans and free my beloved. On that day my wayward offspring will learn that a mother's guidance is never redundant and once lost, will be forever mourned.'

'You will destroy your own creations?' I felt her judgement harsh.

'No, I will allow them to destroy me,' she advised, 'in the hope that my compassion will touch that untapped potential to feel in them all.'

I felt she was being overly optimistic in trusting that her death would emotionally affect the majority of Nefilim in any way. 'And if it does not?'

'Then the Nefilim will eventually destroy themselves. They believe they have discovered the secret to immortality in the Orme substance they inject themselves with. It's the same gold-derived powder that they use to power the shield of their dying planet, but they are deluded to believe it will sustain any body indefinitely. This substance may grant supernatural power, but when taken in large and frequent doses, it will trap a soul inside its physical body. Once severed from their soul-group, they will be rendered infertile and cease to reproduce; my little ironic gift to the nihilists of the divine plan. If they believe that there is nothing beyond the life that they are living, then it will be so. The only thing that will save the Nefilim from cosmic extinction and a place in the Satan's army once more will be the activation of their emotional bodies through exercising love, compassion and wisdom.'

'They will find themselves in the dark universe, and will not advance further in the universal scheme, but go round and round through the two lower universes until they learn their lesson.' I saw the wisdom of it. 'Still, it is clear that some of the Nefilim have tapped into their Grigorian spiritual legacy.'

Tiamat nodded to agree. 'If not for Enki, Anu and Ninharsag, all the Grigori would have been wiped from existence by now ... or rather, kept apart from it. For sleep and death are brothers that are hard to tell apart in some instances.'

'*What?*'

'You are not alone in your slumber.' Tiamat motioned to the ball of energy and within it I saw a vision of my brothers sedated in modules laid out in a row.

'Anu, Ninharsag and Enki appealed your case to the great Pantheon of twelve, but by nine to three they voted that the Grigori were too powerful to remain in existence, or to instruct humankind, who are the race currently bearing the brunt of their merciless desire to wield power and accumulate riches. A desire that is now shared by the branch of the reptilian species that the Nefilim sought to enslave.'

In the sphere of energy I saw a great battle between the reptilians and Nefilim; the latter hovered over the battle on small flying transports, out of reach, whilst humans, mutants and monsters from the labs of Ninharsag confronted the hostile enemy, being devoured by the reptilians as they advanced. The field looked more like a feast than a battle! The Nefilim fired their weapons indiscriminately into the throng from above, killing fighters from both sides.

'How did this happen?' No sooner had I asked the question than I realised the answer. 'The virus. The Nefilim released it?'

'The infected reptilian was freed by its kin during a rebellion against the Nefilim, and having acquired your talents and a very self-serving smart virus, it quickly established itself as their leader.'

'The reptilians took the Nefilim capital?'

'No,' she clarified, 'this war is unfolding on the planet where human consciousness was to develop, but I fear there will be no humans left by the time my spawn have finished airing their grievances upon one another.'

'This is my fault! I should never have come here.' My worst fear had come to pass. I had been turned against the humans I was meant to protect in the last universe, and now I had failed to protect them in this universe also.

'The soul of every uninfected human slain by the Grigori in the dark universe was delivered into this one,' Tiamat addressed my unvoiced guilt. 'You were destined to come here, as were the Fallen Elohim … but unlike you, they do not remember their dark past. Their instinct is still selfish rather than selfless.'

'But what was the point of saving those souls, if they are only to be tortured in this universe as well?' I appealed.

'It is not for you to fathom or judge,' she advised. 'That is the job of the Logos. It is for you to *guide* humanity —'

'No. I cannot stand back and watch them suffer knowing I am the cause. I want to be involved!' I beseeched her to think of a way.

'I could encourage those few Nefilim who are well disposed towards you to release you — but then they will be declared traitors, and war will be declared on them and you. Then the Grigori will find themselves slaying the Nefilim, and the humans you were sent to protect, who will also be battling the reptilians and the creatures of my wrath.'

'No, I would not place those who are protecting the Grigori at any further risk.' It struck me then, what could be done. 'Araqiel incarnated into the Nefilim race to awaken the emotional body they lack. So allow me to join with humankind, to develop the mental body they require to rise above their pitiful lot.'

Tiamat's face went blank at the suggestion — I could not tell if she was for or against the notion.

'If indeed you can inject the souls of the Grigori into the human consciousness matrix,' I proposed, 'we could deal with your rogue children in a more covert fashion … as is your way.'

'You learn fast, Dragon,' Tiamat served me with an odd look of consideration. 'That is not in the plan. That said, you are not the first to suggest this.'

227

'Am I not?' I was pleased to have support, however anonymous.

Tiamat continued to stare at me, as she considered how to best pursue the subject. 'The Nefilim Lord Enki has always deeply desired to have sons, but has been unable to seed a male with any of his mates. He has turned to Ninharsag to fashion him human sons, as intelligent as any of the Nefilim. To grant Enki's greatest wish would be a clear sign of my favour and draw him out of his melancholy. Before the Grigori, I had not an appropriate soul to match to the chore.'

'The Grigori are a match?' I inferred.

'On a physical level that seems the case,' she said. 'By splicing human genes with yours, Ninharsag has fashioned the perfect bodies to fulfil her brother's request, and they are more beautiful than the Nefilim, in her opinion.'

'Bodies?' I queried the plural curiously and was prompted again to peer into the sphere of chaos. There was an image of a male of the human species, bearing a remarkable resemblance to my Grigorian self, and next to him was the paragon I had entered this universe to find. Yet the image appeared to be only an artistic impression. 'Are they real?'

'This is a developmental projection of how these bodies will appear when fully grown.' She waved a hand before the sphere and the image changed to one, more realistic, of many human embryos gestating, some male and some female. 'This is what they look like at present.'

Shock reverberated through my being as the realisation caused the fire in my chest to swell, which to me vindicated that I had found the right path. 'I have been seeking aspects of myself that have never been realised.'

'Interesting.' Tiamat still did not sound convinced.

'Why must we only be Watchers?' I was distressed by the proposition of defying divine will; was this a test? I thought back to my time in the council of the Watchers, and to my meeting with DK — clearly at least one of the Grigori had resigned himself to entering the human consciousness stream, just as he had entered the Nefilim consciousness stream. 'To join the human consciousness stream, you would have to split my soul-mind into twin souls?'

'Such is the polarising aspect of this universal scheme. But the divide is only on a physical, emotional and mental level, to aid you to develop those subtle bodies. On a causal level, you will always be one. Just as on the highest levels of existence, you and all the Grigori are one.'

I grasped the premise and yet I knew Watchers were not meant to be involved. If we cheated this situation, were we ultimately opposing the divine plan? That was the Satan's way.

Tiamat seemed wary and was sorry to advise me: 'You have already exposed the reptilians and the Nefilim to the Satan's influence.'

The statement sparked the realisation that the reptilian carrying the virus now had access to the grimoire about the Fallen that had been programmed into the mind-eater. 'How did I expose the Nefilim?'

Another vision in the sphere before me allowed me to view Ereshkigal, reforming all the melted seals left in cryogen modules inside *Leviathan*. Having collected all seventy-two, she spirited them away.

'No!' I protested my failure to leave the influence of the dark universe behind, even though I'd been fooled into forfeiting all control over the situation. 'I can't allow them to summon the Fallen into this realm.'

'Too late,' she said. 'And how easily humanity will be convinced to kneel to his will.'

I was startled by her attitude. 'Are you trying to talk me into defying the divine plan?'

Tiamat laughed. 'You cannot defy the plan, for it is constantly changing according to the choices of all involved,' she advised. 'No being in creation, not even I, can force a soul-mind to submit to any lot. It is the divine plan that every soul chooses its own path ... no one can hold you back from any path you freely choose to pursue.'

It seemed to me that my joining with humanity was what Tiamat wanted all along; but she could not make me volunteer the Grigori for this fate, I had to choose it. 'And what will be my punishment for joining with humanity?'

'There could be no harsher punishment than being human.' She sounded surprised that I was seriously considering it. 'You can't imagine what being mortal is like,' she warned. 'To *feel* … pain, hunger, thirst, sickness, oppression, *death!* Imagine the torment of thousands of lifetimes constantly craving your soul mate and being bound to love and lose them in every one of them.'

'If it is so terrible to be human then what is the purpose of the species? Why are they so integral to the plan?'

'Because humans also know what it is to love, to have compassion, show kindness, feel happiness, joy, solidarity, *peace!* Combine those qualities with great intellect and you have true enlightenment. Only through such processes will any of my children exceed this universe.'

'I cannot see how the Grigori can accomplish our aim if we do not get involved,' I submitted.

'I can aid you in this,' Tiamat said, 'but there would be a condition.'

I felt willing to do anything to secure my greater involvement. 'Ask what you will of me, and I shall see it done.'

'I know that you will, Dragon.' Tiamat neared to stand too close to me once more, and brushing the long strands of hair from my face she gazed into my eyes. 'You and your Grigori were *chosen* to be unique in the four universes, for your memory burns eternal … and thus, any vow you make will never be forgotten.'

'What do you ask of us?' I queried, baffled by how engaging her gaze was.

'It is my dream to see all my children back to source. So once you have raised humanity's consciousness to a frequency where it can transcend to the next universe, you must find a way to deliver the Nefilim and the reptilians you have infected as well.'

I felt Tiamat was asking the impossible. 'How are the Grigori expected to accomplish such a feat?'

'How do you intend to accomplish such a feat with humanity?' she posited.

'By guiding them,' I stated the obvious.

'There you have it,' she concluded, and I had to scoff at the reasoning. 'Neither the Nefilim nor the reptilians will ever listen to what a human has to say.' I had seen what the Nefilim thought of humans, they were just slave labour and pets! To the reptilians they were just a food source!

'The same could have been said of you, once,' Tiamat pointed out. 'You listened to a mere human, and were enlightened.'

Her point was valid, and yet I felt compelled to stipulate. 'I can only speak on my own behalf in this matter, I cannot bind my fellow Grigori to such a vow and such a fate.'

'They will follow you, you know this,' Tiamat annihilated any delusion I entertained of acting alone. 'They followed you into this universe and they will follow you into the next. And that is well, for you cannot hope to accomplish all you must alone. It may seem from your current perspective that you are but one being among the Grigori, but you are in fact all of the Grigori in one being. And that being must now decide what its role in this evolution shall be … Watcher or Dragon?'

A sudden and excruciating stabbing pain ran down through my neck and all through my chest, blurred my response and sent my consciousness plummeting into darkness.

PART 3

SYMMETRY OF CHAOS

10

THEN, WHEN AND NOW

The pain intensified as consciousness drew him back into the present. Dan had felt the sting of cold steel pierce his flesh before, but in this instance there was no warning or putting the agony aside and recovering his wits — the strike was paralysing. The foreign object wedged through his left shoulder and down into his chest restricted his attempts to draw breath. He opened his eyes, but there was only darkness, and a taste of blood in his mouth.

'Didn't see that coming, did you, *Dragon?*' a raspy voice uttered in his ear from behind him.

It was then Dan fathomed his situation — he was seated in meditation, in the chamber of En Noah, at the lake house on Kila. There was no doubt who his attacker was, and it was now clear to him how Dragonface had managed to stay one step ahead of the timekeepers, since their failure to destroy him back on Earth. 'The virus carries my talents,' he wheezed, and tears of horror and remorse flooded his eyes.

'That's right,' Vugar was elated to inform. 'Including your eternal memory.' He revelled in the victory, which the mind-eater had obviously been planning for some time. 'And there is no hiding from your own recollection.'

The claim thrust an emotional dagger through Dan's heart. He couldn't imagine how the timekeepers could get around that impediment, being that Azazèl was the storehouse of Hudan's experiences too. 'Why didn't you just kill us ... at Yin?' Dan recalled how the reptilians had been avoiding him in that battle; if Dragonface possessed all Azazèl's power, he could have killed him and his brothers easily.

'Well, I felt I owed you a favour, being that you were the carrier who brought me into this universe, and served me up a soul-group upon arrival,' it jested, before the scornful tone returned. 'Yet since you annihilated all my people on Earth, I've lost that sentiment.'

The speed of his demise meant that Dan did not have the strength and focus needed to will his soul-mind home to AMIE. To his great regret, everything he'd learned in this universe would be swept from the conscious recollection of Lucian Gervaise. But all was not lost, for he still clutched the thought recording orb that En Noah had given him to use during the session. He tucked the device between his legs, hoping that in the darkness it would not be noted by his assailant. 'The reptilians ... are not ... your people,' Dan gargled, and spat blood, feeling the life draining from him rapidly.

'I have been eating my way through them for over three hundred and eighty thousand years, so it would seem time supports my claim,' the virus informed via his reptilian host. 'When I entered Edin, I took over the replication program of reptilians that Ninharsag left behind and I became their creator. Tiamat could not stop me then, and will not stop me now.'

Dan had only just recollected his vow to deliver the reptilians from this universe and now that hidden objective would be mislaid once more — obscured among the thousands of lifetimes of experience stored in his cosmic memory banks. The revelation was more defeating than the blade through his body, but if what Noah said was true about the thought recorder picking up on unconscious memories, then the vow had been recorded. Still, the virus would be aware if Hudan was enlightened, and would endeavour to prevent her from keeping their vow to Tiamat.

'So now, old *friend*,' the virus summed up, 'you can die knowing that there is nowhere in this universe where your soul mate and unborn child will be safe from me. And I assure you, their deaths will not be so swift and merciful as yours.'

The blade was quickly withdrawn, whereupon Dan keeled over, and the brief relief of the sword's removal was immediately succeeded by panic, as he choked and drowned on his own blood.

Wu Geng was on watch duty, and was alerted when the two unconscious seers he was guarding began to surface from their deep trance. Aysel was twitching a little, Hudan was trembling violently.

'Governor!' He ran to the stairwell and yelled downstairs to alert the others. Song, Huxin and Rhun wasted no time in teleporting themselves upstairs to join him.

'Are they okay?' Wu Geng queried Rhun.

'They're coming out of it,' the governor confirmed to allay Wu Geng's concern.

Aysel opened her eyes first. 'The Dragon,' she said, sitting immediately upright. 'Vugar is with him.'

'Are you talking about —' Rhun's query was cut short as Hudan let loose a bloodcurdling scream.

'Dan!' She awoke, hyperventilating and when she sat upright tears spilled from her eyes. Her distress was so debilitating that Hudan nearly collapsed once more, but Song rushed to her support. 'Take me to him, quickly!'

Song nodded to affirm, and scooped Hudan up in his arms to teleport her directly into the meditation chamber two floors below.

'I'll get Noah to switch on the lights,' Rhun advised. 'Everyone stay alert and stay together.'

The room was in darkness as Song set Hudan down on her own two feet.

'Dan?' she called into the silence, and when there came no reply, she began to panic. 'Please, *please*,' she appealed to the universe to let her premonition not have come to pass yet.

But as the lighting in the chamber engaged to reveal Dan's body crumpled in a pool of blood, her heart plunged into the pit of her stomach. 'No, no, no … I am supposed to have more time …'

Usually her trances brought glimpses of future events, not present instances, and she was angry at the cosmos for being so cruel. 'What was the point of giving me the prophecy, if I could not act on it?'

The shock stole her last ounce of energy, and she dropped to her knees and crawled to his side. 'Coward!' she cried out to curse the culprit, as she cradled her dead husband in her arms and wept silently. 'I remember our vow to Tiamat,' she told him in a whisper, knowing this had been one of his final regrets. 'I remember *everything*.' The fact pained her, for she was now aware of the obstacle that had been working against them that would be nearly impossible to subdue. 'We will find a way to overcome, I swear it.'

The door to the chamber opened — Telmo, Huxin, Rhun and En Noah entered and were immediately devastated by the sad state of affairs they found within.

'How could this have happened?' En Noah felt responsible, as he had been monitoring the session. 'I heard no struggle from within, and his vital signs showed no change until the second Rhun appeared to alert me of a possible breach.'

'It's not your fault,' Hudan assured Noah, still clutching her dead lover tightly. 'The mind-eater absorbed Azazèl's talents during his time of infection.'

Noah's eyes boggled as he considered the ramifications of this. 'It has access to your eternal memory ... that's where Vugar is acquiring his information.'

'Holy shit!' Song cried. Hudan and Dan were their masterminds.

'I am useless to you now. In fact, I am a danger to you all. The only way to keep Dragonface in the dark about our plans is if I know nothing of them.'

'Shit!' Song protested again. He cast his eyes downward in thought, and spotting the thought-recording orb on the floor, he retrieved it. 'Is this what I think it is?'

Noah nodded to confirm.

'The success of this mission now lies in your hands,' Hudan advised Song, and he appeared both honoured and shocked that she was choosing him to lead.

'You want me to take charge?' Song had suspected Telmo would be nominated.

'Knowing what is on that orb, I believe you have the greatest chance of fixing this mess. But I dare not even consider what I would do, lest our nemesis picks up on it.' Hudan looked back to Dan and was again overwhelmed by grief.

As this was not the time to query the subject further, Song looked to the governor, who had been set on edge by this ambush.

'I should go and see if my wife has also awakened, as she may be able to shed more light on this matter.'

'Shall I come with you?' Song offered.

Rhun declined with a shake of his head. 'There is a large guard surrounding her, I will be perfectly safe.'

The governor walked Song into the adjoining room in order to speak his mind. 'You should start formulating a plan to get out of here, or none of the timekeepers will leave this universe with their memory intact.'

Song nodded; the timekeepers needed to leave! Still, getting Hudan to agree to return to their rightful universe without her child was not an option; nor was leaving Rhun to contend with Dragonface alone. *There must be a way round this that would satisfy everyone.* Song was determined to fathom this mind-fuck of a situation and clutched the bloodied orb in his hand tightly. 'We've not endured through everything, to be beaten by a goddamned virus!'

'I share that sentiment completely,' Rhun assured him, 'and don't think I don't know that the deaths of its victims are on my head. I should have listened to Avery before our coup at Bayan Har Shan.'

'You saw a chance to take out your enemy and you took it,' Song reassured him. 'Who wouldn't have?'

'Someone who has learned that nothing good ever comes from destruction ... my parents drilled that into me!' Rhun appraised his actions in retrospect and shook his head, baffled by his lack of vision.

239

'Everything has a rightful place in the scheme of things, but in my eagerness to return home, I overlooked that, and now I am paying the price.'

Song shook his head in argument. 'Had you not taken this route, we would never have known about the virus, thus your people would never be safe from threat. Sooner or later Dragonface would have stumbled upon Azazèl's memories of this planet, and …' He shrugged. 'Everything happens for a reason,' Song quoted some more of Rhun's parents' philosophy at him and the governor could not argue it.

'We can only hope it is a *bloody good* reason,' Rhun forced himself to better spirits, thankful for the pep talk.

'We will get this sorted,' Song vowed. Rhun had been his father during Song's life in Zhou, and he'd been Zeven's father back in his universe of origin. 'We've been in worse situations than this.'

Rhun raised both brows and roused a smile. 'Hell yes, do you remember the Lahmuian mutant?'

Song hadn't really taken the time to look into his lifetime as governor here on Kila, during which time Rhun had been his vice-governor. 'I can't say that I do, but it sounds dangerous.'

'You tamed the damn creature before the eyes of the entire Pantheon of the Nefilim, who expected you to kill each other, and you saved my arse in the process. It was pretty epic.' Rhun waved off what was obviously a fond memory, and Song felt empowered by the tale.

'So I did good?' He grinned, chuffed.

Rhun had to laugh at the understatement. 'It wasn't just my parents who led the Nefilim to enlightenment in the end; you played a very big hand in that, and were entirely responsible for the deliverance of the children of Demuzi,' he told him in no uncertain terms. 'You have a mind for strategy that is every bit as astute as Dan or Hudan. I have no doubt that you can navigate us through this enigma. The truth is, not in any of the lifetimes I have known you, have you ever let us down.'

'Whoa,' Song was overwhelmed by Rhun's faith in him. 'I should really brush up on some of my history in this universe.'

'Some thought recordings for another time.' The governor pointed to the device in Song's hand. 'But for now, focus on that one, and I'll be back to brainstorm a solution presently.'

Wu Geng remained with Aysel, while their companions vanished downstairs. 'Are you all right?'

'No,' Aysel shook her head, as she recollected what she had seen in trance. 'The Dragon is not Vugar's only target, there is another.' She ceased her inward contemplation and looked to him.

'Who?' Wu Geng pressed for more information.

'A woman, I don't know who she is,' Aysel insisted. 'I've never seen her before, she is not one of your crew.'

'Then what would Vugar want with her?'

Aysel, emotionless at the best of times, appeared to lament the reason. 'She is pregnant, and Vugar intends to eat the foetus, for it is no ordinary child.'

As Wu Geng was kept uninformed, he had no idea who this woman might be. 'Are you strong enough to teleport yourself to her? Or I could assist?'

'I am fine.' She buckled her dragon belt, which none had dared touch, and then took hold of Wu Geng's hand. 'Be ready.'

They both drew weapons and prepared to face the worst on their arrival.

In the wilderness where Wu Geng and Aysel manifested, the elements were in an uproar, but they were not the first to arrive on the scene. The Lord Avery stood before an unnatural dark mist and it was repulsing the elemental lord's attempts to penetrate the dark field using his elemental forces or his own brute strength.

'I'm the one you want!' Avery yelled over the din of furious winds whipping about in an attempt to break through the barrier of shadow.

Vugar laughed, turning his hostage to face her beloved. 'I don't want *you*, it's your pain, hatred and fear I want.'

'Why did you leave the Otherworld?' Avery asked his sobbing wife.

'I sought to advance the pregnancy, if just a little at a time.' She shook her head, knowing now how ill-considered that desire had been. 'I wanted to surprise you.'

'Surprise!' Vugar placed a claw around her throat.

'I'm so sorry.' Her gaze sought her husband's forgiveness and expressed her undying love.

'No!' Avery summoned all the elements of the air to him, and took a running jump at the shadow which repelled him with equal force. He hit a tree and fell to the ground, winded.

'Avery!' the hostage protested.

'Vugar!' Aysel drew his attention as she unsheathed her belt.

The cosmic light was blinding, but the sound of Vugar's mocking laughter made it clear that he was still present and undeterred. It seemed that not even the divine light of her protector could penetrate the dark force protecting him.

A horrid cracking sound silenced the sound of the woman's protests.

'Shut off the light!' Avery demanded, as naught could be seen through it.

Aysel complied, immediately sheathing her weapon. The light retracted in time to witness Vugar rip the tiny foetus from a long, bloodied wound in his victim's belly and eat it before the distraught eyes of its father.

As the lord's anger welled, so too did the fury of the wind intensify; lightning suddenly lashed the sky, trees burst into flames, and rain began to pour.

Vugar did not look worried as he licked the blood of the dead child from his fingers; if anything the dark shadow protecting him appeared to have grown stronger. 'Thanks for lunch … very revitalising.' The reptilian vanished, along with his dark mist, leaving the mutilated body of his kill behind.

Avery yelled out his anger until he was reduced to tears, and looking to his wife; he wanted to go to her, but was so filled with remorse that he wavered in his stance.

242

The clash of forces ceased, and the world fell silent as if in mourning — all that could be heard was the sound of the rain falling in empathy with Avery's tears. Wu Geng was mortified by what he'd just witnessed and he didn't even know the woman.

'How has Vugar become so powerful?' Aysel didn't understand why the cosmic light had not frightened him off as it had in the past.

Wu Geng looked to her and held a finger to his lips in silent appeal that she discuss such matters later, out of respect for the dead.

'Oh dear goddess,' uttered the governor as he arrived on the scene with a beautiful woman Wu Geng had never seen before.

'I was right.' The woman gasped back her tears and ran to the dead woman's side.

'Rhun!' Avery found his feet and his anger. 'This is your fault!' The lord literally went flying into his brother and knocked him to the ground.

'I know it is!' Rhun agreed, before he was slammed in the face by his brother's fist.

'Stop it!' The female Rhun had brought with him looked up from inspecting the victim. 'Your bickering will not bring your child back!'

Landing one more good slam to Rhun's face, Avery backed off him, too drained of emotion to continue. 'Fallon was never supposed to die.' He fell to his knees and wept for her loss.

'But she is immortal like the rest of us, so how can she have been vanquished thus?' the lady asked of Rhun, tears filling her eyes. 'A DNA-destroying weapon perhaps?'

'That would be my guess,' Rhun was sorry to concede as he gathered his battered wits.

'When are you both going to advise our council about this threat to all the human tribes?' She sounded surprised at them both.

'Sybil —' Rhun staggered to his feet.

'It is no matter,' she decided, obviously still angry with the governor, but not about to pursue the argument when they had company. 'Who are these people?'

Rhun only just realised that Wu Geng and Aysel were present.

'You foresaw this too?' Rhun asked Aysel.

'I did,' she confessed, 'but I had no idea who the victim was.'

'You are a seer?' Sybil was suddenly fascinated.

Aysel nodded.

'Did you see beyond this event?' Sybil queried.

'No, I did not.'

'I did,' Sybil advised, approaching the grieving lord to place hands upon his shoulders. 'Do not lament, my brother. This sad event will open you to better ways to achieve your desired outcome that you would not have risked before.'

Avery was bemused by her words. 'Are you implying we can change this?' He looked to her to garner a response.

Sybil nodded to assure him. 'Our ex-governor will lead the way.'

Rhun frowned, bemused by her soothsaying. 'Brian?'

Brian Alexander had been the governor of Kila prior to Rhun's appointment, but he had long since departed this world. Sybil nodded, completely unaware that the soul of their ex-governor was visiting them and that this other incarnation of him was currently residing at Noah's lakehouse.

'Song,' they deduced at once.

The thought recorder shut off and Song emerged from the viewing trance. '*Holy shit*,' was his appraisal. Noah and Telmo had been watching over Zeven while he studied the recording, but his thoughts were already playing through scenarios and the different paths through time that the timekeepers could follow in order to defeat the virus.

'That's all you've got to say?' Telmo appealed, reaching out to take the thought recorder from Song in order to view it himself.

Song avoided the handover, and held the orb close to himself. 'I know what needs to be done.'

'Do tell then?' Telmo challenged, folding his arms in preparation to be unimpressed.

Song shook his head in all seriousness. 'Too risky.' He knew the answer would annoy Telmo, being the control freak that he was.

Telmo opened his mouth to express his discontent when Noah intervened.

'I agree, we should not discuss it, unless we have cause.' The historian looked to Song, and his expression queried what their next move should be.

'We are just going to trust that Song knows what he's doing?' Telmo was very uncomfortable with that idea.

'We are,' Noah concurred, serving Song a smile of support. 'What do you need from us?'

'Nothing really,' Song knew the reply was pushing his luck with Telmo, yet it was the truth. 'I need the girls.' He stood and headed back into the meditation chamber, where Huxin was sitting with her grieving sister. She'd pried Hudan away from her dead lover's body, and covered his remains. They were still seated on the floor, and Song joined them.

'I have a plan,' he assured Hudan.

'You can't —'

'Tell you, I know,' Song pre-empted her concern. 'So I need you both to do exactly as I ask, without question.'

Where normally they would have mocked such a request, they both stared wide-eyed at him a moment and then nodded in agreement.

'Good,' Song was glad to get no argument. 'I need you both to return to AMIE with me immediately.'

The request brought a gasp from everyone present, including Telmo who had followed Song into the chamber to hear his resolve.

Hudan gripped her stomach. 'I cannot.'

'Trust me, you can.' Song advised surely. 'And you will.'

Hudan was clearly panicked.

'I know how hard it is for you to relinquish control,' Song ventured, 'but you gave me command because you claim to trust me, and now I need you to prove it.'

Her gaze drifted to the cover under which Dan's body lay. 'Can I not lay him to rest first?'

Song clicked his fingers to regain her full attention. 'No,' he instilled in her once she was focused on him. 'It would be a waste of time.'

'Song.' Huxin was surprised at him. 'What difference could it make?'

'All the difference,' he assured. 'I am not being callous, just honest.'

Hudan gathered her shattered sensibilities, as she quietly considered her circumstance, then said, 'I will do as you ask.'

'I appreciate that.' Song was truly honoured by her faith.

'What about me?' Telmo wondered why he was being left out of the equation.

'You can't help us in this phase of the mission,' Song stood to inform him. 'In fact you may even be a hindrance.'

'You are not going back to AMIE without me!' Telmo was not of a mind to miss out on going home.

'Would you argue my order, Telmo?' Hudan stood to exert her influence.

'No,' he assured her, 'of course not, but —'

'Song is in command now,' she insisted, 'and, knowing what I know, I would suggest we follow his orders to the letter. No argument.' She gazed back to the cover under which Dan's body lay. 'If we are not all on the same page, we don't stand a chance of defeating this curse and its vendetta.'

When Rhun entered the chamber looking like he'd just been in a boxing match, Song was concerned. 'What happened to you?'

'I happened.' The Lord of the Otherworld entered behind his brother, still angry, until he saw the blood and the covered body on the floor. 'Not Dan too?' He moved to comfort Hudan when she nodded.

'I need to speak with you both,' Song said, as he prevented Avery from approaching Hudan, and directed both him and Rhun back into the other room.

'You have a plan?' Avery queried before yielding to the request.

Song nodded and then looked back to Noah, 'I would speak with you also.'

'But not me?' Telmo was getting very frustrated.

'That's correct,' Song informed him. 'You stay put with Wu Geng and Aysel.'

The role reversal had Telmo fuming. 'If this is personal —'

'It isn't,' Song assured him. 'I promise you,' he added as his crew mate was still perturbed.

'I think I know why you must stay,' Noah said in the hope of easing Telmo's frustration, 'I believe Song's reasoning is sound.'

'Have I done something adverse that I am not aware of?' He didn't understand why his input was suddenly redundant.

'Quite the contrary,' Noah assured.

'Here.' Song thrust the thought recorder into Telmo's hands, impatient at wasting time arguing the point. 'If you must know, you can view it once we are gone.'

Upon entering the adjoining room with the governor, Avery and Noah, and finding Wu Geng and Aysel there, Song asked them to join the others in the meditation chamber, so he could confer with those he needed to.

'You still don't trust me,' Aysel commented, rolling her eyes, as she complied with the instruction.

'Actually,' Song waylaid her, 'for the record, I do trust you. I believe I know who your dragon guide is …'

The claim surprised Aysel.

'We are fighting for the same cause,' he stated. 'So now it is you who must trust me.'

'I trust Wu Geng,' she proffered, looking to him to gauge his thoughts on the matter.

'I am certain that Song wants this adversity resolved in favour of the greater good as much as anyone here, including me,' Wu Geng told her, and Song appreciated his support.

'I have factored the desires of everyone into my plan, and trust me, if we play our cards right, we shall all get what we want,' Song vowed.

Wu Geng appeared indifferent, knowing his desires ran contrary to most of the timekeepers' main objectives. 'For Aysel, I hold no fear of that. As for myself, I doubt that very much.'

'*Don't.*' Song was unable to say too much on the matter. 'There is a place for every being in this universe,' he shot a glance at Rhun, having drawn upon his recent resolution, 'and we shall help you find yours, that's a promise.'

Wu Geng was stunned, and although clearly grateful for the reassurance, he hesitated to believe it. 'In the big scheme of things, my desires matter little.'

Song shook his head, frustrated, and moved in close to whisper in his old nemesis' ear. '*You were right all along.*' Song pulled back to see Wu Geng utterly flabbergasted, his expression full of question. 'But for now,' Song went on, not at liberty to expand on his confession, 'you are one of us, and we shall not abandon you, in this universe or the next.'

Wu Geng clutched Song's right arm below the elbow, and Song returned the gesture, to shake on it. 'That intention is mutual,' Wu Geng pledged, ahead of escorting Aysel into the meditation chamber.

Noah closed the door behind them and their eyes fell on Song.

'Now, what the hell is going on?' Avery was not in a patient mood.

'I can summon you from the Otherworld to anywhere in the physical realms, is that correct?' Song directed the query at the Lord of the Otherworld.

'Correct,' Avery verified.

'Excellent,' Song resolved. 'Those of you who wish to be involved at this time, go to the Otherworld and await my summons.' He turned and headed for the meditation chamber.

'What about telling us the plan?' Avery was in no mood to be put off, and moved to extract the information from Song by teleporting himself into his path.

'Not here,' Song emphasised, despite the lord's dark mood.

'He is right to refrain,' Noah cut in before Avery retaliated to the response with force.

'My wife and unborn child lie butchered!' the lord stressed, as Noah held him back from the new timekeeper commander.

'Not for long,' Song insisted, and the comment pacified the lord to a degree. 'Just do as I ask.' He waited for confirmation from the lord and, jaw clenched in frustration, Avery moved out of Song's path. 'I would see you gone, before I depart,' Song asserted.

The request did nothing to appease Avery's mood, yet he complied nonetheless and vanished in a huff. Noah followed suit without question.

'I regret the responsibility for my mess has fallen in your lap,' Rhun stated in parting.

'Your actions have provided me with clarity,' Song granted, 'and this sidetrack will grant access to a far greater highway.'

'It is my greatest hope that you are right about that.' Rhun vanished to join his brother in the Otherworld.

'Mine too,' Song uttered quietly, and steeled himself to stay the course.

Inside the meditation chamber, Song was met by silent bemusement from everyone therein, and as much as he wanted to set their fears at rest, if he did, they would surely fail. Hence, he looked to Huxin and Hudan. 'Let's do this.'

With a wry smile of confirmation from them both, all three of them lay on the floor of the chamber.

Hudan was close to Dan's covered body, and noting his hand protruding from the shroud, she placed her hand on his. 'See you in the next one.' She looked to the ceiling to allow her welling tears to roll down her face. She drew a deep breath for strength, and placing her free hand on her belly, closed her eyes to mentally stave off her fears for her child.

'When will you be back?' Telmo appealed, fearful that he would never see them again.

'Before you know it,' Song retorted, although Telmo was left dissatisfied with the answer.

'We are returning to the day we left?' Huxin assumed.

'No,' Song advised, 'to exactly one Sermetic year prior to our leaving.'

Huxin frowned upon casting her memory back to that long forgotten time. 'But nothing was happening then.'

'That's exactly why I picked that destination,' Song explained. 'Mission Log Day one thousand, three hundred and fifty-six … the day following my daughter's ninth birthday.'

'Thanks for the reminder,' Huxin grinned, 'but I do believe I awoke with a splitting headache that morning.'

'We all did,' Hudan complained.

'See, we all remember it,' Song rested his case. 'I'm guessing you won't remember the next day half as clearly.'

'He's right, I don't.' Huxin reconciled herself to the miserable homecoming, as did Hudan.

'What have I missed?' Jahan arrived on the scene to forestall their departure once again. 'You're leaving?'

Huxin sat up to address his concerns, but Song reached up and, grabbing her shoulder, urged her to lie back down.

'Focus,' he ordered, 'we don't have time for this.' And with a mournful look in Jahan's direction, she closed her eyes to comply.

'Watch out!' Song heard Wu Geng cry as a commotion erupted, and he snuck a glimpse.

Ling Hu leapt at Wu Geng as Jahan reached for his weapon to fire at Vugar and several other reptilians that had forced their way into the chamber. For a moment Song considered raising himself to help fend off the attack, but if they failed to return to AIME their best route to ridding this universe of the virus would be cut off.

'Don't look, just go!' He encouraged the girls beside him, to join him in pouring their entire focus into leaving these bodies before they were slain. *No pressure,* he quietly mocked their goal.

His last conscious wish was that his female crew mates could maintain the concentration needed to join him back on AMIE, as convincing the crew of the vital urgency of this mission on his own would prove highly problematic.

11

ORIGINS

His body being rocked woke him with a start, and his eyes parted to set blurry sights on the depths of deep space beyond the window in his sleeping quarters. 'What … what is it?' The throbbing of his head urged his eyes closed once more.

'Daddy? You told me to wake you if you were not awake by now.'

His body was rocked a few times more.

'And you're not awake.'

'I'm awake,' he mumbled, his mouth as dry as the surface of Sermetica. 'Just stop with the shaking, or I'll be sick as well.'

'I made you tea.'

In a burst of consciousness, it hit Zeven that he was in bed on AMIE, and the little voice begging his attention belonged to his daughter. 'Ray?' His eyes shot open and immediately flooded with tears, due to both his sorry condition this morning and the relief of seeing his only child after an age without her.

'Yes, of course,' she was amused by his doubt, placing the tea on the bedside table. 'Who else would dare wake you in this condition?'

'Baby girl,' he sat upright and pulled her close to him in a tight embrace, savouring the smell of her dark hair.

'You have to stop calling me that,' she hugged him gladly and then pulled back to remind him. 'I turned *nine* yesterday.'

Zeven grinned. 'You could have turned a hundred and nine, you'd still be my baby girl.'

Ray rolled her eyes, freed herself and patted his chest in reassurance. 'Whatever floats your boat, Dad.'

He looked aside to find his wife, Aurora, still sleeping off the celebration of the previous day alongside him, and leaning over he kissed her bare shoulder and savoured her scent also.

'She won't be happy if you wake her,' Ray warned, 'we promised to let her sleep in today.'

Zeven was very tempted not to honour that promise, but withdrew to a less tempting distance.

'So are you going to get out of bed of your own accord, or shall I be forced to lift you out of there?' Ray folded her arms and raised both eyebrows in question.

She had some cheek, Zeven considered, as she could make good on that threat. For Ray had no psychic talent of her own, but could tap into the talents of any psychic in her close vicinity; meaning at present she had access to his psychokinesis.

'Threaten me, will you?' He jumped out of bed and threw her, squealing, over his shoulder.

'You told me to!' she insisted through her unbridled laughter, as he tickled her. 'I brought you tea!' She defended her own good intentions.

'Have some respect for the dead,' Aurora stirred to complain, and brought their game to an end.

'Shhh!' Zeven put Ray down.

'Your bad,' she pointed out.

'I accept that,' Zeven held up his hands in truce, as he backed towards the bathroom.

'See you at breakfast,' Ray instructed, suspecting he might just return to bed. 'If you're not in the mess by the time I finish my cereal, I'm coming looking for you.'

'Message received and understood,' he assured her. 'You are the best alarm clock *ever*.'

'The prettiest too,' Ray grinned, on her way out the door.

In the bathroom Zeven did a double take in the mirror, and stopped to stare at himself returned to his own body. 'Man, it's good to see you,' he told his reflection. 'I honestly thought I'd never lay eyes on you again!' He'd left this body back on Kila, what seemed like an eon ago. 'Home, sweet home.' He whipped off the clothes he'd fallen asleep in, and stepped into the shower.

The hot water pelting down upon him brought Zeven fully to his senses. His reasons for returning to AMIE were foremost in his mind, but it was the first occasion since his dying day in ancient Zhou that time was on his side and he stole the opportunity to relax. His body was so used to being on alert every waking second, it felt unbelievably good to just take a breath.

Recollections of all that had happened since leaving AMIE played through his thoughts, and it was exhausting just thinking about it.

'No one said this timekeeper shit would be easy,' he reminded himself.

Yet, at the same time, he wouldn't have missed out on his experience in the other universe for all the tea in China. *If I hadn't gone, I wouldn't even remember that China existed … or Kila, or the Otherworld either!* The premise made him smile, and he was glad and proud to be who he was: timekeeper, Chosen, Grigori! Psychic may still have been largely a dirty word in this universe, and there was a time when he had dreaded his own developing powers, but now, Zeven never wanted to go back to being an average, naive citizen of the United Star Systems again. He'd had a glimpse of the big picture, and he loved being one of the artists who had developed the ability to consciously paint that canvas. Most just saw the universe as a finished work, created by another for them to admire on their way through life, but he knew that it was a continual work in progress, actively moulded to perfection by those with the will to turn their existence into great art.

Time to begin drafting my current part of the masterpiece, he resolved, switching off the shower to get to it.

Walking the long curving corridors of the AMIE craft again was very consoling for Zeven, even though the place was like a ghost ship this morning. In the mess hall, Ray sat by herself eating breakfast, and he gave his daughter a wave upon entering.

'You only just made it.' She finished her last spoonful and got up to return her plate to the dish disposal at the end of the service counter.

'I thought we were eating together?' Zeven queried after Ray hugged him and headed for the door.

'It's a school day.' She noted the time on the clock on the wall. 'And first period is starting already. Later, Dad.' She waved and ran out the door.

As Zeven's stomach was not feeling particularly disposed towards eating this morning, he was about depart the cafeteria when he heard someone clanking about in the kitchen.

Upon investigation, he found Ringbalin stocking the fridge with fresh produce from his greenhouse.

The AMIE craft was comprised of six different modules, one of which, Module C, was entirely devoted to horticulture, and was the largest and most successful greenhouse ever to be launched into space. The reason for the success of AMIE's botany experiment was entirely due to the work of the man before him — Ringbalin Malachi, whom he'd known as Fen Gong in ancient Zhou, and as En Noah on Kila.

'Balin!' Zeven startled the botanist.

'Oh, hey, Starman,' Ringbalin replied after he recovered from the fright, and returned to his chore. 'I didn't expect to see you up this early.'

'Starman,' Zeven grinned upon hearing the name, 'it seems an age since anyone called me that.'

'Well, you have so many names these days,' Ringbalin explained. 'The royal name you were born with, the name your adoptive parents gave you, the name you got given while you were living on Frujia … I never know what to call you. Your nickname is the only constant.'

The botanist's view made Zeven laugh. 'You don't know the half of it.' The statement was a joke, but it caught in Zeven's throat and made it ache. Ringbalin didn't recall their time in ancient Zhou or on Kila because Fen had been brutally killed by Dragonface before he'd been given the chance to return his soul-mind here with his multi-universal memory still functioning.

'Song?'

Zeven swung around to find Taren with a questioning look on her face. 'Hudan,' he replied, and she breathed a sigh of relief.

'Not another name?' Ringbalin jeered, as he carted his empty trays past them, and was surprised when the captain's wife unexpectedly became teary eyed upon sighting him. 'Is something the matter, Doc?'

'Not at all,' Taren gasped back her emotion and smiled. 'It's just so good to see you.'

'Okay …' Ringbalin found this perplexing as she saw him every day and never reacted like this.

'Don't mind her,' Zeven moved in close to Ringbalin to whisper, 'she's probably still tripping from all the mescaline we consumed last night.'

Taren whacked Zeven's shoulder for being so forthcoming.

'What?' Zeven defended and then stressed, 'You're the one acting *strange*.'

'Well, it's a *strange* kind of day,' she retorted.

'Sure is,' Ringbalin decided he was heading back to the isolation and safety of his greenhouse.

'Now, do you want to tell me why I abandoned my unborn child in another universe?' Taren queried in a whisper once they were left alone.

'You've slept on Kila now,' Zeven explained, as he led her towards the table furthest from the door. 'So you can go back to any morning prior to our leaving, and rejoin Dan and your unborn child, and both shall be alive and well.'

'Of course they will,' she was excited to realise, so excited she kissed Zeven's cheek.

This was one of the few setbacks of time hopping — you could only jump into a body during its last unconscious state prior to your target day. Once you had slept, or been knocked unconscious, you could return to that moment in time.

'Control yourself, woman,' he eased her back, pretending he didn't appreciate her adoration, and Taren withdrew and folded her arms to hear him out. 'Vugar said there was no place in

255

that universe where you would be safe from him, which made me realise the virus has never been in this universe and cannot trace us or your memory here, and even if it could, it would have to have an incarnation living here to get to us. So, here seemed the best place to regroup and base this operation from.'

Taren grinned; she was fairly impressed with him, Zeven could tell.

'You can say it,' he prompted, smiling, pleased with himself, as they both took a seat.

'Say what?' She fobbed off the offer. 'You haven't told me how you plan to rid that universe of the virus yet.'

'Am I late?' Jazmay wandered into the mess, holding her head and wearing very dark shades over her eyes.

'Huxin?' Zeven checked her status.

'Sorry?' she rasped, heading for the water dispenser to pour herself a cup. 'Are you still tripping, short-man?'

'That's Starman, Jaz,' he corrected.

'Not from where I am standing.' She hazarded a laugh, but decided it hurt too much. Still, it was true, Jazmay was taller than most of the men on board AMIE of whom Zeven was the shortest.

'She didn't make it.' Taren was devastated, as Jazmay had been time-hopping with her as long as Zeven had.

'Make what?' She approached and collapsed into a chair at their table.

'Nothing,' Taren forced a smile to downplay the tragedy. 'It's no matter.'

'So then,' Jazmay placed her crossed feet up on the table. 'What are we going to do about Dragonface?'

'Aww!' Taren hit her feet, annoyed by the scare.

'Really, Jaz … are you trying to give me a fucking heart attack?' Zeven grumbled, as he stopped trying to figure out how he would manage what he had to without her.

'You were both so sucked in!' Jazmay chuckled despite the obvious pain it caused her.

'This is serious!' Taren stressed, having nearly had heart failure herself.

256

'No,' Jaz corrected, 'this is *paradise*, not having that bloody virus breathing down our necks.'

'Hear, hear,' Zeven granted.

'You're pretty smart, short-man,' she warranted.

'You're pretty brave to keep calling me that,' he retorted, and Jazmay, being the stunning Phemorian beauty that she was, just served him a huge smile.

'So what's the plan, *Star*man?'

'We go back to when we first came through the Eternity Gate and stop Ninharsag ever injecting the virus into the reptilian line.'

'I think I've missed something?' Jazmay sat forward.

'You were there,' Zeven assured her, 'your Grigori name is Gadriel. And there were others on this crew like Leal and Swithin who could also be of aid if we can teach them how to regress into their past lives as we have learned to do.'

Taren frowned, unsure if dragging more of the crew into this disaster was really a good idea.

'And I can fetch Lord Avery, Rhun and Noah from where they await my summons in the Otherworld, as they were there also,' Zeven summed up.

'Correct me if I am wrong,' Taren cut in, 'but I was without a working body throughout the entire time of which you speak.'

Zeven grimaced. 'Yeah, it's true, you'll have to sit this mission out.'

'Damn,' Taren hated the sound of that. 'So say you stop Ninharsag injecting the virus into the reptilians,' she challenged, 'then what do you plan to do with it? Fly it back through the Eternity Gate and into the dark universe?'

'Whoa!' Jazmay was a little alarmed by what she was hearing.

'If I have to,' Zeven boasted. 'We have no use for the *Leviathan* after that and it could be a good way to dispose of those seals for good, too.'

'Okay, that would mean the virus won't be in the reptilian race, so how do you think that will affect the situation that the Ji family find upon occupying the Yin capital in ancient Zhou?'

'We'll have to return to ancient China to find out —' Zeven began.

'No, I couldn't go through all that again,' Taren refused.

'Not all,' Zeven advised, 'just go back to a few days before Jiang Hudan died to, say … the day before Hudan married Ji Dan and got herself pregnant.'

'Jiang Hudan and Ji Dan never married.' Taren gasped on the revelation — she could not count the amount of times she'd been told that and did not listen. 'If I never got pregnant there would be no impediment to prevent me returning here once we straighten out this mess.'

Zeven served her a knowing wink. 'We need to take out the virus before we venture back to Zhou to check out the reptilian situation at the end of Song's reign. But with any luck the events that lead to the destruction of the Dropa craft will play out very differently to the last two times that that situation at Bayan Har Shan has been revisited by one of the Chosen.'

Taren raised both eyebrows, her mind boggling at the scope of his vision and at the million things that could go horribly wrong with screwing around with events so vastly spread out through time. 'You know the risk you run when you attempt to rework one instance in time too often?' Taren cautioned.

Zeven nodded and shrugged. 'It's the only way through that I figure will get that virus off our tail, and set things to rights on Earth and Kila.'

'I hate to put a fly in the ointment, but there is a flaw that you may not have considered,' Taren winced.

'What's that?' Zeven challenged, feeling that he'd thought everything well through.

'What if you go back to your Grigori existence and forget everything that has gone before, as we did in ancient Zhou?'

'Shit, she's right,' Jazmay realised. 'Then we'd have to live our lifetimes over in that universe.'

'Lucian is tapped into the Akashic memory,' Taren pointed out. 'And even then it took him half his life as Ji Dan to tap into the talent! The only one of us who retained all memory during our time in ancient Zhou was our Shifu.'

'Telmo!' Zeven wanted to kick himself for leaving him behind now.

'Did I hear someone call my name?' Telmo entered right on cue, yet despite the coincidence, chances were he remembered nothing of their latest mission.

'If I didn't know better,' Taren ventured to say, 'I would think you were just waiting to hear your name called?'

'Well, it was either come back here, or be eaten by a bunch of reptilians, so I opted for here.' Telmo came and took a seat.

'What about the others? Wu Geng, Aysel, *Jahan*?' Jazmay asked even though she knew the answer.

'It matters not,' Telmo forced a grin to avoid the unpleasant topic. 'I'm guessing we are just about to change all that.' He looked to Zeven, wearing an expression that begged for an apology.

Zeven felt he owed Telmo an explanation. 'The only reason I didn't want you on board on this mission was because —'

'I was one of the Nefilim at the time.' Telmo knew why.

'You remember?' Zeven was surprised, as Telmo surely couldn't have had time to view the orb, and could not have brought it wih him when time-hopping.

'Of course I remember, *I was there*,' Telmo emphasised. 'I am the only one among you that is fully plugging into the Akashic memory. You have realised that you need me for this mission. Thus, here I am. Sorry to have defied your order … but then again, I'm not really.'

'Whatever … yes, we need you,' Zeven corroborated.

'I know,' Telmo concluded and Taren shook her head in wonder.

'You get more and more like Taliesin every day,' she noted, sounding unsure if that was a good thing.

Telmo looked her way and grinned. 'Let's not bring the dark ages into this; it's confusing enough already.'

'I second that motion,' Jaz held a hand up. 'I need coffee.' She picked herself up and flounced towards the machine that would supply her with a cup of the said brew.

'Not only can I awaken your timekeeper memory in your Grigorian counterparts, but I can also train up Leal and Swithin, as I did all of you back on Kila,' he concluded.

Zeven was frowning. 'How long have you been listening in on our conversation?' Zeven had thought they were keeping their voices down.

'I wasn't,' Telmo claimed, 'it is just an elementary conclusion that you'd want to utilise them. You are not the only one with a brain, you realise?'

'Well, at least you are admitting I *have* a brain now,' Zeven bantered, 'so I guess that's a step in the right direction.'

'You did great, Starman,' Taren finally awarded him his due, as she gripped his arm across the table. 'I for one am very grateful, just to be able to eat breakfast and not want to throw up.'

'I want to throw up,' Jaz rejoined them at the table, with her beverage in hand.

'Actually,' Taren thought about eating something and decided she did feel a bit seedy, 'maybe tomorrow.'

'Shitty morning, all,' Lucian entered the mess and, with a meek wave in their direction, headed straight for the coffee machine. Thankfully, the captain did not notice how petrified his crew were to see him.

'What do we tell the captain?' Zeven queried in a whisper and all at the table leaned into a huddle to discuss the vital matter.

'We have to tell him everything … especially if you want to get other crew involved,' Taren insisted on the quiet.

'That's a lot of explaining,' Zeven stressed.

'I can retrain the captain in past life recall, then we don't have to explain it, he'll just remember?' Telmo proffered.

'But he won't let you regress him unless he understands why,' Taren pointed out.

'Are you all whispering to be considerate,' Lucian asked as he approached, 'or did I miss something?'

'Ah. Funny you should ask …' Taren stood to 'fess up.

'Oh dear.' Lucian was wary, because he knew his wife well! Clearly he was already regretting getting up this morning.

'Perhaps you should sit down,' Taren suggested, 'it's rather a *long* story.'

After an hour of playing fill in the blanks over breakfast, Lucian had heard enough. 'Khalid is on our side now?' He had to laugh.

'No, seriously,' Taren backed up what Telmo had been saying.

Lucian smothered his mirth, and frowned in an attempt to give them the benefit of the doubt. 'Can any of you give me some proof of all this?' Clearly, he suspected that their story was an elaborate hoax to catch him out in his hungover state.

'I plan to summon forth the Lord Avery, his brother Rhun and En Noah to aid us in this mission,' Zeven advised.

Lucian sat forward in his chair, unsure if he had heard correctly. 'From Kila?'

Some of their crew, including Lucian himself, had visited the universe parallel before, so he knew they weren't inventing the other universe of which they spoke. He knew his wife had made a vow to the governor of Kila to return there to warn him of the reptilian threat at some point in the future; he was just finding it hard to believe they had already done this, and so much more.

'I'm summoning them from the Otherworld, actually,' Zeven corrected. 'That's where they are, right now, waiting for me to call them to strategise.'

Lucian gazed about at the nodding heads, confirming their pilot's words. 'Is anyone else on the crew aware of this?'

All present shook their heads in accord, and Lucian quietly considered how best to proceed.

'From what you've said, I assume time is not a major factor in this mission at present?' the captain put to them, and again they all shook their heads in response.

'Then, keep this to yourselves, and we'll meet in my conference room in an hour.' Lucian stood to depart, and looked to Taren. 'Can I have a quiet word, my dear?'

She hated when Lucian called her 'my dear' as it always meant she had earned his disfavour. 'In your office?' she guessed.

'Yes, indeed.' He sounded none too impressed as he led off towards said destination.

Once inside the captain's office, the door closed. Lucian sat on his desk, folded his arms and raised his brow in expectation of a confession.

'What can I tell you, it's the truth.' Taren held both her palms outwards to appeal her innocence.

'So you are telling me that I learned not only how to teleport and time travel, but how to project my consciousness into a past life incarnation that wasn't even in this universe?' He was sure he was being led down the garden path on this one. 'I know things have been a bit boring on board lately but why pick me to torment?'

'It is because we were playing a waiting game with Khalid at this point of time, that Zeven picked now to return to AMIE,' Taren stated. 'I kid you not. During our time on Kila this time around, you even tapped into your eternal memory, *and could again*, if you'd just let Telmo instruct you. You only need to log back into that memory and get an update, then you'll know we're not bullshitting! There is some serious shit going down on Kila. I saw you slain before my eyes not a few hours ago.' The shock of it came back to haunt; Taren began to physically tremble, and took a seat to stay her nerves.

'You're not kidding.' Lucian came to sit beside her on the lounge, sounding rather disappointed to be finally accepting of the idea.

'I wish I were joking,' she assured him.

Taren was concerned that if Lucian did obtain total recall of the events in that other universe, he would also recall her pregnancy, which she rather hoped to reverse on the quiet. Wanting a child as he did, Lucian might object.

'That must have been distressing, seeing me killed?' he allowed, whereupon he was overwhelmed by a hug.

'It will never come to pass. Once we are done, Ji Dan will have a very different end.' Taren considered that was true in more ways than one. If Hudan refused to marry Ji Dan, she would also have to avoid becoming involved with him once Rhun brought the timekeepers together at Bayan Har Shan — that was going to prove harder than destroying the mind-eater virus.

'If you are bluffing, then you're a consummate actress,' Lucian decided, at which point his hug was replaced by a whack to the gut.

'I'm not lying!' Taren stressed again and stood frustrated to pace about. 'How many more times am I going to come to you with something like this, which, I might add, always proves to be true, before you will realise this is *me* you're talking to and strange situations are bound to just spring up out of nowhere! I thought you'd figured that out before you married me?'

'Ouch!' Lucian rubbed where she'd hit him. The muscles there were like stone from working out in the gym, so she knew she hadn't physically hurt him. 'So this is the way you treat your dearly departed husband, is it?' He grinned to imply he did believe her.

'So, you're in then?' She sat back down, returning his amorous smile.

'I might be persuaded to come on board,' he suggested, lying back on the lounge and placing his hands behind his head. 'You've got about three-quarters of an hour to win me over.'

'I doubt it will take that long.' She lay herself face-down on top of him, eager to take up the challenge.

'So, were we lovers in this past life we visited?' he asked.

'I was a vestal virgin of an ancient order of shamanistic priestesses, and you were a widowed and celibate sage of the royal house of Ji,' she told him honestly.

'That does not sound very promising,' Lucian grinned, realising how sex starved his soul mate must have been.

Taren grinned and shrugged. 'We have a lot of catching up to do.' Her kiss conveyed her great eagerness to be compensated.

'I feel more disposed towards your cause already,' he allowed as Taren raised herself to strip off her clothes.

'The best part is, we have to sit this mission out, you and I.' She discarded her suit and crawled back on top of him in her underwear.

'I am definitely in,' he submitted, and Taren laughed.

'That took all of two minutes,' she claimed victory for the challenge, leaning in close to him to invite another kiss.

'Which means we can spend the remains of the hour far more gainfully …' Lucian proposed, 'not talking at all.'

Zeven arrived in the conference room fifteen minutes early for the meeting, in order to do some preparation. In accordance with the law of three requests, he summoned Lord Avery and his companions forth from the Otherworld to brief them on the plan, which they were all most eager to hear, once Zeven had explained his reasons for delaying the conversation until now.

'It was a smart move,' Rhun considered, and even Avery had calmed down.

'Are you all familiar with your Grigorian personas?' Zeven asked.

'Sacha,' replied Avery.

'Armaros,' Noah confirmed with a smile.

'Not a clue,' announced Rhun.

'Penemue,' all his associates advised at once.

Rhun was a little taken back by the verbal onslaught. 'Okay then … thanks for the heads-up.'

'Penemue is important because I need him to prevent Ereshkigal from stealing the seals from cryogenics in the *Leviathan*,' Zeven explained.

Rhun frowned, distressed. 'I definitely have some homework to do on this one.'

'It's a very small window of opportunity you are talking about here,' Noah was concerned. 'There were only a few hours at most that the virus was actually incubated and contained.'

'I know exactly where I was at the time,' Zeven pointed out, 'as Azazèl's phantom came to see me right after he saw the virus contained in the labs of Ninharsag.'

'I was in the great library with Enki,' Noah confirmed.

Zeven looked to Rhun to advise him, 'Penemue was on the *Leviathan*.'

Rhun nodded pleased to have been accounted for, and they all looked to Avery.

'I'll have to get back to you on that,' he admitted, and Rhun was doubly pleased to learn he wasn't the only one with regression work to do.

'Oh, damn.' The captain entered to see Zeven's company, which confirmed his prior story beyond a shadow of a doubt. 'Harrowed to see you gentlemen,' he explained his reaction, as Taren entered behind her husband and gasped to see their colleagues from another universe inside.

'Best hope that Ringbalin and Mythric are nowhere about.' She was relieved when the door closed behind her.

'I've met my past-life incarnation before and there was no harm done,' Noah advised.

'I haven't,' Rhun obviously felt kind of weird about that.

'Ringbalin doesn't remember any of that; for him it hasn't happened yet, and Mythric doesn't even know about your universe, let alone his place in it.' Taren frowned. 'We'd best keep all this on a need to know basis.'

The door opening behind Taren gave everyone a start, until they saw it was Jazmay and Telmo.

'Even when I'm on time, I'm late,' Jazmay commented removing her dark glasses, when she saw they had company.

'Gang's all here,' Telmo rubbed his palms together.

'And I thought we were going to have a fairly simple, straightforward year this year,' the captain commented, taking the seat at the end of the conference table as Taren locked the room closed.

'Never mind, we'll have this done and be out of our way in no time,' Taren took a seat, and looked at her team mates hopefully. 'Right guys?'

Everyone's perplexed expressions did nothing to reassure Lucian, and he resigned himself to just co-operate. 'So tell me then, what do you need from AMIE?'

Lucian had no qualms with hosting this mission, his only sticking point was getting Leal and Swithin involved.

'Leal, or rather Sariel, was with me at the time in question,' Zeven explained, 'it would help a lot to have him consciously cooperating, because even then he was one of our best telepaths and a technological whiz.'

'I see,' Lucian considered this. 'What about Swithin?'

'I don't know where he was placed in all this, only that Bezaliel, his Grigorian counterpart was there,' Zeven said. 'I just figured the more Grigori we had on side the better.'

Lucian frowned. 'Well, I will not order my crew to comply, but I can have them paged, and you can put the case to them and let them decide for themselves.'

'Good call,' Zeven gave Lucian the thumbs up, fairly sure that Leal would come on board. He was not so sure about Swithin, however.

'I would also recommend we brief Kassa on all of this, and get her medical assessment of the risk.' Lucian put forward.

'We've done this kind of thing before,' Taren posed, wanting to get as few of the crew here involved as possible.

'Well, not exactly,' Rhun pointed out, 'as you've never actually attempted returning to a body you have left behind in an unaltered timeline before, you've only jumped into bodies of the timelines you were altering.'

'My head hurts,' Jazmay complained. In her hungover state she was having difficulty following all the quantum time theory.

'What Rhun is trying to say,' Telmo pointed out, 'is that if we misjudge our return, our bodies could shut down, as we are really placing them in a voluntary state of coma.'

'And that being the case,' Lucian felt his suggestion warranted, 'I will feel much easier about this with our medical advisor overseeing the proceedings.'

'Are you out of your fucking mind!' Swithin was strongly opposed. 'I was born in this universe and here is where I intend to stay!'

'Where is your sense of adventure and discovery?' Zeven appealed. 'Isn't that why you joined the AMIE project in the first place?'

'No,' Swithin insisted, sharply. 'I joined AMIE to make money! Which, by the way, I didn't!' he reminded the captain, who was also his brother. 'I didn't ask to be a psychic space pirate! I think we are already in enough shit, don't you?'

'Fair enough,' Lucian granted, 'you can leave.'

Everyone's attention turned to Leal, who appeared wide-eyed and rather overwhelmed by the premise also. 'Sure, I'm in … sounds like a hoot.'

Kassa, AMIE's doctor, who was also Leal's wife, frowned to indicate that she felt her husband was being rather flippant.

'Aww,' Swithin waved Leal off as an idiot. 'You're all insane.' He moved to leave, and Lucian caught his arm to stop him.

'Not a word of this to anyone,' the captain instructed.

Swithin frowned, as if his brother was daft. 'Who the fuck would believe it?' He exited the room and the door closed behind him.

'Charming fellow,' Avery commented dryly.

'And always wasn't,' Rhun added to the mirth of those who remembered Caradoc from the dark ages.

'Good to have you on the team,' Zeven was relieved his co-pilot had agreed.

Leal shrugged off the decision as simple. 'It's not every day you get to work with people from another universe and a being from another dimension,' Leal grinned — his spirit of adventure was alive and kicking.

'Kassa, what are your thoughts?' The captain sought her professional opinion.

'I am inclined to agree with Swithin,' although she was sorry to curb their enthusiasm. 'What you are doing could be very dangerous.'

'But if you were monitoring their bodies throughout the event, you could minimise that risk?' Taren pointed out.

'Well yes, but I would still strongly advise against it.' She looked to her husband, hoping that he would appreciate her judgement and decline.

'I left my body for much longer periods in ancient Zhou,' Taren informed Kassa.

'How long will the mission itself take?' the captain queried.

'As far as you are concerned it should be practically instantaneous,' Telmo estimated, which was a relief to Lucian.

Kassa was also becoming a little more well disposed. 'Should it take longer, I have equipment in the medical rooms that could aid to sustain you indefinitely, but if all goes to plan, that should not be required.'

'So you will help us?' Taren clarified, hopefully.

'Better that than to have you all wake up dead,' she resigned herself to giving assistance reluctantly.

'What are the chances of us failing to return as planned?' Leal was looking a little more worried.

'We haven't failed yet,' Zeven assured. 'You just return to the minute you left.'

'Then we head off to our next meeting point,' Telmo concluded.

'Which will be?' Lucian was curious.

'We'll decide that once this first phase of the mission is completed,' Zeven advised. 'But rest assured, you shall wake tomorrow morning, and it will be as if none of this drama ever happened.'

Lucian didn't appear to quite believe that, or if he did, he felt a little odd about it. 'Do you need me to do this past life regression?'

'Probably not,' Taren piped up to say, 'we are not needed for this phase of the mission, and the you we left behind on Kila remembers everything.'

'The dead me,' Lucian stated with a good serve of irony.

'The day before we returned here, you were perfectly fine,' she assured him.

'So,' Lucian was perplexed by the unfolding paradox, 'shall I remember the sum total of what we've been through in the end?'

'You should do,' Taren allowed, after thinking it through. 'A large part of it, anyway.'

'Yeah,' Zeven agreed, 'whether we revisit you on Kila or just meet up with you in ancient Zhou, you should return with memory intact, including this memory, but excluding the past-life regression you did before your untimely death … because Dan got killed, so that memory will be wiped if we go back and change the situation.

268

As we already know what Dan learned from that regression, there is no need to revisit it and expose you — him — to death by Dragonface again.' He backed Taren up, suspecting why she would rather Lucian remain ignorant to the situation they'd left behind on Kila.

'Well then I guess I should take most of you down to the meditation chamber in module D, and see if we can't get you remembering the period in question.' Telmo stood to get them organised. 'It should only take a few hours to get everyone up to speed.'

The captain nodded to concur. 'I'll seal off access to the recreation module for the day, so the rest of the crew should remain ignorant of your presence here. 'When you are ready to embark on your quest,' Lucian ordered, 'we'll get you up to the medical quarters where Kassa can monitor the proceedings.'

'Right you are, Captain.' Telmo gave him the thumbs up. 'Follow me, all.' He vanished — Rhun, Avery, Noah and Jazmay followed.

'I feel rather inadequate suddenly,' Leal commented aside to Zeven.

'Not to worry,' Zeven grabbed his crew mate's arm. 'We'll have you jumping time and universes in a few hours.'

Leal appeared a mite concerned about that, as did Kassa, as Zeven vanished with him.

'I'd like to learn how to do that, too.' Lucian was undecided about foregoing the session in the wake of their departure.

'You will,' Taren assured him, 'about a year from now.'

'But don't you intend to change the event that lands us in another universe?' He figured he would never end up on Kila.

'True,' Taren agreed, 'but the you who will return with us just prior to those event changes will have already been through everything of which we speak.'

'This is making my brain hurt,' Kassa frowned as she attempted to wrap her mind around their conversation. 'Why did you have to pick the hangover day from hell to do this?'

'We all remembered it,' Taren stated the simple truth.

'We certainly will now.' Lucian said, still a little perturbed about the whole affair. 'How can you be so sure this is the right thing to do? That you won't just create some huge inter-universal time disaster?'

'My thoughts exactly,' Kassa concurred.

Taren rested her hand against the piece of stone that the timekeepers still residing in this universe at this time wore on their upper arm as protection.

These amulets had been dubbed Juju stones, as they linked every one of the timekeepers to the entity who was the sum total of the Grigori — their group soul, *Azazèl-mindos-coomra-dorchi*. The same entity whose exit from their universe they would seek to safely facilitate one year from now, in hopes of preventing their sabbatical in the universe parallel from ever eventuating. The Juju boosted their own psychic power, prevented others from seeking them via psychic means, and linked them energetically to the cause of their highest good.

'When I think about what we are planning,' Taren answered them both, 'I feel no pain from the stone, so I can only assume that our oversoul is at peace with our decision.'

If their intention was not in line with the highest good, the Juju stone let them know by causing their arm to ache. Lucian, who was well aware of this, was placated, as was Kassa to a degree.

'I cannot argue that reasoning,' Kassa admitted, heading for the door. 'I'll be in my office when you need me.'

Taren was quietly comforted also, and when she considered reworking her last few days in ancient Zhou, there was no protest from the stone either: not that Taren imagined there would be, when she would most likely be setting history back to the way it should have been.

When they received Telmo's 'good to go' message, Lucian and Taren headed down to the medical chambers to see their team off and await their return.

'My main concern is for Leal to be comfortable doing this and not feel obliged to go on this mission, which is *way* beyond the call of duty,' Lucian explained to Taren, as they the entered the medical room where the team were gathered in the waiting area.

'So you, Avery and Noah should head immediately to Rhun's aid,' Zeven was saying to Jazmay. 'Armaros' emotional influence will hopefully sway Ereshkigal to our cause.'

'The Sumerian Goddess of the Dead,' Noah stated, showing that he knew of her from previous adventures with the Chosen Ones. 'How can I influence the emotions of a creature with no emotions?'

'The Nefilim have emotions, they're just not in touch with them yet,' Zeven pointed out.

Still, Noah was uncomfortable. 'I know Armaros discovered his power to influence the emotional states of living things back on Nibiru, but I have never really exhibited this talent, not to the same extent as Ringbalin or Fen.'

'You've got it,' Zeven served Noah an ironic look. 'I can hardly believe it is me telling you to have a little faith in yourself.'

Noah chuckled, amused by his point. 'I'll do my best.'

'Hey, Captain,' Leal noted he and Taren had entered and was excited to see Lucian. 'Check this out!' The co-pilot vanished.

Lucian was startled by a tap on the shoulder; he spun about to find Leal. 'Ta-dah!' the co-pilot announced, 'I'm officially a timekeeper now.'

'I'm very happy for you ... I think?' Lucian concluded, frowning and smiling in turn — clearly Leal was hyped about the proceedings and not fearful at all.

'Well, I must say I am impressed,' Kassa considered, as her husband hadn't had the ability to teleport when he woke this morning.

'We've always had this talent, right from our very beginning.' Leal passed on what he'd learned. 'It's just a matter of remembering that we did, made easier by the fact that all Grigori retain their eternal memory; and how in tune we are with our Watchers denotes how much we can remember. And seriously, you ought to get a load of where we are headed!' Leal added, enthusiastically looking to the captain. 'It's a shame you were without a body at the time.'

Lucian looked to Taren bemused. 'Now I'm disembodied?'

'*We* were disembodied, yes,' Taren answered with a grin, to emphasise it was nothing to worry about. 'We were off speaking with the mistress of primordial creation and chaos at the time,' she advised just to add to his confusion.

'That's how the Grigori ended up in the human consciousness stream,' Zeven added.

'And why this mission is so important, because in return for having our wish to be directly involved with the evolution of human consciousness granted we undertook to raise humanity's consciousness to a point where it could enter this universal scheme; also the Nefilim and the reptilians,' Telmo added.

'We took care of the Nefilim a hundred years ago,' Rhun outlined. 'We didn't know about the injustice the Grigori and the Nefilim had done the reptilians until just recently.'

'Well, you all seem to be on the same page,' the captain granted, although he didn't understand half of what they were talking about. 'If you feel prepared, best get this done and over with.'

'Are we all clear?' Zeven queried and everyone nodded in accord.

'No matter how tempted you may be to alter situations back there, just stay focused on our objective.' Avery added. 'Or god knows what effect it might have on both the future of the Earth and Kila.'

'Affirmative,' Zeven replied on behalf of the team, who were nodding and giving the thumbs up. 'See you all back here in a couple of minutes.'

'Your beds await!' Kassa motioned them through to her main chambers, where she had several beds assembled, and monitoring equipment set up. 'Come in and we'll get you all hooked up.'

12

CONTAINMENT

'Timekeeper awaken.'

After a vague moment, Noah realised that he was standing in the body of his Grigorian counterpart in the garden beyond the door of the grand library on Nibiru, where he was keeping company with the Nefilim lord, Enki.

'I have no idea what that means,' he was explaining. 'Only that Anu instructed that I should tell you this upon finding myself in the garden with you this day.' As his company still appeared a little stunned, Enki asked. 'Do you know what it means?'

'I do indeed,' said Noah, reaching out to a long stem lined with flowers yet to bloom. He loosely wrapped his hand around the stem and, running his touch along the stalk, its flowers burst into full bloom.

'Good gracious!' Enki was amazed, and Noah gave a chuckle.

'Well, what do you know, I can do it,' he consoled himself.

'You have the power of the creatrix running through you!' Enki concluded. 'If only my children were so inclined and gifted.' The lord appeared awfully disappointed that this was not the case.

'The Grigori, with the aid of Tiamat, will bring your desires to life in time,' Noah assured the lord.

'You know of this?' Enki was shocked to his core. 'How?'

'Why, Tiamat, of course,' Noah advised. 'She knows it was not your choice to imprison her son in ice.'

The lord drew back in fear that his part in the affair was known. 'I begged the Pantheon to let Kingu go, but they —'

'It is no matter,' Noah advised, 'Tiamat sees all, and is watching right now.'

Enki was suddenly wary and uncomfortable.

'I know that you have been ordered by the Pantheon to sedate me in this instance and to see me escorted to a similar cryogenic containment in the labs of Ninharsag,' Noah challenged, and what little colour that existed in the Nefilim's lord's face drained away. 'But it is Tiamat's wish that you refrain, for I have something I must do for her.'

'Will you release Kingu?' Enki assumed, worried about the backlash from his peers.

'No,' was all Noah would say on the matter, 'that situation has nothing to do with the Grigori. But the situation that is about to unfold in the labs of Ninharsag is of concern to us, as it will have far-reaching ramifications.'

'Has this something to do with your timekeeping?' Enki realised that Anu must have known of this pending situation also.

'You are wise, lord, yes, it does,' Noah granted.

Enki pulled the sedation device from his stately robe and tossed it away. 'What would Tiamat like me to do?'

'Go to the labs of your sister and prevent her from resisting the will of my brothers,' he instructed.

'Where are you going?' Enki was concerned. 'There is a sedation order out on all the Grigori, this city is not safe for you.'

'Exactly the reason that we must move quickly.' Noah closed his eyes and thought of Sammael.

Armaros appeared in the path of Sammael and Sariel as they headed towards the entrance of the prison level beneath Nibiru. 'Timekeepers?' he said, halting them in their tracks.

Given an instant to collect their wits and look about, Zeven gave Noah the nod of approval. 'Good job?' He looked to Sariel beside him. 'You with us?'

'Yeah?' Leal frowned, feeling between his legs. 'But my genitalia seems to have gone missing?'

'No,' Zeven advised, 'you just haven't been assigned any yet.'

'Then how do I piss?' Leal wondered.

'You don't piss, you don't eat, you're immortal!' Zeven looked to the end of the corridor to note the door opening.

'But —' Leal was bemused.

'Forget it, we gotta motor,' Zeven pointed out the Nefilim guards emerging from the door ahead of them. 'They're about to knock us out. Go wake Sacha and Gadriel,' he bid Noah, who vanished.

'Follow me,' he advised Leal, who was like an animal caught in the headlights as he watched the alien force raise weapons and move towards them.

'Never mind,' Zeven grabbed hold of his companion and envisioned them both outside the lab of Ninharsag.

Penemue was obviously surprised to see Armaros, Gadriel and Sacha return to the *Leviathan*. 'I thought you were sightseeing?'

'We have a situation,' Noah informed, 'timekeeper.'

Penemue observed himself, and the situation he was in, with an expanding grin. 'It actually works! Ha!' This was the first time Rhun had time-jumped in this fashion.

'Well, if you are done being chuffed with yourself,' Avery proffered via Sacha's body, 'we have an appointment with the Queen of the Underworld.'

'You're Lord of the Otherworld. Won't you have some influence on her?' Rhun queried.

'The Otherworld and the Underworld are entirely different places, on entirely different levels of consciousness.' Avery filled him in. 'I have no authority or influence over the dead, she does.'

'Oh goody,' Rhun mocked, as he looked to the security monitor before him and saw the lady in question appear in their cryogenics facility. 'Speak of the devil.'

They all moved around behind Rhun to view their target.

'I have a question,' Noah raised a finger to query. 'Do I need to be touching a subject to exert my emotional influence over them?'

'No,' Jazmay advised from within Gadriel. 'Or at least, Ringbalin and Fen discovered they only needed to be in the vicinity.'

'Then you should go ahead and distract our guest.' Noah observed the lady on screen coming to a stop before one of the modules and taking an interest in the floor of the interior. 'I won't be far behind.'

Under the guiding hand of her incantation, Ereshkigal watched the seal before her reforming into a solid mass, and when it had, she reached out to take hold of the solid item.

'Dismissed,' Avery commanded.

Her enchantment over the elements broke, the reformative energy scattered, and the golden insignia melted over the floor of the module once more. Angered and curious, Ereshkigal looked to the three Grigori entering the chamber to see who dared override her will — something that had obviously never happened before.

'Which of you dares to defy the Queen of the Dead?' She removed her hood to stare them down.

'That would be me.' Avery held a finger up to claim responsibility. 'But what you should be asking yourself is *how* I did it? The answer … my vibrational frequency must be more influential than yours.'

Ereshkigal was not amused. 'Impossible. You have come through the Eternity Gate from the lesser universe, where all the rejects from this evolution are cast. I know as I watch the souls of the damned cast there every day.'

'We are all capable of rising beyond our humble beginnings,' Avery advised graciously.

'There is a portal to the dark universe in the Underworld?' Rhun queried finding Ereshkigal's claim interesting.

'Of course, for those who choose that path. It is a one-way passage,' she cautioned, 'and all souls are inevitably brought to bear before me prior to judgement.'

Avery noted Armaros appear behind their target and kept talking to keep her distracted while the sage cast his glamour. 'Well, I am sorry to disappoint you, but you shall never have the pleasure of seeing me before your throne. For I am Lord of the Otherworld, and the elementals you seek to exploit with your conjuring are *my* subjects.'

'That is a lie.' Ereshkigal's eyes narrowed. 'There is no such place.'

'Indeed there is, only none of your ilk are developed enough emotionally to frequent it,' Avery enlightened her. 'For there is another one-way portal in your realm through which the souls of righteous humans are returned to Tiamat's reincarnation loop, and they pass through my realm to reach her matrix.'

Ereshkigal was wide-eyed. 'No one, bar myself, knows anything about the workings of the Underworld! For no one dares go there but I.' Clearly she sought to know how this newcomer had come by his information.

'Are you so used to lies that you cannot tell when the truth is staring you in the face?' Avery replied kindly.

The dark Nefilim lady did not lash out, but rather her entire demeanour softened as she felt Noah's influence. The anger in her frown turned to curiosity as she turned about to find Armaros at her back.

He smiled amicably upon being discovered.

'You?' She was perplexed as she took a step closer to him and then reached out a hand to make contact with him. 'You are so *warm*.' It seemed a wonder to her; despite that she was touching the breastplate of his metal armour. 'What is that energy?' Ereshkigal was compelled closer and wound her hands about him to hug him close.

'That is joy,' Noah told her as she pressed herself against his Grigorian form.

'It's so … magnetic.' She nestled her head into his neck, and Noah looked wide-eyed in panic at his companions as Avery served him the thumbs up.

'You are *mine*,' Ereshkigal uttered, and a shadow creature formed behind them, swallowing Ereshkigal and Armaros, before dissipating altogether.

'What?' Rhun gasped, as did they all.

'Well, Armaros certainly distracted her from the seals,' Avery proffered.

'We should go after him,' Rhun advised Jazmay, who quickly agreed with him.

'I'm going to conceal our ship a little better,' Avery said, 'and prevent any other alien tourists from finding these seals.'

Avery waited to see his Grigori brother gone, but in the end Rhun only gave a disgruntled moan. 'What is wrong?'

'We are still *here*.' Rhun pointed out the obvious.

'You can't follow Armaros,' Avery deduced.

'Let me guess,' Rhun hypothesised. 'Ereshkigal has complete autonomy in her realm?'

'I do in the Otherworld,' Avery concurred. 'So in all likelihood, you are correct.'

'Don't you know this stuff?' Rhun was annoyed they had not foreseen this possible complication. 'You are supposed to know everything!'

'About the age I am from! Not even the soul who was the Lord of the Otherworld before me has come into being yet, so how the hell would I have knowledge of this point in evolution? Even the Otherworld is still forming!'

'What about all that shit you just said to Ereshkigal?' Rhun challenged. 'How did you know that?'

'I was just theorising really,' Avery confessed.

Rhun was gobsmacked. 'You were lying.'

'How are we going to get Armaros back from the goddamned Queen of the Dead?' Jazmay cut into the argument. 'If we can't get in, he can't get out.'

Avery shrugged. 'I guess we find something Ereshkigal wants more than Armaros and trade her for him.'

'But the only thing she might want more are these seals.' Jazmay outlined their conundrum.

'We can't be entirely sure about that,' Avery posed. 'From what I know of Ereshkigal from studying history under En Noah as a lad, she is not a very social creature.'

'Yeah, so? She wanted to check our ship for souvenirs from the dark universe, what of it?' Rhun attempted to speed things along.

'I wonder if that was why she met with Anu just prior to the Grigori arriving on Nibiru?' Avery postulated. 'Or was there some other reason?'

'Maybe it was to get permission to search our ship?' Rhun theorised, 'but Anu would not have granted her request.'

'En Noah did mention that Anu seemed very dark at his kin following that meeting,' Jazmay recalled.

'That could have had something to do with the Pantheon voting to put the son of Tiamat and the Grigori on ice,' Rhun posited.

'Maybe there was more to it?' Avery advised they investigate. 'Telmo is obviously residing within Anu, or none of the timekeepers would have awakened.'

'I'll go see Telmo,' Rhun volunteered. 'You go tell Zeven what has happened,' he delegated, and from within Gadriel, Jazmay nodded to affirm.

'And I'll get creative with this lot.' Avery referred to the melted seals, scattered throughout the chamber.

'Jaz,' Rhun prevented her leaving. 'Penemue never left the *Leviathan*, and so never met Anu.' This meant he could not teleport to the target, having neither the image of the person nor the place he wished to reach.

'We did,' Jaz referred to Avery and herself, who, along with the rest of the Grigori had been brought through the porthole system from their ship in Orion to the capital on Nibiru. 'We were taken to Anu's Worlds Chamber before being given leave to explore the city. So I'll drop you off.' Gadriel slapped a hand down on Rhun's shoulder and vanished with him.

Upon materialising in Anu's Worlds Chamber, Rhun was thankful for Jazmay's forethought in landing them behind the large throne therein. Their target was in the middle of an important meeting that Rhun would not have relished interrupting with a sudden appearance.

'If we do not send you back to her in the Underworld, she has threatened to raise the dead to outnumber the living!' Anu was saying, and Rhun peeked out from behind the throne to see whom Anu was addressing.

Even though he was so much younger, less jaded and less Orme addicted, Rhun recognised the Nefilim lord as one he would have dealings with at several points in the long distant future. *Nergal.*

'I am one of the great Pantheon of Twelve, not a subject to be traded for favour!' The young Nefilim warrior strongly objected to the proposal, as the bodies of the unconscious Grigori were dragged into the chamber by Nefilim guards and dumped in rows for counting. 'I would not return to that revolting place if it were the last in existence! The only reason I went to Irkalla in the first place, was because no one else dared go.'

Interesting that this was the Nefilim lord that Ereshkigal would grow old and debauched with. In that long-distant future time Ereshkigal was no longer mistress of the dead, for she too would become Orme addicted and earthbound.

'I have already refused,' Anu advised. 'I just thought it prudent to advise you that Ereshkigal is obviously most eager to meet with you, as it is clearly a matter of great urgency and importance to her.'

Rhun had his answer. Avery was right, there was more to Anu's discontent with his children than was evident the day that the Grigori had first arrived. Ereshkigal had obviously fallen in love with Nergal already, and was prepared to go to war to possess him; but did that sentiment still stand now that she had become infatuated with Armaros?

'There is far greater sport here, in the land of the living.' Nergal motioned to the bodies on the floor. 'There are still several of them missing, and I want them found! Search the science labs,' he advised the guards, who doubled their speed to exit the room and respond to the order. 'This has been grand target practice for our forces,' Nergal gave Anu credit for the strategy.

Rhun ducked back behind the throne not wanting to tempt fate, yet at the same time resenting that his brothers had been used for sport. Jaz, in the form of Gadriel, was not looking too pleased either.

'You go,' Rhun mouthed the words.

His companion gave him a nod, and vanished.

'Well, I wouldn't wish to keep you from your entertainment.' Anu ended the meeting.

'It was a good idea to let them split up,' Nergal commented on his way out. 'Easier to catch off-guard in small groups, whilst maximising the training potential.'

As the large door to the chamber closed behind Nergal, Rhun frowned, wondering whose side Anu was on. Rhun had already got the answer he'd come looking for, so perhaps he shouldn't risk making contact with Telmo, whose consciousness was hopefully residing in Anu.

'I'm on the side of history,' Anu said as he came round the back of the throne and found Rhun. 'We both know the Grigori end up in cryogen, never to be revived, or how would you be here? Still, that doesn't mean we can't solve our little problem before that happens.'

'Ereshkigal has kidnapped Armaros and taken him to the Underworld,' Rhun outlined their little hiccup.

Anu raised both eyebrows, seeming almost pleasantly surprised. 'And Nergal will stop at nothing to hunt the Grigori down.' He smiled in conclusion: 'There seems to be an opportunity here for everyone to achieve what they desire.'

From behind the rows of hanging sacs of developing humans, Zeven and Leal observed the main lab of Ninharsag beyond the large glass windows that divided the two areas. The Nefilim scientist was in the process of moving their still-contained, unconscious commander out of her bio-containment room, and her little grey friends were replacing the incubator Azazèl was occupying with another empty incubator.

'Perhaps the infection of the reptilians was not a last resort, but a foregone conclusion?' Zeven commented to his companion.

'Of course it is.'

A third person answered and startled the Grigori to an about-face to find Enki. 'Once we infect one of reptilians we have

281

engineered, the royal strain of reptilians of Alpha Dranconis will no longer wish to claim them as part of their group consciousness, and will want them as far away as possible to avoid risk of infection,' the Nefilim lord explained. 'Thus our workforce on Ki shall be secured, and we will move the genetic breeding program there permanently, without fear of invasion.'

Ki was another word for Earth, which Enki had been given governance of. Zeven shook his head at their forethought and their distinct lack of regard for all involved. 'Well, your reptilians, besides being smart, are very aggressive. When they rebel they will release their diseased kindred and infect their entire brood on Ki with the most evil minded, blood-lusting creature that ever inhabited the dark universe … even its creators feared it!'

Enki frowned in light of the information. 'Can you see the future?

'I've been there,' Zeven advised, and Enki was truly aghast. 'We're here to prevent that disaster from happening.'

'My human sons shall truly be a wonder,' the Nefilim lord was excited by the prospect of their coming into being.

'Yes, we know,' Zeven emphasised, 'we were them! Infused with greatness further along in our human evolution by your Nefilim son, Marduk.'

'I will have a Nefilim son!' Enki was fit to explode with excitement.

'Provided you stay in the favour of Tiamat.' Zeven got the conversation back on track. 'The creatrix knows this virus is not of this universe, and that it is going to cause everyone grief. So we have been charged with finding a way to return it to the dark universe.'

'There is a portal that leads to the lesser universe from the Underworld, so I am told,' Enki advised, 'but getting into the realm of the dead without dying is tricky.'

'One would have to be invited?' Zeven posed, and Enki nodded to concur. 'Ereshkigal is your twin sister, don't you have some influence with her?'

'I do not see very much of her since she chose the Underworld over the outer world,' Enki advised. 'I am not as adventurous you see, and have never longed to delve into the deepest depths of the creation where Kur and the Dark Guardians abide.'

'She actually chose to be Queen of the Dead?' Leal concluded.

'Oh yes, she loves all things unknown, no matter how dark, ugly or painful,' Enki said.

'Fabulous,' Leal commented, not liking the sound of that.

'First things first,' Zeven looked back to the lab of Ninharsag. 'We need to deal with your older sister.'

'She's not dangerous,' Enki stepped out into the walkway. 'She is Tiamat's greatest advocate, as their work goes hand in hand.' He encouraged them to follow him in taking the direct approach.

'Could be a trap,' Leal uttered his view quietly aside to Zeven.

'It isn't,' Enki turned back to assure them. 'Your friend Armaros encouraged me to lose my tranquillising device in the garden.'

'And who gave you that device?' Zeven probed, although they'd gone too far to abandon their course of action — Enki triggered the doors of the lab that opened to allow them entry.

'It will be fine,' the lord sidestepped the question.

'You're here.' Ninharsag had obviously expected her brother to arrive with several sedated Grigori, not two conscious ones, and she quickly closed the metal sheath on the window of the incubator containing their commander. 'Your commander will need time to recover,' she said, standing to address them.

'He certainly will …' Zeven commented with a laugh. 'Since you have returned him to cryogen and are planning to use his soul, along with the rest of the Grigori to spawn the next generation of breeding humans.'

Ninharsag was mortified, and looked to her brother accusingly.

'I said nothing!' Enki was surprised by just how well informed the Grigori were. 'They are time walkers.'

'Timekeepers,' Leal corrected.

'Look,' Zeven honed in on Ninharsag, 'we are not here to stop your research and development, we are here to save it from a noxious threat.'

'The virus,' she assumed.

Zeven nodded. 'It will not be the solution you hope. It will escape and serve the Nefilim a formidable rebellion on Ki. It must be sent back to where it belongs.'

'And the Grigori will all volunteer their souls to my research?' Ninharsag asked.

'More than willingly.' Zeven avowed. 'You have the word of Sammael.' He motioned to himself and her sights shifted to his Grigori companion to see if this resolve was unanimous.

'Affirmative,' Leal assured her, 'I like having genitals.'

Zeven elbowed his companion for the unnecessary wit.

Ninharsag considered the situation a moment, and then, passing her hand over a metal plate on her desk, she opened the outer door to bio-containment. 'It's in there,' she invited them to go help themselves.

'I trust it is still frozen?' Zeven queried before investigating.

'Of course,' she replied.

With a nod of thanks, Zeven headed towards the open door, quietly considering that the Nefilim scientist had given up her new and powerful virus rather more easily than expected.

Leal followed Zeven then hesitated, as his telepathic mind picked up on a thought. 'She's lying —'

The trigger action of a weapon firing was heard behind them.

Zeven turned, expecting to be hit before he'd fully done so, but instead he found a dart poised in mid-air, and watched it drop to the floor.

'Not subject!' stressed all of Ninharsag's little grey helpers at once, as they pointed to Zeven. Leal picked up on the thought of the Greys and conveyed it to Zeven who was appearing very annoyed.

'Yes, very good,' Zeven acknowledged his unexpected allies, who were acting out of efficiency rather than favouritism. 'Not subject!' Zeven looked back to their superior. 'That was a rather foolish play, considering you have no idea what I am capable of.'

'Give me that!' Enki grabbed the device off his sister. 'You're going to ruin everything! Did you not hear what they said?'

Ninharsag glared at her little brother, as if he was the idiot. 'I do what the Pantheon tells me, or they stop my research altogether.'

'And lose all the slave labour you provide them with?' Zeven queried. 'Not bloody likely! What will stop your research is if this virus leads the reptilians of Ki on the warpath. Release his mind-eater into a soul-group like the reptilians have and you effectively make this menace immortal! And don't think it will kill them all off eventually. It won't, it's smart. It will take your lab and start producing its own food supply! You fear your civilisation on Ki will be invaded by the reptilians of Alpha Dranconis, but believe me, you are about to create a far bigger threat to all the inhabitants there, that is a lot closer to home.'

Ninharsag was expressionless, as she considered her next move.

'She knows the Lord of War will be here at any moment with the bodies of the Grigori that his forces have collected,' Leal was disturbed by his telepathic insight into the mind of Ninharsag. 'They're to be cryogenically frozen indefinitely.'

'Yes, we know that,' Zeven reminded Leal who was looking distressed. 'How else do you think we become human?'

'But what if they knock us out before we return to AMIE?' Leal stressed quietly to him. 'We'll have to live through our entire evolution through two universal schemes, again! We'll never awaken in the reality we left, and if that happens before we deal with this virus —'

'Taren might be left to deal with a very dark future on her own,' Zeven freaked.

'If we don't wipe that entire timeline from existence altogether, and the Taren we knew, right along with it,' Leal ventured.

Zeven really didn't appreciate his theory as the timekeepers could theoretically cease to be. 'We'd lose what little grip we have on all these timelines.'

'We have a couple of problems,' Jazmay announced upon arriving in the guise of Gadriel.

'We certainly do.' Leal pointed to the glass windows of the lab, to where Nefilim guards were entering the incubation room beyond.

'Yep, that's one of them,' Jaz confirmed.

'Ah, for pity's sake,' Zeven complained.

'Ereshkigal has stolen Armaros away to the Underworld,' Jazmay gave her report regardless. 'And we have been unable to pursue him. He'll be trapped there if we don't find a way to get him out.'

'Time out!' Zeven called it; the guards running towards them all froze.

'Good call,' Leal awarded, breathing a sigh of relief, as the two Nefilim in their company gasped.

'You *are* powerful.' Enki emphasised how impressed he was.

'Tiamat tried the subtle approach to dealing with the Nefilim once before,' Zeven informed them. 'This time she is not going to take no for an answer.'

'Not even Tiamat holds sway over the Underworld,' Ninharsag informed.

'That is very true,' Anu spoke up to announce his arrival on the scene, and Rhun was with him in the guise of Penemue.

'There has to be a way to get to the Underworld without dying …' Zeven was frustrated that he was being forced to follow a path that he really didn't wish to tread. 'Ereshkigal is still alive.'

'Nergal is the only other Nefilim to ever gain access to the Underworld and return unscathed.' Enki motioned to the approaching warlord, who eyed over his motionless troops as he passed them.

'Then I guess we want to speak with him.' Zeven willed the warlord's weaponry to materialise in his possession, and when the said paraphernalia appeared in his hands, he passed the haul to Leal, as Nergal entered the laboratory proper, fuming.

'This is high treason!' the young Nefilim lord protested in a loud booming voice, and all the conscious creatures in containment in the lab were disturbed by his hostile presence — except for the reptilian, which was watching the proceedings very intently.

'No, this is a think tank,' Zeven explained. 'We have a little problem to correct before we will willingly submit to the Pantheon's ruling to contain us.'

'Your agenda is of no concern to us!' Nergal came forward to reclaim his weaponry, and Leal ducked behind Zeven, who froze the Nefilim warlord's feet with a thought. As Nergal nearly fell over, the restraint made him even more furious. 'You are going to die, sub-creature.'

'No one is going to die,' Anu announced to make his will clear on that front.

'You may be our elder,' Nergal looked to Anu, 'but you do not have the authority to take liberties with a Pantheon ruling!'

'I have not taken any liberty with the Pantheon ruling on the Grigori.' Anu pleaded innocent. 'The Grigori have submitted, but there has been a complication that we need their help with, if you would just listen.'

'No beings in their right minds would assist with their own incarceration!' Nergal's voice was strained with impatience.

'Who said we were in our right minds?' Jazmay pointed out.

'Yeah,' Leal agreed, 'we just don't like it here very much.'

'What kind of an idiot do you take me for?' the warlord snarled.

'The regular kind,' Zeven proffered, and regained Nergal's full attention. 'So you will be happy to leave one of us at large, will you?'

Nergal teetered in his stance and regained his balance to inform. 'Over my dead body!'

'That's what I thought,' Zeven concluded — the warlord obviously had charge of rounding them up. 'Ereshkigal has absconded with one of my brothers and taken him to the Underworld.'

'Then I shall go there and fetch him back myself!' the Nefilim snarled. 'I don't need you for that.'

Zeven folded his arms in challenge, as Rhun stepped forward to add his two cents to the argument. 'Um … I think you will find that Ereshkigal will not be so eager to invite you down, now that she has a new distraction. Our brother is very attractive to women, you see.'

Nergal growled at the implication — he may not have been able to express love but his adversity to Rhun's suggestion was pretty damn clear.

'We Grigori possess the only other thing that Ereshkigal desires in this world,' Rhun outlined. 'So if you want to succeed in your commission to deliver us *all* to cryogen, then I'm afraid you do need our assistance for bargaining power.'

'I close my case,' Anu concluded his argument with Nergal also. 'No need to have a meeting. Our problems can be sorted quite amicably.'

'They must be getting something for their cooperation?' Nergal was wary.

'Oh, we are,' Zeven assured him. 'I have something I need to toss into Ereshkigal's garbage chute to the dark universe, that is all.'

'Not the virus.' Nergal objected.

'Yes, the virus,' Zeven insisted, extending the lord's immobility from his feet to his neck. 'And if you don't like that, we can just leave you here and we'll take our chances dealing with Ereshkigal by ourselves.'

'Although word has it you don't have an arsehole,' Nergal gritted his teeth, 'it can be arranged, and I'm going to ensure you go into cryogen with a pole shoved —'

'I'm here to ensure that does not happen.' Anu discredited the warlord's vow.

'Wait until the Pantheon hears of this!' Nergal turned his furious sights to Anu.

'They will hear how you allowed the Grigori to run rampant, and I was forced to step in and deal with the situation?' Anu suggested an alternative view. 'I think Ninharsag and Enki will both back me up on that account?'

Nergal looked to his older kindred who nodded to concur.

'So we can just keep this incident to ourselves and handle it quietly, or not.' Anu put the option to Nergal.

'You had better hope you can trust these mutants of yours,' Nergal warned, 'or all your heads will be on the chopping block, not mine. The council are not going to like that you have not administered the virus to the reptilian as decided.'

'They will never know,' Anu assured Nergal rather forcefully, as he gripped both sides of the warlord's head to stare into his eyes. 'From this moment forth you are just going to ignore anything pertaining to that virus.'

'I will,' said Nergal, suddenly passive.

'As far as you know the virus was administered to the reptilian that we will place in cryogen,' Anu dictated.

'Yes,' Nergal agreed.

'You will cooperate fully with this mission, and despite any desire you might have to betray these Grigori, you will do nothing that will jeopardise their wellbeing or their agenda. Is that understood?'

'It is.' Nergal submitted completely.

'Now,' Anu let go of him, and Nergal was a little dazed for a second. 'You will see to having the unconscious Grigori in my Worlds Chamber brought here to Ninharsag for incarceration, and then you will meet us back in my chamber to finalise our mission.'

It didn't take Nergal long to regain his foul mood. 'Your pet will have to release me first.'

Zeven let his hold over Nergal lapse gladly. 'Of course, we really appreciate your assistance in this matter,' he smiled sincerely.

The Nefilim warlord was confused when Zeven was not baited by his insult, and so he looked to his relatives instead. 'Have it your way.' Nergal grabbed his weaponry from Leal, and exited in a huff.

'I have never seen you exert your influence like that, Father,' Ninharsag wondered about Anu's support of the Grigori.

'Well, I like to think that my children can think for themselves,' Anu replied, 'but in desperate circumstances such as this, some are best not given the option.'

'No wonder Taliesin never had children,' Rhun commented and Anu burst into laughter, although it was Telmo's consciousness within the Nefilim lord who got the joke, and he was the only one with a memory that spanned back that far.

'It's all clear now in retrospect,' Anu nodded to concur.

'Well done,' Zeven shook Rhun's hand impressed by his insight and the scheme he'd just aided him to hatch.

Originally they had planned to get rid of the seals and the virus by sending their ship back through the Eternity Gate to the dark universe. But no one really knew how the Eternity Gate worked. With no living soul on board from which to gauge a frequency, they suspected that the *Leviathan* might end up in a higher universe rather than the lesser one. Here was an opportunity to ensure these curses were returned to where they truly belonged.

'How did you know how to push the warlord's buttons like that?' Zeven wondered.

'We've dealt with Nergal before,' Rhun explained.

'Oh,' Zeven was enlightened, although he was not as familiar with their history in this universe as Rhun was.

'You remember the Lahmuian mutant I was telling you about?' Rhun hinted, cryptically.

'He put us up to that?' Zeven boggled at the claim.

'Affirmative,' Rhun concurred.

'Good to know,' Zeven jested, sarcastically. 'I wouldn't want to kill him now and miss out on all that fun later on.' He rolled his eyes, deciding to tread more warily around the warlord.

His gaze drifted to the caged reptilian who'd been observing the proceedings, and although the species were not renowned for their facial expressions at this stage of their evolution, Zeven could have sworn it was smiling.

13

THE UNDERWORLD

Once the initial shock of being spirited away to the realm of the dead by a monstrously large apparition passed, Noah stood looking outwards from the platform of Ereshkigal's throne, situated on the mezzanine level of a colosseum-like structure of stone. The floor, ceiling and back wall of the dark throne annex were writhing with bugs, snakes, spiders and creepy crawlies of all kinds that immediately vacated the area upon the queen's return. Noah had spent a lot of time in the natural world, so the critters did not bother him. And in this Grigori form he was immortal, so they could hardly do him any harm. There was a distinct lack of natural light in this annexed area, apart from the flaming oil fountains positioned at intervals round the mezzanine. The passages that led off to the left and right of him curved around the enclosed central arena and disappeared into darkness. Yet light, and the sound of chaos, poured in through a huge stone arch on the inside curving wall that was directly in front of the throne's platform, and this granted the only view inside the arena. Noah approached the phenomenon cautiously, marvelling at the greatest exemplar of polarity imaginable that lay therein, for it was truly a wonder and a horror to behold.

Besides this one aperture, there were no windows or doors in the huge central circular chamber. Inside, the souls of the dead bled through the walls to take flight into the celestial vortex of light and mist extending upwards through a void in the ceiling, or slide down a funnelling floor that dropped into the abyss of darkness below. Noah was encouraged to note that there were far more souls ascending than descending. Upon considering his memories of life in the dark universe, it was harrowing to witness those souls on the downwards slide. In retrospect, Noah considered that the Grigori had been lucky to have been so prized by Samyaza, but life as a human was truly hell there. Fortunately, most humans in the lesser universe did not have the intellect or experience to imagine a better existence.

'Don't look so glum, they are all going where they most desire to go,' Ereshkigal advised her guest. 'Just because another soul's choices might differ from yours, their desires are just as valid. This evolutionary scheme is not for them,' she explained, as if it were no big deal. 'At the end of days, when all the souls of the multi-verse have reached their goal, they shall move on to other schemes more suited to their development.'

'So you don't judge the souls of the dead?' Noah realised.

Ereshkigal shook her head to confess. 'This set-up,' she motioned to the forces at play within the arena, 'was here long before I ever braved the Underworld. Every soul is their own judge.'

This was exactly what Noah had come to understand.

'This is the most spectacular place to be found in the Underworld,' she said as they observed the comings and goings of the deceased. 'Which is why I built my fortress here. I have a great desire to know the unknown and to reveal patterns unseen. I wanted to achieve something that has never been done before, purely because I am the only one who can.'

'You have certainly succeeded.' Noah looked to the Nefilim woman beside him with more respect and wonder, for she was not at all as he expected, and quite unlike the Ereshkigal he would witness in later years. Even though Ereshkigal was under his friendly spell, it was surprising to realise she was a fellow scholar with similar aspirations to himself, yet she did not appear completely satisfied with her life's work.

'Then why am I still the only one who seems to understand the beauty of the unusual and strange, or that there is knowledge to be gained from knowing true pain and suffering? The creatures who live alone in the darkness still have a rightful place in the great scheme, and desire to be admired and recognised for what they do and who they are. Like Kur, and the other Dark Guardians of the doors to Underworld.'

The monstrous apparition that had delivered both Ereshkigal and Noah to the Underworld had taken a solid form — that of a huge dark dragon, breathing fire, and menacing in appearance. This might have been horrifying to Armaros, as the Grigorian had never seen a dragon, but Noah's mind harked back to his lifetime in the dark ages of Britain, and he was filled with wonder and sentiment, for he'd not seen a dragon since then.

Ereshkigal was quietly impressed that her captive did not run in fear from the beast, nor pull a weapon and attempt to slay it. 'What name do you go by, Grigorian?'

'Armaros.'

'Are you not afraid of the mighty Kur, Armaros?' Ereshkigal took a step closer, finding his lack of fear rather fetching.

'Well, of course I fear him,' Noah maintained. 'Dragons are the most formidable, magical and intelligent creatures in all of creation. That is why they are the champions of Tiamat.'

The beast snorted fire in a non-threatening manner and settled into a comfortable position lying alongside the throne. *I like him better than the last one.*

Noah's eyes widened upon picking up on the dragon's thought.

'Yes,' Ereshkigal placed her hands on the Grigorian. 'He is really very genuine for a creature so revoltingly pretty.'

Noah grinned, unsure if he was flattered or insulted. 'May I ask why you have brought me here, Highness?'

'For company,' she said resting her head upon his shoulder, 'and pleasure.' She nestled her head into his neck again.

'I am a sexless being,' he stated, without spurning her.

'You have a tongue and fingers …' She toyed with his hands and then placed them on her body. 'The energy you exude is amazing! Explore, I command it.'

'But there can be no issue from our relations.' Noah got to the point, although he near forgot it as she guided his hands over her heaving breasts.

'I am already with child,' she advised, with a smile of satisfaction.

Noah swiftly withdrew his hands and stepped away from her. 'Then you must already have a mate.' He played coy and concerned, but he really sought information. He already suspected who the father was.

'He despises the Underworld and refuses to see me,' Ereshkigal advised coolly, as Kur breathed fire to protest the very mention of the subject.

'I am sorry —' Noah attempted to sympathise.

'Why? I'm not.' Ereshkigal lost her amorous mood and retreated to sit upon her throne. 'He only mated with me to gain power over me! Well, I shall not give him the satisfaction. You have given me this clarity, Grigorian. I do not need him. Your presence is one thousand times more agreeable than his.' She raised a finger and beckoned him to approach.

Agreed. Kur seconded his mistress' resolve.

'It is my honour to please you thus,' Noah assured her, staying where he was. 'But hasn't the Pantheon ordered all the Grigori be taken to cryogen?'

Your toy is wanted by the Pantheon? The dragon was disturbed by the news and raised himself. *You were aware of this!*

Ereshkigal was alarmed by the resentment behind Kur's accusation. 'It was a spur of the moment decision, I did not consider —'

You did this knowing he would be sent to fetch the Grigorian back!

'My dearest half brother … that was not the way of it,' she appealed to the creature kindly.

Noah found Ereshkigal's reference to the dragon as half-brother curious; in fact he found everything about Ereshkigal curious. How had she become the sole ruler and only living occupant in the realm of the dead? He felt Kur surely had something to do with her privilege, and at this present moment the dragon appeared none too pleased with the object of his patronage.

You vowed, along with me, to challenge and fight to the very end those who dared to approach the Underworld uninvited! Kur snarled in challenge.

'And if *he* dares come, I shall,' Ereshkigal exerted.

That is what you said last time, Kur now seemed more hurt than angered. *And now you carry his seed!* Kur growled as his anger overwhelmed him once more and morphing into shadow, the creature vanished.

Ereshkigal looked back to Noah. 'Could he be right, do you think?'

Noah had decided to lose some of his loving feeling in order that she might lose interest in seducing him. 'Sometimes, destiny forces us to act in ways we cannot explain, and are not even aware of.'

'I came to my throne in the Underworld in such a way.' Ereshkigal related to his reasoning. 'And as surely as I knew when I met Kur that he could carry me here, where I could be one of a kind with the one who is all kinds … I also know that the father of my child will destroy everything I have achieved here. And still I am drawn towards him. Against my own will, I could not stay my hand!'

'Kur seems jealous of your mate,' Noah observed the dragon was rather dark on Nergal.

'Naturally so,' Ereshkigal validated her companion's reaction. 'For Nergal is Kur's polar opposite in every way: fair of face, yet heartless, cold, and a moronically boring intellectual. Whereas Kur, despite his ferocious appearance, is the most loyal, loving, intuitive and wise being I know. The Pantheon do not like that I live in the realm beyond their influence, or that I have access to powers beyond their understanding. They sent the handsome Nergal to tempt me to abandon my claim here and return to the land of the living. For he will not live here, and if I am to be his wife, I must stay at his side, and he will ban me from visiting the Underworld again.'

'Hence the reason why Kur is so opposed to Nergal.' Noah nodded, appreciating her woes. 'So it appears I am just bait for a much larger fish you wish to catch.'

Ereshkigal looked down to reflect on this, and was saddened to have to nod to affirm. 'Kur's instincts are never wrong.' She snapped herself out of her melancholy and looked back to her guest. 'But before my fate comes calling for me, tell me of the dark universe you came from.'

'We all came from the dark universe,' he replied.

Ereshkigal smiled broadly to learn this. 'Then why can I not remember?'

'Because we Grigori are the only soul-group cursed to remember; the universe has done you a great kindness by allowing you to forget,' he suggested.

'No, for me it is an injustice. I alone among the living in this universe hold the desire to dive into the deepest depths of creation, and by so doing know the deepest depths of my sacred self. This is why I ventured into the Underworld. But here is as close as I can get to the ancient dark ones that are the seat of my soul, I know it!' she insisted.

'That is why you wanted the seals,' Noah realised.

'Yes!' she replied, as if only just realising that she had been distracted from her goal. 'If I cannot get to the dark ones, then I could summon the dark ones to me. Their seals will be safer and more cherished with me than anyone; you must help me acquire them.'

'If you knew the Fallen Elohim like I do, you would know those seals are not safe with anyone outside of the dark universe.' He could not vindicate her wish. 'But you are right in thinking your soul-group harks back to the ancient dark ones of which you speak. Your language, your technology and even the way you think, is all reminiscent of the Fallen Elohim.'

Ereshkigal was not angered by his refusal to aid her with the seals, it appeared she had another idea more inspiring. 'I am adept at reading the thoughts and feelings of others, that is how I came to befriend Kur ... would you share your memories of the dark universe with me?'

Noah was rather impressed that this was a request and not a command. 'If it will help you realise the danger of using those seals, it would be my honour and my duty to share with you what I know.'

'Come, sit before me,' she beckoned him forth once again, and this time Noah complied, approaching to kneel before her.

'You must not fear invoking the darkest of your recollections …' She placed her long slender hands upon his shoulders. 'There is no horror that is too painful for me to bear.'

'I will oblige you in this,' Noah vowed, 'as I understand how vital it is that you know the truth.'

The queen of the dead smiled, excited. 'It is my life's aspiration you are about to fulfil, Grigorian, for which you shall hold my utmost gratitude.'

'You seek to find beauty in all things, but in the dark universe there are beings so pure in hatred and devoid of compassion that no amount of nurture will save them from themselves,' Noah warned.

'Show me,' Ereshkigal urged nonetheless.

'As you wish.' With a heavy sigh, Noah closed his eyes to cast his thoughts back to Tartarus and his dark life spent in imperial service.

Once it was cleared of bodies, Anu held a closed court in his Worlds Chamber, with Nergal and all the Grigori who remained conscious. Zeven had brought the cryogen incubator containing the virus to the meeting with him, as he was not prepared to let it out of his sight — or out of his psychokinetic influence, which was keeping the package powered up and on ice.

'What could you possibly have that Ereshkigal would desire?' Nergal was demanding to know.

'On board our craft are some very precious souvenirs from the dark universe that your lady love has already attempted to steal,' Zeven assured the warlord boldly.

Nergal's mood darkened. 'I have no interest in that morbid piece of work … and anything on board your vessel is *mine*, being that your vessel has been seized by *my* forces.' He motioned to one of the Worlds Chamber screens that displayed an image of the Nefilim base ship that hovered over the *Leviathan*. But Nergal did a double take, when he glanced to the image and found the captured craft had vanished.

'Sorry,' Zeven apologised, 'you were saying?'

Nergal came at Zeven, raising a fist to slam into him, but he found that he could not — the young Nefilim lord's unconscious vow to Anu prevented it. He roared out his anger and then backed down.

'That's not very cooperative,' Zeven pointed out, unfazed. 'But if you would like me to have our treasure brought forth, I can arrange it.'

'What guarantee do I have that, when this quest is done, you will all submit to cryogen as vowed?' Nergal resisted as best he could.

'Unlike you, we fathom what cooperation means,' Rhun commented.

'I will take personal responsibility for the incarceration of the Grigori upon your return,' Anu advised the warlord and then looked to Zeven. 'Tell Sacha to bring them forth.'

Zeven looked to Leal in Sariel's form, and gave him the nod. Leal closed his eyes to send a telepathic message to the Grigorian, Sacha, who was the body Avery was inhabiting at present.

Moments later Sacha appeared in the Worlds Chamber, accompanied by a great clang of metal, as all the seals, still melted beyond recognition, fell into piles around him.

'This is just a pile of junk!' Nergal observed the ruckus with disgust.

'I couldn't agree more.' Avery floated his Grigori form up and over the pile of metal to come stand before Sammael. 'What would you like me to do with this lot?'

'I shall take it from here,' Zeven replied, 'the rest of you can submit yourselves to cryogen.'

Leal breathed a huge sigh of relief, clutching at the void between his legs. 'Thought you'd never ask.'

'Don't screw this up,' Avery uttered quietly to the man they were leaving in charge, then resigning himself to the command, he took a seat on the floor next to where Leal had plonked himself down.

'Bring our brother back to us.' Jazmay sat Gadriel's form next to Sariel and Sacha.

'I have the utmost faith in you,' Rhun gripped his brother's right forearm, and Zeven did likewise thankful for the vote of confidence. 'If you can tame a mutant, the Queen of the Dead ought be a pushover.'

Zeven was amused, as he considered just how many times he'd found himself in precarious predicaments. 'Yeah … I think, if we create our own reality, I really need to question where my head is at.'

Rhun grinned, in tune with that sentiment. 'A conundrum best left for musing in some future time.' Rhun's Grigorian form, Penemue, lay down alongside his brothers. Closing their eyes, their forms fell limp as their spirit consciousnesses took flight back to the future.

'I like these odds so much better,' Nergal grinned.

Zeven grinned back, before turning his sights to the twisted metal piled on the floor. He extended his hands towards the wreckage and raised them, whereupon all the metal floated into the air and liquefied.

'I didn't mean anything by that,' Nergal lost his urge to make trouble, obviously adverse to the thought of being coated in liquid metal. It was a possibility to be feared as the molten air-borne substances divided and re-grouped with their own mineral, either mercury, tin, copper, lead, silver or gold.

'Are you quite sure you are with the program?' Zeven queried Nergal, having no intention of using the substances on the lord.

'Quite sure … but if we could keep the gold —' He attempted to sweeten the deal, whereupon the free-floating gold mass lashed out in a wave in Nergal's direction. 'Keep it, we have plenty!' the warlord decreed and the tumultuous mass became docile once more.

The liquids then formed sheets of fluid that wrapped themselves around the incubator containing the virus, where they immediately hardened and cooled. When the last layer dried, Zeven admired the huge golden orb. 'Much easier to transport.' He looked to Anu who was smiling in approval. 'Summon Kur, we are ready to collect.'

So much was riding on this first phase of the mission, and Taren's non-involvement was frustrating her. What if her team mates never awoke, then what would she do? Start the entire escapade again? The thought was a harrowing one, and her worry must have reflected in her face.

'Now you know how I feel, every time you take off on one of these little inter-time stints without me,' Lucian commented from the chair opposite hers in the waiting area outside the medical rooms.

'I didn't take off without you,' Taren countered. 'You've been right beside me every step of the way, up until yesterday when —' She choked on the memory and fell silent.

'How did it happen?' Lucian was morbidly curious, or silently sceptical.

'It doesn't matter,' Taren looked her husband in the eye. 'It will never happen now.'

'How can you be so sure?' He leaned forwards to query her. 'It was one thing when you were playing around with events in our little world, but now our actions are impacting upon at least two universes. Don't you ever stop and consider this timekeeper venture might be getting just a little out of hand?'

'Of course I do!' She stood to pace out her repressed fears. 'But why give me this talent and all these resources, if they were not meant to be utilised?' She stopped and looked back to the doors beyond which her crew mates lay in coma.

'That was not a criticism, just a bystander's observation.' Lucian held his hands up in truce.

She was tempted to stress again that he'd not been a bystander in all of this, despite how much it probably seemed that way to him at present, but she instead decided to consider the point he was trying to make. 'If we are wrong about this, it will certainly be time to rethink our plan.' Taren was feeling the pressure of risking the lives of her nearest and dearest. Tears of stress were welling in her eyes, as she silently prayed that they were doing the right thing by all involved.

When half the team emerged from the medical room, it felt like her prayers were being answered, but Noah, Zeven and Telmo were not with them.

'How did you go?' Taren was dying to know.

'Hard to say,' Rhun regretted being so vague, and collapsed in a seat. 'We'll know more when Zeven, Telmo and Noah revive.'

The other three wakeful members of the team tiptoed from the room and closed the door in their wake, so as not to disturb those remaining from their repose.

'It's like sleeping with the dead in there,' Jazmay commented once the door was closed behind her and she was able.

'Well, technically, they kind of are,' Rhun replied.

'Don't say that,' Taren appealed, she was stressed enough as it was.

'Maybe we should get Swithin down here, just in case,' Leal suggested to their captain, as Swithin had the power to raise the dead.

'Oh please,' Taren appealed, looking back to the closed doors. 'Have a little faith. When I put Zeven in charge I knew what I was doing. He doesn't know how to fail. The soul-minds with him are the most wise and the most loving beings in all creation. I have the utmost confidence that together they'll succeed.' It was a concerted effort not to choke on that statement, for they were also, apart from her husband, the three souls dearest to her. Life and timekeeping was impossible to fathom without them; thus she chose to ignore any consideration that deviated from the desired outcome. 'They'll be back.'

Throughout the thought transference, the darker the memories got, the closer to Noah that Ereshkigal drew and in the end her form was hugged close to his; Noah was unsure if this was in a bid to comfort him, or get closer to the dark experiences he was invoking.

'I see now,' she said as she peeled herself away from him, and still caught up in her perceptions, she staggered backward to a seat on her throne.

'I have upset you?' Noah queried, knowing the Nefilim did not understand their emotions fully, and perhaps that was why she appeared so calm in the wake of the horrors he'd just made her privy to.

'That was incredible,' she countered his worry, but her tone was hard to read; had he raised her awareness of the dangers of playing with dark universal forces or only excited her more?

The large shadow body of the dragon manifested alongside the throne, but Kur did not bother taking physical form in this instance. *Surprise, surprise, the lord Nergal is demanding an audience, and threatens to smash through the seven gates to Irkalla if you will not receive him.*

Ereshkigal considered the situation and then looked at Kur with a look of entreaty on her face. 'Would you be so kind as to bring him forth to me?'

I am but a humble servant, the dragon said dryly.

'You know that is not true,' she countered.

She truly felt for the creature's feelings. At this point in her life Ereshkigal clearly knew what empathy was. It was a shame the path she was forging now would destroy what emotional understanding she had acquired through her experiences here; but that sad fact was not what Noah had come to the past to change, and he must not do anything that might divert her from her true destiny. Just as his Grigorian persona was here to witness her straying from her path to enlightenment, he and the other Chosen Ones would be there in the future, to aid her find her way back to source once more.

There is another Grigorian with Nergal who wishes to trade some treasure from the dark universe in return for your new toy.

Ereshkigal's eyes lit up upon hearing the news.

Shall I fetch him too? Kur persisted.

Ereshkigal was tempted to console him, but thought better of it. 'That treasure is the true reason I stole the Grigorian,' she stated, and neither being in her company was sure if they should believe that statement. 'So I would be very grateful if you would collect my treasure. Tell Nergal I am prepared to deal.'

As you wish. Kur, seeming slightly mollified, gave his mistress the benefit of the doubt and his shadow form vanished to do her bidding.

'Is that the truth, Nin?' Noah stood and backed away from her to query. 'You were only after the seals? Did you learn nothing from the horrors of my past?'

'Allow me to let you in on a little secret. The Grigori hold no sway over me in my realm, your glamour is wasted on me here.' Ereshkigal looked to him, her eyes glazed with insight. 'But I thank you from the bottom of my empty heart for sharing your memory with me, I learned a *great* deal.'

'Your heart is not empty,' Noah challenged, 'but fuller than any. For you love all the unloved, your presence fills up the emptiness of the Underworld with your being.'

Ereshkigal was unmoved by his flattering observation as she sat back in her throne and allowed the creatures of the dark to crawl and slide over her.

Some might have found this sight repulsive, but Noah could only admire her complete abandon; Ereshkigal was a disturbingly beautiful being.

The dragon portal erupted and spat forth the Grigorian, Sammael, a large golden orb and the Nefilim lord, Nergal. The shadow body moved around behind the throne, then took on a physical form to watch over the proceedings.

Sammael was a little dazed and confused upon landing, but came to focus on Ereshkigal. 'That is a hell of a transport system,' Zeven commented. Looking about to spot the missing Grigorian, he was glad to find him. 'There you are, Armaros, what have I told you about going home with strange women?'

Noah rolled his eyes. Zeven made a joke out of everything; it was his self-defence mechanism for dealing with stress.

'This is not how I expected my treasure to look.' Ereshkigal eyed over the golden orb. 'How do I know they are all there?'

'Because I would not risk leaving any behind in the land of the living to be found by the inept,' Zeven outlined. 'That would be —'

'Dismiss the creature,' Nergal cut into the proceedings to demand, 'I'll not talk Pantheon business with that thing looming over us.'

'Kur is my partner, not my subject,' Ereshkigal advised, 'and I don't believe he wishes to leave.'

'You are wasting my time,' Nergal seethed, pulling from his weapons belt a baton, which he proceeded to bash on the ground until it lit up, bright as the sun.

Kur released a booming screech, and cries of pain were heard from all who had the voice to complain. The dragon and the creatures of the night fled, and their Queen was left shielding her eyes from the sudden light.

After a few moments the flare dimmed to a bearable level, and the Nefilim lord passed it to Zeven ahead of climbing the few long-platformed stairs that led to the throne. 'I've had enough of being summoned to this cesspit of repugnant existence that you call home! No more playing Queen of the Dead for you!' Nergal slapped Ereshkigal hard across the face and, grabbing hold of her by the hair, he dragged her from her seat. 'You are coming home with me!'

'I will never come with you, never!' she spat at him and resisted being led.

'Then you will die!' Nergal pulled a blade, and despite that Noah had been told his glamour had no effect here, he had to intervene. Zeven had the same resolve, but Noah beat him to the warlord.

'Kill her and you kill your unborn child,' Noah laid hands upon the Nefilim lord's back, who had his own hands too full to cast the Grigorian off, and to Noah's amazement the warlord calmed.

'Is this true?' he queried in a more reasonable tone, although he still pulled Ereshkigal to standing by her hair.

'That is why I requested an audience,' she replied, the defiant gaze still on her face.

'Then there is nothing left to argue.' He loosened his grip and slid his hand over her hair, as if patting an animal to calm it before a kill. 'You will return with me, you will be my wife and have my child.'

'I will not abandon my realm!' she insisted, whereupon Nergal grabbed her hair again, yanking her head to ensure he had her full attention. 'You will do as you are told.'

'I will stay here with my Grigorian and Kur,' Ereshkigal was used to pain and would not be bullied, which was not making this negotiation any smoother. 'You can take your treasure and you can shove it —'

'Ah …' Zeven stepped in to address Nergal. 'Anu told you that you were not allowed to impede our mission in any way, and I'm afraid that pissing off our hostess is an impediment, so please unhand her.'

Nergal appeared a little stunned by the request.

'Now,' Zeven added to make himself clear.

Nergal found himself forced to comply; he let his captive go and stepped away from her.

Once Ereshkigal was free, she regained her composure and slapped Nergal's face just as hard as he had slapped hers. 'You are a child, *and a fool,* if you think you can torture me into bending to your will.'

Nergal's eyes burned with fury. 'In the land of the living you won't be so formidable.'

'That is why I am not going there with you,' Ereshkigal returned to her throne. 'And if you don't like it here, then you shall never see this child.'

'No child of mine is growing up in this freak show!' Nergal insisted, and Ereshkigal stood, affronted.

Noah had stepped away from the action and was quietly meditating upon sending his love of his own wife to the Nefilim lord, for even if he didn't have any control over Ereshkigal here, that did not seem to be the case with Nergal. Still Noah needed to be able to block out their negativity and find his happy place.

Fortunately Zeven noted Noah's tactic and cut into the negotiations before things got physical again. 'I suggest a compromise. Your wife-to-be and impending child should be allowed to spend half the year in the Underworld and the other half in the land of the living. Whether you accompany them for their stint here is up to you.'

Noah had to smile as he heard Zeven's suggestion, for indeed this was how the legend of the Queen of the Underworld would play out in the Earth legends of the future.

Ereshkigal seemed to be happy with those terms, but looked to Nergal for his opinion first.

The Nefilim warlord appeared to be put on the spot. 'As long as I never have to come here,' he grouched, 'but the child stays with me.'

'No deal,' Ereshkigal decreed, and returned to a seat on her throne.

Zeven was losing patience. 'Then you take him for one half of the year, and Nergal takes the child for the next … work it out, this is not brain surgery! Sheesh!'

'The child stays with me for the first five years,' Ereshkigal proffered, 'then that arrangement could take effect.'

Nergal was seething — he was really not one for compromise.

Zeven knew this and so advised, 'If you don't agree you are in breach of your directive.'

'Imagine that?' Ereshkigal emphasised sarcastically. 'Nergal unsuccessful in a mission.'

'You weren't saying that the last time I was here,' he challenged with a suggestive grin.

'That's because you faked being charming to get your way,' she teased him back.

'That wasn't the least of my talent in that regard,' he moved to approach her again, but Ereshkigal held out a hand to prevent him coming closer. 'Agree to the terms.'

Nergal served her a very amorous grin, as he knelt down before her. 'But we haven't finished negotiating yet.' He pulled her close, and although she pushed her upper body away from him, she wrapped one of her long legs around his.

'I won't submit,' Ereshkigal insisted.

'You already have.' Nergal grabbed her buttocks, as the light from the baton Zeven was carrying faded out completely, and the throne area and its lusty occupants were again shrouded from view by shadow.

Zeven cast the torch aside and turned his attention to the large golden orb, as Noah quietly approached to whisper, 'Now is our chance.' He motioned Zeven to the archway and opposing portholes beyond.

Zeven didn't bother going to admire the view, he just directed his intention towards flinging the golden orb into the void.

The golden orb did not budge, however. A large dragon claw manifested around it, as did the rest of the guardian of the Underworld that was attached. *What do you think you are doing?*

'Oh, shit …' Zeven backed up a few paces just to be able to perceive the grand scale of the creature, but Noah didn't move.

'This treasure is a curse, and it belongs in the dark universe,' Noah told him, glancing aside to note the Nefilim had not been disturbed from their amusement. 'It will cause great suffering to all who touch it,' Noah ventured forward to place his hand upon one of Kur's claws, clutching the orb. 'Ereshkigal included.'

You can't charm me, little creature, the Dragon's thought echoed its amusement.

'I know,' Noah admitted readily, 'but I am aware that you know a lie when you hear one. Ereshkigal claims your instincts are never wrong and that you are the wisest soul she knows. So what does your instinct and wisdom tell you now?'

Kur growled as he bowed his head down low to confront Noah, who stood back palms up in submission. Noah could feel the hairs of his face being singed by the dragon's agitated breaths, as it mulled over the query. At last, it lifted the orb into the air and with a fiery grunt, flung it through the archway. The two Grigori and Kur rushed to the opening to view the orb plummet down; only the golden ball did not plummet, but spun, posed directly between the two opposing poles.

'Goddamn it!' Zeven cussed, horrified. It seemed they had the same problem here as they did with the Eternity Gate: there was no living soul attached to the orb from which to gauge a resonance with either this universe or the last.

'Use your psychokinesis,' Noah suggested.

'Don't you think I'm trying?' Zeven stressed quietly. 'It's not working!'

Well, it does make a lovely ornament. Kur expressed his view.

'What are you all doing?'

Dragon and Grigori turned about to face Ereshkigal.

'Nothing,' said Zeven, sounding as guilty as a child lying to its mother.

'Kur?' she queried her large partner, who was blocking her view into the arena.

It was for your own good, he explained, before Ereshkigal motioned him to move aside and show her what they were hiding.

When she laid eyes on the spinning ball of gold hovering in the centre of the arena, she had to laugh. 'You really didn't think that plan through very well, did you?'

'Get your creature to fetch it out of there?' Nergal suggested as he came up behind Ereshkigal. 'And we will take it back to Nibiru with us, and the Grigori too.'

'My dear husband to be,' she reached back to stroke his face, 'you know nothing of which you speak, so best leave this to me. Kur, take my Lord Nergal back to Anu. I shall join you there presently to formalise our agreement.'

With pleasure. The dragon reduced itself to shadow, which went rushing at Nergal.

'Not without the Grigori —' The Nefilim warlord attempted to protest, but was gone before he could exert any force.

Ereshkigal looked back to the Grigori. 'Well, haven't you both proven yourselves useful?'

'So, you will help us?' Noah tested the extent of their favour.

'The question is more, *can* I help you,' Ereshkigal posed. 'Which depends on how honest your little friend has been with me.'

'How do you mean?' Zeven was up for the challenge. 'I have not lied about anything.'

'If that metal orb is truly comprised of the seals of the Fallen Elohim,' she advised, 'they can be used to summon, contain and control them.'

Zeven saw her plot and was excited. 'Even if we just summoned the principals of the golden outer seals it would be enough.' But looking at the smooth golden orb he foresaw a problem. 'But without their respective insignia, we cannot hold them to it.'

'Can you not emboss the seals on the orb with your power?' Ereshkigal looked to Zeven.

'How do you know about my power?' he queried as his only opportunity to wield any power in her presence had been thwarted by Kur.

'I shared with Ereshkigal my memories of the dark universe,' Noah confessed, realising in retrospect that she now knew all there was to know about his Grigori brothers.

'You did what?' Zeven freaked, but Noah waved him off and looked back to Ereshkigal.

'You said that Grigori have no power here in the Underworld?'

'No power over me,' Ereshkigal clarified, 'and even that is a lie,' she confessed, with a soft seductive smile in Noah's direction. 'Self-defence,' she justified her deception, which could have been another fib to suit her ends; it was difficult to read the Nefilim, especially the females. 'You don't think I am this good natured normally, surely?'

'Well, a good temperament seems to have served you well,' Noah returned her affectionate smile. 'Your worst fear has not been realised, and your marriage will be more accommodating than originally thought.' Still, Noah knew her time in the Underworld would not last forever once her addiction to Orme, extended life and eternal youth got a grip on her, for the substance abuse would anchor her soul in the physical realm.

As Armaros and the Queen of the Underworld smiled fondly at each other, Zeven rolled his eyes. 'I want some of the talent you're having.'

'I am not the one about to save the day,' Noah motioned to the orb. 'Do you remember the seals in question?'

'Thanks to Ji Dan's memories and fine eye for detail, I shall never forget them,' Zeven confirmed. 'There are nine, plus the emperor.'

'Samyaza,' Ereshkigal concurred, and Zeven was shocked by her knowledge. 'Thanks to Armaros' memories, I shall never forget them.'

'No offence,' Zeven commented to Ereshkigal and then looked to Noah, 'but that is dangerous.'

'So is allowing her to summon the principals of the dark universe, but we are about to risk that,' Noah stated in the Queen of the Dead's defence. 'So if Ereshkigal is going to betray us, I feel it will be sooner rather than later.'

'Those seals are easily enough reproduced,' Ereshkigal admitted, 'but why would I wish to dredge the lowest part of my soul experience up into this universe, when I have grown so much since then? I am no fool. To share what I know of the dark universe with anyone would be to destroy the natural order and risk my own damnation. No matter which of the Fallen I once was, I do not wish for my darkest aspect to be at anyone's beck and call.'

'I can't say I would fancy that either,' Noah awarded, gratified by her comprehension of the matter.

'That is why I wanted to ensure I had them all, so that I could dispose of them thusly.' She motioned back to the orb in question. 'So if you would be so kind.'

Zeven was still a little wary about producing the seals for her.

'Well, I could depart and allow you to perform the summons yourself,' Ereshkigal proffered. 'But do bear in mind that time does not exist in the dark universe. As there is a part of me still residing there, so do the Grigori still reside there, and if you were to summon Samyaza and his henchmen, the Satan might be rather curious about how you got here.'

'She has a point,' Noah considered. 'It might be best not to present Samyaza with such a paradox to solve. It could backfire badly on our past Grigori selves, and we might end up being exposed to his virus before being sent through the Eternity Gate.'

'Heaven forbid, no!' Zeven's mind was exploding trying to dispose of just one mind-eater; a couple of hundred of them would see this universe as damned as the last. 'Okay,' Zeven called it, deciding to trust Ereshkigal, and Noah nodded to confirm it would be all right.

If Ereshkigal was again lying about Noah's influence on her, or her enlightened intent, this mission would fail miserably. Yet, his gut told him that he was right to give her the benefit of the doubt. Just because she was Nefilim and would become a great nemesis to them in future, didn't mean she could not be trusted now.

'It's not like we have a lot of choices here,' Zeven turned his focus to the golden orb and cast his mind back to the dark universe, to recall the personal insignia the fallen Elohim all wore emblazoned upon the chest plate of their armour. The circular seals of embossed gold all rose to adorn the surface of the sphere, Samyaza on the top, Bael on the bottom and the eight other principals in two rows around the middle of the sphere. 'All yours.' Zeven bowed out of Ereshkigal's way.

'Before we begin,' Noah who had some experience of conjuring spirits from the sub-planes in the past, informed. 'We need an unbroken circle drawn around this entire central area. Do these passages go right the way around?' He motioned to the dark curving corridors to either side of the throne area.

'They do,' Ereshkigal sounded affronted. 'But why a circle of protection, when the seals will hold the fallen?'

'Just a precaution,' he answered diplomatically — but in the event that Ereshkigal summoned the Fallen and then decided to set them onto Zeven and himself, a circle of protection would contain them and prevent the issue. 'Zeven, if you would be so kind?'

With a thought, Zeven manifested an ultra-violet mark of light on the ground that went shooting off around the central enclosure to the left and within moments the band of light emerged from the passage on the right to join with itself and maintain a solid glow.

'No trust.' Ereshkigal quipped at their safety measure.

'Our only thought is for your welfare.' Zeven grinned winningly, despite lying through his teeth.

'You need fear not, I know what I am doing.' Ereshkigal positioned herself in the centre of the archway facing the area, and as Zeven and Noah still stood observing her every move, she asked, 'Are you waiting for a formal invitation to hide?'

'Ah, right you are.' Zeven turned himself invisible.

Noah decided to conceal himself to one side of the archway, and heading off in that direction, he felt a hand slap down on his shoulder.

'It's cool,' said Zeven, but looking back he did not see his comrade, and looking down Noah couldn't see himself either.

'That's a little off-putting.'

'It is, isn't it?' Zeven agreed. 'But at least you'll get to watch the proceedings.'

That was quite true, Noah considered looking up and into the arena — being able to hide in plain sight was certainly an advantage he'd never known before.

> '*I, Ereshkigal, Queen of the Underworld*
> *and all the souls of the dead,*'

Their hostess began her summons, calling into the great void before her.

> '*I invoke and conjure,*
> *the terrible and invisible God,*
> *who dwells in the void place of spirit.*
>
> *Show thyself within this circle,*
> *in fair and comely shape,*
> *without deformity or tortuosity.*
>
> *Hear me, Bael — the first principal,*
> *Paimon, Baleth, Purson and Asmoday!*
>
> *I invoke thee, Vinè, Balam, Zagan, Belial,*
> *and your leader, who shall not be named,*
> *the mighty, born-less one!*
>
> *With power armed from the divine creatrix,*
> *and the one who is all kinds,*
> *I command you now, appear!*'

The forms of the fallen Elohim began to rise from their seals, growling and cussing at the uncomfortable inconvenience.

Although they began eyeing her in an obtrusive manner, Ereshkigal held her ground; her claim to be fearless was substantiated in her unwavering focus.

'Clever mortal, how have you summoned he who obeys not?' Samyaza moved to fly towards her, only to find his feet firmly fixed in place to the golden seal upon the globe at his feet, which he noted was indeed his own. 'How do you know the unknowable?'

The Fallen Elohim were very beautiful to behold, but their perfect faces and forms did nothing to hide the evil intent that coursed through every fibre of their being. They protested loudly to being stuck at strange angles on the spinning orb — Bael, hanging upside down from the base, was the most agitated of all. 'Cut me loose, cretin —'

'Quiet!' Samyaza ordered his lackeys. He was interested to hear what Ereshkigal had to say.

'I confound you,' Ereshkigal found this a great compliment. 'But you need only know that the seals at your feet bind you all to do my bidding.'

Samyaza laughed at her summation. 'They bind us to appear before you, but for our aid … you must make a *deal*.'

'Must I?' Ereshkigal was equally amused. 'Behold!' She spread her arms wide to bring their attention to the arena, in which the globe restraining them was poised. 'You are at the centre of the circle of living breath, of the one who looks with gladness upon you. There is no deal to be made here, your presence is all that is required.'

Samyaza noted that the golden globe at his feet had begun sinking down towards the dark porthole. 'Release us, and you shall have every spirit of the firmament, and of the ether, and every spell and scourge of creation obedient to you!'

'You cannot give me what I already possess,' she looked down upon his descending person. 'But I thank you, for you are both magnificent and praiseworthy in the eyes of the one who is all kinds. All things of heaven, Earth and dwelling in darkness are in their rightful place, because you are a servant of obedience. I bid you all remain visible to my eyes, until you descend into your dwelling, whereupon you are released of my hold.'

'There must be something you desire?' Samyaza growled, getting more agitated by the second.

'I desire that you return and remain in your dwelling,' she stated kindly, 'until the living breath of the voice of the creatrix is, according to the law, given to you.'

'Fuck you! I obey no one!' he seethed. 'I will be back, and I will find you!'

'I am certain of it,' Ereshkigal said loudly, as their dialogue was drowned out by the growing distance between them, the protests of the Fallen Elohim and the regular chaos within the arena. 'I am living proof that you will return,' she uttered quietly to herself, as the dark ones she had waited her whole life to meet, vanished into the darkened void below.

'That was brilliantly negotiated, Highness,' Noah awarded, as Zeven let him go and they both become visible once again.

'Brilliantly negotiated?' Zeven thought it an understatement. 'That was fucking awesome!' he stressed and gripped his head with his hands, arms spread wide in relief. 'It is done! We did it!' The realisation urged him to rush at Armaros, and jump-hug him.

'*Who* did it?' Ereshkigal queried, indignant.

Zeven let Noah go, turned to the Nefilim woman, placed an arm across his chest and bowed to her. 'The Grigori are indebted to you, Majesty, it is a very great feat you have helped us achieve this day.' He stood upright to find her grinning.

'Our meeting in this instance, when considered on the whole, has been an equal exchange of mutual benefit,' Ereshkigal allowed. 'All debts are paid in full. At least they will be, once I return you to my betrothed.'

'We surrender entirely to your will,' Noah granted. 'The time of our internment is overdue.'

'You said it,' Zeven agreed wholeheartedly, and the Queen of the Dead, found their words perplexing.

314

'You face limbo so willingly,' she noted, 'yet I find it sad such talent and wisdom is to be suppressed for all time. I believe I should appeal your case once more to the Pantheon —'

'No!' Both Noah and Zeven chimed in to insist at once, and Ereshkigal was truly confused.

Zeven leaned in close to have a quiet word with Noah. 'Turn off the charm, will you?'

'I have,' he insisted. 'She is naturally compassionate.'

'That is unexpected,' Zeven warranted.

Noah sidestepped him to focus on Ereshkigal. 'You would never get the majority vote, Highness. It would only make trouble for you on the eve of your engagement.'

'I don't think your betrothed likes us very much,' Zeven was fairly sure about that.

'Have you not observed how I can negotiate my betrothed?' She encouraged them to be more positive. 'I shall take this up with Anu —'

'Really, Majesty,' Noah attempted to sway her, but they were already being swallowed by the dark mist of the dragon express.

In the Worlds Chamber, they joined Anu, who was alone upon his throne, with all the doors closed.

Ereshkigal was concerned to find her suitor was not present. 'Where is Nergal?'

'I dismissed him.' Anu rose and descended the stairs. 'So that we might speak alone.'

'That is well, Father,' Ereshkigal decided, 'for I wish to take issue with the sentence of the Grigori.'

'I thought you might,' he advised her as he gazed into her eyes, 'for at this time in your young life, your heart goes out to all the forsaken.' Anu placed a hand on both sides of her face. 'But you will forget about them now —'

'No,' she gasped, realising what was happening and attempting to pull away, but she could not.

'Yes, you must,' Anu instilled in her more forcefully.

'Yes,' she succumbed to the directive.

'Wipe from your memory all recollection of the Grigori and their cargo —'

'And the dark universe,' Noah cut in to advise; Anu looked to him and raised his brow in question, displeased.

'And the dark universe,' Anu looked back to Ereshkigal to conclude. 'Allow only your encounter with Nergal to remain.'

'As you will, Father,' she replied.

'You may leave me now, your betrothed awaits you beyond those doors,' Anu motioned to the primary exit from the chamber. 'As does your brother, Enki. Would you be so kind as to send him in for me?'

Ereshkigal gasped at the sound of her twin's name, it had been some time since they had seen each other. 'Lingering in the land of the living for a time, shall have some boons … I have missed my less adventurous brother.'

'Your family misses you, most curious daughter,' he assured her. 'It will be a joy to have your company and wisdom more often.'

'Father?' Ereshkigal frowned, 'you were not so well disposed towards me at our last meeting.'

'Well, that is in the past.' Telmo, who was inhabiting Anu's body realised he was probably sounding a little too affectionate for a Nefilim, even one as advanced as Anu.

'A gracious resolve,' Ereshkigal granted and as she departed, her eyes did not stray towards the Grigori present; for her, they were simply not there.

'It will take them a little while to process their reunion,' Anu advised, once the door was closed, 'so we should really get moving.'

Zeven waylaid the Nefilim by grabbing his arm, wishing to address Telmo within. 'I just wanted to say, you've been anything but a liability.' Zeven held out a hand to shake his. 'We couldn't have succeeded in this mission without your help.'

'I accept your apology,' Anu granted. 'But we haven't succeeded yet.'

'I wasn't saying sorry,' Zeven was irked by the assumption. 'I didn't do anything wrong, I was just saying —'

'Guys!' Noah was already laying himself down on the floor, in preparation to depart. 'Argue later. We have a lot of backtracking to do, before we are out of the woods.'

'Right you are.' Zeven joined Noah on the floor, but Telmo choose the throne to put Anu's body to snooze in.

'Enki knows what to do,' Anu advised them as they all got comfortable. 'See you in the next one.'

'Roger that.' Zeven closed his eyes to focus on the minute they had left the AMIE project to venture back to ancient Nibiru. He loved a good adventure, more than any of the timekeepers, bar Taren herself, but it came as some relief to know that this was hopefully the last he would ever see of the Nefilim.

PART 4

BACKTRACK TIME

14

THE THIRD UNIVERSE

As Taren sat waiting for her three remaining unconscious crew members to surface from their regression, she was quietly musing on the illusive tricks time played — for these few minutes seemed to be taking a lifetime to unfold.

She thought back over the events that had brought them to this point, and all the instances in time they had yet to tackle — the notion of facing that totality without the three souls still in question was unfathomable, as were the repercussions if they did not succeed.

'Why did you leave ahead of them?' Taren queried Rhun, Avery, Leal and Jazmay, who had all taken a seat to regain their sensibility of the present — Leal was gripping his privates and silently giving thanks and praise.

'It was Zeven's call,' Rhun clued her in. 'He wanted to deal with Ereshkigal on his own.'

'Ereshkigal?' Taren recalled seeing her in Dan's thought recording. 'I thought you and Noah were dealing with Ereshkigal?'

'Well … the Queen of the Dead took more than just a liking to Noah,' Rhun outlined the complication, 'and took off with him to the Underworld.'

'The Queen of the Dead?' Lucian wanted to be sure he was hearing correctly.

'You let Zeven venture into the Underworld alone?' Taren was astounded.

'No,' Rhun assured her, then added more tentatively. 'Nergal accompanied him.'

'Nergal!' Taren freaked, knowing he was one of the most troublesome among the Nefilim that the Chosen had been forced to deal with in the past.

'Who is Nergal?' Lucian appealed to be enlightened.

The doors Taren had been staring at finally opened and Kassa stood in the doorway to announce. 'All back and accounted for.' She stepped aside so that all in the waiting room could see that Noah, Telmo and Zeven were sitting upright and stripping sensors from their bodies.

This event brought sighs of relief from everyone, but they refrained from entering the chamber to give the occupants time to collect themselves and comprehend their present place in space and time.

Telmo and Zeven were having words with one another, having returned to consciousness arguing. Noah waved them both off and raised himself to come and brief Taren and the others waiting expectantly outside the doors.

When Zeven noticed this, he stripped the last of the sensors from his form and followed suit. 'Why would I apologise when I didn't do anything wrong?'

'Just admit you should have recruited me in the first place,' Telmo replied, bringing up the rear.

'I did admit it!' Zeven argued back.

'Does it matter?' Noah turned back to them as they entered the waiting room. 'We succeeded, that's all that counts.'

'You succeeded?' Taren noted, fit to burst with relief.

'Of course!' both Telmo and Zeven chimed in to boast at once.

'The virus, the seals?' She quantified their claim to success.

'All returned to the dark universe, courtesy of Ereshkigal.' Zeven put her mind to rest and Taren was compelled to hug him.

'I was so worried!' She pulled back to express how concerned she'd been for them all.

'Well, thanks for the vote of confidence.' Zeven was underwhelmed by her reaction.

'I was worried for you, not the mission,' she clarified, as the rest of the crew congratulated each other on their success. 'Rhun said you were dealing with Nergal again, and the last time you faced off with him, you wound up in a pit fighting a mutant!'

'But he didn't have *me* there at that time, to save his arse,' Telmo stated in a grandiloquent manner.

'No, I handled it on my own. Much like this instance,' Zeven scoffed. 'You didn't venture into the Underworld!'

'I didn't need to, when I set you up perfectly for success,' contested Telmo.

'Jeez, they are worse than us!' Avery commented to Rhun, who nodded to agree.

'I say we debate the matter over food,' Leal said, throwing an arm around his wife, and grabbing his stomach with his free hand. 'We may have only been gone a couple of minutes, but I feel like I haven't eaten in an age!'

'Hear, hear,' Jazmay agreed. 'We're not Grigorian now.'

'Thank goodness for that,' Leal concurred. 'Saying yes to Tiamat is the best decision we ever made,' he looked to the captain as he said this and then kissed Kassa, because he could.

Lucian frowned, frustrated. 'Who is Tiamat?'

'Someone we made a promise to once,' Zeven filled him in.

'A promise that has now been executed in full,' Noah pointed out, which inspired a round of applause from the other timekeepers.

'Provided what we've done hasn't drastically affected history in some unforeseeable manner.' Avery was wary not to count their chickens just yet.

'We were very careful not to change anything besides what we went to alter,' Zeven was more confident. 'The big question now is … where to from here?'

Taren, Jazmay, Noah, Rhun and Avery nodded as they considered the query.

'Well, I don't know about you guys but my next stop is the mess,' Leal commented on his way out the door. 'And then I'm back to the flight deck, as per usual.'

'Thank goodness for small mercies.' Kassa was clearly relieved to have the ordeal over.

'Thanks for your contribution,' Zeven acknowledged them both, placing his hands together to emphasise how grateful he was. 'It was most appreciated.'

'Not what I was expecting to be doing today, but it was very educational nonetheless. And now I have a new skill,' Leal warranted it was worth the effort and risk. 'I hope it works out for us in the end.' He waved, as did Kassa, as they headed out to resume their regular routine.

'Well, I guess that's a wrap everyone, good job.' Lucian looked to their three inter-universal guests. 'You'd best return to the conference room, we'll meet you there to discuss your next destination.'

'I'll round up some food for the troops,' Jazmay volunteered as the team from Kila vanished as requested.

'I'll give you a hand,' Taren moved to follow her, but the captain waylaid her.

'Zeven and Telmo can assist,' Lucian suggested. The men in question realised that their absence was being requested, and they both moved to make their exit with Jazmay.

'See you both there,' Zeven commented, serving Taren a look of sympathy — he knew she was in trouble and so did she.

'Okay, what have I done now?' Taren folded her arms, and prepared to be lectured on the extravagance of her problem solving means.

'You tell me,' Lucian challenged. 'What is it that you're not telling me?'

Damn it. Her husband knew her way too well; there was no point denying that there was information she was withholding. 'We screwed up.'

'We?' Lucian raised a brow intrigued.

Taren nodded to confirm, and her pending confession caused an ironic smile to form on her lips. 'We fell in love, when we weren't supposed to.'

Lucian grinned at this. 'So what's new?'

'I got pregnant,' she announced and watched the gamut of emotions unfurl across her lover's face, before landing him with the bad news. 'That issue was a huge impediment to me being able to return here, for there is no safe way to deliver a child from that universe into this one. I would have had to stay and raise the child on Kila.'

Lucian's amazement was replaced by a daze of devastation. He gripped his head with all ten of his fingertips in an attempt to fathom the complications and ramifications of the news. 'Yet you're here now?' He was perplexed by that fact. 'Where is our child?'

'In the limbo between rearranging timelines, I expect,' she said, but the dark look Lucian served her implied he was not as detached from the outcome.

'You left our child in another timeline?' He stood again, and she could not recall ever seeing him so angry.

'I was but a couple of weeks pregnant and the lives of our entire crew were in jeopardy. I had to get them out of there, and they would not leave without me.' She defended her decision. 'What would you have done?'

'Thought of something else!' He backed off a little, but his aversion was still plain.

'I know how dearly you want a child,' Taren's tough exterior began to dissolve. 'But I couldn't stand to see another one of us slaughtered,' her tears of horror spilt down her face, 'not after you.'

Despite how mad he was, Lucian hugged her close to him, and allowed a moment for them both to calm down. 'So that is it then, there is nothing to be done?'

The short embrace did wonders, it felt good to have cleared her conscience and Taren pulled herself together and withdrew from him to confess the rest. 'I will return to ancient Zhou and ensure we do not wed, which is what history dictated.'

'So our child will never be?' Lucian clearly resented the desired outcome.

'That child was never meant to be,' Taren concluded. 'It is not of this universe, and we no longer belong to the time zone, planet or the universe where it rightfully should have been born! In the reality of that world, both of its parents were dead.'

'I want to remember,' Lucian decided.

'And you shall —'

'Not if you go back and change everything,' Lucian was sure of that much.

'Can you not just trust that I have got this —'

'After what you have just told me?' Lucian posed, indignant.

It hurt that he considered she'd done the wrong thing by them, when she knew in her heart that she had not.

'Damn.' Lucian looked to the floor and swallowed hard as he digested the facts. 'I wish I could be as detached from outcomes as you are. I almost wish I hadn't asked.'

'Repeated tragedy has a way of numbing the senses,' she explained her indifference, which Lucian was finding so very unbecoming. Still, this was her self-defence mechanism for dealing with the grief, and she would not lower that guard now, not before her mission was done, or she would collapse into an emotional heap and be useless to everyone. 'Today is the first real victory we've seen in some time.'

Lucian looked to her, and astounded by her view, he shook his head. 'I'm afraid I cannot see it that way.'

'Then we must agree to disagree,' Taren concluded, unhappily, and made a move towards the door to leave it at that.

'Did I even know back then?' Lucian queried. 'Or did you hide the fact from me then also?'

'You knew,' she turned back to state coolly. 'You wanted to make it work, regardless of the risk that posed to everyone else. I resigned myself to your wishes.' She gritted her teeth to endure the ire she felt in this moment. 'But, over your dead body, I relented.' Taren left his presence before she lost control and her psychokinesis started flinging inanimate objects at him.

'Taren!' Lucian called as he came after her, and although his tone was more sympathetic, she needed a moment to decompress, and so teleported herself to the one place in AMIE that always made her feel calm — Module C.

Upon arrival in the greenhouse contained within Module C, Taren breathed deeply in an attempt to allay her surging emotions; her anger turned to guilt and self doubt, and she broke down and wept. 'Damn it,' she scolded herself. 'Don't do this now.' She struggled to draw deep breaths to counter the massive anxiety attack welling within her. The weight and magnitude of the risks they were taking bore down heavily upon her conscience, and she gripped the Juju stone fixed to her left upper arm to seek its guidance. 'Send me a sign. Tell me I'm not wrong about this!'

'You're never wrong.'

Taren looked aside to see Ringbalin a short distance up the pathway from her, planting saplings.

He brushed the dirt from his hands and stood. 'Yet, clearly there is something amiss with you ... can I be of assistance?'

As with his Zhou incarnation Fen Gong, Ringbalin was a calming force; Taren was breathing easier just upon seeing him. In this life he was fair of skin, golden haired and blue eyed, like Armaros, but he had Fen Gong's nature through and through.

Taren shook her head, both to disagree with their horticulturalist's summation of her actions and to decline his aid. 'I'll be fine,' she sniffed back her emotion. 'I just need a stroll through your garden.'

'Would you like company?'

'I always welcome your company —' She had to stop herself from calling him little brother.

'Would you like tea with that?' he suggested with an expectant grin, which Taren returned, realising Ringbalin also knew her very well.

'Do you even have to ask?' She smiled sincerely to accept.

The mug of warm tea was a great comfort to cling to, as they did the rounds of the gardens within the greenhouse; hearing Ringbalin discuss his passion was a pleasing distraction from the strife and stress.

'As riveting as my work is,' Ringbalin posed sarcastically, 'I feel you have other more pressing concerns.'

'I do.' Taren breathed a heavy sigh, reluctant to leave this peaceful pause in the chaos.

'I sense there are strange things afoot today,' he voiced his observation. 'Anything I can be of help with?'

The offer made Taren smile, as she considered that his past life incarnation of Noah was awaiting her presence in the conference room as they spoke. 'You already are helping,' she emphasised, and handing him back his cup, Taren gripped his wrist to get one last shot of his calming energy.

'It was just a cup of tea.' He downplayed his part.

'And a damn fine one at that,' she awarded, feeling much better.

'I thought I'd find you here.' Zeven appeared and startled them both. 'The captain is looking for you.'

'I know.' Taren let Ringbalin go. 'I'm coming now.'

'He's not happy,' Zeven added in warning.

'I am the one who made him so,' Taren regretted to inform. 'But there is nothing to be done about it now.'

'He knows then?' Zeven guessed, without giving away the cause.

Taren nodded and forced a smile. 'But the reprise will play out as it always should have, only then will the issue truly be set to rights.'

Zeven nodded, for he agreed it was for the best; still, it was not his child they were discussing. 'He will forget all this,' Zeven tried to be supportive.

But Taren knew better. 'Ji Dan will forget, sure enough. But when we return here ... Lucian will remember.'

'Maybe by then, he will understand your choices?' Zeven put forward, hating to see their leader doubting herself.

Taren forced a smile and nodded. 'We can hope.'

When Taren entered the conference room, you could have cut the tension between her and the captain with a knife; fortunately the crew had eaten and were ready to get down to business.

'Could I speak with you in my office?' Lucian requested.

'Afterwards,' Taren suggested. 'I'm sure our friends from Kila are eager to get moving.'

'Our discussion could have some bearing on this meeting,' Lucian resented her attempt to put him off.

'No,' Taren insisted, 'it cannot.' She could feel Lucian quietly fuming at her back, as she approached the rest of the timekeepers seated at the table to propose. 'The way I see it, there is little point in us returning to Kila before we gauge what effect our actions have had on the situation in ancient Zhou.'

'I second that motion,' Zeven stated.

'Makes sense,' Jazmay agreed.

'We must return to our rightful universe via the Otherworld,' Avery pointed out.

'We can summon you forth when we get to ancient Zhou,' Zeven theorised.

'And what am I to do in Zhou?' Noah asked, 'I already have an incarnation there.'

'I can bring you back to Kila with me on the chariot,' said Rhun.

'But the chariot won't be there, will it?' Noah answered. 'Not unless you drop by Kila and take it back there, as you did originally?'

'Depending on when we go back, I could already be there and so would the chariot?' Rhun countered.

'But then you'd have to leave your body here and jump into the one that is there.' Avery confused the issue further, as Jazmay groaned and gripped her aching head.

'All I know is that I have an incarnation in Zhou, so I have somewhere to go.' She held up her hands to relinquish responsibility for putting any further thought into the matter. 'If I go back to just before I died then I won't have the opportunity to screw history up too much, before Rhun comes to collect me. Done.'

'Same here,' Zeven seconded her plan.

'Ditto,' Taren agreed, still mulling over the paradox. 'Noah could wait the incident out in the Otherworld, and can return to Kila when you do, Avery.'

'I can summon you back to Kila once we are done in Zhou,' Rhun suggested.

'Um,' Noah hated to put a spanner in the works, 'but won't I already be on Kila, as technically I would never have left?'

'Damn it!' Taren cussed under her breath, they'd created a hell of a paradox for themselves.

'I thought this would be the easy part of the mission,' Zeven owned up to his shortcomings, 'but it looks like I've just quantum jumped us out of the frying pan and into the fire.'

'No, you've done well,' Taren awarded, 'there has to be a way around this.'

'Even if one of the timekeepers attempted to go back to when we left, it will most likely be an entirely different situation that greets us there.' Zeven saw the problem now.

Taren thought harder on it. 'We need someone who is there on Kila already who can summon Rhun, Avery and Noah back, as we timekeepers may or may not have returned there after the mission to ancient Zhou this time around.'

'Jahan!' Jazmay proffered. He'd been Ji Shi — her partner in ancient Zhou — and that same soul-mind was also her partner, Yasper, here on AMIE. 'Jahan is on Kila. We could train Yasper up, and he could go back and summon them forth?'

Taren's eyes lit up. 'That might just work.'

'You want to involve another member of this crew in this?' Lucian was inclined to disagree.

'There is little risk involved,' Taren turned to appeal their case to the captain, despite his aversion to her at present. 'If Yasper can return to his incarnation of Jahan on Kila and summon the Kila contingent back to their rightful place, Noah's paradox is sorted and Yasper can return straight here. Rhun can take the chariot back to Zhou, then summon Avery, whilst the rest of us return to Zhou directly.'

Lucian, perturbed, looked to the rest of the team to find them all smiling in accord with her plan, except for Telmo.

'I don't think that is going to work either,' Telmo offered up his expert advice, having been something of a time lord in the last universe.

'How so?' Taren's head was starting to hurt.

'If the timelines have changed,' Telmo suggested, 'chances are that Rhun and Noah never left Kila, and if they return there —'

'There is going to be two of them,' Taren realised where he was going with this.

'There is only one way of getting everyone back to where they rightfully should be,' Telmo stated. 'We must all, bar Avery, do a body jump.'

'Are you suggesting we leave these bodies behind?' Rhun motioned to his form.

'And jump back into the same body just before you went back to ancient Zhou? The same goes for Noah. Avery will be fine to just return to the Otherworld and be summoned forth again, as he is not bound by the same physical rules as the rest of us. If all is well, as we hope, Kila will not be attacked by reptilians this time around, but regardless you must take the chariot back to Zhou, to the safety of the crystal cavern that served as a meeting place for you and Avery last time around.'

'Check.' Rhun got the picture. 'If there is no Dragonface, there is no chance of him stealing the chariot and starting the entire mess again.'

'Exactly,' Telmo agreed.

'The four of us,' Telmo referred to Zeven, Jazmay, Taren and himself, 'will return directly to our Zhou incarnations just prior to our gathering and deliverance to the Dropa base there.'

'And what is to be done with the Dropa this time around?' Rhun posed to them all.

'Let us gauge how the situation stands now, before making any firm plans in that regard,' Telmo suggested.

'And where does that leave me?' Lucian was curious to know.

'Oh, you'll still be there,' Telmo assured.

'But I won't remember this,' Lucian realised.

'Not until you get back here to AMIE, but you will remember,' Telmo reassured. 'In Zhou however, you, Ji Shi and Fen Gong will be the only ones who shall consciously remember the new history we have created, which is going to be vital to our decision-making process going forward.'

Lucian looked to Taren and the look on his face implied that he saw the reasoning, but at the same time hated that he did.

'It *will* all work out in the end,' Taren imparted the hope that she was clinging to, and Lucian nodded to accept their plight.

'And what shall become of the bodies we leave behind?' Noah clearly felt odd about his impending time/body jump.

'I shall carry them to the Otherworld with me,' Avery offered. 'You never know when having a spare body might come in handy.'

'Don't looked so freaked out,' Zeven slapped a hand down on Noah's shoulder. 'I've body jumped a few times now, and it hasn't done me any damage.'

Noah did not look reassured. 'What if we forget everything? Including going back to Zhou. There is no one waiting on Kila to awaken the timekeepers within us.'

Telmo was already shaking his head to assure they would remember. 'That is more likely when you are jumping into a past life incarnation, rather than your present incarnation.'

'That was true for those of us who returned to AMIE,' Taren pointed out.

'Thank heavens for that,' Zeven breathed a sign of relief, for that was not an instance he'd factored into his plan of attack.

'No offence, short man,' Jazmay laughed, 'but I think your defeat of Dragonface was a sheer stroke of luck!'

Zeven opened his mouth to retort, but Telmo assumed control of the proceedings. 'If we clear the room,' he suggested, 'I can run Rhun and Noah through the consciousness projection process, and see the team from Kila returned to their rightful place.'

'That would be a good start,' the captain concurred. Zeven and Jazmay rose to make an exit.

'What about the rest of us?' Zeven sought to know when they should make their move.

'Well,' Telmo noted the time on the wall clock in the conference room. 'It's just about bedtime, so I suggest you go to bed as per normal and do the jump then.'

'So, does this mean that half my crew may not wake up tomorrow?' Lucian posed. 'How is their body jump different to the one that Rhun and Noah are about to make?'

'A very good question,' Telmo awarded. 'What we have going on here is more like what happens when your spirit inhabits the body of another: the consciousness of that body is suppressed while the invading consciousness dominates. Once that invading consciousness leaves, so will the other return. Rhun and Noah brought their bodies with them, rather than just their consciousness, thus it is that we have an excess body count.'

'Don't say that,' Rhun objected, 'makes me feel like a walking corpse.'

'As are we all, really,' Telmo allowed.

'So, what you are saying is that none of the crew involved are going to remember what happened this day?' Lucian glanced at Taren, not thrilled about that premise, and she smiled awkwardly.

'Most likely not … only you and Leal will remember, until we return here with our current conscious knowledge.' Telmo advised. 'Unless we choose to return to the exact moment we left on this occasion. But the original plan was to return closer to D-day.'

'Fabulous,' Lucian shook his head, hating that his personal feelings paled in comparison to the outcome of the big picture in this instance. 'Well, without my complete recall, I can hardly argue the point.'

'Trust me, Captain,' Telmo appealed, 'this is the only way we might succeed in setting history to rights.'

'Which includes our child never existing.' Lucian brought everyone's attention to the elephant in the room that they were all ignoring, and everyone looked guilty, until Telmo spoke up to solve the matter.

'Even if Ji Dan and Jiang Hudan had wed, which according to history before we screwed with it, they never did,' Telmo clarified, 'Jiang Hudan died the day after, and so would the child have died with her, because fate decreed it was not that soul's time.'

'He speaks the truth,' Jazmay assured Lucian, who looked to Taren, who also nodded to confirm.

333

'That is why I say that soul cannot figure into the equation,' Taren concluded gently, but as she approached Lucian he backed up an equal distance.

'Well then, proceed,' he gave Telmo leave to organise the exodus. 'I'll be in my office if there are any problems.'

'Yes Captain,' Telmo affirmed.

'Happy travels, gentlemen,' he bid farewell to their visitors from Kila, shaking the hand of Avery, Noah and Rhun in turn.

'Thank you, for your assistance, Captain.' Rhun gripped his hand and held it fast. 'Past and present.'

Lucian forced a grin to graciously accept his gratitude, and departing to his adjoining office, the door closed in his wake.

The captain's moody exit left a heavy silence in the room which Zeven broke with a clap of his hands. 'Well then,' he approached and shook hands with the Kila crew in parting also. 'I'll see you back there,' he aimed the comment at Rhun, who was the key to their success now.

'Yes, you will,' the governor assured.

'We're going to finish this,' Zeven assured the Governor of Kila, who nodded firmly in agreement with his incarnated long-time ally.

'You had all better hope my child has not been lost in the timelines,' Avery was restless and eager to move forward.

'We'll get out of your hair then,' Taren aided to speed the process along, waving her people towards the exit door that led to the reception office, and once Jazmay and Zeven had waved farewell and left, she turned back to those team members remaining to add: 'May the Grigori be with us on this one.'

'And always,' Noah granted.

'Goodbye, Mother,' Avery found his humour as she turned to depart, but Rhun thought the comment was in poor taste.

'Considering what has just gone down with the captain, you would bring that up now?' Rhun lectured his little brother.

'What, she's the splitting image of Mother in this body,' Avery pointed out. 'I only meant —'

'Guys!' Taren spoke up to end the argument — it was just a private joke Avery had with Hudan and she'd understood his intent. 'Make me proud,' she decided to play along with the joke, and with a smile, left them to it.

As the door closed behind her, she realised she was already proud of them, and although she had not given birth to the pair in this lifetime, she still felt a tweak of hurt upon being parted from them.

'Well then,' Zeven was suddenly up and away. 'I'm off to bed.' He slapped his hands together and rubbed them, in eager anticipation of the event. 'As soon as I track down my wife.'

'I see you've learned to make the most of these little sidetracks,' Taren commented.

'Yes indeed,' he grinned and nodded to give Taren her due. 'I learned from a master of the art.'

Taren's grin contorted, recalling a precarious situation involving Zeven, a shower, and a mistimed backtrack teleportation event, where he'd busted her for dwelling in a timeline longer than she should have, because Lucian seduced her into the distraction.

Her discomfort must have satisfied Zeven's desire for a reaction, for he waved and departed. 'See you in Zhou.'

'What was that all about?' Jazmay had obviously noted the awkwardness of the moment.

'Zeven's ego,' Taren replied dryly, 'what else?'

Jazmay knew there was more to it, but shrugged. 'Well, I think I'm learning a lot.'

Taren was alarmed, hoping she hadn't got the wrong impression. 'Hey, we were talking about something that happened before either Zeven or I were attached.'

'I wasn't implying there was anything going on between you and short man,' Jazmay laughed, even more enlightened and curious now. 'I meant about seeking my husband out before I leave.'

Taren covered her embarrassed grin with both her hands and then lowered them as she blew off her own betrayal. 'Oh yes … good move, considering how old you'll be when you return to Zhou.'

'Not looking forward to that,' Jazmay mused, 'but then we have the Dropa to make us young and useful again.'

Taren nodded and grinned.

'It's all right for you, you die young,' Jazmay poked her for her mirth.

'Yeah ... your bad, for having a long, blissfully happy life with your beloved and all your offspring,' Taren retorted sarcastically.

'There was that,' Jazmay dwelt upon the time fondly for a moment. 'I'll be off then, to enjoy my youth ... before old age comes around in the morning to bite me in the arse.'

Taren laughed at her reasoning.

'What are you going to do?' Jazmay glanced at the closed door of the captain's office and then back to Taren.

'I'm not too sure there's much I can do.' Taren eyed the door warily.

Jazmay raised both eyebrows, as she backed up. 'Even though you'll be Jiang Hudan in the morning, you could spare Taren Lennox a lot of confusion and worry tomorrow by preventing her husband from waking up mad at her, for no apparent reason.' Jazmay held her hands up to wave off any further comment and leave the decision in Taren's hands. 'See you when I'm old and grey.' She turned about and left.

Taren took a seat in reception to ponder her predicament, feeling decidedly wrung out; it seemed the Ringbalin effect was wearing off, and she needed some real rest.

The sound of a door sliding open drew her attention, and Taren was a little disappointed to find it was Telmo emerging from the conference room, and not Lucian exiting his office. 'That was quick.' Through the open doors she could see the room beyond was now empty.

'Fast learners, the Chosen,' he commented. 'Always were.' His smile seemed more to uplift her than to convey his satisfaction. 'You look tired.'

Taren gave a wry grin, not surprised the fatigue was showing. 'You get that, in our line of work.'

'Only if you allow yourself to become a slave to the lifestyle, rather than allowing the lifestyle to work for you.' He winked as he plonked himself in the seat alongside hers.

This was curious. 'How is it that you are still so chipper?'

336

'I came back here a few days early,' he admitted, 'got myself some rest.'

Taren's jaw waned. 'You cheat!'

'Well, the universe is not going to schedule any down time, we have to make time ourselves. Why don't you take a couple of days to do the same, and patch things up here?' He ticked his head towards the captain's office. 'No one will miss you in ancient Zhou. You'll arrive promptly at your destination, no matter when you choose to depart for it … but you know that.'

'I rather thought that was breaking the rules,' Taren didn't know if she was horrified or overjoyed by the suggestion.

'What rules?' Telmo laughed. 'If there was a rule book, you would be the author.'

'Or you,' she granted, as technically he'd perfected the art in the last universe, long before she had ever got a grip on the practice.

'But dwell too long here …' Telmo warned, 'and you might forget the details of the mission.'

'But,' Taren frowned, 'what effect might that have on the outcome of this universal timeline?'

'You're a timekeeper! If you spend every minute of every lifetime pondering whether you should go this way or that, you'll spend all your time attempting to figure outcomes to moves you are too afraid to make,' Telmo said. 'I have been a time lord and a sage, and as far as I can tell, the theory that within a time-travel paradigm the slightest thing you do might have a profound effect on the future, is *bullshit* … in so far as that is true for every instance outside the time-travel paradigm as well. In my experience, whether you go this way or that, you'll always end up exactly where you are meant to be, exactly when you are meant to be there.'

Taren wasn't sure she fully fathomed his wisdom, being that her brain felt fit to explode from an overdose of esoteric theory this day, but she was rather comforted by it nonetheless.

'Just something to think about.' He stood. 'Me personally, I cannot wait to get back to Zhou and see what has eventuated. I'll give you a full report when you reach Bayan Har Shan.' Telmo moved to depart.

'I'll be right behind you,' Taren assured.

'What have I just been saying?' He did a twirl, waving in the process and departed.

Taren leaned back in her chair and looked over to the closed door. She too was curious to see the outcome of their efforts in ancient China, and the thought of talking through Lucian's grievances with her at present, was not an inviting one. By the time she returned here to AMIE it would be nearly a year from now and this instance would be nothing but a long faded memory. Could she simply trust that her husband would forgive her? She wanted to think so. Or would she return from this mission and discover them estranged from one another? She mulled over Telmo's advice to not do exactly what she was now doing — trying to fathom the best outcome — and just do what her gut told her was the right thing to do.

15

RETURN TO KILA — PART 1

Consciousness dawned and Rhun's eyes parted to behold the most exquisite cleavage in his face — his wife, Sybil, was leaning over him to grab her dressing gown off the bed.

'Rhun, we'll be late —' she was saying, before he grabbed hold of her and she collapsed on top of him. 'Stop it,' she insisted, her amusement contradicting her instruction. 'Did you not hear what I just said?'

'Nope.' He smothered her neck in kisses.

'I said —'

Rhun planted a kiss on her lips to silence her, and rolled on top of her to gain control of the negotiations. 'Is the world coming to an end?' he queried, gripping her hands in his and stretching them up above her head to hold her down.

'No,' she admitted, 'but —'

'Everything else can wait,' he decided, planting his lips in the cleavage he'd been admiring and freeing her hands.

'But you do have an early meeting scheduled with En Noah,' Sybil informed, stroking his dark hair, 'about extending the curriculum at the Immortal Institute to include the Grigori and the Dark Universe,' she concluded, sounding rather baffled by the agenda.

All the events preceding his arrival in this moment came flooding back in a rush and with a pained groan, Rhun rolled off his wife. 'Bastard came back early,' Rhun realised. 'Can I not even have a few hours' grace?' he appealed to the heavens above.

'There is always this evening.' Sybil kissed him briefly in consolation and clambered off the bed to ready herself for the office.

'This evening could be years away,' Rhun mumbled, exasperated; yet he was grateful to discover that his capital city on Kila was not waking to the threat of an alien invasion. 'That's something, I guess,' he decided and reached for his trousers, preparing to launch into the day.

In the reception area outside the governor's chamber En Noah waited to greet them. 'Governor,' he acknowledged Rhun's presence with a grin. 'Nin Sybil,' Noah nodded to wish her good morning also.

'En Noah.' She returned his smile as she took a seat behind her reception desk, and brought up her soft screen to check on the day's agenda.

'I understand your reasons for this meeting,' Rhun stated, showing Noah to the door of his office. 'But did you have to make this appointment so damn early in the day?'

'Apologies,' he replied, 'but I feel we should move on this quickly, and I know how easily you can be distracted.' Noah eyes darted aside to Sybil, as he grinned and entered the office at Rhun's prompting.

'See that we are not interrupted,' Rhun advised his wife.

'Shall I bring tea?' she queried.

'Ah … yes,' Rhun decided, before Noah stuck his head back out the door.

'Ah, not for me,' he countered. 'We might need to go for a wee stroll in a moment, as there is something I wish the governor to look at.'

'After perhaps?' she suggested.

'Splendid,' Noah agreed, disappearing back inside.

'I have a feeling that after … I'm going to need something a lot stronger than tea,' Rhun commented under his breath, as he trailed Noah into the office and the door materialised behind them to close them inside.

'So how long ago did you get back?' Rhun delved straight into the matter, taking a seat in the lounge area and not behind his desk.

'A few days,' Noah admitted and took a seat on the lounge opposite.

'So what is our situation?' Rhun figured his advisor had been doing some investigation.

'Well,' he raised both brows. 'I don't remember back far enough to recall the time before the timekeepers ever landed here, but things seem to be pretty much as they would have been in that event.'

'Hold on,' Rhun was panicked. 'If the timekeepers have never come here then ...' He looked at the historian, horrified. 'You haven't summoned my youngest brother back here yet, have you?' Rhun didn't even dare to breathe the Lord of the Otherworld's name, least he heard and responded by making himself present.

'Well, I didn't see the need before we deal with Zhou,' Noah proffered, 'what's the concern?'

'Do I need a concern to avoid my brother?' Rhun sidestepped the query.

'Not usually,' Noah warranted with a wary grin.

'Maybe we could just never summon him back?' Rhun mulled over an attractive option.

Noah frowned, considering the suggestion rather harsh. 'What has Avery done?'

'Shh!' Rhun urged him not to bandy that name about. 'It's more what he's going to do.' He waved off his worry. 'A matter for after I get back from Zhou.'

'Well, from all appearances, things have been set to rights here on Kila,' Noah warranted.

'A little too right,' Rhun scoffed.

'With any luck, the situation in ancient Zhou shall be as it always should have been, also,' his advisor said, frowning, as the governor appeared quite distracted. 'If you have a concern I wish you'd voice it, you're making me nervous.'

341

'Nothing for you to worry about,' Rhun said surely.

A knock on the door, was cause for further frustration, and as Sybil entered, the governor spoke up. 'I thought I said we weren't to be disturbed.'

'Our son is here, requesting an immediate audience,' Sybil advised. 'He says it's urgent.'

Asher was Rhun's head of defence, so Rhun nodded to allow it, and as Sybil withdrew, he looked to Noah.

'Now don't be alarmed,' Noah cautioned, 'I'm sure it's nothing to worry about.'

'That's blind optimism if ever I heard it,' Rhun stood to greet his son as he entered.

Asher was taller than Rhun, the height came from his mother's side of the family, as did the pale brown eyes and reddish tinge in his light brown hair.

'Apologies for the interruption.' Asher lacked his usual good cheer this morning. 'We have an alien vessel parked beyond our atmosphere requesting permission to land.'

The governor and Noah looked at each other in trepidation a moment. 'Who are they?' Rhun queried.

'They say they are Draconian. Their ship's commander goes by the name of Vugar,' Asher informed and watched both his superiors turn pale. 'You know of him, Father?'

'Déjà vu,' Rhun uttered by way of an explanation.

'Is this how it played out last time?' Noah was afraid to ask.

Rhun nodded. 'Only it was Shyamal in command, not Vugar, and they didn't ask for permission to land, just …' Rhun looked to Noah not wanting to voice the word 'attacked' in front of Asher and cause undue alert.

'Is there something unfolding that I should know about?' Asher queried warily.

'What is their business here?' Rhun asked before setting off any alarm bells.

'Well, that's the curious thing. I suspect they are in the wrong place, for they claim to be seeking the timekeepers?' Asher shrugged. 'In particular they are asking after persons named Sammael, Armaros or Taren.'

'Taren? What the?' Rhun was agape, wondering how they could know her name in particular.

'I told them there are no citizens on Kila who go by those names,' said Asher, 'but then they asked if I knew anything of the Grigori. And as I have heard you mention the Grigori on occasion, I thought you might be of some help with the mystery.'

Rhun was just too mind-blown to speak for a time, and looked to Noah for his thoughts, but he too was having difficulty fathoming how this had come to pass.

'Did they say why they were seeking the Grigori?' Noah rose to query the head of defence.

'Apparently, they have a debt to settle with them,' Asher advised.

'A debt,' Noah mulled over the choice of word. 'That implies they owe us.'

'Why us?' Asher cut in, following nothing of the conversation.

'That could mean payback for something we've done, or it could be sarcasm?' Rhun began to pace.

'I don't think we should speculate,' Noah advised, 'I think we should finish what we started out to do this day, then we might have a better idea of what is going on here and now.'

'And what if I arrive back here to discover we are back where we started?' Rhun appealed, hesitant to go anywhere with a possible enemy ship poised above his city.

'You both think they are hostile?' Asher was unnerved.

'No,' Noah insisted, 'they have done nothing to offend, and we don't want to cause an incident by assuming they will.'

'But you think they might have hostile intentions?' That much was clear to Asher.

'In all honesty,' Rhun looked to his son to advise, 'I really cannot say, but if we can buy me an hour, I can surely find out.'

Noah gave a firm nod, feeling his reasoning was sound.

'So what do you want me to do?' Asher posed, awaiting the governor's instruction.

'Give permission for them to send down a small contingent to a meeting with me in one hour's time,' Rhun instructed.

'If you are going somewhere …' Asher was clearly disturbed by the thought of the governor roaming off, given the present circumstances. 'You should take a security detail with you.'

'We are only going so far as the institute,' Noah advised, 'and I shall accompany the governor there.'

Asher still seemed uneasy. 'If you expect something untoward might be unfolding, I should be the first one to know.'

'And you will be,' Rhun assured him. 'Just give Noah and myself one hour to gather some intel, and all shall be made clear.' *I hope.* He kept that thought to himself.

Asher rarely felt the need to question his father's judgement. 'One hour then,' he granted to confirm the arrangement.

'One hour,' Rhun agreed. 'I'll meet you at the governmental space dock.'

'I would request you meet me here,' Asher insisted, 'and brief me before we proceed to the dock to greet our guests.'

'Done,' Rhun agreed, as Asher took his leave and Noah rose.

'What the hell do we make of this?' Rhun whispered his concern to his advisor once they were alone.

'Let us not waste time speculating,' Noah advised. 'Meet you at the chariot.' He dematerialised, as Sybil entered.

'Where are you really going?' she said once the door had closed behind her.

Rhun knew the clock was already ticking here and that he should waste no time getting to the chariot — the sooner he left, the more time he would have when he returned. Still, if he didn't reply, Sybil would only follow him to find out, and as she was a seer, she might already know the answer, thus lying was pointless. 'Ancient China.'

'Why?' She frowned in disapproval.

'Because I need to go there to understand what is happening here and now,' he confessed.

'You're caught up in a time paradox, aren't you?'

'And I've got an hour to figure it out,' he advised, hoping to speed things along.

'I *know* there must be a very good reason for this,' she advised with a good serve of warning in her voice — hands on hips.

'There absolutely is,' Rhun assured her, appealing with his eyes for her trust. 'Which I will convey you in *great* detail at first liberty.'

Sybil strode forth and kissed her husband in parting. 'Go then.' She stepped away to witness him depart. 'Keep safe.'

Rhun found that notion amusing — there were a lot of words he'd use to describe his life at present, but safe wasn't one of them. 'I shall be cautious,' he vowed, focusing his thoughts upon joining En Noah.

Beneath the Institute of Immortal History was a vault only Noah and the current governor of Kila knew about. It had once housed both of the time-shifting chariots, but the empty space alongside the remaining chariot was an unwelcome reminder of how Rhun and Avery had misplaced its twin. The chariot normally sat in a floor to ceiling box of light that constituted both the alarm system and an electric shield that could inflict enough pain to deflect even an immortal attempting to breach the system — Noah had already switched off the safety measure.

'Sybil?' Noah guessed what Rhun's delay had been.

'Nothing gets past her.' He was rather pleased about that in retrospect.

'A good person to have on board in any case,' Noah suggested, motioning the governor to the chariot.

'True … one less to chew my arse when I return.' Rhun made a move to comply with his advisor's invitation.

'You can count me out as well,' Noah assured him, amused by Rhun's pessimism.

'Back to the old model,' Rhun eyed over the chariot as he approached it — he'd rather liked the revamped model they'd come up with in ancient Zhou, an instance which had now never occurred. 'Once, all I wanted was to escape the responsibly of being

345

governor. But now I would do anything just to have a boring day behind the governor's desk.' Rhun took a seat on the chariot for what he hoped was the last time, and paused to take in the moment. 'You know last time I sat here, I swore that the timekeepers were going to kick Shyamal's butt. And, being that Shyamal was really the product of the mind-eater virus, I would say we accomplished that feat.'

Noah grinned and raised both brows to agree. 'But what effect has that had on the bigger picture?'

Rhun sucked in his cheeks, as he primed himself and his vehicle to make the jump. 'Only one way to find out.' He hit the accelerator, which reduced his person and the chariot to a quantum state of being, and sped them forth to the intended destination.

16

ANCIENT ZHOU

'Timekeeper awaken.'

Taren's eyes parted to behold the snow-covered landscape of Zhou, just as it had appeared days prior to Jiang Hudan's untimely death. She recognised the location as the one she'd been aiming for — she was on the road to Shao to visit her sister Jiang Huxin and her husband Ji Shi.

'Telmo?' She looked about to find she was alone. Yet, she felt sure she'd heard his voice just now, urging her to 'awaken'.

In the snow behind her, she saw the imprint of feet. Someone had been standing behind her, but there were no tracks either leading to, or away from, the prints.

Dear Telmo, doesn't leave any detail to chance. She was glad he'd thought to give her a wake-up call; she remembered nothing before this moment, so she'd obviously needed it.

Taren had chosen to return to this particular spot as it had been where Jiang Hudan had met up with her little brother, Fen Gong, and his tigress, Ling Hu. Yet there was no sign of them beneath the tree where she had found them both sleeping last time this instance had played out.

'Curious.' She pulled her shawl tighter about her shoulders to block out the cold of the misty morning and in so doing realised that she had two free hands — which Jiang Hudan never did when travelling, for she always carried the legendary staff, Taiji.

'Holy mother, where is it?' She began a desperate search of the area.

Taiji was a tall staff of carved wood with a curved hook at its top inset with a glowing stone ball that changed colour and frequency depending upon the the mood and intent of the wielder. Taiji meant the supreme, or ultimate, pole — pole used in the sense of opposing poles. For Taiji granted the wielder a supreme polarity which was non-polar — a perfect state of non-judgement through which to channel the will of heaven. It had been given to Jiang Hudan by her Shifu, the great mother of Yi Wu Li Shan, for safekeeping. This staff was the entire reason that Jiang Hudan was on her way to Shao this day, for she had been charged by Yi Wu to return Taiji to the Dropa to which it had originally belonged.

'Please, universe, Telmo did not take off with it as a joke?' Taren wondered how she would be greeted at the Dropa camp when she showed up without the treasure that had been entrusted to her.

The sound of horses' hooves distracted her from her search as she moved to watch the horseman approach.

'Brother Hudan!' he exclaimed, pulling the horse to a halt and drawing back his hood so that she might see his face.

The sight of Fen Gong, young and vibrant, brought tears to her eyes; she hadn't thought to be so overwhelmed to see him again, but she did miss this incarnation of him dearly, especially after his death. 'Brother Fen,' she exclaimed, choked by her emotion as he sprang off his horse to bow to her in the official manner. It had been some time since they'd seen each other in this lifetime, and his time in the king's court had made him rather civilised. 'It's so good to see you!' She dispensed with the formality of the time, and hugged Fen, who endured her open display of affection with both hands at his side.

'It is a great surprise to see you on the road to Shao, brother?' The joy in Fen's voice made his delight plain, and noting his discomfort she let him go.

'Likewise, little brother,' she replied, her eyes reverting to her search for the staff.

'Have you lost something?' Fen noted her distraction.

'The Taiji staff, of all things,' she replied, knowing Fen was well aware of its importance.

'What is that?' he asked, curious to know more, and Taren was immediately alarmed.

'What do you mean, what is that?' she queried him back. 'It's the long staff I carry with me everywhere!'

Fen's frown deepened. 'Did you take to doing this after I left the cloister?'

Clearly Fen had not the faintest clue what she was talking about. 'You swear you've never heard of Taiji?'

'I swear!' he insisted.

'Interesting.' Taren pondered that she might be looking for a staff that did not exist.

'Why are you on the road to Shao?' Fen asked, more curious about that. 'What reason do you have to leave the House of Yi Wu Li Shan?'

'Well, if you have never heard of Taiji,' Taren thought it was a very good question, 'I must confess, I have absolutely no idea why I am here.'

Fen chuckled at her response. 'You are behaving very strangely, brother Hudan.'

'Why are you here?' she queried, noting something amiss with him. 'And where is Ling Hu?'

'Sorry?' Fen was appearing bemused again.

'Your tiger?' Taren prompted his memory, but his expression only became more perplexed.

'Are you unwell, brother?' Fen was sincerely concerned for her mental health at this point. 'What would I be doing with a tiger? I live at court!'

'Of course.' Taren forced a smile, although inside her chest her heart was beating faster and faster. What else had they changed? What did it all mean? In any event, she wasn't asking any more questions, best just to observe for a time.

'I am heading to visit with our sister,' Fen explained. 'Could that be why you are here?' he suggested, as his brother appeared to be confused. 'We could travel together?'

'Yes, we do,' Taren said, with a smile. That much she was certain of, for Jiang Hudan's death lay in wait, deep in the mountain ranges beyond Shao, just a few days from now.

In the meantime, she would learn about the course of history in this timeline and pinpoint as many variances as she could before meeting up with the other timekeepers. Jiang Hudan had been the first among her ilk to die in ancient Zhou, so she had returned to an earlier period than any of the other team members and would be on her own until she met up with Rhun.

At that moment the sun penetrated the heavy morning mist and it began to break up in the warmth.

'Looks like it is going to be a fine day.' Fen smiled as he turned his face to the sun to absorb the warmth.

Taren smiled at this, for the next few days had been among the most enjoyable of Jiang Hudan's life. 'Yes, it will. I've been greatly looking forward to seeing our brother's new home.'

'Well, she is not our brother any longer. Are you not still mad at her for breaking her Wu creed to marry Ji Shi?' Fen ventured to ask, grabbing the reins of his horse to lead it, as they began to stroll down the road. 'I didn't think you'd ever speak with her again after our Shifu banished her.'

Obviously events had played out a little differently in this timeline. 'She was not granted Yi Wu's blessing to wed?'

'Yes, I know,' Fen was sounding bemused again. 'That's why I never expected that the great mother would allow you see your twin again. Or does our Shifu not know you are here?'

'Oh, she knows.' Taren was sure of that much.

'So you intend to stay at Shao a little while?' He was excited by the prospect of spending some time with his adoptive siblings.

'A few days,' she replied honestly.

'And after that?' Fen queried.

Taren forced a smile. 'That remains to be seen.'

Happy enough with her answers, Fen came to a stop to suggest: 'If we ride, we should make the city by the midday hour.'

'Sounds like a plan.' She waited for Fen to climb on the animal first, and he reached down to give her a hand up to sit on the saddle behind him.

'Our sister will be so surprised to see us both.' Fen got their horse moving at a nice steady pace.

'I have a feeling I'm in for a few surprises myself.' In fact, Taren was quite certain about that.

The location of the Shao stronghold was strategic, located in a valley that opened to the east and surrounded by hills on the other three sides; it was the last bastion of the Zhou empire in the west, and controlled the pass through the Qin Ling mountains of Qiang and the upper Jia-ling River.

At the end of the thoroughfare through town, they came to the stronghold estate and were led by a guard across the courtyard to the stairs of the main house, at the top of which Jiang Huxin stood next to her husband, stony-faced. 'Why are you here?' She wasted no time on formality, but made her aversion known. 'Come to lecture me on the sinfulness of my choices?' She descended the stairs and stopped halfway down to address them.

Fen bowed before her, for her husband, as a duke, outranked him. 'I would never assume to question the King's will in this matter.'

'Of course, you would not, little brother,' Huxin allowed, 'and you are most welcome in my home.' Her eyes fell back upon her twin.

This was not the warm welcome Hudan had received from her sister last time this reunion played out, and knowing what a stick in the mud Jiang Hudan had been about the creed of her order, she suspected Huxin probably had good cause to be at odds with her.

'I can hardly rebuke you for your choices and banishment, when I have made those same choices.' Taren dropped a bombshell, and Huxin was clearly both shocked and delighted — Fen and Ji Shi were just plain shocked.

'What?' Fen gasped.

'I don't believe it,' Huxin scoffed, although a little grin betrayed her hope. 'Not the legendary Wu of perfection? Jiang Hudan would never defy her creed.'

351

'Then explain how I could possibly be here?' Taren challenged. 'The great mother would never allow it.'

'I thought you said that our Shifu knows you are here?' Fen demanded.

'She does know,' Taren informed him. 'When she banished me, she guessed where I would head.' She looked back to her twin. 'I can live without my creed, my order, my power … but I cannot live without my family.'

Huxin's jaw was gaping, as tears moistened her eyes. 'Then I welcome you to my home also, lest you be homeless.'

'That is most gracious of you, dear sister,' Taren grinned having always called her 'brother' before this day.

'Come inside,' Huxin invited, leading the way. 'I should like to introduce you to your niece and nephew.'

'I would like that,' Taren smiled to accept the invitation, despite how odd the prospect seemed — the last time round she had been at the birth of the twins, clearly that had not been the case in this instance however.

This was not the only variation on their history that Taren discovered that afternoon. The change that was immediately apparent upon meeting her niece and nephew was that Jiang Huxin and Ji Shi's brood were no longer a family of were-tigers. Huxin and her offspring were still shapeshifters and could assume tiger forms, but this was just one of an array of animal physiques they could adopt. Ji Shi did not possess any shapeshifting skills but had the ability to levitate, which was more akin to his timekeeper talent, which he had not tapped into in the timeline previous. Huxin, like Hudan, had developed her ability to teleport from one place to another, and Fen's healing talents were as they were before. Taren figured these inherent soul traits had been developed by their Shifu during their time with the Wu on Li Shan.

The mystery of what had become of Ling Hu, Fen's spirit tiger, was solved when Huxin informed she had in fact given birth to triplets — one of which was a tiny albino baby, who had died at birth. Ling Hu had never existed. The remaining twins, Zhen, a daughter, and Kao, a son, were strong and thriving here at Shao.

The rest of the day played out much as Taren remembered, in the company of family, good food, wine and conversation. There was a legendary game of hide and seek played that evening with the twins — for far more difficult than seeking toddlers or tiger cubs was attempting to seek something that might be as small as a mouse, or as scary as a coiled python!

The following day, after lunch, Fen joined Shi in his room of court, which allowed the Jiang sisters some quiet time in the garden to talk. The wind coming off the snow-capped mountains beyond Shao was freezing, but the sun burned brightly in the blue sky above and its warmth was not entirely lost. It was lovely just to sit in the stillness of the moment and take it all in.

'I must say I'm surprised you haven't said a word about Ji Dan since you arrived,' Huxin noted.

Taren was alarmed by the topic, as her relationship with Huxin was so different this time around, how her relationship with Ji Dan had unfolded, she couldn't even guess. 'I do believe that the great mother might have exerted some control over my memory before I left Li Shan, for there is a great haze over my memory of the last few years.'

'You don't remember the Battle of Mu?' Huxin was shocked.

'We defeated Daji,' Taren was fairly sure that was the case.

'Her dark magic proved no match for our psychic skill,' Huxin boasted.

Taren learned that the evil spouse of the last Shang emperor had not been a were-fox, as before, but had been dubbed a fox in character only, as she was so sly and cunning.

'But what of the time after we occupied the Shang capital at Yin?' Taren quizzed. 'Did we find a pit beneath the castle?'

'The dragon pit, where the emperor kept his huge pet lizard men,' Huxin emphasised. 'You were there when Ji Fa and his brothers slayed them all.'

'And Fa was injured?' Taren posed.

'No,' Huxin frowned, 'no one was injured, bar the creatures. We all attended the victory ceremony the following day, followed by Fen's wedding.'

'Fen's wedding?' Taren sat forward in her chair shocked and pleased by the news. 'Of course!' She internalised her reasoning — *if none were injured combating the reptilians hiding out beneath the city, then He Nuan was never killed by Dragonface, and Ji Fa was never infected by his mysterious reoccurring wound.*

'Surely you remember our little brother's wedding?' Huxin maintained, and Taren nodded to appease her sister's disgust.

'So what killed Ji Fa?' Taren queried.

'A broken heart, I suspect,' Huxin voiced her view, 'he never did recover from losing his queen in childbirth.'

'Fen was not there to save her?' Taren figured if there was no Dragonface, then no one had laid the plot to kidnap the healer and leave the Queen in peril.

'Our brother's healing talent is good, but even he could not repair the damage in time to save her life.' Huxin advised. 'I don't know that he's ever forgiven himself for that.'

'Fen was not kidnapped,' Taren concluded, to confirm her prior theory, and then looked to Huxin who appeared most concerned for her.

'Our little brother is right, you are behaving very strangely.' Huxin was distracted as she spied the head of the exterior rushing double-time up the garden path towards them.

'Speaking of Ji Dan,' Taren commented to her sister as they awaited the messenger's arrival.

'My Lady,' the servant began, 'the Master told me to let you know we have another guest …' He seemed very excited. 'Zhou Gong is here!'

Huxin looked to her sister wondering how Hudan had predicted the duke's arrival. 'You knew he was coming here?'

'Call it intuition,' Taren replied.

Huxin nodded to dismiss her servant, and looked back to Hudan. 'But why would Zhou Gong suddenly decide to visit Shao?'

'Your guess is as good as mine,' Taren allowed, and at this point it probably was.

'And I thought winter in Shao was going to be fairly uneventful,' Huxin sat back in her chair to ponder the event. 'But it is shaping up to be rather interesting indeed.'

'Unforgettable, I dare say,' Taren agreed.

There was one last truly important deed that Jiang Hudan needed to accomplish prior to her death and that was to convince Ji Dan to return to be mentor and guardian of the child king, Ji Song, from whom, if history held true to form, Ji Dan had just estranged himself. In the last timeline Jiang Hudan had been the cause of their falling out; but this time there was no telling what their dispute was, nor how they could be reconciled.

The Duke of Zhou did not join the family for dinner, and Taren was not surprised as the last time this instance played out, Ji Dan had not been well and had stayed in his room for the entire evening. But unlike last time, Jiang did not drink her fill of wine by the fire, only water, as she needed her wits about her for this meeting.

Lying awake in her bed, as the hour of the rat spend towards a close, she wondered how exactly to play her next move. Last time she had presented herself at Dan's door, half drunk, but then they'd been lovers, and such behaviour was overlooked. If their relationship had unfolded differently, such an approach would be considered most improper.

Still, if they did not talk and become engaged this night, then they would not wed on the morrow, so Taren had a spare day up her sleeve. Hence, she decided it would be best to let their conversation unfold in its own due course, and wait for Ji Dan to seek her out.

After hours of anxious, broken sleep, Taren rose at the crack of dawn, rugged up and headed outdoors for a stroll in the icy mist that hung over the garden. Breathing the frosty air served to alert all her senses, which were waning from lack of rest. It was exciting to be back in ancient Zhou with her cosmic memory intact, she appreciated being able to comprehend how unique this moment truly was. Jiang Hudan had had no idea that this was to be the last full day of her life — her last day to make an impact on the civilisation that she had helped bring into being and that the female aspect of her soul-mind was about to leave behind.

What concerned Taren most was successfully navigating her coming conversation with the Duke of Zhou, having no recollection of their dealings previous to this day.

Azazèl, please guide me through this. This seemed an odd request really, as the Grigori were causal beings who brought about the will of their physical manifestations, but they also had a much broader view of evolution in its entirety, which was all unfolding at once. *Guide me towards the best possible outcome for everyone involved,* she quantified her request.

As if to reassure her, the sun cleared the mountains beyond; the mist lit up all around her and began to thin and rise. Now that she could see further than her hand in front of her, she spotted the chair where she had been seated with Huxin the day before, and took a seat to watch the cloud haze swirl into the sky and evaporate.

'It is a great surprise to find you at Shao, Brother Hudan.'

Taren witnessed Ji Dan emerge from the mist, and when she cast her mind back to this day — that in the last timeline had been their wedding day — there was a minor difference in Dan's appearance, and that was that he still had the little beard on his chin. This was significant, as the last time around the duke had shaved off this beard to please her. The fact that he still wore it seemed to indicate that they had not been so intimate with each other in this time and place. She was incredibly relieved not to have visited his room last night, for she may have caused a very embarrassing incident.

'I could say the same of you brother Dan,' Taren added, 'although I am no longer a brother of the House of Yi Wu Li Shan.'

Ji Dan did not appear surprised to hear this. 'Could that be because the House of Yi Wu Li Shan is no longer in existence?'

Taren forced a smile — last time they'd had this conversation, this announcement had been a shock to Hudan, but this time she understood the cosmic agenda. 'The time of peril in this land is now over. The great mother and her house have moved on to more pressing trials and times.'

'Shifu Yi has not adequately trained our new king,' Dan voiced his doubts about the great mother's judgement in this case.

'It is for you to train him, Zhou Gong,' Taren advised kindly. 'Ji Fa left that duty in your capable hands.'

'My nephew will not listen to me,' Dan protested, 'he will not adhere to the rule of heaven without Yi Wu's direct instruction.'

'One day he will,' Taren assured him, 'and you will be the cause of that realisation in him.'

Dan shook his head, he did not want to doubt her prediction, yet equally did not wish to believe it. 'Is that why you remained here, despite Li Shan's departure … to sway my decision to resign?'

Taren realised that was precisely the reason. 'How is Zhou Gong to become the brightest star in Tian's sky, without influence in the Zhou court?'

Exasperated with the topic, Ji Dan took a seat beside her and changed the subject. 'And where will you go now that you cannot return to your cloister?'

She forced a smile to be honest. 'I shall be joining the great mother as soon as I have convinced you to return to Haojing and aid our new king with a rebellion that is brewing at Yin.'

Dan's eyes parted wide in horror. 'You're leaving?' He nearly choked on the question. 'Even more than Shifu Yi, or brother Fen, you have been my greatest teacher.'

Taren was choking on emotion now, despite that their parting would be a short one in her reality; for Dan, however, it would last for ten years. 'It is a great honour that you consider me thus, but you have taught me in equal measure. Still, I thought you might be more concerned with the challenges at hand.'

Dan didn't want to take the bait, but reluctantly he did. 'The Wu have foreseen a rebellion?' he queried.

'Is it not written in the Jade Book?' Taren was going out on a limb here, but she hoped it still existed.

The fact that Song was king and not Dan, as the previous king had wished, meant the secret rewriting of the King's will had taken place. The decision to do this was due to that which was decreed in the Jade Book — an ancient treasure secretly passed down through the Ji family from the time of the Yellow Emperor. This book listed the line of imperial succession of the land in chronological order, from the time of the book's creation, until thousands of years from the present. The Jade Book had predicted the rise of Ji Fa and of his son, Ji Song. But as Song was too young to rule, Zhou Gong had been named as the boy king's guardian and ally in the rebellion that was to arise in the wake of Ji Fa's death.

Dan was stunned. 'How do you know about the Jade Book?'

An enlightening reaction for Taren, as Ji Dan had obviously not shared this secret with her. 'I am Wu.' She explained away the detail to get to the point. 'Has the Jade Book proved wrong to date? Do you really want to be the one to prove it so?'

'What I want seems to have very little relevance.' He stood, frustrated with his lot. 'I would rather go wherever you are bound, than go back to the court of another self-serving tyrant in the making.'

'That is not what the Jade Book said of the boy king's reign.' Taren argued on Song's behalf. 'A long-lasting peace is to follow this rebellion. But only you can rally enough support for the new king to put down the eastern uprising, which I feel sure Song's new bride has already tried to warn him about.'

'The wedding never took place,' Dan informed. 'The king's betrothed has run off, I know not why?'

'Could it be because she attempted to implicate Song's uncles in a rebellion, and he thought she was just trying to make trouble and stall their wedding?' Taren suggested, subtracting Dragonface from the equation of what she'd learned of the events following Jiang Hudan's death.

'That is impossible to know. When I went to speak with the bride to be, she knocked me out and escaped, and Song will not speak of what drove her to do this.'

'Because admission would vindicate how much he needs your help,' Taren reasoned. 'Despite that you allowed his bride to escape.'

'A bride should not be seeking to escape!' Dan stressed what was more to the point.

'I agree, I was commenting from Song's perspective,' Taren explained. 'If he thought his chosen bride was just spinning tales to get his attention, her escape would have shattered that delusion, leaving him furious for being spurned, and secretly alarmed that her warning of rebellion could be true.'

'Then he should have advised me of this instead of banishing me for lying on her behalf.' Dan was seated once more.

'Surely, you would not allow pride to take precedence over the will of heaven?' Taren posed.

With a heavy exhalation of resignation, Dan looked to the swirling sunlit mists above. 'I would not.'

They sat for the longest time in silence. Taren did not have to ask after his resolve, for this soul-mind would always do what he knew was in the greatest interests of all. Jiang Hudan may not have been intimately connected to Ji Dan in this life, but Taren still knew what Dan's reservations were. Their soul quest was to seek knowledge and experience that went beyond this earthly state of being, Ji Dan feared that ultimate goal would escape him now that Li Shan had departed this world. 'We all dwell beyond the limits of our living consciousness, where all that is baffling to us now is understood. We strive through many lives to return to this place, until we arrive at the realisation that we never actually left.'

The duke found the premise a pleasing one. 'Strangely, I feel that you and I have already met in such a place.'

'And will again,' she returned his smile with one that was even more confident.

'Well, if this is to be our final parting of the ways,' Dan stood once again, to state more formally, 'I am grateful for the knowledge you have bestowed on me, Shanyu Jiang Hudan, and for your counsel in times of peril.'

'Wise counsel and knowledge are nothing without an open mind to receive them,' she replied, standing also. 'So the honour has been entirely mine, Zhou Gong Dan.'

They bowed to each other.

'Those souls presently residing in this house,' Taren referred to Shao, 'will be firm allies, and can aid you to reach Haojing in time to avert disaster.'

'Will you not even stay to talk strategy with us?' he appealed. 'I would greatly welcome your counsel one last time.'

Taren shook her head. 'You are the most inspired mind in all the land, and I do not cherish the thought of a long drawn-out goodbye with my family.'

'You have not told them you are leaving?' Dan assumed.

She shook her head. 'I have seen both my siblings happily wed, and any ill will that might have been between us has been resolved.'

She had not been given the opportunity to bid her family goodbye last time, so she thought it best to keep to the script. Tonight was also the night that Jiang Hudan suspected she had conceived of their child, so Taren wasn't about to tempt fate, as unlikely as that event seemed from her new perspective.

'Tell them, as I tell you now, we shall meet again upon our dying day.' Her last glimpse of Ji Dan saw him frowning curiously at her missive, and content that all was as it should be, Taren closed her eyes and visualised the snow-capped mountainside upon which Jiang Hudan would meet her end.

'Farewell —' she heard Dan bid her, but the rest of his words were obscured as her body dissolved into the quantum passage that led to her desired destination.

Aware that she was arriving an entire day before Jiang Hudan's death, Taren didn't visualise landing on the icy mountain face that would collapse and claim her life, but in the small patch of trees that stood on the mountainside close by.

'Rhun!' she called, not fancying the idea of spending a night out here in the freezing cold.

Beyond this point, her psychic talent would be rendered useless by a shield that fortified the area around the Dropa ship. The Dropa had a device that made their allies immune to the shield, and as Rhun was in league with these extra-terrestrials, he could psychically move freely through this area.

'Rhun!' Taren panicked a little, turning circles in search of him. What if he had gone back to Kila and not made it to ancient Zhou? '*Rhun*, where the bloody hell are you?'

'Steady on,' he commented as he manifested before her. 'You're early.'

'Better than late,' she commented with a good serve of sarcasm, as she breathed a sigh of relief.

'Dan not in tow?' Rhun looked around behind her.

'No,' she was chagrined to announce. 'It appears that we actually managed to get through a life as just respected colleagues.'

Rhun was grinning.

'What is so amusing?' she queried coolly, although she couldn't completely wipe the smile off her face, either.

'I just can't wait to see the look on his face when he remembers the truth.'

Taren had to admit that was going to be fun. 'So what's news? There are a few alterations to history that even Dragonface's absence doesn't explain.'

Rhun was nodding. 'Actually, the virus' absence does account for everything, you're just not looking far enough back in time.'

'Explain?' Taren was eager to hear his theory.

'Once we gather the entire team, so I'm not explaining this several times over,' he suggested.

'Explaining what?' Taren attempted to pry the information out of him anyway.

'A little problem that we did not foresee.'

'How little?'

'Well, it's a very little problem, for this universe,' he said sheepishly.

'But?' Taren prompted.

'But … you should really discuss this with Telmo,' Rhun declined to pursue the topic further. 'He's the expert.'

'Then take me to Telmo,' Taren requested, knowing of the Dropa shield.

'You can find him on your own.' Rhun hinted at the problem.

'Is the Dropa shield down?'

'You could say that, yeah.'

Rhun's cryptic hints gave her a very bad feeling, and envisioning Telmo she issued an intention to join him.

Snow-capped peaks around her for as far as the eye could see. Taren felt like she was on top of the world, with a floor of cloud far below, obscuring the valleys from view. She knew this outlook well. This was Bayan Har Shan, the site where the Dropa craft had crashed twenty thousand years ago. She turned around expecting to find a complex of caverns behind her — an illusion that masked the defunct alien craft — but all she found was a bare snowy mound, in the middle of which stood Telmo, waving at her.

'Where is it?' she gasped, trudging through the deep snow towards him, her feet so frozen they felt like dead weights to lift. 'Where did it go?' She feared that the reptilians had got hold of the craft sooner than they had last time around. As she neared Telmo she noted him standing on top of the loose snowfall.

'You do make things difficult for yourself,' he commented, grinning at her struggle.

Taren rolled her eyes at the oversight and employed her psychokinesis to rise up and walk above the snow with ease. 'I've been cast between being human and superhuman so many times now, it takes me a while to adjust my perspective.'

Telmo nodded, able to relate.

She noted he had grown a thin moustache and little beard, and it made him appear so much more like a young Taliesin — who had been a master mentor to some of her many incarnations on this planet. This growth also suggested Telmo had been back in ancient Zhou for quite a bit longer than she had. 'So, are you going tell me what happened here,' she queried, 'or do you not have an answer?'

Telmo frowned at her, surprised she would suggest such a thing. 'Well, the simple answer is that the Dropa craft was never here.'

Taren's eyes opened wide in astonishment — for this explained so much. 'Then the Taiji staff never existed!'

Telmo was nodding.

'The Dropa never interbred with the locals and were-people were never created!' she surmised. 'Thus without those genes, we timekeepers only developed our inherent psychic skills here in Zhou. Huxin's offspring must have inherited their psychic talents from their parents.'

'Well, in this universe you were known as the Chosen,' Telmo corrected, 'but yes, that seems to be the case.'

'But how did —'

'Taking the virus out of existence result in this?' Telmo pre-empted her query, motioning to the barren snow cap surrounding them. 'I have consulted the Akashic records on this matter. It turns out that the reptilians led by Dragonface did not just discover this Dropa craft by chance, they shot it out of the sky in the first place and then tracked it here. It was the virus' goal to go in search of the hybrid race of their kind beyond Earth; Dragonface was seeking females to breed a food supply. Those reptilians who survive here are quite happy to remain on Earth, as this is where their food supply is.'

'So without the virus, they had neither the intellect nor motivation to shoot the Dropa down.' Taren was amazed. 'So we've saved the Dropa and Draconians in one fell swoop.'

'Yes, indeed we have,' and Telmo was happy about that. 'But I'm not sure we have done ourselves any favours.'

'What do you mean?' Taren was suddenly alarmed. 'Must we deal with the reptilians remaining on Earth?'

Telmo shook his head. 'We executed our part in Earth's big clean-up long ago, but those events still lie in the future history of this planet.'

'Well, what then?' Taren suddenly recalled why she was seeking Telmo in the first place. 'The little problem Rhun spoke of.'

Telmo sucked in his cheeks and nodded, his brow furrowed as if challenging her to work it out.

'If the Dropa are not here,' her mind began ticking over, 'then Dorje Pema is not here to take Wu Geng under wing and train up the spiritual side of his nature.' She gasped. 'If we awaken Zeven's timekeeper consciousness in Song's body only shortly before his death, then what is to stop him from slaying Wu Geng at Yin — an event that took place decades before Song finally died. When their confrontation at Yin takes place, Zeven won't remember that Wu Geng is an ally! Zeven will slay Wu Geng, as per history, before the timekeepers visited ancient Zhou and changed events there. If Wu Geng is killed he'll remember nothing upon his return to our universe, and he'll be back to being our enemy,' Taren stressed, 'and we'll be back to square one with Khalid.'

'That could be a good thing. It will ensure nothing in our universe will change,' Telmo reasoned.

'But saving Wu Geng's soul could only change things for the better!' Taren reasoned.

'So one would think,' Telmo agreed in a noncommittal fashion. 'But I do not believe that option is really open to us.'

'But Zeven vowed he would not abandon Wu Geng, and he will not forgive himself when his timekeeper memory is activated and he realises that he slayed Wu Geng thirty years before!' Taren felt for her team mates. 'What are Avery's thoughts on all this?'

'I have no idea. Rhun won't allow me, or anyone, to summon him forth.'

'Rhun hasn't summoned him back yet?' Taren gaped at the news.

'Not to Kila and not to here,' Telmo advised.

'Did he say why?'

'No,' Telmo frowned, 'but as Kila is as it was before we or the reptilians ever got there, then I am guessing Rhun has figured that the Lord of the Otherworld's child has never been conceived.'

'Holy shit, you're right.' Taren bit her lip to ponder the oversight and unable to easily solve it, she moved on. 'So what does Rhun intend to do, just leave his brother in limbo?'

'Yes,' Rhun spoke up for himself, drawing their attention to his presence just behind them. 'Until I come up with a solution to make it right.'

'And if you don't?' Taren posed.

'Look … we don't need Avery,' Rhun insisted. 'I just need to do a bit more time-hopping on the chariot, is all. So right now I need to deliver you to the time of Dan's death; you still have a curse to cast upon Ji Song.'

'Wu Geng is the next pick up, if memory serves,' Taren reminded him.

'What you do about him is your choice,' Rhun pointed out, 'but if the timekeepers never landed on Kila, then obviously Khalid didn't either. So he never learned about our quest, never jumped back into the body of Wu Geng, and will have no idea what's going on.'

'He's right,' Taren was devastated. 'Then we've lost all hope of Khalid being on our side when we return to our universe of origin.'

'But we have learned that he has a soul-mind worth saving,' Telmo pointed out, 'so that is something.'

'Hold on!' Taren had a light-bulb moment. 'If the timekeepers have never been to Kila, then only those timekeepers who have returned to Zhou during this final leg of our mission are going to have their timekeeper consciousness intact. There is no point picking up Dan, Fen or Ji Shi, for only Huxin and Song will know what's going on.'

Rhun was nodding, and Taren suddenly felt ill.

'I swore to Lucian he would remember all this,' she said mournfully. 'Now he won't remember any of it.'

'The captain already possesses the talent to tap into the akashic memory, and he can catch up on all he missed,' Telmo reassured her with a smile.

'Across all the timelines?' she queried.

'Of course,' Telmo emphasised.

'Well, that's some consolation I guess, but … damn.' Taren was still frustrated about losing Khalid as an ally.

'The only timekeepers we really need to remember, are you and Zeven,' Rhun stated.

'Why is that?' Taren's curiosity was piqued.

'I have a situation unfolding on Kila that I may need your assistance with,' he confessed.

'But the plan was to go straight back to AMIE from here,' Taren said, worried about taking another sidetrack. 'What has happened?'

'It would be better to see this mission completed, before I brief you,' Rhun suggested. 'But I will say, it shouldn't detain you long.'

'We've thought that before,' Taren said. 'I was only ever meant to be crossing into this universe to warn you about Shyamal's attack, which clearly cannot happen, as the virus that was driving him no longer exists!'

'In a cosmic sense I believe we were brought back here to keep our vow to Tiamat, which was never fully completed,' Telmo said.

'But now that vow has been kept,' Taren argued. 'There is nothing left to be done.'

Rhun was looking a little doubtful about that.

'Is there?' Taren queried more warily.

'Your guess is as good as mine,' Rhun admitted, not wanting to speculate. 'Could we please just finish up what needs to be done here, and I will explain everything once we have collected Jazmay and Zeven.'

Taren's glare shifted to Telmo to get his view.

'A job worth doing is worth doing well,' he advised. 'If we leave no stone unturned, then we ensure that we shall never need to return here again.'

'You know what the problem is?' Taren assumed Rhun had already got Telmo on side.

'It is quite possibly no problem at all,' he allowed, and Taren was a little frustrated.

'And what if we just create another disaster by staying longer than we should?' she questioned.

'You cannot,' Rhun pointed out, 'the future is the future, whatever comes I shall deal with it. All I need is a few hours of your time. Please.'

'Argh!' Taren turned away to vent her frustration — it was difficult to say no to a soul who had once been her son. 'If, when you explain this, the others agree …' Taren turned back to deliver her decision, albeit reluctantly. '… then, I agree.'

Rhun grinned, satisfied with those terms. 'Then let's go get them.'

THE CRYSTAL CAVERN

Before retrieving Zeven and Jazmay, whose incarnations both outlived Jiang Hudan by thirty- to forty-odd years, Taren was first required to make an appearance at Zhou Gong Dan's untimely death — more adequately described as slaughter — as this event transpired only ten years following Jiang Hudan's demise.

Ji Song's insistence that the king's will was the will of heaven and Dan's view that a king must seek heaven's will through homage and divination, had been the cause of a decade-long bone of contention between them. This wedge in their core beliefs eventually drove Zhou Gong to resign as Song's advisor once the king had come of age and the regency was no longer an issue. The young king refused to accept his uncle's departure from office, and threatened to brand Ji Dan a traitor and have him hunted down as such. When Dan defied the king's protest, and Song made good on his threat — having no inkling of the great service and sacrifices his uncle had made to ensure Song's kingship — Jiang Hudan was so angered by the inequity, that she cast a curse upon all the territories ruled by Ji Song. This curse sent raging storms through half of Zhou that flattened crops and upturned huge trees, and could only be broken if the king realised and repented the injustice he'd done the first Duke of Zhou.

The curse cast by Jiang Hudan was the catalyst for the young king's spiritual turn around, which saw Ji Dan's political and social reforms cemented into the cultural and historic landscape of

China, to be used as a guideline for this civilisation for millennia to come. Thus it was imperative that the event took place, to keep history on track.

The timekeeping trio relocated to the glowing crystal cavern hidden deep in the inner Earth that Avery had nominated as a safe place for Rhun to store the time-shifting chariot. With this vehicle Rhun gave Telmo a lift forward in time, to the same cavern about forty years hence, when the timekeepers would be reunited. He then returned to Taren's present, to pick her up and quantum jump her forwards to the same cavern, just a decade after her death.

Upon arrival Taren climbed off the transport to teleport herself to the scene of the crime. 'Without the Taiji staff, I am not even sure I still have the ability to summon the elements to my cause.'

'You learned to wield those powers without the staff before you died the last time around,' Rhun reminded her.

'In another timeline!' Taren stressed. 'I have no idea if Avery and Jiang Hudan even made contact this time around.' Taren had been puzzled by that point. 'How did Jiang Hudan handle the Yin rite without the staff or the aid of the Lord of the Otherworld?'

'She used her own command of the elements to bring down the rains and break the drought in the name of Zhou,' Rhun stated the obvious. 'It makes no difference whether Avery granted you influence over his elemental dominions in this life, timeline, whatever. The point is that he did grant you this power once and has never retracted that gift. Try it, if you don't believe me.'

Taren placed her hands together to focus her chi on summoning the elements of air into her palms. As Jiang Hudan had once taught herself to do, Taren envisioned a positive charge accumulating in her right palm and a negative charge building against her left. Once a significant charge had built up, she drew her hands slowly apart, and the positive and negative charges sought each other, forming streams of blue-white lightning to dance between her hands.

'Whoa,' Taren gasped at her own accomplishment, feeling only a tickling where the streams made contact with her skin.

'If you are satisfied, you should really go,' Rhun suggested. 'Before we have to time-jump backwards because we've missed the event.'

'Dismissed, dismissed, dismissed.' She complied with the law of three requests, and the activity ceased. The delight of her achievement was short-lived as Taren turned her attention to the task at hand, for this was not going to be the joyous reunion it once was. 'I must watch him die.'

'At the risk of sounding callous, it wouldn't be the first time,' Rhun was sorry to say. 'This is the way it was always meant to be.'

'But if the timekeepers never toyed with history, why would Jiang Hudan have appeared upon Dan's death to curse the land?' she reasoned.

'We cannot risk ignoring the event, lest we change history and risk altering the future on Kila,' Rhun debated the issue just as furiously.

Taren was frowning, as much from wishing to argue the matter as predicting his reaction to her next question. 'Are you sure we don't need Avery's counsel?'

'Shh!' he insisted, looking about in the hope his brother had not appeared, and was relieved he had not. 'Believe me, I am right about this.' His large brown eyes implored her trust.

With a heavy sigh, Taren nodded. 'I shall be back.' She closed her eyes and thought of Dan, but that didn't seem to work.

'What's wrong?' Rhun queried the delay.

'I'm thinking of Dan, and no dice.' She shrugged.

'Perhaps think back to the scene of the crime, instead?' Rhun suggested.

When Taren took that suggestion on board, she got some quantum traction and took off.

In her absence, Rhun was feeling anxious, not being as sure of events as he outwardly projected. If he screwed anything up, he could always call on his little brother for aid, but at this point that was a last resort. He did have some idea of how he might right the wrong done to the Lord of the Otherworld and his wife, but it was going to take time to organise, and he wanted to be fully prepared with a solution before facing his brother's wrath.

He was mentally playing through different scenarios of how he might achieve his goals when Taren reappeared — soaking wet and really pissed off.

'You were wrong!' She was dripping like a drowned rat.

'What do you mean?' Rhun hopped off the chariot to speak with her. 'What happened?'

'Nothing happened! Dan wasn't there! The hunting party sent to retrieve him wasn't there either!'

'Damn it!' Rhun turned away to vent his frustration.

'What are you mad about? I'm the one who got drowned,' Taren chided, as she wrung the water from Jiang Hudan's long black hair. 'However, there is some good news.'

'I could use some,' Rhun turned back eager to hear it.

'The cursed storm is already in full swing.' She splashed Rhun with water, as she threw her arms out for emphasis.

'Are you sure?' Rhun wiped himself off, still doubtful. 'How do you know it's not just a regular —'

'There are storms,' Taren said, understanding his doubts. 'And then there is a tempest! The squall I just left was the latter.'

'But how? Who?' Rhun posited, baffled.

'I have no idea!' Taren, having made her point and beginning to shiver, imagined herself dry, and it was so.

'We should speak with Telmo,' Rhun decided, returning to his seat upon the chariot. 'I have to take you to him anyway, before I collect Zeven and Jaz.'

'You're not afraid we might have missed something here?' Taren queried, as she took a seat behind him.

'Fear is a waste of time in our line of work.' He hit the half-orb shaped telepathic control plate, and focused on returning to where he had left Telmo.

Subsequent to the whirlwind of quantum light in motion, their transport arrived in the same place, thirty years on, to find Telmo seated on the luminous crystal cluster that Avery had fashioned into a throne-like chair. In his hand he held another chunk of

370

the glowing crystal that lined the inside of this cavern, and with its light Telmo was reading a bamboo chronicle, much like those Jiang Hudan had written during her time at the House Yi Wu Li Shan.

'Oh dear,' he observed, having looked over to acknowledge their arrival. 'From the concerned look on both your faces, I assume something is amiss. Let me guess, Dan wasn't where you left him.'

'You *know* that?' Taren was a little annoyed that he had not spoken up a little earlier.

'I do *now* that I have been brought forth to the future beyond such events, where I can just read the recent history as written by the local chroniclers of the Zhou court,' he explained. 'In this case, Shao Gong Shi.' He referred to the bamboo scroll he was holding.

'That is Shi's account of Dan's death?' Taren was immediately intrigued, and Telmo nodded. 'Where did you get that?'

'From the Hall of Records at Hoajing, where else?' He shrugged, as if it were nothing.

'That's an important historic document!' Taren freaked.

'I'll be sure and send it back where I found it.'

'Did the cursed storm lead Song to venerate Zhou Gong accordingly or not?' Rhun got straight to the point, as he had other places to be.

'Yes it did,' Telmo was happy to advise.

'Excellent!' Rhun clenched both fists and drew his arms close to himself in a jerking motion, to highlight his small victory. 'Is history on track then, or is there some other disaster I need to know about?'

'Yes. No.' Telmo answered both queries in turn, happy to dismiss Rhun's lingering doubts. 'We're on the right track.'

'Thank fuck for that!' Rhun, who had been through this mission three times over now, was so very relieved to hear it. 'I'll be back.' With a wave of appreciation and a thumbs up, he returned to the chariot and vanished with it, to collect the few remaining members of the team.

'So what did happen to Dan?' Taren found herself a smooth rock to sit on close to where Telmo was seated, to be enlightened.

'Following the construction of the great city of Chengzhou, Zhou Gong dedicated himself to defining the Government and offices of Zhou, penning many defining texts on the subject, to ensure continued aid and service to the common people and society at large. Much like his father, the duke was so absorbed in his work that his own health suffered.'

'He worked himself to death,' Taren concluded, sad, but not entirely surprised.

'It says here,' Telmo referred to the scroll in his hands, 'that the duke was on his deathbed in Feng, and requested to be buried at Chengzhou, to make it clear that he would never depart from King Cheng.'

King Cheng being the name given to Ji Song after the quashing of the rebellion in the East.

'Yet Dan was at Fengjing, Zhou's ancestral home, rather than with the king at his court in Chengzhou?' Taren found the situation at odds with Dan's final wishes.

'In this timeline it eventuated that Zhou Gong did not resign his office, but Song, fed up with the duke's constant overseeing, commanded the duke to Fengjing. Effectively banishing him, without formally having to do so. But Song kept the court healer, Fen Gong, with him at Chengzhou.'

Taren felt this was a rather malicious act, as the pair of scholars worked very well together and were fast friends. Dan gave Fen access to earthly knowledge and wisdom, Fen awarded Dan spiritual insight and was an excellent researcher; Taren imagined that without each other, their daily lives would have been laborious, as there were few others who shared their pursuit to understand the greater mysteries of creation. 'Without Fen to share his workload, watch his health and ensure the duke ate,' Taren's eyes narrowed, 'Song effectively allowed the duke to work himself to death, and Fen was not there to prevent it.'

Telmo raised both brows in challenge. 'Better not to judge, or jump to conclusions.'

'That is difficult when Zeven just drove my other half to his death,' Taren stated, as the whooshing sound of the chariot returning could be heard behind her.

'Well, the cursed storm did bring the original will of Ji Fa to light,' Telmo referred back to the text to distract Taren from the new arrival. 'Whereupon Song discovered the will in which his father, Ji Fa, decreed that Ji Dan be next to rule, and learned that the duke of Zhou had later written a forgery of the document that had made Song king. Upon realising the great sacrifices Zhou Gong had made in order to establish a clear line of succession, Song was filled with remorse and vowed to venerate the Duke, to live by his virtues and govern via the guidance of heaven. The storm reversed on itself. The grain was blown back upright and in the end there was a great harvest.'

'All's well that ends well.'

Taren turned about to find an aging Ji Song — Rhun was already disappearing to his next destination. 'Of all the low things to do!'

'Hey?' Zeven held both hands up in defence. 'Do you really think I would have done that, knowing how pissed off you would be at me right now? I only just got here!' He calmed a little. 'Rhun just gave me a quick brief. I am *very sorry* I was such a little *prick* in one of my *zillion* past lives in *another* universe, okay?'

'Okay.' Taren accepted that. 'I've been a pain in the arse on more than one occasion myself.'

'*You certainly have,*' he agreed, and then noting her scowl, he back-pedalled. 'But not often.'

Telmo had a quiet chuckle at this.

Taren chose to ignore him. 'So who cast the curse of that storm?' She opened the question to both her companions.

'The text is unclear on that issue,' Telmo offered up what he'd read. 'It only mentions that there was a storm. It speculates that it could have been sent by Dan's great ancestors. Others speculated the great mother of Li Shan, Yi Wu, returned to cast the curse to teach Ji Song a lesson.'

Zeven served Telmo the evil eye, knowing Yi Wu was one of his past life incarnations. 'Did you?'

Telmo forced an unconvincing laugh. 'Would I do that to you?'

'Yes!' Zeven didn't have to think twice about it.

'*Most* believe the storm was sent by Tian, to make Song repent his ways,' Telmo put forth one last theory, and he and Taren looked to Zeven.

The old king threw his hands up. 'You are in the body of Jiang Hudan,' he posed to Taren, 'how much of her previous life do you remember now?'

Taren had to admit she saw his point. 'Nothing.'

'And that's how much I remember.' He closed his case.

'So how much did Rhun tell you?' Taren queried.

'He told me I was in the shit over Dan's demise … that we've lost over half our crew including Wu Geng, *damn it*,' he said, vexed about it. 'The Dropa were never here, thus their anti-aging technology is not here to fix these aging bodies!' He referred to his geriatric form, even more aggravated about that. 'The timekeepers never made it to Kila, yet, *insanely*, Rhun needs me to hang about in this old bag of bones, as he now wishes for us to tempt fate *yet again* and accompany him to Kila!' Zeven summed up. 'Did I miss anything?'

'Nope … that's about it in a nutshell.' Taren awarded, as Rhun and his chariot touched down with the aging Jiang Huxin.

'Tell me he is bullshitting about the Dropa not being here to make me young again!' she begged, as Rhun hopped off the chariot to aid his aged team mate safely out.

'I wish!' Zeven dashed her hopes.

'This is not what I signed up for!' Jazmay employed a walking stick to hobble over, but then, being a shapeshifter she transformed into Jazmay Cardea, whose genetic structure was much younger. 'Just kidding.' She offered the walking stick to Zeven, who did not have her talent.

'Show off.' He took hold of the staff and threatened to hit her with it.

'Bring it on, grandpa.' She placed her hands on her long slender hips, to serve up some attitude.

'Great! So I am the only one stuck like this!' Zeven objected.

'I only need you for a couple of hours at best,' Rhun appealed, sympathetically. Rhun had been stuck in an aging body the first time he'd visited Zhou, having been shot with the reptilian Shyamal's DNA depleting weapon, which had caused his immortal twelve-strand DNA to unbraid to the mortal two-strand DNA. This was how a psychically superior race, like the Chosen of Kila, had been overpowered by the lesser evolved, hostile reptilians under Shyamal's command.

'So what is the situation on Kila?' Taren asked noting they were now all present. 'Why do you need us?'

'Vugar has a vessel parked above Kila,' Rhun began.

'Oh dear,' Taren admitted that was a worry.

'He is requesting an audience with the timekeepers. He mentioned Taren by name.'

'What?' Zeven, Taren and Jazmay chimed in at once.

'He knows we were Grigori once, and named Sammael and Armaros by name, too,' Rhun concluded.

'That's impossible!' Taren thought they'd been so careful keeping their movements a secret. 'How could Vugar know?'

'The reptilians are a hive-mind,' Telmo reminded them. 'Their memory is passed down from one leader to the next, and they have been around since before the Grigori got here.'

'No, no, no …' Zeven shook his head as he knew what Telmo was driving at, but couldn't believe it.

'Yes,' Telmo nodded.

'They remember the incident in Ninharsag's lab!' Zeven looked to Rhun, who was there, and Jazmay was cussing under her breath, mind blown also.

'What incident?' Taren appealed to be let in on the event.

'There was a reptilian present when we prevented the virus being injected into their caste,' Rhun explained. 'It heard the entire negotiation.'

'You were mentioned, by name,' Zeven played over the conversation in his mind.

'Armaros too, as he had been taken to the Underworld,' Rhun added.

'And Sariel corrected Enki, when he called us time walkers,' Zeven recollected, 'so the timekeepers were mentioned also.'

'That does seem to explain the seemingly impossible,' Rhun admitted.

'Of course it does,' Telmo sounded as if he knew all this and was just waiting for the rest of them to catch up. 'The question is … does it mean they have hostile intentions, or not?'

'We were doing them a favour?' Jazmay appealed.

'From our perspective, we were,' Telmo cautioned. 'But the reptilians of Earth were far more powerful with the virus than without it.'

'But these are Draconians. The pure bloods who wanted to avoid the virus, and who abandoned the plight of their caste on Earth to ensure it never latched onto them.' Rhun, remembering the devastation Shyamal had once served the Chosen, could only be cautiously optimistic at best. 'Can't you just pop into the future, like you did here in Zhou, and find out what happens?' Rhun posed to Telmo.

'You popped me forward in the chariot,' Telmo reminded him, 'I just thought to take a look while I was waiting around. You could do the same on Kila, but do you really want to risk starting a whole new time paradox there when we've spent so long trying to correct the last one?'

'The Akashic record then,' Taren suggested.

'Think of it as a library,' Telmo explained, 'that has new releases coming in all the time. What happens now is still coming out of the author's head, and won't be released for public viewing until complete.'

'Let's just bloody do this,' Zeven grumbled, 'before I have a heart attack and die!'

'Thank you,' Rhun was sincerely grateful, as the timekeepers had already got way more than they'd bargained for since first landing back in this universe.

'Considering we started all this, it's the least we can do,' Taren awarded, as Rhun backed up to the chariot.

'I'll take Telmo first, and send him back for the rest of you in turn,' Rhun instructed. 'I have another quick errand to run on Kila.'

'Aren't you going to share with the group?' Taren appealed, as Telmo followed Rhun to the transport. All she got was a wave from them both, before the chariot vanished.

'Telmo gets more like Taliesin every day,' Zeven grumbled. 'He's even starting to look like him!'

'And he's just as annoyingly know-it-all,' Taren added.

'That's the pot calling the kettle black, isn't it?' Zeven put it to Jazmay, who'd taken a seat on the crystal throne, but her thoughts were elsewhere.

'Here we are again,' Jazmay noted, 'the original three timekeepers still standing.' She smiled, impressed by their achievements.

'And you both thought I'd never be able to keep up with you,' Zeven raised his eyebrows suggestively.

'And you're still a pervert,' Jazmay added, 'only now you're a short, dirty old man.'

'And you're still a *tease*,' Zeven gave his own view. 'Only now you're … still as hot as ever … lucky me.' He grinned and got one in return.

'You have *both* been just amazing,' Taren didn't often get the chance to say so.

'But I've screwed things up between you and the captain?' Zeven sounded sincerely sorry for that. 'I know I seem to keep doing that, but it really was unintentional.'

'*We* screwed things up, all on our own,' Taren relieved him of any guilt. 'All you have done is put things back the way they should have been. Besides, I am fairly sure Lucian will not be very mad at me when I return, as I lingered on AMIE a little while before I came back here.' She couldn't keep the grin off her face.

Jazmay and Zeven both appeared shocked.

'So did I.' Jazmay dropped the act to admit.

'Yeah, me too.' Zeven shrugged in league with the rebellion.

Taren laughed. 'How fast they learn.'

In a whoosh of sound and air the chariot appeared with Telmo at the controls. 'Next!' He called for someone to get on board.

Jazmay shoved Zeven in the chariot's direction. 'No woman should be left alone with you.'

'I thought you were braver than that?' he commented as he took a seat behind Telmo.

'I'll bring the walking stick to Kila,' Jazmay told him, 'in case you need it after I get there.'

Before Zeven could retort, Telmo activated the chariot and vanished with him.

'How to shut the short man up,' Jazmay chuckled, 'send him three thousand years into the future.'

'*Oh* ... you love and admire him *really*,' Taren suggested, knowing how much they'd been through together.

'No,' Jazmay insisted. 'Why did you ever let him sucker us into bringing him along?'

'Because ... he's always got my back,' Taren admitted, affectionately.

'Yeah,' Jazmay emphasised, 'there's a perverted reason for that!'

The pair of them burst into laugher, as the chariot arrived.

'Sorry I missed that joke,' Telmo commented, as both women struggled to regain their composure. 'But we're on a bit of a tight schedule here ... less than one hour before we meet with Vugar.'

'You go,' Taren urged Jazmay, who teleported herself to a seat on the chariot behind Telmo.

'Right back,' he assured Taren with a wink.

A moment later, Taren was alone in the dim glow of crystals in the cavern.

For the first time she noticed how quiet it was, just the sound of water dripping into pools, and splashing against rock. This was, with any luck, the last time she would ever visit Earth, and she felt strangely sentimental about it. Back in the universe where Taren was from, she changed planets like clothes, and so had never grown very attached, but she had lifetimes of memories and entanglements with this place. She had recollections of experiences in ancient Sumer, Atlantis, China, at the Gathering of the Kings in the 21st century, and of her life in ancient Britain, where her first time leap had stranded her. These lives and times were already written in the ancient future of this universal scheme, however. Thus it was high time she turned her thoughts to the challenges that awaited her once she returned to her rightful universe and time.

'Ready to go?' Telmo prompted.

Only now aware of his return, Taren snapped out of her nostalgic contemplation and teleported herself to a seat on her transport back to Kila. 'Ready when you are?'

'I was ready before we got here,' he commented back with a grin, ahead of hurtling them both forth to Kila.

RETURN TO KILA — PART 2

As Telmo and Taren dismounted, they were greeted by En Noah. 'Welcome back to Kila, Telmo, Jiang Hudan.' He referred to Taren's outward appearance.

She grinned. 'It seems I am to be Hudan a while longer.'

'Yeah, and I'm the oldest looking person on the planet!' Zeven grumbled, to the amusement of everyone present.

'I'm glad you are in such good spirits,' Rhun entered the vault where the chariot was stored. 'If you would be so kind as to follow me to my office.' He vanished and they complied with the request.

Once in the grand governmental office on Kila, the timekeepers felt immediately at home, and Zeven was overjoyed to see a lounge. '*Hallelujah*, I can sit my arse down.' He plonked his aging person upon it.

'I forgot what a great view this room has.' Jazmay wandered out through the open balcony doors, to look down upon the pristine gardens of central park.

'I shall advise Nin Sybil, or our re—' En Noah was offering, when the lady in question entered.

'I never need to advise her of anything,' Rhun acknowledged her arrival with a grin that she returned, until she noted they had extra guests — a couple of whom appeared to have arrived directly from ancient China. 'You brought people from the ancient Earth here?' Sybil's mind was boggling at the trouble this could cause.

'It's okay, really,' Zeven spoke up for the governor. 'We all died first.'

'I don't know that that really helps,' Sybil was courteous to the guest, but then looking at him more closely, she felt an inkling of recognition. 'You remind me of someone?' Her eyes narrowed as she mused this, and then parted wide when the answer came to her. 'Brian Alexander, the last governor of Kila.'

Zeven grinned. 'So I've been told.'

Sybil looked from the body Zeven was in, to the body Taren was in, and then to Telmo. 'Oh my goodness,' she gasped, seeing in them some of the greatest ascended masters that the Chosen had ever known. 'These souls are not even of this universe any more!' She looked back to Rhun. 'Let alone, this time and planet … have you completely lost your mind?'

'That is still open to debate,' the governor conceded.

'Does Avery know about this?' Sybil sank into a trance state a moment, and having a psychic flash, she looked back to her husband. 'Why will Avery be so angry at you?'

'*Please.*' The urgency of Rhun's appeal startled her, so he smiled before continuing more calmly. 'Please don't say his name a third time.'

'Give me a good reason,' Sybil challenged.

'That will take longer than we have to explain.' Rhun appealed for her patience and trust yet again.

'I can vouch for our governor's good intentions,' Noah put forward, hoping to speed her cooperation. 'If anyone is to blame for this mess, it is me … I have been advising him the entire way.'

'Actually, we are to blame,' Taren stepped into the debate. 'We caused the timeline mutation here, and the governor has been aiding us to correct the damage caused by the accidental involvement of the timekeepers in this universe.'

'*You* are the timekeepers,' Sybil was enlightened as to their connection to this instance, 'the ones the Dracon are here seeking?'

'The very ones,' Taren smiled, glad to have taken some of the heat off Rhun.

'That still doesn't explain why Avery will be so mad,' Sybil said without thought to Rhun's earlier request, and seeing her husband's pained expression she gasped, unable to take it back.

When the Lord of the Otherworld appeared to find everyone looking so stunned, he was naturally curious as to why. 'What's going on?' He was surprised to see so many of the timekeepers had already been collected and delivered back to Kila. 'I seem to have missed several legs of our mission.'

A chime sounded from the reception room to notify them someone had arrived at the unattended desk.

'It's Asher,' Sybil stated without needing to check. 'You said you'd brief him before you meet with Vugar.'

'Vugar!' Avery was alarmed. 'He is here?' The Lord of the Otherworld began seething, as the last time he'd seen the Draconian in question, the creature had murdered his wife.

Rhun held up a finger to postpone Avery's answer, so that he could speak with Sybil. 'Keep Asher in reception, I'll brief him en route to the landing pad.'

Sybil nodded and left the room — the door vanished only long enough to allow her passage before immediately materialising in her wake.

'You're inviting Vugar down here?' Avery objected.

'It might be better if En Noah and I handle this negotiation,' Rhun advised his brother, 'why don't you go home for a bit and see your wife?'

'After you tell me what the hell is going on!' Avery directed his frustration at Rhun. 'Why didn't you summon me back when you first got here?'

'I've been a little busy!' Rhun snarled back.

'Gentlemen,' Telmo stepped into the middle of the dispute. 'I can assure you that any precarious situation will not be made easier by discord among the ranks. If you could put personal disputes aside, before we lose our one chance to straighten out this entire quantum fuck up, that would be truly appreciated.'

Rhun took a big breath, and calmed. 'You have to trust me on this —'

'I don't,' Avery insisted.

'Good that you don't get a choice then! You rule the Otherworld, I rule Kila!' Rhun reminded him. 'Dismissed, dismissed —'

'That won't work,' Avery chided, 'as you are not the one who summoned me.'

Rhun drew breath to call for her, and she entered of her own accord. 'Sybil, my love and *loyal* secretary, would you kindly dismiss my brother.'

'No, he's up to something,' Avery appealed, serving Rhun an accusing look. 'I can feel it.'

Though she hated to buy into a disagreement she knew nothing about, she felt she had to side with the governor. 'I'm so sorry, Avery. Dismissed, dismissed, dismissed.'

When his brother vanished Rhun gave a great sigh of relief, although the dirty look his wife was serving him was not at all welcome.

'That won't keep him at bay very long,' Telmo advised. 'Once he catches up with his wife, Fallon … he'll just get her to summon him back.'

'I don't think so,' Rhun said confidently.

'Nin Fallon is here to see the governor.' Sybil folded her arms upon realising that Avery's suspicion was right on the money.

Telmo shook his head at the governor's underhanded insurance measure. 'Fallon was the business you had to see to upon your return here,' he guessed, and Rhun winked in response, looking back to his wife.

'I have a few things to see to first,' Rhun outlined, 'but it is very important I speak with Fallon, so could you make our dear sister-in-law some tea and ask her to please wait.'

'As you wish,' Sybil was beyond wanting to know what the plot was.

'You should all stay put. The less of the Chosen who discover you are here, the better.' Rhun advised the other timekeepers. 'I shall suss out Vugar before I bring him to meet you.'

'Would our other guests like something while they wait?' Sybil suggested half jokingly, as everyone seemed to be taking this event rather casually.

'Tea would be lovely,' Taren took a seat on the lounge.

'Buhula!' Zeven cried — this was a local brew, the name of which meant 'deadly joy water'.

'After,' Rhun vowed, denying the request.

'Tea all round then?' Sybil suggested and departed the room ahead of Rhun and En Noah.

'Let's go,' Rhun cued Asher to come along as he passed through the reception room. The governor acknowledged his sister-in-law, who was seated waiting — she was complementing his plans by looking particularly stunning today. 'You look fantastic.'

'Thank you,' she accepted the compliment graciously. 'I —'

Rhun held up a finger to beg her patience, as he had to keep moving. 'Don't go anywhere.' He walked out of reception, with Asher and Noah in tow, and into the long curving corridor that led to the government's private landing facility. 'The Dracon are on their way down, I take it?'

'Not as yet,' Asher brought him up to speed. 'For although they were happy to accept our invitation, they would not allow their leaders to attend completely unarmed.'

'Fair enough,' Rhun granted.

Both his advisors were perturbed. Noah spoke up first. 'But what if …'

Rhun knew he feared that the Draconians were carrying the DNA-destroying weapon that had crippled Kila in the last timeline. 'When I have no armour,' Rhun shared his reasoning, 'I will make benevolence and righteousness my armour.'

Noah nodded to concede the point, although Asher still looked concerned, as allowing an unknown race of beings to bring weaponry straight into the hub of government was a huge breach in protocol.

'I have to object —' Asher began.

'They are our guests and whatever they need to feel their safety is assured, must be allowed for.' Rhun ended the matter.

'And shall we be armed?' Asher knew better than to ask.

'We shall not,' Rhun instructed.

Asher was not happy, but noted his long-time mentor, En Noah, seemed in agreement with the governor's decision.

For Noah understood, as Rhun did, that if the Dracon planned to make war, nothing was going to prevent that. The Chosen had no defence against the genetic regression technology so they had nothing to lose by awarding the Dracon the benefit of the doubt. Shyamal had a primary weapon that could take out the entire city at once, and if that was the case and intention in this instance, Kila would be in ruins already.

'When I have no divine power,' Noah quoted from the same ancient verse that Rhun had quoted, finding it particularly poignant in this instance, 'I shall make honesty my divine power, and understanding my means.' He nodded in conclusion and agreement. 'So that is how you wish to play this?'

'It is,' Rhun informed. 'I've had enough theorising, strategising and speculation … let's try something completely new and just let events unfold as they may.'

'What a novel idea.' Noah grinned in approval.

Once clearance to land had been given to the Dracon, the governor, Asher and Noah, stood awaiting their arrival in the sparsely furnished foyer of the government terminal, where they could observe the Dracon craft as it landed.

'I won't be kept in the dark any longer,' Asher demanded, upon finding a window of opportunity to do so. 'I want to know what is going on here this morning?'

'This is Grigori business,' Rhun advised, 'that's all you need to know.'

Asher looked cynical. 'That's an oxymoron, isn't it? Causal beings don't decide what is to be done, only the living do that.'

'So perceptive,' Noah commented, proud of his one-time student. 'But the Grigori were not always purely causal beings.'

'You never taught us that at the institute.' Asher had excelled at immortal history.

'It will be a whole new course of study that will be added to the curriculum, just as soon as we finish creating this chapter,' the historian advised.

Asher was confused and then concerned by this. 'What —'

'Just watch and learn,' Noah spoke up over Asher's query. 'Your father's forte is not the art of war, but the art of peace.'

'Thank you, Noah —' Rhun began, but was distracted by the arrival of their guests, who appeared on the runway — no vessel, just two dignitaries, one male, one female — and half a dozen guards. 'They can teleport,' he observed, alerting Noah and Asher to the arrival of the guests. Rhun recognised the female with Vugar; it was Aysel. She had been able to teleport back when they had first met, even with the virus in the equation, so in retrospect, it was really no surprise she still could.

The large transparent doors vanished as the Draconian party entered the foyer, and Rhun approached to greet them. 'Highnesses, Vugar and Aysel, I am Rhun Gwynedd, Governor of Kila, I bid you welcome to the city of the Chosen Ones.'

The Queen of the Dracon was obviously curious and probably wondering how he knew her name, but said nothing of it.

'And we know why Enki chose you,' Vugar proffered, 'for you are the vehicles of the Grigori.'

Rhun nodded once to confirm this was quite correct.

'You appear a lot like your Grigorian counterpart,' Vugar noted. 'We never caught the name, but we remember you were there.' Both reptilian dignitaries nodded in accord.

'Your Majesties, sorry to interrupt,' Asher came forward to join the proceedings.

'May I introduce my son, Asher, Kila's head of defence,' Rhun gave him leave to speak.

'You are curious about our weapons,' Vugar guessed, and with a wave of a claw, one of his guards stepped forward and gave Asher one of the handguns to inspect.

Asher had never seen anything like it. 'What manner of weapon is it?' It was fairly bulky, but lightweight.

'It targets the DNA of your subject,' Vugar outlined.

Noah looked alarmed.

'And enhances it,' the Draconian leader added, to reassure his hosts.

'What?' Rhun regretted that he sounded more worried than surprised.

'We learned eons ago that killing is useless! For you shall only be reincarnating the same wretched souls you send to the grave,' the Draconian leader reasoned. 'But enlighten your enemy, and he will be your enemy no longer.'

'Bravo!' Noah applauded their reasoning.

'From all accounts of the Chosen Ones, we understand there is no need to use this technology on you,' Vugar stated for the record. 'But it is not often that our royal person performs a diplomatic errand such as this, with no reconnaissance in advance, so we needed to see the situation here with our own eyes. And as we note you were gracious enough to meet us unarmed, I shall have our weapons returned to our craft.'

'Ah!' Rhun stopped Vugar, taking the weapon in his son's possession. 'Would you mind if I kept this one?' he requested, noting all present were a little stunned by the request. 'My science adviser would be most curious to see it,' he explained the anomaly.

'Of course,' Vugar granted, 'as a token of our goodwill.' When the reptilian leader dismissed the guards and they vanished, leaving only the leader and his lady companion, Rhun was very surprised.

'I am overwhelmed and honoured, that you would entrust the Chosen with your safety.' Rhun could hardly believe that this was the same being who had murdered half their team.

'There is no risk when we can see the true nature within all, written clearly upon your light-bodies,' Aysel explained graciously.

Rhun smiled as he recalled that Aysel could see auras and had perceived Jiang Hudan's pregnancy thus. 'We have nothing to hide,' he replied winningly.

Aysel seemed not entirely sure of that. 'Yet still you worry?'

Clearly his discord with his brother was evident in his light body. 'I have some personal concerns,' he allowed, 'but none regarding your visit. Although, you have yet to state your reasons for seeking us out.'

'Is the one known as Sammael here, on Kila?' Vugar queried.

'He is scheduled to leave, but delayed to attend this meeting,' Rhun confirmed, and Vugar and his companion were both delighted.

'We should very much like to speak with this Grigorian,' Vugar requested.

'Well, like me, he is Grigorian no longer,' the governor clarified, and both Draconians nodded to acknowledge they understood this. 'Asher. Please escort our guests to my office. I shall be right behind you.'

Asher didn't query the governor's instruction in present company. 'Please, follow me.' He led the Draconians out of the governor's space port and into the gardens located between the offices of government.

As soon as their company were gone, Rhun inspected the gun in his hands. 'Do you think they are telling the truth about this weapon?'

'Yes, I do,' Noah gave his honest opinion. 'Please tell me you did not intend to shoot your brother with that?'

'How else is he going to get his wife pregnant?' Rhun asked. 'Damn it, why did they have to find God now?' He flicked a switch and energy began streaming through the weapon's circuitry, beneath the transparent casing. 'Whoa!' He was mesmerised by how beautiful and elegant it appeared, and then took aim at Noah with it. 'I need to test it on someone.'

'I have no desire to be mortal again,' Noah protested his governor's intention, looking for a place to hide. 'There must be another way?'

'We're pushed for time,' Rhun maintained his focus on his target.

'Can't this wait until later?' Noah appealed — they had a lot going on a present. 'I mean what happens if the Dracon are telling the truth?'

'I guess you rejoin the Grigori sooner than expected. Keep still.' Rhun urged, as Noah ducked for cover behind a solid moulded metal chair. The leader lowered the weapon, and huffed out his frustration. 'This is not the way this was supposed to go.'

'But it has gone as well as you could possibly hope for!' Noah told him. 'We could just explain your problem to the Draconians?'

'How can I explain it, without going into the whole time paradox that led us here? Which does not paint our guest in the best light.' Rhun took a seat, disheartened for the present. 'I was really counting on the Draconians being lying bastards, as usual.'

'Well, that will teach you to underestimate your own divine influence,' Noah came out and took the seat alongside him. 'I commend that you want to fix the injustice done to your brother, but this is the way it was meant to be — the timekeepers were never meant to be here.'

'Avery won't see it that way,' Rhun was certain. 'And I cannot allow a discord to develop between the material world and the elemental realms.'

'If any discord results, it is not your fault,' Noah stressed the fact he seemed to be overlooking.

'I lost Avery the first chance to have a child in one hundred years!' Rhun stood to stress, and his eyes moistened, as his emotion welled. 'I know I give him a hard time, someone has to, in order keep his *massive* ego in check! But I love him, *dearly* … he has saved my arse more times than I care to remember —'

'If memory serves, you have also saved his,' Noah allowed.

'I am his elder brother, that's my job! This is not about me feeling guilty, it's about me wanting my little brother's greatest happiness.' Rhun insisted, passionately. 'I won't dash his only desire. I will give him back his opportunity to be a father, if I have to create another cosmic fuck-up to do it!'

Sybil materialised before them, appearing unusually frazzled. 'Whenever you are ready, gentlemen,' she eyed the colourful glowing weapon in her husband's hands, with disapproval. 'There is an ever-growing crowd of people in your office, awaiting your attendance.'

Noah raised both his brow at Rhun. 'We need to get our priorities straight here.'

Rhun saw the wisdom in that. 'We're right behind you,' he advised Sybil.

'*Right* behind me,' she cautioned, with a look of ire.

'I know today has been challenging, but bear with me,' Rhun rubbed the top of her arm, affectionately. 'I promise the results will be worth it.'

'In fact, they are already a world away from what could have eventuated this day on Kila,' Noah added, reminding Rhun to count his achievements, and not just focus on his shortcomings.

Sybil resolved to smile in encouragement. 'It's certainly not a boring day at the office.'

'I miss boring days at the office,' Rhun told her mournfully; those were the days they locked the doors and made love all afternoon.

'Tomorrow perhaps?' She grinned winningly and stepped away from him. 'But not today,' she concluded with a pout.

'We'll see about that,' Rhun challenged as she vanished, and looked back at Noah, who was admiring the view in an attempt not to note the governor flirting with his wife.

'Do you feel it?' Noah queried still gazing out at the garden.

'What's that?' Rhun wondered.

'Peace,' he advised. 'I feel we've done something incredibly right.'

'That would be a pleasant change of pace for us.' Rhun didn't share his certainty, but appreciated Noah voicing it. 'Onwards and upwards then,' he tried to sound more convincing, as he departed to make their appointment with the final outcome of their timekeeping agenda.

In reception, Rhun found his wife speaking with Fallon, trying to convince her to stay.

'Here he is,' Fallon breathed a sigh of relief when she saw the governor.

'Sorry to keep you, I won't be too much longer,' Rhun assured her from afar with a wave, and proceeded through to his office.

'What could be so important, that it could not be put off for another day?' she asked, but he only held up a finger to implore her patience, before the doors manifested to enclose Rhun and Noah in his office, with the timekeepers and the Dracon.

Asher was the first to approach Rhun as he entered. 'Who are these people?' Asher whispered the query quietly to his father.

'Surely you recognise them?' Rhun posed, evading the question.

'I do,' Asher was annoyed. 'But what are they doing here?"

'I think you are about to find out,' Rhun grinned, and moved to join his guests, who were introducing themselves; but in reality no introductions were necessary — everyone's reputations proceeded them.

'So you are Taren?' Vugar was saying. 'The one the Grigori were so keen to protect?'

'Really?' She hadn't taken that trip back in time, and looked to Zeven.

'We were worried about not making it back to you, and the situation that would have left you in,' he explained.

And Taren tipped her head sideways and smiled, touched that they had been so concerned for her. 'You always come through in the end.'

'Even for those who would seem your enemies,' Vugar granted, looking to Zeven, who the Draconian leader addressed by his Grigorian name. 'We are honoured to meet you, Sammael,' Vugar looked about at all the timekeepers, recognising many of them, 'and all you Grigori.'

Zeven held out a hand in a friendly fashion as Vugar's attention turned back to him.

But the Dracon royals avoided the gesture to kneel down in front of Zeven to the shock of those present.

'You gave up your souls to the Nefilim's cruel genetic experiments on the human race, in order that our soul-mind could be free of a sub-universal virus,' Vugar stated the fact with huge gratitude.

'It amazes me that you remember back to that incident,' Zeven, not as used to being venerated as many of his other incarnations, made light of their adoration, and so crouched down his aging form to continue the discussion at their level.

'"Release his mind-eater into a soul-group like the reptilians have and you effectively make this menace immortal!"' Vugar looked to Zeven, quoting Sammael's words from countless thousands of years ago. '"And don't think it will kill them all off eventually, it won't, it's smart. It will take your lab and start producing its own food supply!"'

'That's word for word.' The fact completely blew Zeven's mind.

'You stood up to our Nefilim oppressors who wished to blackmail us into giving up on our caste on Ki, which we very nearly did,' Vugar explained.

'The Nefilim still led you to believe that they had injected the mind-eater into one of their hybrid reptilians, which they had on ice.' Zeven understood that was the plan.

'As the virus spread to the next most powerful reptilian in the vicinity, we kept our distance from Ki, where that caste were forced into slavery. Due to the genetic imperfections of their genetic structure, and the fact they could not procreate on their own, they developed a taste for humans, whose vital fluids, they discovered, could prolong their lives indefinitely.'

'We saw instances of this in ancient China,' Taren was saddened to recall, and the Draconian leader appeared just as sickened by the fact.

'We only mention this shameful degeneration, in order to assure you that this abuse of humanity will come to an end,' Vugar stated.

'So you made contact with your caste on Earth — I mean, Ki?' Zeven assumed.

'There was one among us that dared to challenge the word of the Nefilim, who instilled in us a long-held belief that our caste on Ki were all infected with disease and beyond salvation.' Vugar looked aside to his companion, to give her credit. 'Even at the risk of being infected and being doomed never to return home, she was determined.'

'That is *very* admirable,' Zeven awarded, as everyone's attention shifted to Aysel.

'Upon making contact with a reptilian hive-mind on Ki, I gained the knowledge of their full history,' she explained. 'Including the memories of their greatest forefather, Kingu, who, in the lab of Ninharsag, bore witness to the Grigori's great sacrifice to save the reptilians from a mind-eating virus.'

'Kingu was the son of Tiamat,' Taren recalled, 'who incarnated into a physical form to warn the Nefilim, but for his trouble he was imprisoned by them in cryogen instead.'

'Thus we of the royal line of the Dracon, now know of the great debt our kind owe yours,' Aysel concluded.

'We appreciate that you acknowledge our aid,' Zeven granted. 'But what I would appreciate more is if we could all stand, or better still be seated?'

'Of course.' Vugar and Aysel rose, and gave Zeven a hand up.

'Many thanks,' he stated, as they let him go. 'Please, be seated.'

Once everyone was comfortable, Zeven resumed. 'What I don't understand, is how did you know how and when to find the timekeepers here on Kila?'

Vugar placed a hand on the ornate dragon buckle on his belt — the same mysterious belt Aysel had used to guide her forth to the timekeepers once before.

'The Dragon's Eye,' Zeven said, upon recognising it.

'You know of it?' Vugar sounded proud the legend had spread so far. 'It is one of our most sacred relics.'

'It detects treachery, as only the pure of heart can stand in its presence,' Zeven recounted what he'd been told of its function. 'It is also deadly to the touch of anyone but its chosen guardian.'

Vugar had been nodding in accord, but that last part of Zeven's tutorial confused him. 'This sacred relic would never kill!'

'My mistake,' Zeven looked to Aysel, suspecting she'd lied to him about that the last time they had met.

'It is our direct connection to the great dragon spirit,' Aysel allowed graciously, 'it only serves the greater good, which is never served by killing.'

'Tiamat,' Taren uttered, having suddenly made the connection. 'Tiamat is the great dragon spirit.'

Vugar gave a nod to grant this was correct. 'Thus, the great dragon acknowledges that the Grigori debt to her has been paid in full.'

This announcement was received with much revelry from those present.

'Those of our kind remaining on Earth shall be quietly tracked down and returned to Fiameadi to be re-educated and assimilated back into our hive-mind.' Aysel added to the mirth.

'And if that doesn't work, you'll just hit them with this,' Rhun patted the weapon in his possession.

Aysel found his suggestion amusing, although a little extreme. 'The effects of that weapon, good or bad, can only be temporary if the character of your subject is contrary,' she explained. 'You cannot enforce enlightenment on a demon, any more than you can force a spiritual master to destroy.'

'Effects, good or bad?' Rhun queried. 'The weapon function can be reversed?'

'It can,' Aysel admitted, warily, almost apologetically. 'But there is a code required to activate the reverse mode, that only Vugar knows, for such a strike against another being would be an extremely malicious act.'

Rhun looked to Noah whom he could tell was silently praying that his governor did not openly ask for the code. The historian need not have feared, Rhun was not as telepathically talented as some of his other siblings, and had learned to turn off this talent as mostly, it just gave him a headache. But he could clearly read the thoughts of another through touching a subject, and had been able to do this from quite a young age.

'Well, I guess that about wraps up everything,' Rhun was eager to get business done, and sort out his little family problem.

'There is one thing that still bothers me,' Telmo spoke up, directing the gripe at the governor.

'And what's that?' Rhun had a feeling he didn't want to know.

'How the "virus" managed to shift Ling Hu through time as it did?' he said cryptically, so that their guests might be intrigued but not offended — it was Rhun who was offended.

'You just had to bring that up again, didn't you?' Rhun challenged.

'The Taliesin in me couldn't help it.' Telmo concurred.

'It's lost in the timelines, just accept that.' Rhun closed the topic for discussion.

Vugar raised a claw, hoping he might be permitted to comment. 'There is another purpose to our visit.'

'I'm so sorry, I didn't realise,' Rhun didn't want to seem rude or unaccommodating. 'Please continue.'

Vugar stood, as all eyes turned his way. If you would like to see us back to your landing dock, I'll enlighten you there.'

Many curious looks were exchanged as the timekeepers accompanied the royals back to where the governor had first greeted them that day, and there in the dock was the time chariot. The sight gave Rhun and Noah a mild heart attack at first, for they assumed the Dracon had somehow penetrated their defences here on Kila to steal the one chariot that remained.

'How did you come by this?' Rhun couldn't keep the panic out of his tone.

'We didn't,' Aysel replied calmly, 'some of our caste on Earth found it buried in an underwater cave after Atlantis sank … our ilk are excellent swimmers.'

'Oh, it's that chariot.' This was the second chariot, the one they had lost! The relief overwhelmed Rhun, as he turned to Telmo, hoping he would now drop the subject.

'Tamat claims it belongs to you?' Vugar was puzzled by Rhun's vagueness on the matter.

'Your dragon guardian is absolutely correct,' Rhun assured the Dracon.

'Our good governor and his brother managed to lose it, when they were lads,' Telmo added, to the Draconians' slight amusement and Rhun's agitation.

'Our caste on Ki never managed to work out its function,' Aysel added, in consolation to the governor's obvious embarrassment. 'Perhaps, with your smart virus however …'

Rhun nodded, following her train of thought. 'The virus had the chariot and was using it all along.'

'That would explain how it knew how to use it, when he first stole it from you,' Telmo was careful not to mention the chariot's twin.

'I thought you said he lost it?' Vugar pointed out.

'It has gone amiss on more than one occasion,' Telmo added to make matters worse.

'As timekeepers you should probably be more careful with your precious treasures,' the older Draconian ruler suggested. 'You can't afford to have just anyone zipping about through time, unsupervised.'

'I have certainly learned a valuable lesson this day, Vugar,' the governor was suddenly overwhelmed with gratitude towards his new allies, who obviously knew what the chariot's function was. 'Only a truly wise and honest being would have returned such amazing treasure to its owner, and not used it to further their own ends —'

'Amazing treasure!' Vugar laughed. 'If you are a timekeeper, perhaps. But to us normal, century-to-century kind of beings, it's a bloody curse!' Vugar looked to Aysel, and she served him a sly wink, before Vugar looked back to Rhun, and held out a hand toward him. 'We would rather leave time and causality in the hands of the experts.'

'Ha!' Telmo suppressed his amusement.

Rhun ignored his old mentor, eager to shake the Draconian leader's hand, for by so doing he garnered the code to unlock the forbidden function on the weapon Vugar had gifted him earlier.

Once the Dracon departed, the first priority was to return the chariot to its twin, in high security under the Institute of Immortal History.

'I'll take it back,' Noah volunteered.

'I shall take it,' Rhun insisted, looking to Zeven. 'Would you mind giving me a hand?'

Everyone present was puzzled by the request as Rhun had psychokinesis — obviously the governor wished to get Zeven alone.

'Not me?' Telmo questioned, since he had been so passionate about finding the missing treasure.

'No, just Song,' Rhun answered simply, making Telmo twice as curious, which made Zeven smile. 'I'll see the rest of you back in my office,' Rhun finalised the matter, then he and Zeven vanished with the time-hopping transport.

'Could you be any more obvious?' Zeven queried upon arrival in the vault, where they landed the chariot back where it belonged alongside the other.

'I need your help with something,' Rhun admitted.

'Shoot!' Zeven was all ears.

'I know that the timelines had altered and so this never really happened,' Rhun outlined. 'But I once promised the Dropa I would take care of Wu Geng, but he was lost, his memory of enlightenment along with him.'

'Don't say any more,' Zeven insisted. 'I already plan to take care of it.'

Rhun wasn't too sure how to interpret that statement.

'I promised I would not abandon Wu Geng, in this universe or the next,' Zeven lowered his voice despite being locked in a vault alone with Rhun.

'How do you plan —'

'Don't ask,' Zeven insisted, and then confessed. 'It's kind of a plan in progress really.'

'Does the timekeeper know your intent?' Rhun wasn't getting the vibe that she did.

'Nah,' Zeven waved off Rhun's caution, 'I think Khalid needs to be a solo project, Taren has enough to contend with.'

'Look,' Rhun was feeling guilty and wary now. 'We just got our timeline sorted out. I don't want to encourage you to do anything that will fuck up yours!'

'I won't fuck it up!' Zeven insisted, and Rhun held both his hands up in truce. 'Remember the mutant!'

'I believe you.' The governor insisted. 'And I do remember, I reminded you.'

'Well good,' Zeven calmed down. 'Surely Khalid can't be any worse than that!' he concluded, sounding unsure if he was trying to convince Rhun or himself.

Upon Rhun and Zeven's return to the governor's office, Rhun was immediately confronted by his son, Asher, who was most baffled. 'What just happened?'

'That, my dear fellow, was history in the making,' Noah replied.

'So, that's it then?' Zeven slapped his hands together, eager to shed his aging form. 'We're free to go.'

'You are,' Rhun granted with a beaming smile.

'I feel better for knowing that Kila shall fare well after we depart,' Taren said. Staying in this universe a little while longer had been well worth it.

'You are leaving?' Asher was alarmed. 'But those of us on Kila have not seen many of you masters in centuries! Some of you never!' Asher looked at Telmo, probably wondering who he was, as he'd been born long after Taliesin had ascended from this world.

'We are timekeepers,' Zeven explained exuberantly. 'We have places to be! I just have one question,' he directed the query at Rhun. 'Where do you want me to dump the body?' He motioned down at his aging form.

'What?' Asher was stunned by his words.

'Thank you, Asher,' Rhun wasn't up for twenty questions. 'The crisis is over, you may leave.'

Asher reluctantly accepted that he was not going to be briefed on this fiasco, but he turned back to their guests, before leaving. 'It has been most intriguing to see you all. Happy travels.' He served Rhun a look that implied he would get the truth sooner or later, and vanished back to his post.

Noah held up a finger to make a suggestion. 'I suggest you all depart from my lake house. I should like to have your bodies put into suspended animation and kept in my Institute of Immortal History.'

'Splendid idea,' Telmo awarded. 'Shall I assume the form of Taliesin for you?' He transformed into the old druid he'd appeared in ancient Gwynedd. 'Or Yi Wu?' He shifted form into the great mother of Li Shan he'd been in ancient Zhou.

'Stop showing off,' Zeven grumbled, and looked back to Noah to complain. 'Really? You want to preserve *this* body?'

'Ji Song is of significant historical import,' Noah reasoned, 'as is Jiang Hudan.'

'Don't tell me you want me to transform back into the old Jiang Huxin?' Jazmay saw the kind look of appeal on the historian's face, and as his soul-mind had been her little brother in Zhou, she could not say no. 'All right, if I must.'

'Only if it pleases you, my brother.' He grinned, playing on their old association.

'Well, at least these forms shall be put to some good use,' Taren shrugged to agree.

'You never know when we might need them again,' said Telmo, and when everyone looked to him to object to the suggestion, he grinned. 'Just kidding.'

Everyone was most relieved to hear him say so.

'Then I shall leave it to you to see the timekeepers gone,' Rhun awarded Noah with his wish, as none seemed to object.

'See you then, gov,' Zeven approached to shake Rhun's hand. 'It's been *real* …' He decided to leave it at that, and nodded to emphasise that there was really nothing more to be said.

'It certainly has been that,' Rhun agreed.

'See you in the next one,' Zeven let him go, and backed up to vex him. 'In that universe, you're my dad.'

'I shan't look forward to that,' Rhun bantered, as Taren approached to say farewell.

'Next time we meet we'll be working together for the Maladaan Secret Service,' she informed, giving him a hug.

'Cool, Mum, thanks,' he teased, as she pulled away.

'Oh, I won't be your mother there, I'm your squad commander,' she grinned at his woeful expression.

'That all sounds … not very ideal,' Rhun admitted. 'What, did I have bad karma to work off or something? And what am I to you?' he asked Jazmay as she approached to shake his hand.

'Absolutely no one,' she shrugged, 'I barely notice you over the sound of how awesome I am.' She served him a cheeky wink. 'But you did good here, Governor.' She gave him two thumbs up and a wave. 'You'll be seeing me.' She vanished — Zeven and Taren left with her.

'Please don't shoot your brother while I'm gone,' Noah appealed, feeling obliged to follow his guests.

'How can I without the code?' Rhun replied, and Noah, reassured, departed after the others.

Telmo had a chuckle. 'He's forgotten about your telepathy.'

Rhun grinned, caught out by how much Telmo remembered. 'We are forbidden to use it *among our own kind*,' he pointed out the loophole in the law he was exploiting.

'Ah!' Telmo was enlightened. 'Well, I guess I should depart and let you get on with devolving your brother.'

'That would be appreciated,' Rhun advised, hiding his sadness at bidding them all farewell. 'I plan to finish work early today.'

'Good for you,' Telmo grinned, as if he knew why Rhun wanted an early mark. 'See you back on AMIE then.'

'So,' Rhun delayed his departure, 'what is your take on me enlightening my brother to his child spawning potential?'

Telmo raised both brows to consider the ramifications. 'Well, I guess the bottom line is that you have obtained some information you feel would benefit your brother. In which case, it doesn't matter how or when you got it, to not pass on that information would really be quite cruel.'

'That's what I think!' Rhun clutched his weapon, obviously looking forward to the event a little too much.

'Have fun then,' Telmo said. 'Play nice.' He disappeared and finally Rhun found himself alone in the governor's office.

'Ah!' He breathed a huge sigh of relief. 'Thank fu—'

'Rhun!' Sybil had entered to remind him. 'Fallon is *still* waiting out here.'

'*Yes*,' he droned, as his second of peace was foiled, but he regained his good cheer. 'I am ready to see her now.'

As Fallon stormed in, annoyed at being parked in reception, Sybil quickly departed, and the door closed. 'You said there was a good reason that you've kept me here half the day.'

'There is,' he motioned her to take a seat, but she refused. 'I've been sitting all morning!'

'Have it your way.' Rhun granted that probably wasn't wise, but grabbed a chair as he approached her. 'I know a way for you to have Avery's child.'

'What?' She was fit to faint with the shock of his words, and Rhun placed the chair behind her and she sank to sitting. 'This is not some practical joke you've planned for Avery, is it? Because it's not funny —'

Rhun was shaking his head. 'No, it can absolutely happen.'

Fallon looked to the strange weapon in her brother-in-law's hand. 'Does that have something to do with this solution of yours?'

'That's why it was so important that I see you today,' Rhun informed. 'I didn't want you to be alarmed when I shoot your husband with it.'

'What?' Fallon was startled by the casual statement.

But Rhun urged her to calm and crouched before her. 'Allow me to explain.'

When Rhun summoned Avery forth, he was alone in the governor's office, and the Draconian weapon was deactivated on his desk. Avery looked about upon arrival, noting they were the sole occupants. 'Where did everybody go?'

'The timekeepers have returned to their universe,' Rhun began. 'Everything in ancient Zhou is back to the way it should have been, the chariot we lost in Atlantis has been returned —'

'What?' Obviously Avery found that claim too good to be true. 'How? By whom?'

But Rhun ignored the query. 'And … and the Draconians, now our allies, are cleaning up the reptilian problem on Earth for us … so, all is right with the world.'

'Oh?' Avery frowned, surprised to have nothing to be mad about. 'Looks like you did good th—'

'There's just one tiny issue that needs addressing?' Rhun held his thumb and finger close together to illustrate how small a detail it was.

'And what's that?' Avery was immediately wary of the impending confession.

'Would you like to sit down?' Rhun directed him to a seat; Avery folded both his legs and sat cross-legged in midair.

'What is it?' Avery asked again.

'Well, as it turns out the timekeepers never came here,' Rhun began.

'Yes, they did, I saw them the last time you summoned me here,' Avery corrected.

'I mean that they were never here *before* our sabbatical in ancient China,' he prompted, and grimaced, hoping Avery would work out the shortcoming for himself.

'But if they never came, the reptilians never shot me with their weapon to render me mortal,' Avery dropped his legs and stood again. 'And my child was never conceived!' he roared, and his anger whipped up and wind blustered through the office.

'That's why I got you this.' Rhun picked up the Dracon weapon and handed it to Avery.

'Do I get to shoot you?' Avery was very grateful for the thought and took aim at his brother, although the weapon was still defunct.

'No, I get to shoot you,' Rhun advised. 'One blast will make you mortal, which means you can *conceive with your wife*.' He wriggled his eyebrows a few times.

'No way!' Avery objected, although he couldn't wipe the smile off his face.

'It's the only way,' Rhun was happy to advise him.

'What if I am stuck as a mortal?'

'You can't be,' Rhun informed him, merrily. 'The weapon has a reverse function. So hand it over, and face fatherhood like a man.'

Avery appeared game. 'If you are lying to me about this …'

'I'm not. I have your wife waiting in reception and she has the keys to the governor's guest house for however long you need it.' Rhun wiggled the fingers of his outstretched palms, beckoning his compliance. 'And I might add that Fallon is looking particularly stunning today.'

Avery tossed the weapon at his brother. 'I'm in.' He assumed target pose, chest out, hands on hips. 'Hit me.'

'You know you can always count on me for a little tough love, my brother.' Rhun fired up the weapon, which lit up in splendour.

'Whoa, cool,' Avery admired it, until Rhun punched in the code to reverse the function of the weapon, whereupon the rainbow light circuitry turned dark and dense as crude oil. 'Are you sure you know what you're doing with that thing?'

Rhun looked it over, appearing a little perplexed. 'Pretty sure,' he decided, as he fired a single dark pulse of energy at his brother.

'Ah shit!' The impact blew Avery into a full backwards flip, which landed him face down on his stomach, winded and mortal. 'Ouch!' He couldn't move for a moment he was so stunned by the pain.

'Welcome to the real world, buddy.' Rhun put down the weapon and walked over to give his brother a hand to his feet.

'You suck!' Avery informed him, despite being grateful for the aid.

'You won't be saying that an hour from now.' Rhun slapped him on the chest a couple of times, which Avery decided hurt as well.

'Thanks very little for your help, but I can take it from here,' Avery disentangled himself from his brother, and headed for reception.

'Just come and let me know when you want to be shot back into the etheric world,' Rhun commented after him.

Avery sidetracked to collect the said weapon from Rhun's desk. 'I think I'll have my wife see to that, if it's all the same to you.'

'You have to reverse the weapon, using a code only I know,' Rhun grinned.

'Do it!' Avery handed the weapon to his brother, who obliged his request and handed the weapon back. 'You did gift this to me, after all.'

'I wouldn't want to deny Fallon the pleasure of shooting you,' Rhun granted. Avery was very tempted to shoot the governor with it, but Sybil entered.

'Just leaving, were you, brother-in-law?' she queried politely. 'Your wife is going to go insane if someone doesn't take her out of that waiting room soon.'

'Are we good?' Rhun appealed for his brother's absolution, and Avery grinned.

'I'll let you know.'

'Well, if it doesn't happen now, it isn't my fault,' Rhun teased, and Avery turned back to retort.

'Oh, *stop* you two,' Sybil demanded. '*Go home* …' she bade Avery, and then turned her sights back to Rhun, '… to your wives, and be grateful for everything you have achieved.' She slinked up to the governor and he welcomed her kiss.

'All right, already, I'm leaving.' Avery took the hint.

'And lock the door on your way out,' Sybil and Rhun insisted at once.

'Yeah, yeah, I know the drill.'

As soon as the door closed, Sybil cooled a little and pulled away. 'Finally, a chance for you to explain to me what happened today?'

'No, no, no,' Rhun pulled her back close to him. 'Do you have any idea how many years it is since I made love to you?'

'No,' she answered, and smiled, as Rhun's hands were all over her. 'I have no idea, why don't you tell me?'

'At least *thirty*. Give or take the time I spent time-hopping about.' He kissed his wife's neck and raised her up to carry her to the lounge.

'You don't expect me to fall for that old "yesterday I got lost for thirty years" trick, do you?' she challenged his story as he threw her down on the lounge, and crawled on top of her.

'You're the one always telling me I should put work aside more often.'

'When have I ever told you that?' She laughed.

'Right now,' he commanded, in a playful manner, 'or I'm sacking you, divorcing you, whatever it takes.'

Clearly, it was difficult for Sybil to put aside her determination to get some answers, which made Rhun appreciate her amorous grin of defeat all the more. 'You're the boss,' she relented and raised her upper body to kiss his neck

'And for once,' he realised, as he lapped up the affection of his sweeter half, 'I am truly grateful.'

His recent travels through time had been a huge wake up call for Rhun. How could he have ever regretted his vocation, history, lineage or plight? Life without the companionship of the other souls who comprised the Grigori was inconceivable; as great as their earthly burdens and destiny were, Rhun knew now that he did not want to be anyone, or live any life, other than the one he had Chosen to lead.

EPILOGUE

GROUND ZERO

Through the lingering light haze of her quantum jump, which had numbed her senses as efficiently as a deep sleep might, Taren's waking consciousness detected a disturbing distant sound that was both foreign and yet familiar. In a rush of awareness, the sound grew louder.

As alien as the sound of a crying baby was to Taren, the intensity of the wail woke her nonetheless. Her breasts ached with a vengeance, like they had been pumped full of air and were fit to burst, and upon inspection, she was horrified to find they had doubled in size and her T-shirt was dripping wet.

Lucian stirred beside her, and reaching across he gave Taren a nudge. 'The baby,' he mumbled, and sank back into sleep.

'The baby?' Taren finally put two and two together, and was horrified. 'We have a baby?' She sat up and shook her husband furiously.

'What?' Lucian protested at being forced into a fully conscious state.

'We have a baby?'

'I know,' he mumbled, 'and boy, he sounds hungry.'

'It's a boy?' She was stunned.

'Well, yeah.' He sat up to support his dozing form on his elbows, and yawned.

'Holy shit!' Taren panicked, as she had returned to her body on

407

AMIE only one week before Khalid was due to cause the disaster that had cast many of them into another universe.

'Oh!' Lucian was enlightened and amused at once. 'You're back.'

'Yeah, I'm back,' Taren stressed. 'Only there appears to be a lot more of me now.' She referred to her swollen breasts, and all Lucian could do was laugh. 'How is this funny? We face off against Khalid in less than a week!'

'Well,' Lucian controlled his mirth, 'look on the bright side, you missed the birth.'

'Yeah!' She was nearly hysterical. 'I missed the pregnancy, birth and everything I probably learned about being a parent! I don't even know our son's name!'

'Danon,' he informed to calm her.

'Dan.' She smiled delighted, being that Ji Dan would have been the father of this child.

'You approve, I take it?' Lucian climbed out of bed to fetch the soul in question, as Taren was quite obviously too petrified to do it, and once lifted from his cot, Danon fell silent.

'Does he do anything?' she asked in a panic, knowing Zeven's daughter had been performing psychic feats from a very young age.

'Well, he cries, belches and creates a lot of dirty nappies,' Lucian advised as he carried the bundle over to where she was seated on the bed. 'But far and away his favourite pastime's gorging himself on your breasts.' Lucian held the child out to her.

'Seriously?' Taren was momentarily stunned by the request. 'I've never done this.'

'You've been doing it for mouths,' he downplayed her fear, and placed the child in her lap.

The sight of the dark-haired babe, sucking so hard on its own fist that it appeared it might devour it, broke her heart wide open, and as she held him close, he went into a frenzy, trying to nuzzle his way through her shirt. Then she raised the barrier and within moments, Danon had latched onto her aching breast and began sucking madly; which came as a relief to both mother and child.

'Told you so.' Lucian kissed her forehead, and she was overcome by the serene bliss of the moment.

'When I asked does he do anything,' Taren recalled her earlier query, 'I mean does he have any psychic talent.'

'Not that we've noticed,' Lucian advised. 'But give me a break, he's only three months old. He hasn't even got teeth yet.'

'Oh, I'm not in a hurry to find out,' Taren assured him. 'We've got enough to worry about.'

Lucian had to chuckle. 'And you don't know the half of it yet.'

Taren's brief bliss departed, and she was panicked again. 'What could possibly be more shocking than this?' She referred to the child in her arms, but Lucian appeared to wish to defer that news for the present.

'I think you should just take a moment to catch your breath,' he sat down beside Taren, to admire her and their babe. 'Whatever we did out there, where you've been … awesome job,' he awarded her her due. 'Danon is safe here with us, and not stuck in another time and universe. I was wrong to doubt —'

'No —' She felt he had just cause to.

'Regardless,' he persevered. 'You did the right thing, and that's all you need to know.' Lucian bent down and kissed his son's forehead, and then looked back to Taren. 'As far as the rest of what evolved here in your absence … well … that shall reveal itself soon enough.'

BIBLIOGRAPHY

de Laurence L. W., *The Lesser Key of Solomon*, Kessinger Publishing, Kila MT USA, 1916.

NOTE: Not surprisingly, my main references for this book were various books from my past trilogies. Those I referred to are listed below.

Dreaming Of Zhou Gong (Book 1: The Timekeepers)
The Universe Parallel (Book 2: Triad of Being)
The Light-field (Book 3: Triad of Being)
Tablet of Destinies (Book 2: The Celestial Triad)
Masters of Reality (Book 3: The Ancient Future Trilogy)